WHITE HOUSE

WHITE HOUSE

DAVID HAGBERG

A TOM DOHERTY ASSOCIATES BOOK / NEW YORK

WHITE HOUSE

Copyright © 1999 by David Hagberg

This book is printed on acid-free paper.

A Forge Book
Published by Tom Doherty Associates, LLC
175 Fifth Avenue
New York, NY 10010

Forge® is a registered trademark of Tom Doherty Associates, LLC

Grateful acknowledgment is made to the Associated Press for the permission to print the material found on page nine.

Library of Congress Cataloging-in-Publication Data

Hagberg, David.
      White House / David Hagberg.—1st ed.
          p.   cm.
      "A Tom Doherty Associates Book."
      ISBN 0-312-86682-8
      I. Title.
PS3558.A3227W48   1999
813'.54—dc21   99-26076
                                       CIP

First Edition: August 1999

Printed in the United States of America

0 9 8 7 6 5 4 3 2 1

This book is for Lorrel.

ACKNOWLEDGMENTS

Grateful acknowledgment and thanks
are given to my friend, editorial assistant,
typist and advisor, Nancy Nebel.

SEOUL (AP)—A high-ranking North Korean defector says North Korea has nuclear and chemical weapons capable of "scorching" South Korea and Japan, South Korea's intelligence agency revealed Tuesday.

Hwang Jang Yop's reported disclosure is the most credible testimony so far that North Korea has developed tactical nuclear weapons. The isolated Communist nation has denied having a nuclear weapons program.

One of 12 members of the North's highest decision-making body, Hwang is the top North Korean official ever to defect. When he arrived in Seoul on Sunday, Hwang said he fled to warn the world that North Korea's 1.2 million-member military is preparing to unleash a suicidal war.

PART ONE

DEPUTY DIRECTOR OF OPERATIONS,
CENTRAL INTELLIGENCE AGENCY

ONE

CIA Headquarters

Kirk Cullough McGarvey had nearly lost his life three months ago in Moscow. Although the pain he felt from his wounds had already begun to fade, the scars, both physical and mental, would never go away. This time his daughter, Elizabeth, had almost been killed, and he blamed himself.

He pulled up at the CIA main gate in his leased Nissan Pathfinder a few minutes before 8:00 A.M. Friday. It was a beautiful summer morning with a perfectly blue sky and almost no haze. Everything that had to be said after the operation—the summaries, the debriefings, the contact sheets and budget lines and weapons reports—had been gone over in endless detail with the headhunters in Internal Security. Yet he was answering the summons again, as he had been doing for twenty-five years.

"The general would like to see you tomorrow morning, eight sharp."

Tommy Doyle, deputy director of Intelligence, had phoned last night. He supposed that the DCI wanted to have a final word, as he himself did. In fact he had a lot to say, most of which Roland Murphy was not going to like.

He gave his driver's license to the uniformed security guard, who checked his name from a list then handed the license back. "Visitor's parking lot is on the left, sir."

"Thanks," McGarvey said. Coming back from Moscow he'd been angry because of the way the Company had bungled everything, and had involved his daughter against all rules of ethics and decency. But that had faded. Most of the people responsible were gone.

The grounds were lush and August green, the trees in full foliage as they'd been the first time he'd come here as a young case officer from the Agency's training facility near Williamsburg, Virginia. He'd been full of ambition, a real sense of purpose, "gung ho," as his instructors described him, but with some inner demons that drove him to excel beyond the level of any trainee before or since. Now it was very nearly over. After a quarter-century of service to his country, good times and bad, he was getting out.

He had to show his license again to the guard at the visitor's lot, where he found an empty parking space, then walked up to the main building. Bad times, he thought. He'd had plenty of them. The men he'd killed in the line of duty weren't a legion, but there were a lot of them. He remembered each of their faces, the look in their eyes when they died. Anger, rage, disappointment, surprise. They were flesh-and-blood human beings with dreams and ambitions like anyone else, their lives ended suddenly by an assassin's bullet. Bad men, Phil Carrara would have said, but men nonetheless. Not fair, they'd wanted to say at the end. And he had empathy for them, the killer for his victims. It was a special bond like no other. He agreed, it had never been fair.

Nearing fifty, McGarvey was tall, with the physique of a rugby player and the coordination of a ballet dancer. He had thick brown hair, gray at the temples, and a wide, honest face that many women found handsome. His eyes were deep, sometimes green, other times gray and almost always filled with emotion, an attitude that he knew something, had seen things that most people couldn't know, let alone understand. His friend Jacqueline said he had Dr. Zhivago eyes from the movie staring Omar Sharif. He ran and swam everyday, rain or shine, unless he was in the middle of an operation, fenced when he could find a worthy opponent and honed his skills with firearms on any firing range or gun club that would have him.

But it was never enough. He never felt as if he were completely ready. He always doubted his competence, always pushed himself to the limit.

It was over, he told himself again, passing through the automatic doors into the main reception hall. And after this morning's meeting he was going to try to convince Liz to get out while she still could. One spook in the family was enough. He didn't want his daughter following in his footsteps, despite the fact she was very good, very dedicated and, according to what he was hearing, the best student at the Farm, maybe even better than he was.

Tommy Doyle, the tall, thin, dapper-dressing deputy director of Intelligence, was waiting for him at the security checkpoint in the lobby with a visitor's pass.

"Thanks for coming out this morning," he said. "The general asked me to bring you directly upstairs, the others should already be in his office." He seemed harried, but McGarvey had seen the look before.

"Others?"

"Yeah," Doyle said, handing McGarvey the pass. "We have a situation brewing in the Sea of Japan." Doyle was one of the old school, the "Club," and along with the late Phil Carrara, who'd been deputy director of Operations, Larry Danielle, the deputy director of Central Intelligence and General Murphy, he had been responsible for bringing the CIA back from near emasculation after the Carter administration.

"I'm out, Tommy. That's what I came to tell him this morning. It's the only reason I'm here."

Doyle's lips compressed. "Maybe that's not possible right now."

"It's the way it's going to be."

Doyle faced him. "Ryan is gone and the situation in Moscow has stabilized for the moment, if that's what's worrying you. All we're asking is that you listen to us, for Christ's sake. You can give us that much."

McGarvey glanced over at the inscription on the marble wall. "And ye shall know the truth, and the truth shall make you free." John VIII: 32. In twenty-five years he'd heard so many lies that he sometimes doubted if anyone here had ever read the biblical quote.

He put the security pass on a chain around his neck, nodded tightly and fell in beside Doyle back to the elevators.

Santiago, Berlin, Lausanne, Lisbon, Paris, Tokyo and three months ago, Moscow. His past came crushing down on him like a load of bricks as he rode up to the seventh floor. Each incident had been started by a man or men with the frightened, uncertain, desperate look that he was seeing now in Doyle's eyes. A "situation" they called such things. Already McGarvey could smell the stench of death.

It was exactly 8:00 A.M. when they entered the large, well-appointed office of Roland Murphy, director of Central Intelligence. The general was seated at his desk watching CNN and drinking a cup of coffee. He was a large man with thick arms, a broad, square face and deep-set eyes beneath bushy eyebrows that were patient rather than cynical, as one might expect. He'd survived four presidents as DCI and was considered one of the toughest, most competent men ever to sit at this desk. He was apolitical, and no president was willing to replace him for fear of what his loss would mean to the CIA.

Seated across from him was Carleton Paterson, the patrician former New York lawyer who was the agency's new general counsel.

Murphy muted the sound on the television. He motioned toward an empty chair. "Thanks for coming out here this morning."

Lawrence Danielle, aging, stoop-shouldered, his jowls looser, his hair thinner and whiter than the last time McGarvey had seen him more than two years ago, came from his office adjoining the DCI's and laid a bundle of files on the desk. "Good Morning, Kirk. How are you feeling, wounds healing and all that?"

"Good morning, Larry," McGarvey said. "I'll live."

"I should hope so," Danielle said brightly. Unlike the others he still seemed to have his sense of humor. But then he'd been around even longer than Murphy. He was deputy director.

When they were all seated, Murphy called his secretary and told her to hold everything until he advised her differently. "Coffee?" he asked McGarvey.

"No."

Murphy studied him for several seconds. "I've never believed that assassination solved anything. But I was wrong this time, and you were right. If you hadn't killed Tarankov, Russia would have become the same threat to the world that Hitler's Germany was."

"It remains to be seen." McGarvey shrugged. Now that he was here he decided that he had no final words after all. It no longer seemed to matter. Seeing the worried looks on their faces had dissipated his anger. "I'm here, what do you want?"

"We need your help."

"I won't accept another assignment, General."

"I'm told the DGSE wants Ms. Belleau to return to Paris," Doyle said. "Will you go back to France with her?" Jacqueline Belleau worked for the French secret service. She was in love with McGarvey, and after the Moscow operation she had come to Washington with him.

"I don't know," McGarvey said.

"I'm not offering you an assignment," Murphy said. "I'm offering you a job."

"Doing what?"

"Deputy director of Operations."

McGarvey had to laugh. "You have to be kidding."

"You're the perfect man for the job, Kirk," Danielle said reasonably. "No one has your operational experience. And you say that you won't take another field assignment."

"I'm out," McGarvey said. "And even if I wanted the job, which I don't, my appointment would never make it through the Senate. I was a shooter. No one in their right mind would even consider me." McGarvey looked at them. "I'm an anachronism, remember?"

"You have too much valuable experience to waste teaching Voltaire to a bunch of kids who couldn't care less," Murphy said.

McGarvey looked out the bullet-proof windows behind the general's desk. Outside was freedom from knowing the frightening secret of just how fragile the world really was. In here they waged a constant battle that never seemed to have an end. And it was up to the deputy director of Operations to see that the war was fought efficiently in a way that seemed to make the most sense. With the most honor.

That had never seemed clearer than during the Rick Ames affair. Fifteen or twenty good people had been killed because no one inside this building, the deputy director of Operations included, had bothered to ask the most obvious question: How could Ames afford an eight-hundred-thousand-dollar house, and thirty thousand a month in credit card bills on a salary of fifty or sixty thousand?

Ames had sold out to the Russians, and every agent he'd identified had been murdered. Blood had been shed. A river of blood because of bullshit, timidity and indifference. And still the battle raged on.

He studied the general's eyes. Everything was different now. Less clear than it had been during the Cold War when we knew who our enemy was. We'd been the good guys and the Russians bad. But times had changed. Now just about everyone was a potential enemy. No place was truly safe; not New York City, not Oklahoma City, not Waco.

So who was left to fight the battles, McGarvey asked himself. The incompetents? If that were the case then we'd already lost.

"I'll listen."

"Good," Murphy said, and he seemed genuinely relieved, as did the others.

Paterson took a form from a file folder. "Before we get started we'd like you to sign this. Outlines your responsibilities to the information you'll be given this morning. Most of it is classified top secret or above."

McGarvey signed the document without reading it and handed it back. A brief look of annoyance crossed the general counsel's face.

"What's going on in the Sea of Japan that has you worried enough to offer me Ryan's old job? If it's Japan, you have a lot of good people in this building who know more about them than I do."

"Your name was put up two months ago," Danielle said. "But the decision was to give you five or six months to catch your breath after Moscow." Danielle shrugged apologetically.

"There was an underground nuclear explosion in North Korea twelve hours ago," Murphy said. "It was at one of their abandoned nuclear power stations on a deserted section of their east coast. A place called Kimch'aek."

"Was it a test, like India's and Pakistan's?"

"That's how it's going to play when the story breaks later today. The White House is going to stonewall it, at least for the time being, because frankly nobody knows what the hell to do. At the very least calling it an underground test is going to put a lot of pressure on Kim Jong-Il."

"The Japanese are already screaming for help," Doyle said. His mood was brittle. "They want us to move the Seventh Fleet into the Sea of Japan as a show of force."

McGarvey watched the interplay between them. "If it wasn't a test, what was it?"

"The North Koreans were using the place to stockpile what we believe were five working bombs. Three days ago they started moving something out of there in a big hurry, and then this happened." The general looked tired. "There were North Korean soldiers there, and civilian technicians, when the blast occurred. Maybe as many as two hundred of them."

"An accident?"

The general shook his head. "The skipper of one of our Seawolf submarines on patrol in the area spotted a Japanese MSDF submarine about five miles off the coast, possibily communicating with someone in the power station. Could be they sent a team ashore to verify what the North Koreans were storing there."

"Either that or it was a kamikaze team," Doyle said.

"If it had been a test, Pyongyang would have made a statement by now," Danielle put in glumly. "It's not something Kim Jong-Il would sit on."

"The *Seawolf* radioed back that the Japanese submarine was damaged in the blast and sent up an emergency beacon. The Japanese are sending rescue units."

"Which the North Koreans will try to block," McGarvey said. He thought that he'd lost his capacity for surprise. But he wasn't so sure now.

"It gets worse," Murphy said. He looked as if he hadn't slept in a week. "Within two hours of the explosion, a pair of Chinese Han class nuclear submarines were spotted leaving the inlet at Qingdao and heading into the Yellow Sea."

"Not much of a threat. They're rust buckets."

"It's more of a political statement, I should think," Danielle said.

"Are we going to send the Seventh Fleet out there?"

"The President is considering it," Murphy said after a brief hesitation. "But for the moment the bulk of the fleet is still at Yokosuka. If we send them into the Sea of Japan, Kim Jong-Il will take it as a direct threat."

"So what?" McGarvey asked. "He won't attack us or Japan, he's not that stupid. And sending the Seventh would be a clear message: Back off. Even the Chinese would stand down just like they did a few years ago when Taiwan held its elections. Nobody is going to start a shooting war over there. And North Korea has lost its nuclear weapons."

"The explosion had an estimated yield of twenty kilotons," Doyle said. "One bomb. We think they had five, four of which they'd managed to move out of there."

"I don't buy it, General," McGarvey said. "They're not going to start a war they couldn't win."

"Unless they're nudged," Doyle said. He took a couple of photographs from a folder and handed them to McGarvey. "Do you recognize either of these men?"

Both pictures were of the same two old men seated across from each other in what appeared to be a Japanese teahouse garden. They were dressed in expensive-looking business suits. In one photograph a geisha girl was serving them something, and in the second picture she was gone.

McGarvey looked up. "Should I know them?"

"The man on the left is Hiroshi Kabayashi, who controls the Bank of Kobe. The other man is Shin Hironaka, the former director general of defense. They were part of the group, that, along with Sokichi Kamiya, nearly brought down the government two years ago, and damned near got us in an all-out shooting war with Japan."

"I thought they were in jail."

"These pictures were taken ten days ago in Nagasaki," Doyle said. "About thirty miles south of the Japanese navy base at Sasebo where we think the disabled submarine came from."

McGarvey studied the photographs, a flood of memories coming back to him. The old men looked happy, even confident. Conspirators again, or just two old friends having tea?

"They call themselves superpatriots," Doyle said. "Unfortunately that's about all we've found out about them so far."

"Who's running operations these days?"

"Dick Adkins," Murphy said. "He's a good man, but he doesn't have your operational experience. Something he himself admits. Dick recommended that you be offered the job, and I agreed with him. We all did."

McGarvey handed the photographs back to Doyle.

"Well?" Murphy asked.

"Convince the President to get Seventh Fleet out of Tokyo Bay, then have Tokyo station find these guys, kidnap them if need be, and find out what's going on. But don't screw around. It looks as if you don't have much time."

"I meant the job offer."

"I'll think about it," McGarvey said.

"Goddammit," Doyle said.

"I said I'll think about it, Tommy."

Murphy nodded after a moment. "Very well. But as you say, we don't have much time, so don't take too long."

"I won't," McGarvey said.

Doyle got to his feet. "I'll take you downstairs."

Murphy stopped McGarvey at the door. "The DO is in shambles, Kirk. It's gotten beyond Dick's control. We need someone like you to put it back together." The general ran a hand across his eyes. "It was Ryan."

There were a dozen things McGarvey could have said, but he held his reply in check. Howard Ryan had hurt a lot of good people because of Murphy's blind devotion to expediency. The former DDO had been a wizard on the Hill. The CIA had been run into the ground under his leadership, but relations with Congress had risen to an all-time high.

The Farm
Williamsburg, Virginia

Elizabeth McGarvey crossed the creek fifty yards behind the operational exercise area and, keeping a narrow strip of woods between her and the edge of the confidence course, raced to the rear of a complex of concrete bunkers. She held up against the bole of a large tree to catch her breath and tuck her medium blond hair in her fatigue cap. The noon sun was behind her so that anyone looking her way would be partially blinded.

She was a pretty woman of twenty-three with intelligent green eyes, an oval face with high, round cheekbones and a slender figure hidden by a black jumpsuit. She exuded self-confidence. Her mother, who came from old West Virginia money, and her father, who had been a field officer with the Central Intelligence Agency before she was born, were divorced. Because of the separation, her parents had overcompensated with love and permissiveness so that she was spoiled. She was used to making decisions for herself.

By now the instructors would be wondering where she had gotten herself to. The object of this exercise was for her to approach the bunkers, take out the two guards, get inside, kill the commandant, steal his briefcase and get back out to the ops center in the safe zone.

But it was a trap. They knew which direction she was supposed to be coming from. She'd found that out last night by breaking into the operation officer's computer.

Stepping out from behind the tree, she ran the last twenty-five yards down a gently sloping grassy field to the featureless back wall of the west building.

In the distance she could hear the rattle of small arms fire on the range and the crump of an explosion, then another. She loved this, every minute of it. Her mother warned that if she wanted to attract a man she would have to exchange her war paint for makeup. But unless she found a man like her father, she didn't care.

At the end of the bunker she took a quick look around the corner. Two guards were hunched down behind a sandbag barrier. Impossible to take both of them out before an alarm was sounded.

Change the rules. She'd read her father's record; he'd never played by any rules except his own. It was one of the reasons he'd survived in the field for so long.

She laid her head against the rough wall for a few moments, going over everything she'd learned from the CIA field officer trainers for the past three months since Moscow. A wicked smile finally curled her lips. When all else failed, try the unexpected. She could almost hear her father saying something like that.

Checking her paintball pistol to make sure that it was ready to fire, she stuffed it in the web belt at the small of her back, then unzipped the top of her jumpsuit and pulled it down around her waist, making sure that she could still reach her gun.

She pulled off her sports bra, stuffed it in a pocket, took a deep breath, then let out a shriek and leaped around the corner.

The two guards, caught completely by surprise, turned toward her, their mouths dropping open as she leaped around like a crazy woman, frantically slapping her arms and shoulders and back.

"Ants!" she screamed desperately. "Ants! Help me, I'm on fire!"

Both men leaped over the sandbag barrier and came running, their paintball rifles slung over their shoulders. They were not much older than she was, both of them ex–Green Berets.

When they got within five feet, Elizabeth pulled out her pistol and shot both of them in the chest, bright orange paint covering their fatigue shirts, stopping them in their tracks.

"Shit," said the guard whose name tag read Jones, falling back.

"Sorry, gentlemen, but you're dead," she told them sweetly, as she holstered her pistol. "Now, if you'll be so good as to lie down, with your heads turned, I'll get dressed."

Jones laughed. "I may be dead, ma'am, but I'll be damned if I'll turn around."

The other instructor, named Gomez, was laughing too. He shook his head. "They warned us that you might try something cute."

Elizabeth put her bra on and pulled up her jumpsuit top and rezippered it. "Macho pigs," she said brightly, pulling out her pistol again.

"Yes, ma'am," Jones happily agreed.

The flag of Iraq flapped gently in the light breeze above the entryway as Elizabeth ducked inside. She waited a full minute for her eyes to adjust to the relative darkness before sprinting down the narrow corridor. She flattened herself against the wall next to the commandant's door, then rolled left, kicked it open and burst into the small office, sweeping her gun left to right.

The briefcase sat in plain sight on top of the unoccupied desk and even before Don Billings, the instructor playing the role of the commandant, stepped out from behind the door and wrapped his arms around her, she realized her mistake.

For an instant she tried to struggle free, but then willed her body to go limp in his arms. "Dammit," she said softly.

"Nice try, McGarvey, but I was watching from up front," Billings drawled. He was from Memphis, and the first time she sat in on one of his classes she'd pegged him as a smarmy, oily bastard. His hands were on her breasts. "Nice," he said in her ear.

She slowly turned in his arms and raised her face to his, her lips parted in a seductive smile. "I'm glad you approve," she told him, her voice husky.

He started to kiss her, when she grabbed his testicles and squeezed hard. His face turned white and he reared back on his tiptoes.

"Nice balls," she said, then she let go, stepped back and shot him in the chest at point-blank range. "You're dead."

Billings was enraged. "Fuck," he said through clenched teeth.

"Keep your hands to yourself, Mr. Billings," she said. "Next time I won't be so gentle."

"This exercise is over."

"Tell it to your wife."

"Goddammit, your approach wasn't in the scenario."

Elizabeth laughed, the look on his face was rich. "Neither was yours."

She grabbed the briefcase, slipped out of the office, waved merrily at the two guards, then made her way back across the creek. It was Friday, the late-summer weather beautiful, and as she walked she sang a little French song her father had taught her on one of his infrequent visits when she was a young girl, the day and nearly everything about her life just now absolutely perfect.

Kirk McGarvey parted the venetian blinds in the ops officer's office as Liz marched up the hill, her shoulders back, the briefcase in her left hand, the paintball pistol in her right as if she were willing and able to take on the world. His heart swelled with pride. The failure rate for the exercise she'd just successfully completed was almost one hundred percent.

"She's on her way up," he said, turning back to the ops officer.

Paul Isaacson, a big, red-faced Swede originally from Minnesota, laughed. "The apple doesn't fall far from the tree."

"I want you to flunk her out, Paul. I want her out of here as soon as possible."

"You're kidding, right?" Isaacson said seriously.

"No, I'm not." There was a flutter in McGarvey's gut just thinking about her back in the field.

"I can understand your reason. My own daughter, Chrissy, is about her age. But hell, Kirk, she'd find a way around me, just like she did this morning." He shook his head. "She's not the kind to take a simple no for an answer. Anyway, I'm not going to do your dirty work for you. If you want her out, you can fire her when you take over the DO."

McGarvey looked sharply at him. "Where the hell did you hear that?"

"The word's out," Isaacson said. He and McGarvey went way back together. Though Isaacson had never wanted to be chief of station, he'd handled just about every foreign desk at Langley. In one way or another he'd been involved in almost every assignment McGarvey had ever been given. For the past five years he'd been in charge of training the new kids how to survive the first couple of crucial years in the field. He'd not lost any of them because those graduated under his tutelage were ready. And he still had an inside track at Langley for the simple reason that he'd trained half of the current staff in Operations, and the other half wished he had. He heard things.

"Well, I told the general no."

"Right," Isaacson said. He wasn't convinced. "Are you taking Liz for the weekend?"

"Unless her class is going to be busy."

"Hell week doesn't start until the twenty-fifth, so we're taking it easy on them right now." He popped a videocassette out of the recorder behind his desk and gave it to McGarvey. "Her only real mistake was not checking for hidden cameras."

McGarvey chuckled. "She's not going to be happy."

"What about Don Billings? He was way out of line, but if he'd really been an Iraqi commandant it would have been worse."

"They're even. And I expect he'll think twice the next time he wants to grope a woman."

Isaacson gave McGarvey a long appraising look. "Working behind a desk would be different than being out in the field. You'd have to get used to the idea of sending green kids out there, who in your estimation wouldn't know how to wipe their own noses. Might be some tough calls." He glanced toward the window. "But it'd be a shame to throw away your experience, even if the Company has treated you like shit. I know a lot of guys over there who'd like to see you take the job. They'd feel more comfortable than they did under Ryan."

"I'll get her back to you Sunday night."

"Do that," Isaacson said. "But give her a chance, Kirk. You had yours, don't take this one away from her."

"Maybe she'd be one of the green kids I'd have to send out."

"Maybe," Isaacson said. "That's the whole point of this place."

McGarvey nodded, then headed out to where his daughter was perched on top of a picnic table with several of her classmates, all of them young men who eagerly hung on everything she was saying. He was even more unsettled than he had been in Murphy's office this morning.

*   *   *

It took Liz less than twenty minutes to shower, change clothes and pack a few things, then meet her father outside the barracks where he was smoking a cigarette. It was a few minutes before one, and the Farm was already winding down for the weekend. She looked bright and innocent in a crisp white cotton blouse, short khaki skirt and sandals, her hair pulled back and still damp.

"Are we having dinner with Jacqueline tonight?" she asked, tossing her bag in the backseat. She had a bittersweet look on her face.

"We're meeting her for drinks at Jake's at four, so we're going to have to hustle," McGarvey said. "Do you know something that I don't?"

"Just girl talk," she said mysteriously. "But I'll let her tell you." She gave her father a look that said it would be totally useless for him to try to pry anything else out of her.

The Farm was in Camp Perry off Interstate 64 outside of Williamsburg, about 150 miles south of Washington. Traffic was moderately heavy but moved well.

When they were away McGarvey gave his daughter the videocassette. "Paul gave this to me. Presumably it's the only copy."

"What is it?"

"You might want to take a look and then get rid of it. But don't let your mother see it."

Sudden understanding dawned on her face and she looked from the tape to her father. "Hidden cameras?"

"All over the place."

A rueful smile curled her lips. "Did you see it? Everything?"

McGarvey nodded. "They're going to come down on you pretty hard at Monday's debriefing."

"I got the briefcase, Daddy," she retorted defiantly.

"If that had really been Iraq you wouldn't have made it."

"I gave them a distraction."

McGarvey had to laugh. "One that's going to make the rounds this weekend."

"Billings is a prick."

"He's one of your primary instructors, and you've still got a lot to learn from him if you'll keep your mouth shut long enough to listen."

Liz gave her father an appraising, manipulative look that McGarvey caught. He'd spanked her once when she was a little girl for the same thing. "I thought you wanted me out," she said.

"Don't play games, Liz. And don't count on the operational experience you got in France and Moscow, because you didn't do such a hot job. Nearly got yourself killed, as a matter of fact."

She lowered her eyes. "I know, Daddy."

He wanted to take her in his arms, cradle her, protect her. But she was too big for that now. It was something he should have done years ago, but never had. "I want you to get out of the Company, or at least out of the DO. But if you're going to do a thing, then do it right."

"I know," she said, looking up. "I'm a McGarvey."

"Don't forget it," McGarvey said, trying to be stern.

She smiled warmly. "Never happen."

Georgetown

Jake's was a trendy new sidewalk cafe on Canal Street much frequented by the younger set of Washington's movers and shakers. Traffic was heavy by the time McGarvey and his daughter arrived a few minutes before four. They found a parking place a block away and walked back to the crowded restaurant.

Liz hadn't said anything else about Jacqueline, but it hadn't been difficult to figure out what was going on from her odd mood. The two of them had been doing a lot of talking over the past couple of weeks. Jacqueline had even driven down to Williamsburg to take Liz to dinner. And at the odd moment Mac's old teaching position at Delaware's Milford College had come up. Jacqueline had even reread his partially finished book on Voltaire and had made a few suggestions, from a Frenchwoman's perspective.

They had to wait for the light to change before they could cross at the corner. Jacqueline was seated at a sidewalk table near the entrance, and when she spotted them she waved gaily. She was wearing the pale blue Hermés scarf McGarvey had given her in Paris. It was like a wedding ring to her, a mark of possession.

Time finally to settle down? he asked himself, crossing the street. He was afraid of it.

She was Mediterranean classic. With a pretty oval face, dark eyes, a flawless olive complexion and rich, sensuous lips. She had the earthy look of Sophia Loren. Like the actress, she was aging beautifully, and would continue to do so. But whatever else she was besides that, she was an intelligent and very capable French secret service officer.

She raised her face to him, and McGarvey kissed her before he sat down.

"Liz has a secret which she refuses to share with me," McGarvey said. "Girl talk."

Elizabeth pecked Jacqueline on the cheek, then rolled her eyes. "I'm going to the ladies' room. Be back in five." She gave her father a significant look then was gone.

"She's a wonderful girl," Jacqueline said, watching her thread her way between the tables. She turned back. "Like you in many ways."

"Stubborn."

Jacqueline nodded. "And a little bit difficult." She averted her eyes. "Lonely."

"That's one of the reasons I want her to get out of the business."

"It won't happen unless she wants it. I don't think even you could force her to leave."

The waiter came. Jacqueline was drinking a kir, and she ordered another. McGarvey ordered a cognac neat; he figured he was going to need it.

"She's been talking about her mother. What does she have to say about all this?"

"Katy doesn't want her to follow in my footsteps."

"Neither would I, if I were her mother," Jacqueline said.

McGarvey studied her troubled face. He'd been against her coming back to Washington with him. There were still too many issues unresolved from his past. Dangerous issues which could hurt her. But she wouldn't listen to him, or to her control officer in Paris. She'd resigned, but the DGSE had simply placed her on an extended leave of absence.

"Is that what these past couple of weeks have been all about, Jacqueline?" he asked. "You want me to get out of the business and take my old job at Milford? Finish the book? The two of us settle down in a little cottage by the Chesapeake? Happy forever after?"

His remark hurt her, which is what he'd intended, because he was frightened again for her safety. "You're a real shit," she flared, suddenly angry, her French accent thicker than usual. "Who do you think you are, Candide? Wandering through life an innocent. No blood ever sticks to your hands?" She shook her head in frustration. "*Merde*. Who made you God anyway? Judge, juror, executioner? You kill anyone you want and nothing happens to you. It slides off your back because you've convinced yourself that what you're doing makes for a better world. Well, killing never solved anything. Don't you understand? Can't you get that through your head? You can't fix the world with a gun! *Salopard!*"

It was as if she had plunged a knife into his chest, directly into his beating heart. "Go back to Paris," he said softly.

She said nothing, and he waited. When he'd lived in Lausanne, the Swiss police had sent Marta Fredricks to watch over him. Like Jacqueline she'd fallen in love with him, and like Jacqueline she'd followed him after a particularly bad assignment. It had gotten her killed. He was desperately afraid for Jacqueline. As he was for his daughter. The only one finally clear was his ex-wife, Kathleen. She was safe. It was one of the few constants in his life.

"I love you, Kirk," Jacqueline finally said, reaching for him.

"I know," McGarvey said. He kept his hands folded on the table in front of him.

Her face dropped again. "I must know if you have any feelings for me."

"You want me to make a decision so you can tell it to Paris," McGarvey said hurtfully. "So you can justify your decision not to return."

Jacqueline was fighting back tears. This moment had been coming for a long time. "I want you to be safe."

"You want me to marry you. But first I have to give you my word that I'm out of the business, permanently, otherwise you'd never be able to return to France, even for a visit."

It was the reason for Liz's bittersweet mood. She liked Jacqueline, but she still held the faint hope, almost a fairy-tale hope, that somehow her mother and father would get back together. If he married Jacqueline, Liz's impossible dream would fade even farther into the background.

Jacqueline met his eyes and nodded.

"Return to Paris, Jacqueline," he said. "You have a life back there, a home, roots, family. I can't give any of that to you."

"But I love you," she said defiantly.

"That will fade," McGarvey said, hating himself for what he was doing to her. But he'd known it would come to this from the beginning, and yet he'd been selfish enough, lonely enough, not to end it before it had begun.

Jacqueline studied his face for a very long time, her eyes filling. "It's eating you alive, my darling," she said very softly, almost a whisper. "Get out while you still can, if for no one's sake except your own."

She gathered her purse, got up and headed for the exit as Elizabeth returned from the bathroom.

"Jacqueline?" Liz called out.

McGarvey was about to turn back to his daughter, his mood dark, his emotions rubbed raw by what he had just done, when he noticed a black

Mercedes E320 darting through traffic on Canal Street toward them at a high rate of speed and accelerating. There was a man in the front passenger seat and one in the backseat, the windows down. Assassins, something in his gut told him. They were meant for him. Somehow they knew that he would be seated outside this restaurant at this moment.

Jacqueline started to turn back at the same moment the Mercedes passed the restaurant entrance and the man in the backseat tossed something out the window.

"Bomb!" McGarvey shouted. He shoved the heavy wrought-iron patio table over on its side as he jumped up and reached for Elizabeth.

The package fell short at Jacqueline's feet.

McGarvey caught Elizabeth's wrist and dragged her to the floor as the bomb went off with a tremendous flash and bang, glass and metal fragments tearing through the fifty or sixty restaurant patrons who'd had no time to react. People screamed in terror and agony even as glass shards continued to fall around them.

The patio table McGarvey had pushed over had saved him from the brunt of the blast, which had taken out the front of the restaurant, the wrought-iron fence and striped awnings. Traffic had come to a complete halt, several cars nearest to the restaurant damaged by the explosion.

McGarvey raised up in time to see the Mercedes round the corner to the right on 31st Street, the wrong direction, he thought, if they were trying to get across the river on Key Bridge. They would have to double back on South Street.

Two police officers trailed by a civilian came running across the street. Jacqueline was gone, the spot where she'd been standing nothing but a smoking crater two feet deep.

"Oh God, Daddy?" Liz cried weakly and McGarvey turned to her.

Her right side from the waist up was a mass of blood and gashed flesh, glass sticking out of dozens of wounds, and a six-inch piece of smoking metal was jutting from her side just below her left armpit. She was looking up at him, her eyes wide.

"The bastards were after you," she said through clenched teeth.

"Here!" McGarvey shouted. He was at the edge of panic. "Over here!"

"How's Jacqueline—" Elizabeth tried to raise up.

"Take it easy, Liz." McGarvey held her down. "Over here!" he shouted. "We need help!"

Elizabeth looked down at her wounds. "I'm okay, Daddy. Did they get away?"

The civilian reached them. "I'm a doctor," he said, pushing McGarvey aside. "Over here," he called to one of the cops carrying a first aid kit.

Elizabeth looked up into her father's eyes. "Is Jacqueline dead?"

He nodded.

"Get the bastards." She mouthed the words.

McGarvey was torn by indecision. Jacqueline was dead, his own flesh and blood lay gravely wounded at his feet and there was nothing he could do about it. But then a black rage rose up inside of him. Once again his little girl had been put in harm's way because of him. This time the bastards had hurt her badly. They'd torn her body, shed her blood. But for a split second she would be dead like Jacqueline, her body torn into a million pieces of flesh and bone.

All of that from the instant of the explosion was less than thirty seconds. Already the doctor was opening the paramedics' kit and was attending to Liz. Other people were coming to help.

McGarvey stepped back, Liz's eyes still locked with his. She nodded and smiled grimly. "Go," she whispered.

McGarvey turned and sprinted out of the restaurant, slipping and nearly falling on the glass and gore. He reached the street and raced toward Wisconsin Avenue, the opposite direction the killers had taken. At the corner, traffic had slowed, and in the distance he could hear sirens. Some people had gotten out of their cars to see what was happening.

The Mercedes was nowhere in sight. But it had to come back this way, because there was no other route out other than the ferry terminal under the freeway at the foot of Wisconsin Avenue. Unless it had made a U-turn on 31st Street, in which case he'd lost them already.

Taking out his pistol as he ran, he switched the safety off. A half block away, just before the canal bridge, he moved out into the street between parked cars. The farther away from the blast, the more normally traffic flowed. Most people a block away from the restaurant had no idea what had happened, except that a man with blood on his side and carrying a gun was running up Wisconsin Avenue.

Traffic parted as he crossed the bridge, and then the Mercedes was heading directly toward him.

McGarvey stepped into the middle of the street and raised his gun. People on the bridge stopped to stare, scarcely believing what they were witnessing.

"Get down!" McGarvey shouted at them. "Get down!"

The Mercedes accelerated directly toward him. McGarvey walked toward it, firing at the windshield, one measured shot at a time, like a bullfighter calmly walking into the charge of a two-ton animal bent on his destruction.

He could see the glass starring, then shattering. Fifty feet away the car suddenly swerved left and smashed into a bridge stanchion, then careened right, crossed both lanes and finally crashed into the concrete railing.

The front passenger door popped open and a slightly built Asian man dressed in a dark shirt and slacks leaped out. He had a pistol. McGarvey fired three shots, all of them catching the man in the chest, driving him backwards half into the car.

The driver was dead and the rear-seat passenger jumped out the other side. McGarvey crossed behind the car and fired one shot, missing as the man ducked down behind the fender. McGarvey's gun was empty, the slide locked in the open position. Still moving around the back of the car, McGarvey ejected the spent magazine with one hand while pulling out a spare magazine from his pocket with his other. He rammed it home and released the ejector slide as the second man suddenly leaped up, smashing a karate blow to McGarvey's right collarbone, making him drop the gun, his arm and hand instantly numb.

He parried the Asian's next blow with his left forearm, and before the killer could come around to the right, McGarvey hooked his foot behind the man's right ankle, pulling him completely off balance and pitching him backward to the pavement.

Before he could recover, McGarvey dropped down hard, his knee in the man's groin, his forefinger and middle finger in the man's eyes.

"Who sent you?" McGarvey demanded, the blackness threatening to block out all sanity. He couldn't see anything but his daughter's bloody body and the smoking crater where Jacqueline had been standing.

The man clapped his hands against the sides of McGarvey's head, a fierce pain shooting through his ears into his skull. McGarvey drove his fingers through the killer's eyes, deep into the man's skull, then picked his head up by the eye sockets, blood spurting out, and slammed his head against the pavement, once, twice, a third time until the man's body went limp.

"Christ!" McGarvey pulled his bloody hand away, the black rage slowly dissipating. People at the sides of the street looked at him in horror. Traffic had backed up on both sides of the canal bridge, and sirens were coming from all over the city. He wiped his hand on the dead man's shirt front. He'd gone berserk, completely out of control. No force on earth could have stopped him from destroying the three men who'd hurt his child. Now nothing mattered except getting back to her.

He stumbled backward off the killer's body, retrieved his gun and holstered it at the small of his back as he headed back to the restaurant.

The first of the police units were arriving at the canal bridge as

McGarvey rounded the corner onto Canal Street into a scene of utter bedlam. Dozens of ambulances, fire-rescue units and police cars had already arrived, and others were coming in as the first of the wounded were being taken away. A pall of smoke and dust still hung in the air. Glass littered the entire street from shop and office windows that had been blown out by the blast. People were everywhere, some of them rescue workers, onlookers gawking at the carnage and others affected by the explosion wandering around in a daze.

"Hey, you can't go in there," a cop shouted as McGarvey pushed his way through the crowd.

"My daughter is in there," McGarvey said.

"She'll be okay, buddy, people are taking care of it." The cop tried to steer McGarvey toward one of the paramedic trucks, but McGarvey pulled away.

"My daughter's in there," he repeated himself, and he shoved the cop aside. "She's hurt. I'm going to her, okay?"

The cop saw something dangerous in McGarvey's eyes, and he backed down. "Suit yourself." He turned away.

Elizabeth, strapped onto an ambulance gurney was just being wheeled out of the devastated remains of the restaurant as McGarvey reached the spot where the exit had been. She was unconscious, her face pale, her blond hair matted with blood.

"She's my daughter. Where are you taking her?" McGarvey asked the paramedics.

"Columbia."

"You're taking her to Georgetown. It's almost as close and it's better," McGarvey said. He was having trouble focusing.

"We don't have time to argue—"

"We're going to Georgetown, and I'm coming with you. Do you fucking understand what I'm saying?"

The attendant opened his mouth to argue, but then nodded. "Yes, sir," he said. "Georgetown."

TWO

The White House

Ever since he was a boy growing up in war-torn Formosa at the end of World War II, Joseph Lee had wanted to make his mark on the world. Dressing in the Lincoln bedroom for cocktails with President Lindsay and the boorish first lady, his dream was nearing fruition. His ambition then, as now, was the same as the Japanese goal in the thirties: an East-Asian co-prosperity sphere. One hemisphere, one power. He was one of its new architects, and he would be one of its major players.

His San Francisco–born wife, Miriam, came from the bathroom as he struggled with his bow tie in the gilded mirror above the dresser.

"You're all thumbs," she said, her voice and movements like a little bird's. At five feet she was only four inches shorter than her husband. In Taiwan, where they maintained one of their half-dozen homes, they were normal-sized. But here, in the land of giants, and especially next to President Lindsay, whom the press described as "Lincolnesque," they were practically midgets. She was fond of telling her husband this as often as he would listen to her. His response was always the same: A true measure of people is their net worth in assets, influence and friends, not in inches above the soles of their shoes.

"We treat our guests considerably better than this," he said. The bedroom was shabby.

"But this is the White House," she replied, finishing with his tie. She looked up into his face. "I'm just so darn proud of you, Joseph. Not even an American citizen and you have brought me here like this." She let her eyes stray around the room with obvious happiness. "My parents would have been so proud."

Lee cracked a narrow, thin-lipped smile. "So would mine," he said. "But for different reasons."

She gave her husband a shrewd look. "They wanted to have this by force. You've gotten it by finesse."

Outwardly his wife was a diffident Chinese-American of the old school. In actuality she was as astute in business as her husband, and she helped manage their nearly four-billion-dollar ventures with an iron fist. After thirty-five years of childless marriage they were extensions of each other.

It was a few minutes before six when he put on his tuxedo jacket and helped his wife with the corsage the staff had sent up an hour ago. The house was shopworn, but the service under this administration was good.

"What do you suppose they'll want to talk about?" his wife asked. "Money for the vice president's campaign?"

"I would think they'll want to know our reaction to the business in North Korea."

"It's not made the news yet."

"That won't last much longer."

Her eyes crinkled at the corners, as they did when she was figuring the odds. Her favorite event was the Hong Kong horse racing season, from which she always came away a big winner. "There could be an advantage to be gained by the correct timing."

"Or disadvantage," Joseph Lee said.

"Yes, that too, but profit can be found in the most unlikely of places." She let her eyes stray around the bedroom again, mentally rearranging, redecorating. "I'll speak with Mrs. Lindsay. It's time that I get to know her." She smiled. "Waterloo, Iowa. What a strange place to be from."

Georgetown Hospital

McGarvey cleaned up and went down to the hospital cafeteria a few minutes after ten, unable to get the vision of what he had done on the bridge out of his mind. The few people seated at the tables did not object when he switched off the television, though the networks were running specials on the terrorist attack. Fifty-eight people had been hurt, and eighteen had been killed. But it would be days, perhaps weeks before all the bodies were identified. Some of them had been so badly torn apart it would take DNA analysis to make sure who they were.

Jacqueline was dead, and there wasn't a thing he could do about it. Nor could he turn back the clock on his daughter's injuries because that would have taken him all the way back to the day he'd joined the CIA.

He got a cup of coffee and went to a corner table. His hand shook a little. He'd been close to death before, but this time the people he'd most wanted to protect had gotten hurt despite his best efforts. He hadn't been good enough, fast enough, and in the end he had lost all control. Nothing had mattered to him on that bridge except destroying the monsters. He lowered his head and closed his eyes, a deep depression threatening to block out his sanity. Three more dead men and a city street filled with broken glass and blood. God almighty, when would it stop?

He looked up as the chief surgeon Dr. Edwin Magnuson, still dressed in his scrubs, came in, spotted McGarvey and walked over. He was in his forties, tall and heavily built. He looked tired but satisfied.

"Your daughter is going to be fine," he said. "It'll be some time before she gets back to one hundred percent, but it'll happen."

McGarvey let out his pent-up breath, the veil of depression lifting a little. "Thank you," he said. "May I see her?"

"I'm keeping her in the ICU at least through tonight, so I want you to wait until we move her." The doctor gave him a serious smile. "There's not a whole hell of a lot you can do for her. She'll be fine. She just needs time to heal."

The relief was sweet. "Will there be any permanent damage? Any disability?"

"Too early to say, but I think she'll come out of this with nothing more than some scars, which a competent plastic surgeon can all but eliminate. I'll give you the name of a colleague of mine. One of the best in the business."

"How are the others?"

A dark look crossed the doctor's face. "Let's just say that your daughter is a lucky young woman to be alive and back in one piece."

The vise around McGarvey's heart closed again. He had almost lost her twice in three months, but now that he knew his daughter was going to be okay he came back to Jacqueline. There was nothing left of her to repair. What pieces they found would probably fit in a very small rubberized bag for transport back to Paris.

McGarvey lowered his head, not sure if he wanted to weep or lash out at somebody or something. The killers were dead, but they had been directed by someone.

"Time for you to get some rest," the doctor said sympathetically. "You look as if you could use it."

"You're right," McGarvey mumbled, but there wasn't going to be much time for rest now. Or for Milford and his job as a teacher, or for the book on Voltaire Jacqueline had wanted him to finish. No time even to mourn Jacqueline, no time to walk away from a twenty-five-year history that had once again caught up with him.

Once Liz had been stabilized and taken into the operating room McGarvey had telephoned his ex-wife at her Chevy Chase home, but she wasn't there, nor did the message on her answering machine say where she was or how long she'd be gone. He left a message for her to call the hospital as soon as possible. It was all he could do for the moment, all he was prepared to do. He needed to work this out for himself first.

Meeting with the general at Langley bothered him more than he wanted to admit. And seeing Liz at the Farm hadn't done much for his already morose mood either. He had gone over the sequence of events a dozen times, looking for something, anything that might give him a clearer understanding. It was possible that the attack has been nothing more than a random act of terrorism. Many of Washington's brightest and best could have been expected to be there at that moment. He wanted to believe that scenario with all of his heart, because it was the least complicated for him. But he was having trouble with the timing. And with the fact the killers had been Asians.

Too many coincidences.

Something was floating around at the back of his head, some memory, some connection, something he should know that would give a reason for this afternoon's attack. Something to make sense of. Something he could understand. If it was there, it would come, he thought.

When he looked up the doctor was gone, and two men in rumpled suits were coming toward him. Cops, he mentally catalogued them. They had the look. Probably federal.

"Mr. Kirk McGarvey?" the taller of the two asked. He was very tall and fit, in his thirties with short hair and wire-rimmed glasses. His partner, who was almost as tall, but with gray hair and wise eyes, was probably in his fifties and looked like an aging street thug or Teamsters boss. He stood back and to the left.

"Who are you?"

The cop took out his ID. "I'm Special Agent Bob Salmon. Federal Bureau of Investigation."

The other cop held out his ID, a dangerous look on his face. He held himself like a boxer. "Thomas Kosiak," he said. "You McGarvey?"

"What can I do for you?"

"We asked if your name is McGarvey," Kosiak said.

"Yes, it is. What do you want?"

"You're coming with us."

"My daughter just came off the operating table, and I still haven't got in contact with her mother," McGarvey said. He knew what they wanted.

Kosiak unbuttoned his suit coat.

"We'd like to ask you about the bombing this afternoon," Salmon said. "Several witnesses place you at the scene."

"I was there."

"It doesn't look as if you took a hit," Kosiak said. "You were lucky." His eyes tightened. "Get to your feet."

"Am I being charged with something?"

"Not yet," Salmon said. "Let's go."

"Give me your card, and I'll call you in the morning after my daughter wakes up," McGarvey said. The situation was accelerating, and he didn't want it to happen. But he wanted to stay at the hospital until he talked to Katy. He didn't want Liz to be alone.

"Mr. McGarvey, believe me when I say that we do not want to use force unless we have to," Salmon said, his voice level. "But you are coming with us one way or the other." Salmon was respectful, and Kosiak was wary.

"What's it going to be?" Kosiak asked.

McGarvey finished his coffee and got to his feet. There was no doubt that they had placed him on the Canal Bridge, and there were going to be a lot of questions he was going to have to answer. He withdrew his gun, ejected the magazine, cycled the live round out of the chamber, reloaded it in the magazine and handed the gun and clip to Salmon who sniffed the barrel.

"This gun has been fired recently."

"Yes, it has."

FBI Headquarters
J. Edgar Hoover Building

They arrived at 10:45 P.M. McGarvey was taken directly upstairs to a small fourth-floor conference room, with space enough for only ten people around a mahogany table. There were no windows in the solemn, no-nonsense room. The drive over had been in silence, giving McGarvey time to work out his options. Foremost among them was that he needed his freedom if he was going to find out who tossed the bomb, and why. He was going to be tied up here answering questions, and there would be a CIA Internal Affairs investigation into why the man they'd proposed as DDO had killed three men in broad daylight in front of a dozen witnesses. They weren't going to buy a father's rage. He was a trained intelligence officer who should have been in better control of himself and the situation. But time was critical, and whatever it took he had to get out of here.

He closed his eyes and he could see the bright flash, feel the concussion, smell the burned Semtex, hear the screams, the jingle of falling glass, and see the look of agony on his daughter's face. Christ, it was happening all over again. He was unable to protect the people he loved, and now it was another link in the heavy chain that he had to drag with him.

They'd parked in the underground garage, and after they signed in, rode up in an elevator, the building very quiet. Salmon brought in a carafe of coffee and several mugs, then laid out several ruled pads and a small tape recorder.

They were joined by a third man, well dressed, perhaps in his early forties, whom McGarvey took to be a senior agent or division head. Salmon and Kosiak were deferent toward him.

He sat across the table from McGarvey, laid a file folder down and switched on the tape recorder.

"I'm Fred Rudolph, assistant director of the Bureau's Special Investigative Division. Has it been explained why you've been brought here for questioning?"

"No," McGarvey said.

"Have your rights been read to you?"

"I'll waive them."

"State your name and current address for the record."

He'd rented a small apartment in Georgetown a dozen blocks from the sidewalk cafe. He gave them that address.

"Are you aware that charges may be brought against you depending on the outcome of our investigation and this interview?"

"What charges?"

"Three counts of murder," Rudolph said, looking directly at McGarvey.

He nodded. "They tossed the bomb."

Rudolph's lips pursed. "You admit it?"

"They were trying to get away," McGarvey said. "I had to take out the driver, and after that it was self-defense. Believe me, I didn't want it to happen that way."

"The last one was quite a mess," Rudolph said dryly. "Witnesses said you went berserk."

"I shouted for everybody to get down."

"They said that too." Rudolph glanced at the other two agents.

"How'd you know they'd be coming up Wisconsin Avenue?" Kosiak asked.

"It was the only way out. After they tossed the bomb they went the wrong way on Thirty-first. It was a dead end, so they had to double back."

"Let me get this straight. You witnessed the bombing?" Rudolph asked.

"I was in the restaurant, and I saw the car coming."

"That's what we figured. But how is it that you managed to get out of there without an injury?"

"I saw what was about to happen, shoved over a table and pulled my daughter to the floor."

"Saved yourself and your daughter, but no one else," Kosiak said with a smirk. It was all McGarvey could do to keep from going across the table after him.

"There wasn't much time to do anything else," McGarvey said, holding his temper in check. His nerves were rubbed raw.

"But you did look up in time to see which direction the terrorists took," Kosiak said. "Then you ran out, leaving your daughter and a lot of other seriously injured people to bleed to death on their own."

"A doctor and a couple of cops came from across the street. They were more qualified than me to help the wounded," McGarvey said.

Rudolph and the others exchanged glances, and he checked something in his file. "Where are you working now, Mr. McGarvey?"

"I'm a teacher. Milford College, in Delaware."

"That must be quite a school," Rudolph said. "Are all the teachers down there armed and dangerous like you?"

McGarvey didn't answer.

"Did you know those men?" Salmon asked. "The guys you took out on the bridge?"

"Never saw them before."

"The car was rented yesterday in Baltimore, on a valid D.C. driver's license with a gold Visa. But there's no such name or address. Same with the ID on the other two men, valid but nonexistent names and addresses. Does that ring a bell?"

"It's more sophisticated than your ordinary terrorist," McGarvey said, his thoughts racing ahead.

"That's what we thought," Rudolph agreed. He shoved a file folder across to McGarvey. "What do you make of that?"

The folder contained a half-dozen photographs of McGarvey, some taken outside his apartment in Paris, and one showing him coming out of CIA headquarters in the Nissan Pathfinder. A single sheet of paper contained a partial transcript of a phone intercept from McGarvey's apartment to Jake's. Jacqueline had telephoned this morning to make the reservation.

"They knew you would be there," Rudolph said. "We found this in their car. It would seem that the attack was meant for you. Can you tell us why?"

"No," McGarvey said, and it was the truth, or almost the truth. The only thing that had changed for him in the past twenty-four hours leading to the attack was Murphy's job offer. "Did you find the bug?"

Rudolph shook his head. "If there was one on your phone, or at the junction box under the street it was gone by the time we got to it this evening." He held his peace for a few moments. "Do you still work for the CIA, Mr. McGarvey?"

"I don't work for the CIA," McGarvey said. "But they've offered me a job."

"Doing what?"

"I can't say."

"Might this attack have something to do with that job offer?"

"I don't know," McGarvey said. There were no processing stamps on the back of the photographs, nothing on the single sheet of paper to give any clue who'd been watching him or why. The Paris pictures could have been taken anytime in the past year, but the photograph of him coming out of CIA headquarters had to have been taken in the past few days. He'd picked up the leased Nissan on Tuesday. And the transcript was from this morning. The list of those people who knew he was being offered the DDO wasn't very long, but starting at the White House it contained some pretty powerful names. If, as Rudolph had asked, the attack was related to the job offer it raised some very disturbing possibilities. Like who had the most to lose if he became DDO? Was it something out of his past after all?

"What about their fingerprints? Have you found a match in your files?"

"Not yet. Our best guess is that we won't. They're probably foreign nationals. Possibly Japanese. We're asking for their help."

"Good luck," McGarvey said.

"Goddammit, was this one of your fucking operations gone bad?" Kosiak yelled.

The agent's outburst stunned them all.

"Get him out of here," McGarvey said. He could feel his control slipping.

"What are you going to do, big man, pull my fucking face off?"

"The attack wasn't my fault," McGarvey said tiredly. "And I don't want a confrontation with you. I'm not the enemy."

"How the hell do we know that? You don't have a recent background. No U.S. driver's license, no voter registration card, no gun permit. Hell, you haven't even filed an income tax return, that we can find, for the past ten years. Who the hell are you?"

"I've lived in Europe for a long time."

"You're a fucking cowboy."

"That's enough," Rudolph cautioned mildly enough to make McGarvey wonder if they were setting him up. Good cop, bad cop. Rudolph made a show of shutting off the tape recorder. "We'll need a detailed statement from you, of course. But then the question will be what do we do with you?" He shook his head. "You've committed a number of crimes which must be answered for. Murder, working out of your jurisdiction, discharging a firearm for which you have no permit, leaving the scene of a crime, actually of two crimes, failure to fully cooperate with a federal investigation."

"I want to know what happened as much as you do," McGarvey said.

"Tell me about Ms. Jacqueline Belleau. We found her purse. The French embassy is very interested in her. She was a friend?"

"Yes," McGarvey said.

"Had you known her long? Was she a good friend?"

"We were close," McGarvey said.

"You spooks stick together, is that it?" Kosiak said.

"Were you aware that Ms. Belleau was an employee of the French secret service?" Rudolph asked blandly. "The reason I mention this is because our counterespionage division has a file on her. There was an incident with a Canadian at the United Nations a few years ago. The boy committed suicide, and Ms. Belleau was asked to leave the United States. Were you aware of this?"

"Not all the details," McGarvey replied cautiously. He had no idea where Rudolph was taking this.

"Yet three months ago she got a visa to return here apparently with no problem. Can you explain that?"

"No," McGarvey said. "What's your point?"

"Just this. There is an outstanding federal warrant for your arrest on unspecified charges. It was issued about four months ago. So far as we could tell the warrant was still valid this afternoon." Rudolph's eyes never left McGarvey's. "Odd thing, but when I went to check on it for further details this evening, I was told that the warrant was a dead issue. It was no longer in force."

McGarvey shrugged.

"Point is, Ms. Belleau's name was also on that warrant," Rudolph said. "Would you care to comment?"

"I can't."

"You and she were more than friends, you were working together on something that probably resulted in the attack at the restaurant this afternoon in which a lot of innocent people were hurt or killed." Rudolph's thin lips compressed. "That's the part that gives me the most difficulty. Why didn't you take your troubles elsewhere?"

"We weren't working on anything," McGarvey said.

"Well, the thing is, I don't believe you," Rudolph said. "The CIA is not cooperating with us on this one, so I've been given the authorization to take this investigation wherever it leads." His beeper chirped, and he glanced at it then looked over at Salmon and Kosiak. "Take him downstairs and read him his rights this time. We'll keep him here until morning when we can transfer him to the metropolitan police." Rudolph got up. "I'm sorry about your friend, and about your daughter's injuries, Mr. McGarvey. But there were other people at that restaurant whom you should have considered." He gave McGarvey a last look then left.

"On your feet," Kosiak said, with obvious relish.

McGarvey got up. "Do I get a phone call?"

"Depends on how well you behave yourself." Kosiak turned McGarvey around and cuffed his hands behind his back.

He and Salmon led him back down the corridor to the elevator, where they had to wait for the car to come up from the first floor.

"Did the car rental agency in Baltimore say which one of the three rented the Mercedes?" McGarvey asked.

Kosiak gave him an elbow in the ribs.

"You're going to learn to control your mouth, CIA boy," Kosiak said.

The elevator door opened when Rudolph called to them from the end of the corridor. "Wait up."

They turned as he and Tommy Doyle came down the hall. The FBI man was mad, and he seemed embarrassed. "Take the cuffs off him."

"Sir?" Kosiak asked.

"I said take the handcuffs off Mr. McGarvey. There's been a mistake."

For a second Kosiak wasn't going to comply, but then he hauled McGarvey around and did as he was told.

"Stop at the counter downstairs; your weapon will be returned to you," Rudolph said.

"If you come up with anything, please let me know," McGarvey said. "So far as I can, I'll do the same for you."

"I appreciate that," Rudolph said tightly. "Now get the fuck out of here."

En Route Back to the Hospital

As a matter of routine, deputy directors had a car and driver at their disposal, but Doyle drove his own, a BMW, this evening. He was shook up and he drove fast and erratically.

"Tell me that was a simple act of terrorism and you happened to be at the wrong place at the wrong time."

"They had a tap on my phone, so they knew Jacqueline and I would be there. The Bureau found a file with part of the phone intercept and a half-dozen pictures of me."

"Did you recognize them?"

"No," McGarvey said. "They might have been Japanese: at least that's the Bureau's thinking. No fingerprint records. All their IDs were good fakes. So it wasn't a simple hit-and-run; they were professionals, they knew what they were doing, except for the one mistake."

Friday night traffic was heavy on Constitution Avenue as they passed the Ellipse, the front of the White House illuminated in the distance.

"The general wants to see you as soon as possible," Doyle said. "And IA has already opened a file." He shook his head. "We got word from the hospital that Elizabeth is going to be fine."

"Have a guard put on her room, would you, Tommy?"

"As soon as we heard, we sent a couple of people over from Security. They'll stick around for the duration." Doyle glanced over at McGarvey. "How about you?"

"I'll be fine." McGarvey hoped that they'd send someone else after him. One on one. He'd give almost anything for the opportunity to have a heart-to-heart chat with one of them. Next time he would be thinking a little straighter than he had on the Canal Bridge.

"Sorry about Ms. Belleau. From what we hear she was on the way out and took the brunt of it."

"Yeah," McGarvey said softly. He was reliving the exact moment the package dropped at her feet. He was on the deck with Liz, the table overturned, and Jacqueline was just turning around, her mouth opening as if she was about to say something. Then there was the flash and bang and she was gone.

"Do you want me to drop you off at your place?" Doyle asked. "You look as if you could use a couple hours sleep."

"I need to get back to the hospital."

Doyle shook his head. "What's your take on it, Mac? Someone from one of your old operations gunning for you? The Japanese have no love for you, that's for sure."

"I hope it's that simple."

"Because if it isn't, then someone wants you dead because of the DDO thing," Doyle said. "And that would lead to some pretty heavy-duty places that none of us would care to go."

"You'd better start putting together a list of everyone who knows I'm being put up for the job."

"Won't be much of a problem on our side of the river, but there's no telling who on the President's staff knows. They're planning on ram-rodding your name through the Senate, so there're a few key people on the hill who already know. Lots of opportunity for a leak."

"You only have to look for two factors. A connection to the Japanese, or to me. Could be something we missed during one of my past assignments."

"I don't understand," Doyle said.

"If they know me well enough, they might guess I'd go through operations with a fine-toothed comb if I signed on as DDO. Could be we missed something the first time around that has them frightened now."

"No telling what old wounds we'll dig up," Doyle said. "Nobody's closet is totally clean."

"Throw a stick into a pack of dogs, and the one that yelps is the one that got hit."

"Except some of these dogs have teeth, and they might bite."

"Again," McGarvey said.

"Right," Doyle agreed morosely. "Again." He glanced over at Mc-Garvey. "Are you taking the job?"

"I don't know."

Georgetown Hospital

Dick Yemm from the Office of Security in the Directorate of Management and Services was seated outside the door to the ICU on the fifth floor when McGarvey got off the elevator. Despite the overheated corridor he wore a dark windbreaker. He got to his feet, his compact motions fluid and sure. He looked dangerous.

"Good evening, Mr. McGarvey."

McGarvey couldn't place the man's face. "How's she doing?"

"They're not saying much, except that they expect to move her upstairs to a private room about eight. I've got someone up there now checking it out."

"Anyone give you a hard time about being here?"

"No, sir," Yemm said, a faint flicker of a smile at the corner of his mouth as if the idea were ludicrous.

"Has my ex-wife shown up yet?"

"No, sir."

"She'll be here sooner or later. Do you know what she looks like?"

"I'll recognize her," Yemm said. "Now, if you don't mind me saying so, Mr. McGarvey, they're not going to let you in there to see your daughter, and anyway you look like shit. So why don't you go up to her room—it's six-oh-two—and catch a few hours sleep. If anything changes I'll get word to you."

McGarvey took out his cell phone and called the night duty officer at Langley. "This is Kirk McGarvey. Do you know who I am?" His eyes never left Yemm's.

"Yes, sir."

"I'm at Georgetown Hospital. DM and S sent someone over to keep an eye on my daughter."

"Yes, sir. Dick Yemm. He's a good man."

"Pull up his file and describe him."

"Don't need his file, Dick's a friend of mine. Short, dark, skinny, ugly as hell with a big mouth. That about cover it, sir?"

"Thanks." McGarvey broke the connection.

Yemm cracked a slight smile. "I was wondering if you were slipping, or if everything I heard about you was a crock."

McGarvey returned the smile. "Keep a close eye on her."

"Will do, sir."

McGarvey went upstairs to the sixth floor, explained to the floor nurse who he was and went back to the room Liz would be brought to in the morning. Peter Weisse, the second security officer from Langley, was seated outside the room.

"There are two beds, Mr. McGarvey, you might as well take one of them," Weisse said respectfully.

"If anybody shows up let me know."

"Will do, sir. Do you want me to have one of the nurses get something for you?"

"No," McGarvey said. Weisse closed the door behind him, so that he didn't see McGarvey walk to the window and take a cigarette out of the pack with hands that shook so badly the simple task of lighting it was almost impossible.

McGarvey came slowly awake as the first light of dawn began to tinge the windows red. For a moment he wasn't sure where he was, but it all came back to him about the same time he turned and saw his ex-wife standing at the window looking outside. Her head was bent, her narrow shoulders slumped, and her normally perfectly coiffed blond hair a mess. He hadn't realized how much he needed her until now.

"Hi, Katy," he said.

Kathleen McGarvey turned slowly to face her ex-husband. She'd been crying, something else out of character, and her makeup was a mess. "How are you feeling?"

"I'll live," McGarvey said, sitting up and swinging his legs over the edge of the bed. "Did they let you see Liz?"

She nodded. "They weren't going to at first." She looked away for a second. "She's a mess, but her doctor says she will heal."

"They'll be bringing her up here later this morning." McGarvey got a cigarette. "I'm sorry it took so long to get a message to you."

"I was with friends in New York." She was tall and slender, with sharply defined features, high, delicately arched cheekbones, full lips, brilliantly green eyes and a classic beauty. She was fifty, but could pass as an haute couture fashion model anywhere in the world.

"When did you get in?"

"A couple hours ago." Commercial airlines did not fly in the early morning hours, which meant she'd probably chartered a plane and bullied the pilot to fly her back to Washington. She was an inventive, forceful woman when she had to be. It was one of her attributes that McGarvey admired most.

"You must be tired, Katy."

"Kathleen," she corrected. "Tell me everything that happened, exactly. The television networks haven't got it right yet." Her eyes sparkled. "I have to know," she said with subdued passion. She was strung out. "Where were you when it happened? Where was Elizabeth?"

"Are you sure that you're up to this?"

She gave him an exasperated look, as if he were a complete idiot for asking such a question. But there was something else at the back of her eyes. Fear?

"I picked up Liz at the Farm for the weekend. We were meeting Jacqueline for drinks and then dinner later," McGarvey said.

"They didn't say anything about her. How is she?"

"Dead," McGarvey said quietly. "She was leaving, going back to France, but she didn't get any farther than the exit when the bomb landed at her feet."

Kathleen reached out a hand against the window frame to steady herself. "I'm sorry, Kirk. Truly sorry. Elizabeth said that she was a good friend to both of you."

"I have a habit of putting my friends and family in harm's way," McGarvey said. He'd known that facing his wife would be difficult.

"Where was Elizabeth when the bomb went off?"

"Coming back from the bathroom. She saw that Jacqueline was leaving, and she called out."

"Then what?"

"I saw the car coming, the guys in the front and back, windows down. It didn't fit, something wasn't right. I don't know. Instinct." McGarvey was back there. "I shoved a table over, grabbed Liz and hit the deck." He looked into his ex-wife's eyes. "But I was too slow, she was too far away and she got hurt." He shook his head. "I didn't get a scratch. All those people killed, torn apart, and Liz was cut to shreds, and there was nothing I could do for her. It was too late." He hung his head. "Twenty-five years too late."

Kathleen came to him, took the cigarette and stubbed it out in a water glass, then took him in her arms, his head against her bosom. "You saved her life. If you hadn't seen the car coming and recognized the monsters for what they were, and if you didn't have your reflexes, your abilities, your strength and courage, our baby would be dead. Whatever else happens, whatever anybody says to you, my darling—including me—you saved our daughter's life. Don't forget it. Please don't forget it."

Twenty-five years for what, McGarvey thought bitterly. What difference had he and people like him ever made? Had he saved the world from Communism? The Soviet Union had disintegrated of its own accord, with perhaps a nudge from the Star Wars initiative dog fight, but he'd had no direct part in it. And certainly there were no major changes in Chile or Europe or Japan because of what he'd done in the name of good old-fashioned, red-blooded American loyalty. Almost every night he came back to the faces of the people he'd killed. Their look of fear, of surprise and pain at the end, would haunt him forever, because in a large measure they had died for nothing. It was a game, with human lives the score.

"Did you know who they were?" Kathleen asked.

"No."

"Will they catch them?"

"They're dead."

Kathleen stepped back and looked down at him.

"A doctor came from across the street. As soon as he was with Liz I went after them."

"On foot?"

McGarvey nodded.

She looked at her husband for a long time, a strange, almost dreamy expression on her pretty face. "Did they say anything to you?"

"No."

"But they're dead. You're sure of that? They won't stand trial and maybe make some sort of political statement. Maybe get charged with second-degree murder, God only knows what?" She was starting to shiver, but there was nothing McGarvey could do for her.

"They're dead."

"Good," she replied reasonably. "But your coming back has created another problem too." She gave him a searching look. "Are you involved in another project?"

"They've asked me to come back to work for them as deputy director of Operations. But I don't know if I'll do it. It doesn't mean anything to me now."

"Well, it better," she said. "Because they almost killed your daughter, and they've come after me. You are the only one who can stop them."

The same fist as before closed over his heart. "What are you talking about, Kathleen?"

"In the last three days I've received two phone calls and one e-mail that crashed my computer. Nothing works. It's a virus or something. They want me to tell you to back off. They blocked my caller ID, so there's no way of tracing them. I laughed at them." She looked toward the door. "I didn't think they'd go after Elizabeth."

"Was it the same voice for both calls?"

"It wasn't human," she said. She was starting to come unglued. "It was a machine-generated voice. You know, the same computer voice you hear when you call somebody at their office. You get fucking choices."

"They want you to tell me to back off from what?"

"It was a warning, not a dialogue," Kathleen said. She searched his eyes. She'd given him comfort, and now she was asking him to repay the loan. She needed his reassurances. "Someone from your past wants you scared off or dead, and they're willing to come after your daughter, your girlfriend and me." She laughed at the edge of hysteria. "If I didn't know better I'd say it was that pompous ass Howard Ryan. He hated you, and he's certainly capable of something like this. You ruined his career, after all. Made him look like the fool he always was. But it couldn't be Ryan. Not like this. Could it?"

"It's not Ryan," McGarvey said. He got up and took her in his arms. "I want you to listen to me, Katy. They weren't after Liz, and they're not after you. It's me they want. And now they know that when they come after my family I'll hit back, so you're going to be okay."

She studied his face. "It's not going to be okay. Not since Greece. They're playing by a different set of rules now. Everyone is. You can get killed for parking your car in the wrong spot. It's crazy out there." She shook her head. "You, of all people, should know that."

McGarvey got an outside line and phoned the Operations duty officer at Langley. It was the same man from last night. He was pulling an all-nighter. "I want somebody watching my ex-wife," he said. "She's been receiving threats for the last three days."

"I'll have to clear this with Mr. Adkins when he comes in—"

"Do it now," McGarvey said without raising his voice. "It would mean a lot to me."

The OD didn't hesitate. "You got it, Mr. McGarvey," he said. "Do you know her whereabouts now?"

"She's with me at the hospital. Pull up her file, but I want her house and movements covered. She's had two blind telephone calls and one e-mail with a virus, warning her to make be back off."

"Makes it Company business, in that case, sir."

"That it does," McGarvey said, looking at his ex-wife. She was watching him, a defiant, proud look in her eyes that made him feel like he was twelve feet tall. Why had he ever let her go? It was beyond all reason.

THREE

SSN21 Seawolf
Sea of Japan

Commander Thomas Harding sat at the tiny desk in his cramped compartment writing a letter to Suzanne, his wife of twenty-three years. It was a few minutes after 10:00 A.M. Greenwich Mean Time, the time zone they kept aboard while on patrol, which made it around 7:00 P.M. local. The sun would be setting soon, but three hundred feet beneath the surface there was no such concept as night or day, only the watch system.

He'd been on duty almost continuously since the nuclear explosion and he was starting to get short-tempered, though it didn't show in his letter, nor would his crew ever suspect. COMSUBPAC's orders had been precise: Stand by and monitor.

It was exactly what they were doing. But it bothered Harding that if Washington was taking the incident seriously the word hadn't filtered down to the *Seawolf* yet. In some respects it was as if the Pentagon had expected something like this to happen. Even the North Koreans were making no response, though something would have to be happening ashore.

He'd moved them twenty-five miles farther southwest where they hovered just off the continental shelf. If the need arose they could go deep and hide in the subsea canyons that paralleled the Korean coast. So far there'd been no need.

Twelve hours ago a lone Japanese rescue vessel showed up and in six hours had pulled the crew off the stricken submarine, doing absolutely nothing to hide the reason they were operating so far inside North Korean territorial waters.

Harding put down his pen and leaned back in his chair. Something funny was going on out here, and he had a gut feeling that it wasn't over by a long shot.

He was the son of an MIT professor of engineering who taught that every cause had an effect, and every effect had a cause. But the world wasn't quite as neat as it was taught in science classes. Especially if man and his institutions were figured into the equation.

The Japanese MSDF had apparently sent a party ashore at the supposedly abandoned nuclear facility, and through either sabotage or an accident had set off a nuclear explosion. And nobody was doing anything about it, except wait and see. That made absolutely no sense.

He pulled down the growler phone. "Conn, this is the captain. Anything new from sonar?"

"Negative, Skipper," officer of the deck Lieutenant Karl Trela said.

Harding wasn't satisfied. Something was gnawing at his gut. "Tell them to look again, real close. I'll stand by."

"Yes, sir."

He glanced down at the unfinished letter to his wife. It would have to wait until later. The Japanese simply did not throw away valuable assets such as a submarine worth several hundred million dollars. Nor did the North Koreans ever miss an opportunity to rattle a few sabers. But none of that was happening now.

Trela was back. "Nothing, sir. Water's clear all around us. Do you want to start a search pattern with the twenty-three?" The TB-23 was a thin-line sonar array that could be unreeled more than three thousand feet behind the slowly moving submarine. Consisting of an array of hydrophones, itself nearly a thousand feet in length, the system could detect low frequency noises at extremely long ranges. But the submarine had to be moving in order for the system to work.

Harding thought it out. "Not yet. Bring us to periscope depth. I'm on my way."

"Yes, sir."

Harding pulled on a fresh shirt, grabbed a cup of coffee from the officers' wardroom and went up one level to the control room. The boat was already on its way up and everybody aboard knew that something was going on. The captain was on the prowl, things were happening. But the mood radiating outward from the control room was one of calm. Always calm. Harding insisted on it.

"Passing two hundred fifty feet," Trela reported unnecessarily.

"Very well," Harding said. Trela was new to Harding's gold crew, but he'd come from the *Mississippi* highly recommended. He was still trying to prove himself on the *Seawolf*. Harding called the radio shack. "This is the captain."

"Yes, sir."

"As soon as you can raise your masts, I want a passive all-band search. But it's going to have to be a snapshot, because I'm not going to give you much time."

"Aye, Captain."

The executive officer Lieutenant Commander Rod Paradise came in, buttoning the top button of his shirt. "Am I missing something?"

"I'm going up to take a look."

"I see," Paradise said, a faint smile at the corner of his mouth. "You're supposed to be getting some rest."

"There's no traffic, Rod."

Paradise shrugged, but then realized the point the captain was making. "Should be some commercial traffic to the southeast."

"Nothing," Harding said.

"Passing one hundred feet, Skipper," Trela reported.

Paradise pulled a phone from the overhead. "Sonar, this is the XO. How's it look?"

"Nothing, sir. My displays are all clear."

"Very well."

"Level and steady at six-zero feet, sir," Trela said.

"Prepare to dive on my command," Harding said. He raised the search periscope and made a quick 360-degree sweep. The western horizon was tinged red. The seas looked as if they were in the eight to ten foot range, and the weather looked cold.

"Conn, ESMs, I have two contacts, designated Romeo One and Romeo Two. Orions, bearing one-six-five, course three-four-five, estimated speed four-two-zero knots."

"Are their search radars active?" Paradise asked.

"Roger."

Harding retracted the periscope. "Get us out of here, Karl."

"Dive, dive, dive," Trela ordered.

"Make your depth three hundred feet."

"Aye, Captain, make my depth three hundred feet," Trela responded crisply.

The boat's deck canted sharply forward. Harding called the radio shack. "ESMs, this is the captain. Were we detected?"

"Negative, Skipper. At least I don't think so. They were fifty miles out and making maximum speed. They weren't doing any serious looking, they were beatin' feet."

"Sonar, this is the captain. Are we still clear?"

"Yes, sir."

Harding and Paradise went back to one of the plotting tables where the captain laid out the course and bearing of the two sub-hunter aircraft. They were American made, but Seventh Fleet would not have sent them out here, which meant they were Japanese MSDF.

"They know where their submarine is sitting on the bottom, which means they're out here looking for someone else," Harding said. "Us?"

"Could be," Paradise said, studying the chart. "Or it could be that they're expecting a response from the North Koreans now that the sub has been abandoned."

"They'll be sending help."

"Most likely."

Harding smiled gently. "In that case we'll have a ringside seat. I kind of like that." He turned to Trela. "Belay the dive, and prepare to bring us back to periscope depth."

"Are we going to phone this home?" Paradise asked.

"We'll give them time to get past us first. They shouldn't be looking over their shoulders."

The White House

DCI Murphy's Lincoln Town Car limousine pulled up at the west portico a couple of minutes before 9:00 A.M. His bodyguard Ken Chapin opened the rear door for him and escorted him inside, where he took the stairs down to the situation room. This morning he felt every minute of his sixty-five years, and for the first time he could remember he thought about his retirement. He had served four presidents, this one no better or worse than the others, and he was fairly well insulated from Beltway intrigues, but the pressure of his position was finally wearing him down. Like McGarvey said, maybe he too was an anachronism. Maybe all the Cold War warriors needed to be put out to pasture. New enemies, new problems, new imperatives were looming on the horizon, trouble spots like Iran, Iraq, Pakistan and now North Korea and perhaps even Japan, were blossoming all over the globe.

A secret service agent greeted him at the bottom. "Good morning, General."

Is the President here yet?"

"No, sir."

Murphy hesitated at the door, shifting his briefcase to his left hand. He'd been thinking lately of getting back to his forty-two-foot Hans Christian sloop on the Chesapeake, the same kind of boat Walter Cronkite used to sail. In fact they'd been in the Bermuda race twice, neither of them winning, and he had to feel that those had been simpler times. But then they'd all been unsophisticated then by comparison to now. He used to quote Shakespeare to Cronkite just to show that he ran the CIA with something a step above a bureaucratic sensibility. Light verses, silly even: "As if we were God's spies." A snatch of something else from *King Lear* had been running around inside his head lately, and it wasn't so light. "The weight of this sad time we must obey; Speak what we feel, not what we ought to say." Maybe that was the trouble after all, perhaps only men like McGarvey had ever known how to speak the truth.

Most of the President's crisis team had already arrived and were talking quietly among themselves around the highly polished oblong table. Murphy took his place on the left next to Thomas Roswell, director of the National Security Agency, General Arthur Podvin, chairman of the Joint Chiefs of Staff, and the other three Joint Chiefs of Staff.

To the right of the President's position were Harold Secor, his national security adviser, a studious Harvard professor whom the media maintained was the most intelligent man ever to hold that position, and Secretaries Jonathan Carter of State and Paul Landry of Defense.

Roswell had been saying something to General Podvin. He turned to Murphy and slid a bulky file folder over to him. "These came over from the National Reconnaissance Office just before I took off. I don't think you've seen them yet." Roswell was a stern-faced man who dressed impeccably, as if he'd just stepped from a CitiCorp board meeting. He had a sharp mind and ran a tight shop in an agency three times the size of the CIA.

Murphy studied the first of what appeared to be high resolution

KH-13 satellite photos of Japan's three main islands. Numerous areas were highlighted in red, and he recognized them for what they were, Japanese air force and navy bases.

"The Japanese are on the move," he said.

"Across the board, Roland. Looks as if you were right, they're expecting trouble."

Murphy flipped through the rest of the two dozen photos. "What about the Koreans?"

"Not a thing." Roswell gave him a searching look. "How about your sources on the ground. Anything happening in Pyongyang that we should know about?"

"It's quiet."

"Too quiet," Roswell said. "What the hell are they up to?"

The President came in, took his place and when everyone was settled he looked around the table. "We have a lot of ground to cover this morning, so let's get started. Roland, give us what you have and we can go from there."

"Yes, Mr. President. In the past forty-eight hours there've been some disturbing developments in North Korea, the Sea of Japan and on the Japanese main islands themselves." He took a leather-bound folder from his briefcase and handed it down the table to the President.

"Much of what we've put together comes from one of our own submarines which happened to be on patrol off the North Korean coast and spotted what the captain thought was an unusual situation."

"The *Seawolf*," Admiral Howard Mann said. "I know the skipper, Tom Harding. He's one of the best. Whatever he has to say you can take as gospel."

"As you all know by now, there was an underground nuclear explosion Thursday at a supposedly abandoned nuclear power station on North Korea's Sea of Japan coast. At the moment our best estimates are that it was in the fifteen to twenty-five kiloton range, about the same strength as the bomb we dropped on Hiroshima. To this point we have no information from Pyongyang or any of our other resources on the ground, although the South Korean CIA has promised something by this afternoon. Apparently they've sent a team to Kimch'aek, which is the coastal town nearest to the site." The truth, Murphy thought. Every director before him had learned that as far as the administration they worked for was concerned, the truth was relative and highly subjective.

"What you may not fully appreciate is that we do not believe the explosion was a test. Nor do we believe it was caused by a problem with the abandoned reactor. In fact we think the explosion was caused by sabotage and involved a nuclear weapon." Murphy paused a moment. "One of five that we believe the North Koreans have managed to build over the past seven years."

It was a bombshell. The men in this room were not dumb, but they were accustomed to dealing in hard cold facts. Although there had been speculation that the North Koreans were developing an active nuclear weapons program, there'd never been any direct evidence.

"Can you support that, General?" Secretary of Defense Landry demanded. He obviously felt as if he'd been left out of the loop on something critical to his job. "Hell, the entire country is an accident looking for a place to happen."

"During the 1997 Seoul debriefings of Hwang Jang Yop, he told the South Koreans that five gun-type weapons—that is, nuclear devices using U235 rather than plutonium—had already been built or were nearing completion. Until now there has been no confirmation. Yop specified that the weapons were in the twenty kiloton range and would be stored at one of North Korea's coastal nuclear generating stations. Over the past five days there has been some intense activity at Kimch'aek that we've been trying to evaluate. They were moving something out of there in a big hurry and under a great deal of secrecy. Apparently the Japanese beat us to the punch."

"Are you saying that the Japanese sub delivered a suicide crew to destroy the facility?" the President asked.

"It's likely they sent a team ashore to gather proof that the North Koreans did in fact possess nuclear weapons. For whatever reason they may have found themselves in a situation where escape was impossible, so they did the only thing they could to prove what they'd found. And that was to explode the bomb."

"Have all five of them been destroyed?" Landry asked.

"Just one," Murphy said. "The other four had already been moved out."

"You say that we monitored the previous activity at the station. Do we know where they took the four weapons?"

"No, sir. We have no resources on the ground, and the weather closed in, making our satellite useless for about twenty hours. By then it was too late. The bombs could be anywhere in North Korea." Murphy spread his hands. "The South Koreans are sending people in, but it's anybody's guess if they'll have any luck, or just how long it might take them to come up with some answers."

"In the meantime the situation out there is getting even worse," the President said.

"That it is," Murphy said. "The crew from the stricken Japanese submarine were rescued overnight, with no interference from the North Koreans. But Captain Harding reported that a pair of Orion sub-hunter-killer aircraft are searching the waters in the vicinity of the downed submarine. We've confirmed that the aircraft are Japanese, from the MSDF base at Sasebo, but the question is what are they looking for? We don't have that answer yet."

"They know where their damned submarine is located," General Podvin said. "Do they suspect that we've got one of our subs in the area?"

"Tom Harding doesn't think so," Admiral Mann said. His manner suggested he could not listen to any criticism of his sub driver.

"The *Seawolf* is still standing by out there, is that correct?" the President said.

"Yes, sir."

"Is there any possibility that the Japanese will find them?"

"Given enough time and assets, it's possible," Admiral Mann conceded. "But it's more likely they're looking for North Korean submarines, although we don't have any evidence that Pyongyang has made such a response."

"How soon before the two Chinese submarines reach the area, assuming that's where they're heading?" the President asked Murphy.

"Submerged they're capable of making twenty-five knots, which could put them on site in another fifteen or twenty hours. But they're still running on the surface, at twelve knots, which means they won't be showing up for another three days. Gives us time to sort out the situation." Murphy glanced at the photos Roswell had handed him, the line from *King Lear* coming back to him again. "But we have another developing problem that might lead to an even more disturbing conclusion."

"Okay, for now the *Seawolf* says where it is, because without reliable satellite data they're our only source of information," the President said. "Or are you going to tell me that this other problem will make that impossible?"

"It depends on the Japanese," Murphy said. "We have some National Reconnaissance Office satellite pictures of the Japanese main islands. It appears that most, if not all, of their military installations have gone to a full state of readiness."

"We're not finished with our analysis, but the photographs seem to be fairly conclusive," Roswell said.

Murphy passed the file around the table. General Podvin shook his head. "I've heard nothing about this."

"They're keeping it quiet," Murphy said. "In the past they've always informed us when they were conducting any sort of an exercise, especially one of this magnitude. But this time they haven't."

"Why not?" the President asked. "What disturbing conclusion are you suggesting?"

"The Japanese wanted proof that North Korea had in fact developed operationally ready nuclear weapons. Apparently they have the proof now, and they intend to do something about it."

"By invading North Korea?" Secretary of State Carter asked incredulously.

"The North Koreans have the Taepo Dong ballistic missile with sufficient range and power to lift a nuclear weapon the seven hundred miles to Tokyo," Murphy said. "Even if Kim Jong-Il has no intention of doing something as insane as that, the mere fact that he now has the weapons and the capability to do it is enough to make the Japanese very nervous. It's almost as bad as when the Russians tried to put nukes in Cuba."

"It's those goddammed Chinese submarines," Admiral Mann said. "It's going to end up a Mexican standoff, with the *Seawolf* caught in the middle."

"What do we do about it?" the President said. "Tokyo will deny everything, and we can hardly tip our hand by admitting the *Seawolf* is up there. Pyongyang is stonewalling it. And the Chinese are merely on a routine patrol. Nobody is doing anything wrong."

"The Japanese are not going to war, I can guarantee it," Secretary of State Carter stated flatly and he looked around the table challenging anyone to dispute him.

"Unless they were nudged," Murphy said.

The President gave him a bleak look. "What else does the CIA have?"

"It's possible that alert is an after-the-fact reaction to a situation that caught Tokyo by just as much surprise as it did us."

"Wait a minute," Carter said. "You're not going to tell us that this was another renegade submarine captain, like a couple of years ago, because we're not going to buy it. I'm recommending that we get word to Tokyo, Pyongyang and Beijing to back off immediately. And I'm willing to leave this morning to personally deliver just such a message."

"Shuttle diplomacy won't work this time, Mr. Carter, just as it wouldn't have worked in Cuba, because like Castro, Prime Minister Enchi may not have all the facts, or be completely in charge of the situation."

"Jesus Christ, General—" Carter said, but the President held up a hand.

"Proceed, Roland."

"On pages fifty-seven through sixty-two you'll see photographs and dossiers on two men who were seen meeting near Sasebo eleven days ago. The stricken submarine was home-ported there, and that's where the Orions are based."

The President's eyes never left Murphy. "Who are these men?"

"Hiroshi Kabayashi and Shin Hironaka, part of the organization that nearly brought down Enchi's government two years ago and almost got us into a shooting war."

"Hironaka was their director general of Defense," General Podvin said. "The sonofabitch is in jail."

"Not anymore."

"But he's no longer directly involved with the government or the defense establishment," Podvin said. "I know that for a fact."

"I shouldn't have to ask if your source is reliable," the President said. "It is."

"What you're saying is that these two men may have formed another organization—a *zaibatsu*, if I remember the Japanese word—to manipulate their own government."

Murphy nodded. "That's what we believe."

"To do what?"

"Protect Japan against the nuclear attack by North Korea that Hwang Jang Yop warned about in 1997."

"The man was a maniac," Carter said. "No one believed a word he said. Even the South Koreans dismissed most of his story as rubbish."

"That's just the point, Mr. Carter. Seoul didn't believe it, we didn't and neither did Tokyo. But someone did, and they're doing something about it."

"Okay, assuming what you've told us is true, what do you think we should do?"

"Get Seventh out of Tokyo Bay, as the Japanese requested."

"And send them where?"

"The Sea of Japan by the northern route over the top of Honshu. In the meantime inform Prime Minister Enchi that we also detected the underground nuclear explosion at Kimch'aek, and we're going to investigate."

"With the entire fleet," Admiral Mann said disparagingly. "That's going to send them one hell of a message."

"Better than having the fleet bottled up if something should occur. It'll give us time to work out our other options."

"Which are?" the President asked, a flinty note in his voice. He wasn't liking what he was hearing.

"We want to interview Kabayashi and Hironaka."

"You'd have to kidnap them to do it," Carter said.

"That's a possibility," Murphy replied, not backing down. "We're working on a number of scenarios now."

"Can you pull it off, General?" Secor asked. "With plausible deniability in case something goes wrong?"

"I don't know the answer to that. It's something we're working on."

Secor turned to the President. "Even if Enchi is in the dark we could get in some real trouble if this blew up in our faces. There are other considerations."

"What about the Russians?" the President asked Murphy. "Has there been any activity at Vladivostok?"

"Not yet, but they are certainly aware of what's going on."

"Will they become a factor?"

"I don't think so."

"How long would it take for Seventh Fleet to be ready to sail?" the President asked Admiral Mann.

"Twelve hours, if we want all our crews aboard. It's summer and one-third of our people are on leave, most of them in Japan."

"How long before the CIA can come up with a reasonably tight plan to grab these two Japanese?"

"I should have something by this afternoon," Murphy said, but it was just a guess and it was clear that the President understood it.

"Before anything else happens I want to see those plans in writing on my desk, including contingencies if something should go wrong. In the meantime have Seventh prepare to sail." The President glanced up at the wall clock. "I want them ready to get underway by nine this evening. But they're to stay put until I give the order."

"Yes, sir," Admiral Mann said.

"I want this kept from the media for as long as possible," the President warned, "No screw-ups." He looked around the table but no one said anything. "If there's nothing else, we're finished here for this morning."

Everybody gathered their papers and headed out, but the President motioned for Murphy and Secor to remain. When they were alone he picked up the telephone. "Send Pierone down." Dr. Gerald Pierone Jr. was director of the FBI.

"How is McGarvey holding up?" the President asked. "It was his girlfriend, the Frenchwoman, who was killed, wasn't it? And his daughter hurt?"

"Yes, sir," Murphy said. "I haven't spoken to him since the bombing, but Tom Doyle has. McGarvey is holding up okay, but he's mad as hell."

"So am I. But is he mad enough to take the job?"

"I don't know. I wish I did, but he's had a lot of crap thrown at him in the past six months. First the business about his parents, then Howard Ryan's handling of his daughter and now this. But it was his idea to get Seventh Fleet out of Tokyo Bay and round up Kabayashi and Hironaka."

"Does he think kidnapping them is possible?"

Murphy had to smile. "With McGarvey just about anything is possible if he's motivated."

"I would think that the attack on his daughter and girlfriend would be plenty of motivation," Secor said, wide-eyed behind his wire-rimmed spectacles.

"I wouldn't care to put it to him quite that way, Harold," Murphy said.

"I didn't mean that as crassly as it sounded, and you know it. We've all had our share of crap, as you put it, thrown at us. Doesn't stop us from doing our jobs. At this point we need him." Secor came from a privileged family, he held doctorates in history and political science and before he'd been tapped for government service he had been head of Harvard's department of history. He didn't know the meaning of personal adversity.

"I'll be talking to him soon. Right now he's with his daughter and ex-wife at the hospital."

"Bring him over here, and I'll talk to him if you think it'll help," the President said.

"That won't be necessary. McGarvey will only take the job if he believes he can made a difference," Murphy said. He had to wonder if in the end any of them made any difference.

Dr. Pierone walked in and set his briefcase on the table. "Good morning, Mr. President."

"Morning, Gerald. I asked the general to sit in on this since the investigation concerns one of his people."

Pierone turned to Murphy. He was a medical doctor. Before he'd been appointed to head the FBI, he'd served on the boards of four major hospitals and an HMO. "If you're talking about McGarvey, he's our prime resource. He was right there in the middle of it, and he took out three terrorists in the middle of Canal Bridge on Wisconsin Avenue in front of a dozen witnesses. We'd very much like to finish interviewing him."

"Our Internal Affairs people are handling the investigation, and if they come up with anything of value to your case we'll hand it over, naturally," Murphy said.

Pierone was fuming. "Twenty people are dead and three others prob-

ably won't make it. We want some answers, because this was no
Oklahoma City. The attack wasn't some random act of terrorism. It was
directed. And at the very least Mr. McGarvey will have to stand a coroner's
hearing on the three men he killed."

"We'll see about that last part. But if you're right about the rest, and
I'm not saying that you're not, we may be in for some further trouble,"
Murphy said heavily. On the way over he'd decided to hold nothing back,
no matter how disturbing it might be.

"You're talking about somebody from McGarvey's past, right?" Secor
said. Murphy thought that the President's national security adviser looked
diffident.

"It could have been a reaction to proposing him as DDO."

This was news to Pierone. "I hadn't heard about that. But the list of
people who did know could be a start."

"There are only a few of us at the CIA, plus the President's staff, and,
I'm assuming, a few key people on the Hill."

"That's right," the President said, tightly. "These terrorists were
Asians?"

"Yes, Mr. President," Pierone said. "We don't have any identification
on them yet, their fingerprints are not in our files, but we're working with
Interpol and a few other international agencies."

"Could they have been Japanese?"

"It's possible, even likely."

The President shot Murphy a significant look. "Where's the FBI's
investigation right now?

"We're interviewing witnesses," Pierone said. "Naturally we want to
talk to McGarvey. Of all the people who survived, his would be the most
useful testimony." He turned again to Murphy. "What has he said to your
people?"

"He thinks the attack might have been directed at him by someone
who doesn't want him taking the job."

"That's not what he told my people."

"Since then he found out that his ex-wife has received a number of
anonymous threats warning her to convince her husband to refuse the
job."

"Is the CIA making a connection between McGarvey and someone
in Japan who might want him dead?" Pierone asked.

"It's one of the possibilities I think you should consider."

"Then I think it'll be a good idea if I send someone over later this
morning to begin liaising. I don't want this to turn out like two years ago.
We still haven't fully recovered."

"There are other considerations here," Secor said.

"The only consideration is that there's been another terrorist act on American soil. The fifth in as many years. And if you want to bring down an administration, just stop protecting the people. Or become perceived as ineffectual in stopping terrorism."

"Your point is made," the President said. "The CIA will fully cooperate with you, in so far as the investigation concerns domestic issues. But if foreign evidence is uncovered that in our opinion directly involves your work you'll be given access to that material as well. In the meantime, Mr. McGarvey is off-limits unless he turns down our offer."

"We'll debrief him and send along the pertinent details," Murphy conceded. It was clear that Pierone thought his hands were being tied, which in fact they were.

He nodded finally. "Then I'll do my best, Mr. President."

"That's all I can ask," the President said.

Harold Secor walked over to the office of Tony Croft, the President's adviser on foreign affairs, in the Executive Office Building a few minutes after ten, a worried frown on his professorial face. The President was meeting with the national Democratic Party chairman in the Oval Office and would be tied up for at least a half hour. It gave Secor a few minutes to sit in on a meeting that he considered politically explosive.

Croft and a half dozen of his staffers were seated around his office with Stewart Dewitt, the President's assistant for economic affairs; Clinton Scott, special consultant to the President for fund-raising activities and Joseph Lee, the major foreign contributor to President Lindsay's re-election campaign. Considering all the media attention over the past three or four years on political fund-raising activities, the Taiwanese businessman's presence here was dangerous, and Secor had told the President just that. But Lee was willing to continue contributing large sums of money, for so-called soft access to the White House, and the administration was willing to keep receiving it.

"Good morning, Tony," Secor said. "I hope you don't mind if I just sit in the corner for a few minutes. I promise to behave myself."

"Always glad to have you aboard, Harold." Croft laughed heartily. He was a corpulent man whose clothes seemed to be tailored for a man three sizes larger. He usually looked like an unmade bed. "Have you met our distinguished guest, Mr. Joseph Lee?"

"I can't say that I've had the pleasure, though I've certainly heard a lot of good things." Secor had purposely kept himself at arm's length. He shook hands with the slightly built man whose eyes held a look of amusement as if he'd just been told an off-color story.

"I'm sorry that my wife and I missed you and Mrs. Secor for cocktails and dinner last night. But the President and Mrs. Lindsay were most gracious."

"Perhaps next time."

"Yes, of course."

One of the staffers brought a chair, and Secor sat down near the door. "Please go ahead, Tony. I only have a few minutes before I have to get back."

"Actually we were just about finished here," Croft said. "I've gone over in rough terms the incident at Kimch'aek and the response, or rather lack of response from Pyongyang, and Mr. Lee was about to give us his words of wisdom on what effect this situation might have on the region."

Secor was stunned, but he covered his discomfiture without missing a beat. Croft would not have discussed the situation so openly unless the President had given his okay. "I would be most interested in his views."

"I can only truly speak for Taipei, but I think my government's reaction must be very similar to Singapore's, Malaysia's, the Philippines's, and of course Japan's. Kim Jong-Il is quite simply insane, and he means to embroil the entire region in an all-out war."

"One that he cannot possibly win," Secor said.

Lee turned his bland gaze to Secor. "The chances are very much against him winning such a conflict. But his chances for survival should he do nothing may be, in his perception, even less. An animal with its back to the wall is likely and capable of doing some amazing things."

"Do you think such a conflict is likely?"

"I truly wish that I could say no with certainty, but there are other factors to consider. Such as appropriate responses."

"By whom?" Secor asked. He could scarcely believe he was having this conversation.

"By someone with a firm hand," Lee said without batting an eye. "A government willing to take decisive steps, shall we say, definitive steps, to rein in Kim Jong-Il."

"Is this a message we should take to President Lindsay?" Croft asked.

"I discussed the issue with the President last night, but of course at the time I did not have all the facts. It is, I suspect, why he wished you to brief me this morning."

"Do you have any sense of exactly what these definitive steps should be?" Secor asked.

Lee smiled and shrugged. "I am a businessman, so naturally my immediate concern is to keep the peace in the region. A protracted war never benefited anyone—neither the loser nor the winner."

"That I can agree with wholeheartedly," Dewitt said, practically falling all over himself with good cheer and bonhomie. The President still owed eighteen million from his last campaign, plus legal fees, and the vice president was already gearing up for a major campaign fund-raising push.

Secor suddenly got to his feet. He couldn't take any more of this. "It was a pleasure meeting you, Mr. Lee. I hope that you and your wife are having a good visit." He smiled. "But unfortunately duty calls, so I'll leave you in these gentlemen's capable care."

Croft shot him a concerned, worried look. "Do you have a few minutes this afternoon, Harold?"

"Of course," Secor said. "Have a good day." He shook hands again with Lee and left, concerned that they were all chasing too recklessly after the bitch goddess money. It was something else that had fallen on deaf presidential ears.

Georgetown Hospital

McGarvey was having a cup of coffee in the sixth-floor waiting room, sun shining brightly through the windows, when Kathleen came down the corridor. She'd gotten no sleep overnight, and she looked all in, but some of the worry was gone from her face, and she held herself a little more erect, more like the old Kathleen, than she had earlier this morning.

"She's awake, and she's asking for you," Kathleen said.

"How is she?"

"The doctor just left. He said she'll be on her feet in a few days." Kathleen gave her ex-husband a searching look. "She can go back to work in a few weeks, but it'll be six months before she's back to normal."

"Did he say if there'll be any permanent damage?"

"Some scars that can be taken care of, but other than that no permanent *physical* damage." Kathleen looked away momentarily. "She's only a baby girl, Kirk. Make her quit. Tell her that she can return to her job in New York with the UN." Kathleen shook her head in desperation. "I don't know how much more of this I can live with."

"If she won't quit, I'll have her fired."

"We were able to divorce each other, but we cannot divorce our daughter." Kathleen was shaking. "Oh, Christ, Kirk, I don't want to lose her. I'll die if anything else happens to her, can't you understand that?"

"I'll do what I can, Katy."

"Kathleen," she corrected automatically. "You're going to have to convince her that she has to leave. She has to do it of her own free will. She's as bad as you are, she wouldn't let you fire her. Nobody could fire her, because she's your daughter." Kathleen closed her eyes. "It was my fault. I could have turned her against you when I had the chance. Especially after Greece, but I didn't."

McGarvey's heart was aching for his ex-wife. If he could he would have gladly taken her pain into his own body, erase it from her as if it had never been there. He could have done that a long time ago, but not now. He remembered the night he returned from Santiago and she'd given him the ultimatum. She wanted him to choose between her or the CIA. She didn't know that the CIA had already fired him, but at the time it would not have made any difference to him. His terrible fault was that he hadn't even tried to explain it to her that night. Instead, he'd walked out of the house without looking back. He'd run to Lausanne, Switzerland, where he'd hidden himself as a bookstore owner until the CIA came to him for the first of many freelance assignments. By then, coming back was impossible.

Elizabeth was a mass of bandages, an IV drip attached to her left hand and a wire from the monitor to her left arm. Her mother had fixed her hair, but she'd refused any makeup. She looked pale and very small in the middle of the hospital bed, but her face lit up when McGarvey came in.

"Daddy, am I ever glad to see you. Nobody wants to give me a straight answer."

McGarvey pecked her on the cheek, it was all he could do not to take her in his arms. "You look a lot better than you did yesterday. How do you feel, Liz?"

"Like I've been hit by a Mack truck," she said sharply. "Next question?"

"I take it that your talk with your mother wasn't entirely successful."

Her lips compressed and she fought back a tear, but she didn't turn away. "She simply doesn't understand."

"Understand what? That she loves you and that she's worried about you?" The same vise was clamped on his heart seeing how battered she was. She was extremely brittle. "And being a smart aleck will get you nowhere. They were trying to kill me, Liz, and they damned near succeeded. It was blind luck that you and I got out of there alive. Jacqueline wasn't so lucky. So before you condemn your mother, think about Jacqueline's mother. What do you suggest I say to her?"

"You got the bastards, Daddy. Mother told me about it. They never had a chance."

"I was lucky," McGarvey said.

"Bullshit!"

McGarvey's fear suddenly turned to anger. "You willful little bitch, do you think all of this is some little game for your pleasure? Twenty people are dead; real people whose families are mourning for them and wanting to find out who did it and why such a terrible thing happened to them. Do you want to say something to them? Some smart-ass, flip remark? Something about how your father killed three men in front of a dozen people who will probably never walk down a street in broad daylight and feel safe for the rest of their lives?"

Elizabeth refused to cry or back down. "I'll tell them that without men like you the carnage would be a hundred times worse. And they'd better thank their lucky stars that you were able and willing to do what you did."

"You're wrong, Liz, and this time your mother is right. She's probably been right all along."

"Don't say that, Daddy," Elizabeth said softly, the words choking in her throat. "Ever since I was little and found out that you worked for the Company, it's what I wanted to do. I used to dream about it. About working with you, about making a difference, because without the Company we'd all be in serious trouble." She closed her eyes for a moment. "You're all I have to believe in; don't take that away from me."

McGarvey's heart was aching. "If you're going to believe in something, you need to know all there is about it first."

"I know enough."

McGarvey shook his head, an infinite sadness coming over him. "No you don't. And maybe it's time I told you everything, starting with your grandparents."

"May I sit in on this?" Kathleen said from the doorway. Her anger had changed to compassion.

"Come in and close the door, Katy."

Washington, D.C.

"PARA/MEDIC is on the move," the radio in the Perfection Cleaning Company van blared. The FBI surveillance vehicle was parked in the Corcoran Gallery of Art parking lot on E Street. The primary team was watching the White House from a suite in the Hay Adams Hotel.

FBI Special Agent Paul Kuchvera pulled out into traffic and shot up 18th Street in time to spot the black Mercedes limousine with Virginia plates passing the Renwick Gallery on Pennsylvania Avenue across the street from the Executive Office Building.

"Unit Two, we have the subject in sight," Special Agent Mark Morgan, riding shotgun, radioed.

"Is PARA/MUTUAL traveling with the subject?"

"Affirmative."

As the Mercedes entered Washington Circle, Morgan took three photographs showing the limo, its license plate and the clearly defined landmark. The date and time were automatically stamped on the negatives.

The FBI, under the orders of the special prosecutor investigating illegal campaign funding, which in the last presidential campaign had set an all-time precedent for the huge amounts of off-shore money, had concentrated the bulk of their efforts over the past six months on Joseph Lee. His code name was PARA/MEDIC, his wife's code name PARA/MUTUAL.

It had come as no real surprise that Lee and his wife had been invited to spend the night in the Lincoln bedroom and attend a lavish reception and dinner at the White House. But what had come as a surprise was that one of their sources inside the White House told them that Lee had attended a briefing earlier this morning with Tony Croft and some other staffers and special assistants. Not only had Lee's money, the source of which was also under intense scrutiny, gained him and his wife access to the President, it had also apparently gained him a voice that the White House policy makers were listening to. It made Morgan mad thinking that while his father had won the Medal of Honor early in Vietnam, he and his family did not have the ear of the President or anyone else in government for that matter, while a wealthy Taiwanese businessman, not even a U.S. citizen, did.

Kuchvera was an expert driver, sometimes tailing directly behind the limo, at times dropping back behind several cars, and sometimes even passing, only to fall back again, so that by the time the Mercedes crossed the Key Bridge and headed north on the George Washington Memorial Parkway, they were certain they had not been spotted, though it was likely that Lee's people knew that they were under surveillance.

"They're heading for home," Morgan said.

"Looks like it," the taciturn Kuchvera agreed.

Morgan got on the radio. "We have subject north on the G.W. Parkway. Looks like they're heading for OREGON." It was the codeword for the Lees' palatial home overlooking the Potomac River between Langley and Great Falls Park. It was something else the average hardworking American couldn't afford, and every time Morgan thought about it, he was frosted. This op had become something personal to him, and it was going to give him a great deal of pleasure to be there when the sonofabitch was knocked off his perch.

FOUR

Tanegashima Space Center
Tanegashima Island, Japan

It was five o'clock in the morning when Frank Ripley hauled himself out of bed and stumbled into the pocket-sized bathroom to splash some cold water on his face. Just about everything in this country was tiny. And after three weeks the confinement was starting to get on his nerves. Aboard the shuttle, and during his three months on *Mir*, it had been different. There you expected to be confined. Besides, the science was exciting, and weightlessness made everything seem larger because you not only lived on the floor, but you were able to live and work on the walls and ceilings too. Here the only things full scale were the fourth-generation H2C multistage rocket and boosters, the vehicle assembly building and the big gantry at the Yoshinabu launch complex down on the beach.

Only a few days to go, and if the launch went off without a hitch he and his NASA Tiger team of expediters would be out of here, back to Houston where they could get a steak dinner that didn't cost a month's salary—the steaks here were small too—and be among people who smiled and actually meant it.

He was in front of the visitors' housing building in his sweats and jogging shoes at five-fifteen, the predawn air thick with humidity and redolent with the smells of the sea and something else he could only describe as Oriental: a sort of sweet soya sauce and fragrant wood chips odor. All around him for as far as he could see were various buildings and structures illuminated in a complex jumble of lights and shapes, very reminiscent of the Kennedy Space Center after which Tanegashima was modeled.

Although the tension among the staff and security people had taken a quantum leap for some reason two days ago, the armed guards were used to his morning runs. They no longer stopped him to check his identification, which he'd learned always to take with him after the first day, but they never waved or cracked a smile. It was as if the Japanese were seriously pissed off that they had to put up with the American team.

"Frank, hold up."

Ripley turned around as Margaret Attwood, dressed in MIT sweats, jogged up to him. They embraced, and she gave his butt a playful squeeze. There was nothing indirect about her.

"Morning, Maggie. I didn't think you'd be up this early."

She grinned. "Good sex gives me energy." She looked toward the VAB and beyond it the broad gravel road that led to the brilliantly lit launch complex three miles farther. The giant H2C would be trundled to the pad later today, so this would be the last morning they could jog out there and back.

Like most astronauts, Ripley was not a large man. At five eleven with short cropped hair, a spare compact body and lean features, he gave the appearance of being agile, like a gymnast without a spare ounce of meat on his frame. But Maggie was even smaller, the Olga Korbet of the astronaut corps, and almost pretty enough to be a model or actress. In fact NASA had used her in some of their television advertisements and promotional videos. In three months she would ride the shuttle up to *Freedom*, the international space station, for a six-month stint which would give her the record for the longest any American woman stayed in space. She was looking forward to the assignment with a lot of enthusiasm. She was divorced and there were no children for her to miss. Her husband, jealous of her career, had tried to bat her around the night NASA had selected her for astronaut training. When the fight was over she had a bloody nose and a couple of bruises, but her husband had to be taken to the hospital with a broken arm and collar bone, a couple of fractured ribs and a dislocated hip. The next morning she filed for a divorce which he did not contest. Her nickname for a long time afterwards was Mighty Mouse, but no one messed with her.

An open Toyota Land Cruiser with National Space Development Agency markings passed on the road; the two uniformed guards glanced at them, but didn't slow down.

"Is it just me, or is something going on?" Maggie asked as they jogged toward the VAB.

"Prelaunch jitters."

"I went over to Hiroshi's office before dinner last night to talk to him about the locking collar problems we've been having. I'm not sure about the fix they installed. But he refused to see me. His secretary said that he had a busy schedule and was flying up to Sasebo." Hiroshi Kimura was the chief engineer in charge of satellite preparation, and of necessity he had more contact with the five-member NASA team than any of the other project engineers and scientists. He often flew to the Mitsubishi Satellite Design Center in Sasebo overnight, returning in the morning.

"He's got a full plate."

"He didn't go. After I left your place, I went for a walk down by the payload building. I saw him coming out."

"Did he see you?"

"Damn right he did, but he didn't say a thing to me, didn't even acknowledge my presence."

"So he had a change of plans," Ripley said. "Come on, Maggie, I think it's you who's getting prelaunch jitters now."

"Three days ago he was the old Hiroshi, at least, he was still pretending to tolerate us. Suddenly I don't even get a nod. It's the same with everyone else. Nobody's saying a thing. Hell, they don't even want to make eye contact."

"Has Hilman said anything to you about it?" Among the other NASA advisory team members, Hilman Hammarstedt, a metals stress management engineer, was at fifty-three the oldest, and the only one who'd never been an astronaut and never wanted to be. A dour, emotionless man, he never told a lie, never exaggerated and was above all a consummate listener and judge of people.

"He brought it up to me yesterday when you were at launch control. Wondered if he had BO or something. Neil and Don noticed the shift in attitude too." Neil Johnson was an electrical engineer, and Don Wirth was their metallurgical engineer. They'd both completed astronaut training and were waiting for assignments on *Freedom.*

"What'd you tell them?"

"We've got a job to do, and when it's done we're out of here."

Ripley nodded. "Good advice. If the Japanese have a bug up their asses, then so be it. In the meantime they want to link their satellite with our space station so they're going to have to put up with us a little while longer."

"The rub is that I like the Japanese. They're neat, organized and polite."

"Raw eggs mixed with rice as a breakfast treat I won't forget real soon." In his opinion Japanese food was even worse than the rations he'd endured aboard *Mir,* although slices of frozen raw salt pork eaten with canned black bread and reconstituted onions came close. Susan, his ex-wife, who'd had pretensions of becoming the wife of a ranking air force officer at the Pentagon and becoming involved in the Washington scene, could not understand what she called his "blue-collar" thinking. Right now he'd give a week's pay for a McDonald's Quarter Pounder with cheese, large fries and a real Coke.

Payload Building One

Working with the NASA Tiger team for twenty-one days straight without a break had not softened Hiroshi Kimura's attitude toward Americans; if anything he'd become even more distant than in the beginning. There was no doubt that he was a brilliant man and knew everything there was to know about satellite design and construction, but he walked around with a permanent chip on his shoulder. Ripley and his crew rode over from the visitors' mess hall where they found him in the diagnostic center overlooking the main assembly bays where the Greyhound bus–sized satellite was being made ready to load aboard the H2C.

Ripley sent his people downstairs and knocked on the open door. "Good morning, Hiroshi."

Kimura, dressed in white coveralls like everyone else, was studying a display over the shoulder of one of the technicians seated at a console. He looked up, his narrow black eyes expressionless. "Good morning, Major. Did you get my message?"

"What message is that?"

Kimura's bland expression didn't change. He said something to the technician, then motioned for Ripley to follow him back to his office down the corridor. The airless little room was furnished only with a desk, on which sat a computer monitor and keyboard, and a stand on which was displayed a perfect scale model of the satellite which the Japanese called Hagoromo II, the veil of the angel, after the 1990 Hagoromo which achieved lunar orbit, making Japan only the third nation ever to achieve such a feat.

Ripley sat down across the desk from Kimura and handed him the line-item diagnostic test manual.

"Margaret has some concerns about the upper locking collar which we'd like to work on this morning. In addition I've marked a dozen tests I'd like redone. Some of the original data seemed contradictory."

"The locking collar has been brought up to specifications." Kimura opened the thick manual to the first of the pages Ripley had marked with paper clips. "This has been done, the data is on your terminal."

"Wasn't there yesterday," Ripley said.

"We did the testing overnight." He flipped the page. "This has been done too."

"Margaret said she saw you down here. Works the same at the Cape, you know, last-minute tweaking. We can't seem to avoid it. But I'd like you to look at the rest of the items, some of them in our opinion are crucial."

"Everything is crucial." Kimura looked up from the manual. "Why did you bring this to me this morning?"

"Because this stuff is important. And it's my job, remember? We're here to ask questions, for which you'll give us the answers. Then you ask us questions, which we'll answer. When we're finished you'll put the satellite into mid-Earth orbit and a few days later it'll rendezvous with *Freedom*. Nobody wants this project to fail."

"Nobody is talking about failure."

"That's why we're here to make sure there are no glitches, so that when the satellite is transferred to the pad tomorrow and strapped aboard your space ship we'll all have a reasonable expectation that everything works like it's supposed to."

Kimura was angry, Ripley could feel it, but the Japanese showed no emotion whatsoever. "This is not Cape Kennedy."

"Nor is *Freedom* a Japanese space station, it's international. And three of my people will be flying aboard her soon, so I have a vested interest to make certain everything is right."

"There are two Japanese astronauts aboard at this moment, so I too have, as you say, a vested interest in making certain that all goes as it should." Kimura ran a hand across his forehead, a gesture so unlike him that Ripley had to think it was simple theatrics. "These last days have been trying." He cracked a faint smile. "Prelaunch jitters, I believe you call such nervousness."

Ripley kept his surprise from showing. They were the same words he'd said to Maggie this morning. A term he'd never heard the Japanese use. "Then we can do the tests?"

"Naturally, though it will cost us additional time. But we want this mission to develop fully without glitches as much as you do."

"Okay, I'll get my people on it right away, maybe we can cut the time, and get the bird out to the pad tomorrow on schedule. We're willing to work with your team all night if it's necessary."

"Major, I want you to understand that, like you, I too must follow orders. Sometimes I may not necessarily agree with what I am told, but then neither of us knows everything. Seeming contradictions may not be in fact so."

"Let's just get Hagoromo II into orbit and then we'll get out of your hair. Make everybody happy."

Kimura nodded.

"Oh, you said you had a message for me?"

"Thomas Hartley would like you to telephone him in Houston." Hartley was NASA's *Freedom* Foreign Missions Project manager and Ripley's boss.

"Fine, I'll get my people started on the diagnostics and run over to my office."

"You may call from here."

Ordinarily Ripley would have taken him up on his offer, it would save time because his own office was in a separate building near launch control two miles away, but he wanted to have some privacy. "That's okay, I'll probably have to pull out a couple of files."

"I can send somebody over for whatever you need."

"Don't bother, Hiroshi." Ripley took the test manual, nodded curtly and went downstairs to the main assembly bay. After he got his people started with the tests, he headed across the base, wondering what the hell was going on.

Ancillary Administration III

Ripley parked in front and went up to his second-floor corner office that looked across a complex of pipes and electrical conduit toward the low, circular launch control facility. Admin was busy this morning, but no one said a word to him; it was as if he didn't exist.

It was a little past four in the afternoon in Houston when Ripley got through. Hartley seemed out of breath, as if he'd just run up a flight of stairs. Like a lot of men in key positions at Houston and the Cape, Hartley was an ex-astronaut. In the eighties and early nineties he had amassed more shuttle time than any pilot or mission specialist before or since. He'd logged more EVA (extravehicular activity) hours than anyone else, and when he found out that he had developed a heart murmur, and would never get a chance to fly again let alone spend time on *Freedom*, he slid not so easily into a desk job. He became a gourmand, and almost overnight his weight shot up to nearly three hundred pounds. The running joke was that Thiokol refused to design and build a new solid rocket booster that would be necessary to lift his increased bulk into orbit because of the lack of funding so the only thing open was a ground job. He took it good-naturedly most of the time, but every time the shuttle launched he went into a funk for a couple of days afterwards. He wanted space.

"How's it going, Frank?" Hartley asked.

"Everything is looking good. We're running some final diagnostics on the bird today, but she should be ready to load on schedule tomorrow."

"Is the H2C on the pad yet?"

"It's going out this morning, providing the weather holds, which it looks like it will." Ripley glanced out toward launch control. A lot of cars were parked in the lot. "So, what did you want to talk to me about this morning?"

"About you and the mood over there," Hartley said almost too casually. "Are you running into any difficulties?"

"What kind of difficulties?"

"Oh, I don't know specifically. Are you getting full cooperation? The diagnostics are looking good, no one messing with anything?"

Ripley turned away from the window so that he could watch the corridor through his open door. He wished he'd closed it. "What the hell are you talking about?" he said lowering his voice.

"I flew up to Washington last night with Unger for one of the damnedest meetings I've ever attended in my life." Carl Unger was the director of the National Aeronautics and Space Administration. He spent more than half of his time in Washington because his job was more political than scientific or technical even though he was a Cal Tech physicist who'd run Los Alamos until his appointment to NASA.

"Meeting with who, about what?"

"That's the hell of it, Frank, we met in Unger's conference room, but I didn't know half the people there, and no introductions were made. But the topic of conversation was you and the launch in three days. Will it go off on schedule?"

"If we can finish the diagnostics over night, there should be no delays," said Ripley. "Now do you want to tell me what you're talking about? In English."

"I've got to ask you one more thing first. And believe me, Frank, I'm just as mystified as you're going to be, because no one explained it to me. I was just told to ask and report back to Unger. Have you noticed any change in attitudes by the Japanese over the past forty-eight hours or so? Anything, any incident no matter how slight that has struck you or the others as out of the ordinary?"

"Nothing slight about it, Tom. It's as if we've all been infected with HIV. No one wants to come near us, let alone talk to us. What's going on?"

"Can you give me a for instance?"

"I think they're bugging our conversations," Ripley said. He explained Kimura's uncharacteristic use of the term *prelaunch jitters* so soon after Ripley had said the same thing to Maggie.

Hartley hesitated for a beat, then he laughed, but it wasn't like him. Nor was his too-jovial tone of voice. "You've been away from home too long, Frank. I told them they were barking up the wrong tree. The Japanese have always been tight on security. I can't blame them. We seal the Cape up a few days before a launch. It makes sense, considering all the crazies out there."

It was a stupid mistake on his part, speaking his concerns on an open line, and Ripley felt like a fool. If someone was monitoring his conversations, they would certainly have a bug on his telephone. But he was an astronaut not a spy.

"You're right, we have been here too long. But the problem is that Unger has become too much of a politician. He's trying to make points on the Hill. He's probably trying to convince anybody who'll listen that the Japanese couldn't pull off this launch without NASA's help. My guess is those guys you met with were reporters, and Unger promised them some kind of a scoop. You know, ex-astronauts saving the Japanese bacon."

"That's about what I thought," Hartley said too loudly. "When you get back, Jo and I will have you guys over for a barbecue and a couple of beers." Hartley despised backyard cookery and hated beer. Ripley figured that Hartley was telling him that he understood something unusual was going on out here. Engineers had a hard time with hidden meanings.

"I'll tell the others."

"Do that," Hartley said. "See you in a few days."

After he hung up, Ripley turned again to stare out the window, even more confused than before. If he'd read Hartley right, something had apparently happened in the past couple of days to make the Japanese even more sensitive about security than they normally were. Whatever it was had apparently got the attention of the top brass. What Hartley had really said was that he wanted Ripley and his Tiger team to keep their eyes and ears open and their mouths shut. They were supposed to spy on the Japanese.

Payload Building One

It was 9:00 A.M. when Ripley got back. Guards had been posted at the door and he had to show his ID before he was allowed inside, where he pulled on paper booties over his shoes and a paper cap over his scalp and went into the assembly bay.

Hagoromo II, which was to dock with *Freedom* from where it would send a series of probes to the moon, was attached to a massive trolley arrangement that allowed it to be carefully moved to and from a loading crane that would place it on a huge truck for transport to the launch pad. Because of the increased size of the new H2C, the satellite could not be mated to the rocket in the vehicle assembly building. It had to be done on the pad until a larger VAB was constructed.

Towering nearly forty feet above the floor, the gigantic satellite was twelve feet in diameter in its stowed position and weighed nearly ten metric tons. It was to be the largest object ever sent into earth orbit by any country except the U.S. and Russia, and it would mark Japan's first serious entry into the space launch business. Not even the French Arianne rockets could launch such a complex payload into orbit.

Once it rendezvoused with *Freedom*, gigantic solar panels would extend like the wings of a butterfly to a distance of 150 feet on each side. Narrow beam antennae and compact satellite dishes would be uncovered, as would a dozen variously shaped probes that would be used to study everything from the solar wind to the Earth's magnetic field and the forces of microgravity caused by the bulk of the international space station itself.

Almost completely sheathed in gold foil for heat management in space, only six access panels at various points on the big satellite were open, exposing the electronic circuitry within, to which were attached cables and leads from a dozen pieces of test equipment. As many technicians, including the four NASA Tiger team members, were putting the satellite through its electronic paces in a procedure called fault tree analysis. One by one, each point in each circuit was artificially brought to a failure mode, and the results were monitored and analyzed. So far the Japanese-designed redundant systems seemed to work perfectly.

Maggie was studying the display on a Tektronix frequency spectrum analyzer and she looked up. "Did Hartley give you the usual pep talk?"

"He's invited us for some beers and a cookout when we get back," Ripley said. "Just like old times."

She gave him a double take. The others were out of earshot for the moment. "What are you talking about, Frank?" she asked in a low voice.

Ripley reached over and adjusted a control on the scope. "I'm not sure, but Hartley wants us to keep our eyes open. Something's going on that has the brass worried. They've even posted guards on the front door now."

"About the Japanese, the launch?"

"I guess so. He wanted to know if we'd noticed any change in attitudes around here over the past couple of days."

"What'd you tell him?"

"Not much, because I think we're being spied on." He told her about the conversation he'd had with Kimura.

Maggie stepped back. "What the hell is going on?"

"Take it easy and do your job. But watch what you say and keep your eyes open, okay?"

She wanted to argue but she didn't.

"I'll get the word to the others. In the meantime, how are the diagnostics coming?"

"Everything is suddenly within specs, Frank. And I mean *everything*. Until now I was happy, but I'm not so sure anymore."

"Don't go looking for something that's not there," Ripley warned.

She managed a smile. "That's why they pay us the big bucks. But this isn't going to take us six hours. We're already mostly done. Don has okayed the locking collar. He says it was replaced last night."

Ripley glanced up at the portalift platform raised to the top of the satellite. Don Wirth, their metallurgical engineer, was lying on his stomach inspecting the retaining bolts that held the collar in place. "How do you know?"

"He put his initials under one of the latches. They were gone this morning."

"You're kidding."

Maggie shook her head.

"Kimura is going to have a bird when he finds out."

"They probably haven't noticed. The collar was bad, so they replaced it. If Kimura was going to say something he would have nailed us with it first thing this morning." Maggie was smiling as if she had a secret.

"What?"

"They won't find my initials."

Astronauts had the biggest egos in the world, and there were times when they acted like children. The practical joke had risen to an art form at Houston and especially at the Cape. But their hijinks were never at the safety of a mission. Never.

"Maybe that's why they suddenly got pissed off at us. They don't take jokes lightly."

"I did it a half hour ago."

"Are you going to tell me where?"

"Nope," she said, smiling sweetly. They would never have anything more than a casual affair, which also was quite common among the engineering staff, but Ripley did care for her, and he suddenly found that he was worried about her and the others. Hartley's strange phone call had set him off.

He glanced up at the diagnostic center windows. Kimura, his hands behind his back, was staring down at them, a frown on his face.

"They want to treat us like hell, we'll give it right back to them," Maggie said. She smiled and waved at Kimura, who just stared at her. "It's a one-way street with them, Frank. They take our technology, but they don't give anything back in return." She looked at the towering satellite. "We don't know one-tenth of what's inside this bird."

"We've seen the blueprints and schematics."

"That's right, but we never got to look inside from the mainframe out. That was all done long before we got here."

"What are you getting at?"

"I'm going to spend six months on *Freedom* with this thing attached to it. I'd like to know a little more about it than I've been told, that's all."

Ripley looked up again at the bay windows. Kimura was gone, but he retained the impression that they were being watched. Hartley's warning was beginning to seem ominous, and the sooner they were out of here the better he was going to feel.

FIVE

Baileys Crossroads, Virginia

Howard Ryan's house was a surprisingly modest split-level on a large lot with a lot of trees, shrubbery and rose bushes in full bloom. The backyard overlooked Lake Barcroft, and getting out of his Nissan in the driveway a few minutes after 7:00 P.M. McGarvey could smell a charcoal grill in action somewhere. Some kids were shooting buckets in a driveway down the street. The neighborhood was very pleasant, not at all what McGarvey had expected.

Ryan had two children, but the young man who answered the door in a T-shirt and cutoffs came as another surprise. He was the spitting image of his father, but whereas Ryan almost always seemed to be scowling, his son, who McGarvey figured was fifteen or sixteen, had a big grin on his face.

"Mr. McGarvey?"

"Yes."

"Dad's in back." The young Ryan led McGarvey through the pleasantly furnished house and through the big kitchen to the patio where the elder Ryan, dressed in swim trunks, was reclining in a chaise lounge next to the pool, while his twelve-year-old daughter was swimming. Ryan's son raced the last few feet and jumped into the water next to his sister, swamping her.

Ryan's wife, Evangeline, dressed in a tennis skirt and polo shirt, glanced nervously at McGarvey from where she was slipping steaks on the built-in grill. McGarvey got the impression that the scene had been staged for his benefit, to show him that Howard Ryan wasn't such a bad guy after all. It was a Ryan insulation factor, one of the tricks he'd used to stay in power so long.

"Well, I never expected to see you as a guest in my home." Ryan motioned McGarvey to the chaise lounge next to his. "Care for a drink?"

"A beer will be fine," McGarvey said.

While Evangeline went into the kitchen to get the beer, McGarvey watched Ryan making a point of watching his children playing in the pool. Even in swim trunks the former Wall Street attorney looked like he was dressed in his habitual three-piece suits. As general counsel for the CIA he had been nothing short of brilliant, and for a few years the agency had enjoyed an unprecedented run of excellent relations with Congress and the White House. When he'd been made deputy director of Operations, however, he'd become a dangerous fool and had caused the agency almost as much harm as Aldrich Ames. After he was fired, he started up a consulting firm for congressional relations. His chief clients were the CIA and the National Security Agency. He was still well connected.

In a way, McGarvey figured his coming here was an exercise in futility. And seeing Ryan relaxing with his family in this setting was depressing. It brought home to McGarvey what he had given up in service to his country. His work, so far as he could see, had never made a difference, except that his ex-wife and daughter had been placed in harm's way. No matter what kind of a fool Ryan was, he had this.

"I didn't come here to make trouble," McGarvey said. "We could have met on neutral grounds."

Ryan turned a skeptical gaze to him. "The advantage would have been yours. I suppose congratulations would be in order, except for that horrible terrorist attack. Will your daughter recover?"

"Physically, yes."

Ryan looked at his own children again. "I hope so," he said wistfully. "I never meant for the situation in Russia to get so out of hand. Poor judgement on my part." He shrugged. "I should never have become DDO. It was a mistake, I can see that now. I was out of my depth. But I don't love my country any less than you do."

Ryan had sent Liz into a situation in Europe in which she was way over her head, and it had almost cost her her life. General Murphy had finally fired him because of it, and had McGarvey been able to get to him at the time, he might have killed the man. Now it didn't matter, though it had nothing to do with Ryan's disingenuous admission.

"I don't expect you do, which is why I've come to ask for your help."

Ryan looked at him with genuine surprise and a little pleasure tinged with suspicion. "With what?"

"Somebody doesn't want me to take the job."

"You think the attack was meant for you and was directed by someone who knew there was a good chance you might escape unharmed. By killing a lot of innocent bystanders they hoped that pressure would be brought to bear to force you to step down. Is that what you're intimating?"

"Something like that."

Ryan looked startled. "Good heavens, you can't possibly think that I had anything to do with it?" Ryan absently touched a scar on his cheek. He'd almost been killed by an assassin's bullet meant for McGarvey a few years ago. "I may be a lot of things you don't like, but not that."

"I think you might try to cut me off at the knees legally or politically, but not that way," McGarvey said. Ryan seemed genuinely relieved, but he was still suspicious.

Evangeline brought the beer, handed it to McGarvey without a word then went back to the grill. She seemed a little frightened. McGarvey figured his name probably wasn't a household word, but it had been mentioned.

"You know a lot of people in town, I want to know what you've been hearing."

"There's a lot of turmoil in Russia, if that's what you're talking about. The Mafia is doing business as usual, but I don't think they would make any effort to have you eliminated, though that kind of terrorism is right down their alley. They simply would have nothing to gain or lose by you becoming DDO. Nor would what's left of Tarankov's old regime. They're trying to hang on until the dust settles. Nobody knows what'll happen after the elections. Could just all be swept under the rug and forgotten, a course of action I'd certainly recommend."

"Not the Russians," McGarvey said. "I'm guessing it's the Japanese again."

"Because of that thing with Kamiya and Guerin Airplane Company?"

"Something else has come up. It hasn't hit the media yet, but it will."

Ryan looked over at Evangeline at the grill. "Pull the steaks off the heat for now, sweetheart. I won't be long." He got up, grabbed a terry cloth jacket and motioned for McGarvey to follow him back into the house.

They went into the study on the opposite side of the house from the pool, and Ryan closed the door. In addition to books, the walls were filled with framed photographs of Ryan with several presidents and congressional leaders, as well as a number of certificates of recognition and his law degree from Harvard.

"I used to make everyone sign the secrets act acknowledgement before I would brief them. Now that the tables are reversed all I can do is give you my word that anything said won't leave this room unless we both agree to it first. But you have come to me for help."

McGarvey nodded. "Fair enough, Howard." He thought that Ryan wouldn't dare cross him again. "The day before yesterday there was an underground nuclear explosion at an inactive power station on North Korea's east coast."

Ryan whistled long and low and sat back in his chair. "Was it the reactor? An accident?"

"One of our subs spotted a Japanese sub that probably put a party ashore. The explosion was most likely sabotage, but it wasn't the reactor. It was probably a North Korean nuclear weapon. One of five."

Ryan's mind was going a thousand miles per hour, obvious from the look on his face. "What's Pyongyang saying?"

"Nothing. Neither is Tokyo. But the Chinese are sending in a couple of submarines."

"The North Koreans have said or done nothing?"

"So far."

"All right, what does this have to do with you? Where are you seeing the connection, because frankly from what you've told me, this is nothing more than the Japanese taking a threat seriously enough to do something about it. What does your taking the DDO slot have to do with them?"

"Two of Kamiya's people, who were in jail until recently, were spotted together near Sasebo, the base from which the submarine sailed. And the terrorists Friday were Asians. Lots of coincidences."

"That part wasn't in the papers either," Ryan said. "Have they been identified?"

"Not yet. But the FBI thinks they were Japanese."

Ryan thought it out. "You've gone up against the Japanese twice in the past four years, and they lost both times. As DDO you'd be an even bigger thorn in their side. Could it be that simple?"

"What do you think?" McGarvey asked.

"It could be that easy, or it could be somebody else from your past gunning for you. Or both." Ryan thought for a few moments. "What do you know about a man by the name of Joseph Lee? A Taiwanese businessman?"

"Never heard of him."

"He's a heavy hitter. From what I've been hearing—and this is very hush-hush—Lee and his wife are under investigation by the FBI for illegal campaign contributions. Sam Blair is the special prosecutor, and he's one tough bastard."

"What does Taiwan have to do with this?"

"Nothing. Point is that Lee's background is suspect. He may have some connections with the Japanese government. His business interests include a number of think tanks in Hong Kong, Singapore, Seoul and Tokyo. As it turns out he's in town now, meeting with President Lindsay. Matter of fact he and his wife spent last night in the White House. I think he'd be worth a look. Maybe he's somehow connected with Kamiya's old crowd. He's worth something over four billion dollars, and guys at that level have connections with just about everybody. If he is working with the Japanese he might be interested in seeing you dead, or at least forcing your nomination to be sidetracked."

"Can you find out more for me?"

Ryan shrugged. "I guess I owe you," he said. "But this goes all the way to the White House, so you have to understand that in my position I'm going to have to be damned careful. I have a lot to lose here. If I were you I'd search the Agency's records to find out if you even had any connection with Lee or any of his business interests. Might be a starting point. That, and ID the terrorists, see if they can be traced back to one of Lee's businesses."

"Will you help?"

Ryan nodded. "Like I said, I owe you. But what about your daughter? Is she going to be okay?"

"She's a tough kid, she'll survive."

Ryan smiled. "She'd have to be, wouldn't she. For what it's worth, I'm sorry, but at the time I thought I was doing a good job so I made a lot of mistakes. And part of it was that I hated you."

"I know," McGarvey said. He got up to go.

"Did you really think that there was a possibility I had something to do with the bombing?"

McGarvey looked at him. "It crossed my mind, but I dismissed it almost immediately. You might have been a lousy DDO, but you're not a murderer."

"Thanks for that. I'll leave word at Langley if I come up with something."

"Do that," McGarvey said, and he left, his feelings about Ryan confused.

CIA Headquarters

Because of the crisis in the Sea of Japan, the CIA was on emergency footing. Tommy Doyle met McGarvey at the front entrance at 8:30 P.M. and took him upstairs to his office.

"Where've you been?" Doyle asked settling down behind his desk.

"Am I being followed?"

"We're watching your apartment. You haven't been there all day, and you left the hospital at two."

"I drove down to Milford to check on my house and tell them I won't be taking the teaching post after all."

Doyle was strung out. He raised his eyebrows. "Are you coming aboard?"

McGarvey had fought depression all of his adult life, starting when he'd discovered by chance that his parents might have been spies for the Russians during the war. He used to tell himself that the CIA had made him what he was. An assassin. But you couldn't make a lamb into a leopard by simply painting spots on its fleece. So he'd come to accept who and what he was, but after each assignment he fell into deep depressions which sometimes lasted months. He'd also learned that his only way out was by action. Not necessarily another assignment, but physical or mental action of any sort. One step at a time, beginning with the first. Fencing, swimming or running to the point of absolute exhaustion. Pushing himself to his limits, and then pulling up a reserve and continuing. The exercise gurus talked about the release of mood altering endorphins, but for McGarvey, pushing himself was simply one method of clearing his mind, bringing his entire being into the sharp focus of self-preservation.

He'd told all of that to Katy and Liz this morning at the hospital. And they'd listened without comment. Afterward he'd driven to Milford on the Chesapeake, where at Slaughter Bay he had run ten miles in the sand.

Back in Georgetown, he'd spotted the surveillance unit outside his apartment, sneaked past them into the building next door, where he took to the roof, crossing to his own apartment building. He'd taken a shower; changed clothes; dug out his emergency kit of spare passport and identification papers including credit cards, ten thousand dollars in cash and his gun, silencer and spare magazine of ammunition hidden in a fake laptop computer, then left the apartment the same way.

From the time he'd left the hospital until he'd shown up at Ryan's house, he'd made no decision. He'd simply given himself the option of running to ground if need be. He'd thought of going to Japan on his own to seek out Kabayashi and Hironaka, working independently as he had most of his life. But he didn't think there was anything to be accomplished there. Even if they admitted there was some kind of a plot to make war on North Korea, he would be no closer than he was before in finding out who had killed Jacqueline and nearly killed his daughter. For that he was going to need the CIA, and Ryan had provided him with the first possible clue. The rest would have to come from his past, documented in the Agency's archives.

"Is Murphy here?"

"Yes. I'll tell him we're on the way over." Doyle reached for the telephone.

"Wait a minute, Tommy," McGarvey said, and Doyle drew his hand back. "We've known each other for a long time. Am I going to get the runaround here?"

Doyle smiled wistfully. "You better believe it. Bureaucratic bullshit comes with the job. But I have a feeling you'll find a way to cut through most of it. Dick Adkins is a good man. He knows what he's doing, and you won't get anything but a hundred percent from him. No resentments."

"Whose idea was it to offer me the job?"

Doyle shrugged. "I don't know, but the consensus was that you were just what we needed, but that there wasn't a chance in hell that you'd take it."

"Why?"

"You can answer that yourself," Doyle said. "But Carrara used to say that if you ever got rid of that chip on your shoulder you'd make one hell of a DDO."

"Has it been that bad?" McGarvey asked, but he knew it had been.

Doyle looked at him for a long moment. "Do you want the truth?"

McGarvey nodded.

"You're afraid of responsibility, of commitment, and you've been running away all of your life on one big adventure after another. One relationship after another. You say you leave to protect the people you love because being around you is dangerous. From where I sit, I think that's a load of crap. If I want to protect someone I stick around and do it. I don't take off."

Doyle's words were like hammer blows between his eyes, all the more so because McGarvey knew that they were true.

"Let me hazard a guess, Mac. You got past our people outside your apartment and picked up your gun and papers. Either that or you've stashed them somewhere you can get to them easily. A little hidey-hole somewhere."

"Is that the consensus around here too?"

"Screw the consensus. No one is going to beg you to take the job, and frankly Howard Ryan was probably right when he said you were a prima donna pain in the ass. But if you can stop for one minute blaming everybody else for who and what you are, there are a lot of good people in this building—including me and the general—who think you'd be the most effective DDO there ever was. The bullshit would definitely stop at your desk, and we could get back to kicking some serious ass around here."

Coming back he would be facing his own past in living color, a past McGarvey had to admit he'd been running from all of his life. He no longer knew if he had the stomach for it. But seeing Liz lying in the hospital bed gave him resolve.

"Call Murphy," he said.

Dulles International Airport

"It's too bad we can't follow him." Mark Morgan watched Joseph Lee disappear through the security arches leading to the blue concourse. They were scheduled to pull another twelve-hour shift, but now that Lee was leaving their jurisdiction, it would be up to their Los Angeles field office, which would have him only long enough to watch him switch planes for Honolulu and then again for Taipei.

"I don't get why he's not taking his own plane," Kuchvera said. "Unless it's down with a maintenance problem. Something we're going to have to check out. But you gotta ask why he's in such a big hurry all of a sudden."

It didn't make sense to Morgan either. Lee's secretary had called from his home barely three hours ago to make the last-minute reservations. United to L.A. and Honolulu, and then Taiwan Air to Taipei. It had come out of the blue, and they had to scramble to alert their field officer. But until Lee actually left U.S. soil, he'd have a tail.

"If I had to make a wild-ass guess, I'd say he learned something at the White House and wants to get back home with it as soon as possible." He looked at Kuchvera. "Something so hot he couldn't even trust it to his encrypted phone line."

CIA Headquarters

McGarvey and Doyle walked over to the DCI's office and went straight in. Murphy was just finishing up a phone call.

"How is your daughter?" he asked, hanging up.

"The doctor says she's going to come out of it just fine." McGarvey said. "But I want a guard kept on her and my ex-wife for the duration."

"No problem. And as soon as Elizabeth gets out of the hospital we'll put her and her mother into a safe house. That's if they'll stand for it." Murphy was genuinely concerned about them, and it gave McGarvey some comfort. "As of this moment Seventh Fleet is ready to sail, but they're not going anywhere until the President gives his word."

"Convince him to at least get them out of Tokyo Bay. But the logical place for them is going to be off North Korea's coast."

"I tend to agree with you, but he also wants to know how we're going to get away with kidnapping Kabayashi and Hironaka."

"We're not, at least for the moment. They wouldn't tell us anything we don't already know. At this point the situation out there is still a political one. If we can put the Seventh between Japan and North Korea before the Chinese submarines show up, and before either North Korea or Japan does something stupid, we have a good chance of heading off a confrontation. Or at least delaying it. Has there been any word from Pyongyang or Tokyo?"

"Nothing."

"What about Seoul? Have they sent someone up there?"

"They have, but there's been no word yet," Murphy said.

"Anything new from our submarine?"

"The Japanese have sent a couple of P-3s from Sasebo, and they're running search patterns."

"Will they find her?"

"I'm told it's possible," Murphy said. "But if Seventh Fleet shows up it'll become a moot point. Podvin would like to avoid a confrontation, but under the circumstances no one is suggesting that we simply ignore what's going on."

McGarvey glanced at Doyle, and he knew what the DDI was thinking. "What about Internal Affairs?"

"These kinds of investigations tend to take a long time. What you did on the bridge was crude, ill thought out and dangerous, but I don't think anyone will recommend you stand trial for it. A lot of us have daughters too."

"I'll take the job, if it's still open, General."

Murphy nodded. "As of this moment you're my acting DDO, until we can get Senate confirmation. I'll inform the President. Carleton will work with the White House staff on a strategy, something that'll make sense."

"We'll have to sanitize his background," Doyle suggested.

A faint smile crossed the general's face. "Larry can work with records on that bit of legerdemain, but Mac is going to have to help out. In the meantime Dick will have to get him up to speed. The sooner the better."

"Tomorrow," McGarvey said. "I'm going to do a little digging myself."

"Do you think that the bombers were directed by someone out of your past? Have you any idea who or why?"

"I'm going to need Otto Rencke."

Murphy sat back. "I was wondering when his name would come up. Is he still in France?"

"He's gone to ground somewhere; maybe Rio, but I'll find him and convince him to come back with no repercussions."

Murphy had to smile at that. "I wouldn't know where to start, because if I made a mistake he'd wipe out every computer in the building."

"It'd be better to have him on the inside," Doyle observed.

Murphy nodded after a moment. "I've been wrong about a lot of things, Mac. About you, about Otto. But I don't want to compound my mistakes by being even more wrong now than I was before. You're getting a shot here, but it's your last shot. No vendettas, no rogue operations. As you're fond of saying, 'Don't shit the troops.' I expect the same from you, complete honesty."

"Don't try to micromanage me, General. Just let me do my job."

"Fair enough, but don't blindside me either." Murphy got up and extended his hand.

McGarvey took it and looked into his eyes. "Thank you."

SIX

The main display, which covered the back wall ninety feet wide and thirty feet tall, showed the real-time position and track of every U.S. intelligence-gathering satellite in orbit. Ranged in semicircular tiers facing the board were the individual control consoles from which satellites could be directed and to which downlinks provided the data, some of it electronic emissions monitoring, but most of it high-resolution photographs or infrared images. Far Eastern Division night supervisor air force Captain Louise Horn, seated above and behind her six console operators, nervously lit a cigarette, as she always did when something of interest crossed her board, and immediately placed it in an overflowing ashtray.

A half-dozen or more heat blooms had suddenly shown up along China's northeast coast, leaving tracks heading south into the Yellow Sea. She didn't have to ask what they represented; she knew, and she shivered in anticipation. They had been waiting for three days for this development.

She dialed up a large scale map of that section of coastline on her console master display and quickly clicked and dragged the pointer icon on reverse headings from the IR tracks, all of them originating, as she expected they would, from three coastal cities.

Next she pulled up the short list of available Key Hole and Lacrosse satellites, which would be coming up on the region within the next hour and computed tracks, times and camera angles so that the two available birds could take real-time images of the ships at sea, if that's what they were, and automatically downlink the digital signals produced by the CCD, or charge coupled device, aboard. One of the satellites was already in position, and within seconds data began to flow on the downlink. She brought up the first images on an adjacent screen and waited impatiently for the computer to enhance the pictures.

The NRO was an air force agency that until the freedom of information decade of the eighties had been so supersecret that only a select few people in the business even knew it existed. Responsible for all intelligence-gathering satellite operations and reconnaissance aircraft overflights, the agency shared its product with the CIA and the National Security Agency. In the past few years there'd been a fight going on between the two spy agencies for control of the NRO, which still primarily employed air force officers and technicians for the day-to-day data-gathering and photo interpretation duties.

Louise Horn, who'd graduated third in her class at the Air Force Academy, had originally wanted to fly jets. But at six five, she was too tall, and with an IQ bordering on the brilliant range, she was too smart. Here is where she belonged and she knew it. She was a mole in her burrow who never saw the light of day except coming to or from work, but the NRO was an exciting place to be, because it was from here she had the ability to eavesdrop on the entire world. The ultimate voyeur's playground.

It was one in the afternoon in the Yellow Sea, the cloud cover was only partial, and the first KH-13 satellite was about 45 degrees above the horizon, the conditions perfect, yet even Louise was startled by the clarity of the pictures.

She immediately started the transfer of data upstairs to Major Hubert Wight, the chief night duty photographic interpreter, then telephoned him. They were old friends.

"Hi, Bert. I'm sending something hot up to you."

"I'm printing it now. Looks like the *Tianjin* from Qingdao." The warship was a Russian-built Sovremenny class destroyer that had been delivered along with her sister ship, the *Fuzhou*, a couple of years ago. At 7,900 tons, the 511-foot warships carried Helix ASW helicopters and were armed with SSM and SAM missiles, eight Gatling guns, torpedoes and a pair of six-barrelled antiship RBU 1000 rocket launchers.

"That's not all. I'm showing at least six strong IR tracks originating from Qingdao, Lushun and Xiaopingdao, all of them heading southeast." They were the three major bases in China's North Sea Fleet.

"Okay, this is what we've been expecting. What else can you put in position? We've got another cold front coming through, so we're not going to have much time."

"You're seeing Yankee-three, and I have Whiskey Clipper–four coming in range within eighteen minutes."

"Where are they heading, Louise?"

"My projected track takes them between Cheju and the South Korean mainland. Means they're in a big hurry."

"They sure as hell aren't heading for Taiwan."

"Could be an exercise."

Major Wight chuckled. "Sell it to the navy, because I'm not buying it. The *Tianjin* is on the same track as the two submarines they sent. Does that tell you anything?" Major Wight was Louise Horn's mentor; she'd hooked her career rise with his, and there were times like this when she was glad she'd done it. He was a no-nonsense straight shooter who didn't hold it against her that she was smarter than him.

Louise manipulated some controls on her primary console while the image of the second target was being enhanced. "If she goes to best cruising speed of thirty-two knots she'll catch up with the submarines in about thirty-six hours."

"Good work."

"Here comes the second target. Another destroyer?"

"You betcha. That's the *Fuzhou*; they definitely mean business. Is that all from Qingdao?"

Louise switched back to the wide view on her primary console on which she'd picked up the heat blooms. The area displayed was the entire northeast coast of China. "That's it for now. The other four tracks originated from Lushun and Xiaopingdao. We're going to have to wait for Whiskey Clipper–four."

"Okay," Major Wight said. "I want you to keep with it. Soon as you get something solid get it up here. In the meantime I'll prep these and get them next door."

"What's going on out there, Bert?" Louise asked. Her only problem, if it was a problem, was her curiosity. She wanted to know not only what she was looking at, but why it was happening and what effect it was going to have.

Major Wight chuckled. "Ours is not to question why. But I'd suggest if you're planning on taking your next leave in Tokyo, you cancel it."

"I hear you."

"Listen, Louise. This is hot, and you've done a damned fine job down there. It won't go unnoticed."

"Thanks."

"Onward and upward," Major Wight said, and he disconnected, leaving Louise Horn to light another cigarette and stare at the big board. What the hell was going on out there, she wondered.

Tanegashima Space Center
Payload Building One

"How about that?" Hilman Hammarstedt observed emotionlessly.

"What the hell?" Ripley said. He was driving the van back from lunch with his Tiger crew, Hammarstedt was riding shotgun.

"Looks as if they're pulling a fast one," Hammarstedt said.

The huge payload transporter vehicle was backed up to the open bay doors of the payload building. A gigantic crane was delicately loading the Hagoromo II satellite under a dust-proof shroud on the flatbed. The move to the clean room on the launch gantry wasn't supposed to have taken place until tomorrow.

Periphery barriers were set fifty meters around the truck, and Ripley had to park the van on the west side of the building. Someone said something to Kimura, who was watching the loading procedure from an open NASDA Toyota. He looked over, then stepped down and came across the parking lot, ducking under the barrier tapes. Several armed guards were conspicuously present.

Kimura reached them as Ripley and the others got out of the van. "We may be getting some weather overnight, so it was decided to move the satellite now," he explained, his mood brighter than usual.

"We haven't finished our tests," Ripley said.

"Ah, yes, we finished them for you. It's the weather." Kimura glanced over his shoulder at the satellite. "I have my orders."

Maggie stepped forward. "Are you taking us out of the loop, Hiroshi?" she demanded. "Because if you are we'll have to report that we can't possibly sign off on this launch." Before the satellite would be allowed to dock with *Freedom*, the NASA Tiger team had to certify that the bird was ready to fly in space. It was part of the agreement.

Kimura seemed genuinely surprised. "Heavens, no. As soon as we have everything secured in the white house you'll be able to continue with your prelaunch sequence. In fact this will give you more time to do your jobs. We don't want to rush anything. This must not fail." Kimura looked at them. "In addition to the very large investment in yen, this project represents a great deal to Japan. It is our national honor at stake here."

"You should have informed us," Maggie said.

"We would not interrupt your lunch."

"Okay, we're here as observers, let's observe," Ripley said.

He and the others started toward the barriers when Kimura handed a piece of gold foil a half-inch wide by three inches long to Maggie.

"Your reputations have preceded you, of course. But for this and the locking collar, we would have been correct in sending you all home. But no one here wished to delay the launch while waiting for a new team to be sent from Houston."

Kimura turned and walked back to the truck, leaving Maggie to stare at the neat initials she had pressed into the foil, and she got a chill up her spine.

Georgetown Hospital

McGarvey spent a couple of hours on one of the CIA computers trying to find Otto Rencke on several international Usenet news groups without luck. But he left word in enough places that he didn't think it would take long for his friend to surface. It was a few minutes after eleven by the time he made it back to the hospital. The guard posted outside Liz's room knew McGarvey but didn't know where Kathleen had gone.

"She got out of here a half hour ago, sir. Dick Yemm is with her, so if you want to know where she is right now I can call him."

"Did she say when she was coming back?"

"No, sir."

The hospital was very quiet at this hour. The nurses at the floor station across from the elevators talked in hushed tones. Liz was asleep, her television tuned to CNN, the sound very low. He watched her for several minutes, bile rising up in the back of his throat again thinking how close to dying she'd come, and finally feeling the pain of Jacqueline's death hitting home. Doyle was right, he had been running away from commitments all of his life. If he had done what Jacqueline had wanted him to do, it would not have saved her life. But if he had forced the issue, forced her to stay in France, she would still be alive. At the time it had been another instance of ducking his responsibilities. He'd known in his heart of hearts why she followed him, what she wanted, and that was something he could not give to her. He was not husband material, not for Jacqueline, nor for Marta Fredericks, who'd lost her life chasing after him.

Liz stirred in her sleep, and McGarvey went to turn off the television.

"Don't turn it off, it helps me sleep," she said, groggily.

"Did I wake you, sweetheart?"

"I've been drifting in and out," she said. "Just lying here is driving me nuts. When can I go home?"

"The doctor says in a couple of days. Can I get you anything?"

She smiled tiredly. "A Big Mac and a Coke." Her expression suddenly darkened. "Jacqueline never had a chance, did she?"

"No." McGarvey pulled a chair over to her bedside and sat down. He closed his eyes for a second, instantly reliving the moment when the bombs went off with a flash and bang.

Liz reached out and touched his face. "You look tired, Daddy. Maybe you should get some sleep."

"I was on my way home. I just stopped by to check on you. Did your mother say where she was going?"

"Home to take a shower and change clothes. She said she'd be back in the morning." Liz studied her father's face for a long second. "Is Mom going to be okay? This has gotten to her pretty badly. She's having a rough time of it."

"She'll be all right."

"I don't want to worry her, but I can't change who I am." She looked away. "After what you told us this morning, she can't ask for that. It's not fair."

"Your mother sees it differently."

"My mother is a manipulator," Liz flared, and she instantly regretted the remark, her eyes suddenly filling. "Shit, what a dysfunctional family we are. Grandma and Grandpa were targeted by the Russians. Aunt Sally won't talk to us. And my parents are divorced. What am I supposed to do, how am I supposed to act?"

"Take it easy, Liz."

"If Mother were here, she'd make you say Elizabeth, not Liz."

She wanted to continue being angry, but McGarvey grinned at her, which eased the mood.

"Are you taking over the DDO?"

One thing about his daughter, she never dwelled on any topic of conversation for very long. She'd been a dynamo from the moment she'd been born. "I told the general yes."

"Thank God for that. With Ryan gone and you running the show upstairs, maybe the CIA will get back on track, because you've got to admit the Company has been dropping the ball a lot lately. Even I saw what was going down in Russia before anybody upstairs would admit there was a problem." Liz blinked. "Whoever hit the restaurant is going to try again. They'll probably go ballistic once the word gets out."

He'd decided not to tell his daughter about the threats her mother had received on the phone. But Liz was bright enough to realize that they were in danger too. She'd seen the guards on the door and knew that her mother had left with one. "That's a possibility we're going to have to watch for."

"As DDO you get a driver and a bodyguard, don't you?"

"That's my choice, but you've got a bigger one you're going to have to face."

Liz's lips compressed and her eyes narrowed. She was digging in her heels, the same way her mother did when she knew she was going to be pressed on something disagreeable. "It's the doctor's call when I can get out of here and back to the Farm."

"I want you to quit."

"No way," she said softly.

"Not the CIA, just fieldwork. I'll put you on the Russian desk."

"Where you can keep an eye on me."

"That's right."

"What if I were a man?" she flared. "You'd jump at the chance to hire me, with my operational experience."

"You're not a man, and you're not just somebody off the street, Liz."

"That's Mother talking. She wants me to get married, have babies and join the Junior League, take up tennis, volunteer for something." Her voice was rising. "She wants me to settle down, and you want a son."

The remark hurt. This was a lot worse that he'd thought it would be. "A son would have been nice," he said slyly. "Of course, by now I would have taught him how to use a gun, how to defend himself, hand-to-hand combat, knives, clubs, fencing foils. He'd certainly know how to swear and spit and tell a good joke."

She looked forlorn. "I can't spit."

He smiled, his heart filled with sadness for all the years he'd missed with her. "I was never good at it myself; Grandma and Grandpa didn't approve."

She raised her free hand to her eyes to hide her tears. "Oh, Christ, Daddy, I'm so scared. I don't want to disappoint you or Mother."

McGarvey got up, gently took her hand away from her eyes and wiped her tears with his handkerchief. "You could never disappoint us." He kissed a spot on her forehead that wasn't bandaged. "We love you for exactly who you are. And it's I who've disappointed you, but I'm going to try to make it up, if you'll let me."

She held his hand tightly and searched his eyes. "I won't quit," she said in a small but defiant voice. "It's what I am, what I want to do. Is that so wrong?"

"No, sweetheart, it isn't," McGarvey said tenderly. "I just wish you'd picked something else."

"It's what I wanted to be ever since I was a little kid in school. And I'm getting good performance reps at the Farm, at least as good as half the men."

"You're at the top of your class, and I'm proud of you, even if you're just a girl."

She finally managed a smile. "That part was your fault. I didn't have anything to do with it."

McGarvey looked at her for a long time, and he could feel his strength returning, flowing into his daughter by dint of his will. It wouldn't heal her wounds, but it was all he could do for now. "I love you, Liz," he said.

"I love you too, Daddy."

"Now, I want you to get some sleep. I want you out of here as soon as possible."

She nodded.

He kissed her forehead again. "Sleep, and that's an order."

"Yes, sir," she replied, her eyes beginning to droop. "Maybe you should check on Mother. She could use a pep talk too."

Chevy Chase

Sitting in his car in the country club parking lot across the street from Kathleen's two-story colonial, McGarvey telephoned Dick Yemm's mobile number. The Security Service agent's van was parked half a block away. The upstairs bedroom lights were on, otherwise her house was in darkness.

"Yemm."

"This is McGarvey, how's everything look?"

"It's been quiet until you showed up, sir."

"You have me spotted?"

"When you came in. I recognized the car and scoped you with the low light."

"When's your relief due?"

"Another six hours," Yemm said. "You thinking about coming over, or are you going to stay there all night?"

"I don't know yet."

"Don't mean to get nosy, sir, but Mrs. McGarvey probably could use some company. She seemed pretty strung out to me."

"Thanks," McGarvey said. He broke the connection and phoned Kathleen's number. She answered on the second ring. She sounded brittle.

"Hello, who is it?"

"It's me."

"Are you at the hospital?"

"I just came from there. Elizabeth is sleeping. How about you, Kathleen, how are you doing?"

"I've been better," she said. "Are you at home, Kirk?"

"No. I'm across the street in the club parking lot."

She didn't hesitate. "Care for a nightcap?"

"I'll be right over." McGarvey drove across the street and parked beside Yemm's gray government issue van.

The Security Service agent rolled down his window. He was drinking a cup of coffee. "Good evening, sir," he said. The passenger seat was filled with electronic equipment including a computer monitor and keyboard.

"Are you monitoring her phone lines?"

Yemm nodded. "Yours has been the first since we got back here. We've got bugs on the doors and windows and inside too, in case someone tries to get in from the back."

"Good," McGarvey said. "Shut down the inside bugs for now, would you?"

"Sure thing," Yemm said. He brought up a screen and typed in a few commands. "It's done, sir." He looked up. "I heard you were taking over the DO. Congratulations."

"Not much of a secret," McGarvey said wryly.

"Not in this town."

Kathleen, dressed in a terry cloth robe, her hair wrapped in a towel, opened the door for him as he crossed the veranda. She'd been crying, her eyes were red and puffy, a slight flush on her cheeks.

The grandfather clock in the hall chimed once for the hour as she let him inside and closed and locked the door. For a long moment or two they stood very close, looking into each other's eyes. She was strung out, but she seemed a little relieved now that he was here.

She handed him her wineglass. "There's an open bottle in the refrigerator. Why don't you pour me some and get yourself a drink and come upstairs. I have to finish my hair."

"Are you sure this is what you want?"

She chuckled. "I'm sure I want a glass of wine." She went up the stairs leaving him standing alone in the empty hall.

He listened to the sounds of the house for a few seconds, then went into the kitchen where he poured her wine. He fixed himself a brandy at the sideboard in the living room and then went upstairs where the door to the master bedroom suite was ajar.

The bathroom door was open too. Kathleen was drying her hair at the vanity when McGarvey set the drinks on the table in front of the settee in the sitting room. The rooms, like Kathleen, were perfectly done, feminine without being overly frilly, with expensive furnishings, thick carpeting and several pieces of very good art on the walls.

"You may smoke if you want," she called from the bathroom. "There's an ashtray on my nightstand."

McGarvey went into the bedroom to get the ashtray. The big bed was turned down, the lights low, soft music playing from the stereo. There was a package of Kool lights and a gold lighter on the nightstand, two half-smoked butts in the ashtray. He brought them into the sitting room.

"When did you start smoking, Katy?"

"Kathleen," she automatically corrected. But then she grinned sheepishly. "Sorry, old habits, I guess."

"Me too," McGarvey said.

"I started smoking this summer," she said, brushing her hair. "Didn't seem much reason not too, even though it's another stupid habit. Probably kill me sooner or later." She laughed without humor.

"Maybe we should both quit."

"Sounds good to me." She finished in the bathroom, shut off the light, came into the sitting room and sat down on the edge of the couch. She pulled her robe primly over her knees.

McGarvey handed her the glass of wine.

"Light me a cigarette, please."

He did it, and she smoked without inhaling, holding the cigarette like a movie starlet. She looked as if she were on the verge of falling apart, breaking into a million pieces, holding on with everything in her power and trying to hide the effort.

"Elizabeth will be getting out of the hospital in a couple of days. I'm going to put her up at a safe house. I'd like you to go with her."

"For how long?" Kathleen asked reasonably.

"Until we find out who tried to kill me and who is threatening you. Will you do it?"

"We don't have much of a choice, do we?" she asked. "Are you taking over the DO?"

"Yes."

"Good. At least you'll be around more than before. That'll make our daughter happy."

McGarvey had to look away for a moment, unable just then to face his ex-wife. "She won't quit."

"I didn't think she would," Kathleen said. "Please look at me when you're speaking."

He turned back to her. "She'll be recuperating for a while, and afterward I'll make sure her training is delayed."

"That won't last forever."

"If need be, I'll quit and take her out with me."

Kathleen's left eyebrow rose. "You'd do that for her?"

"If it comes to it. I don't want her to get hurt."

Kathleen studied him, as if she were trying to gauge his true meaning and figure out what to say next. "Is that why you were sending Ms. Belleau back to Paris, because you thought something was about to happen?"

"She wanted to marry me."

"Why not, Kirk? Elizabeth said she was a lovely woman, intelligent, warm, a spy like you."

"I'm not ready to be someone else's husband."

Kathleen was taken aback, and her hand shook as she put down her wine and stubbed out her cigarette. Her moods were mercurial, and she seemed angry now. "The trouble with you is that you never understood women. You're coming close with your daughter. But she's a special case because she'll accept you on any terms. With her you don't have to make any compromises. That's not the case for the rest of us."

"I know."

"You know," she said harshly. "After all this time, with your daughter lying in a hospital bed, all you can say is that you finally know?"

McGarvey put his drink down, a great weariness coming over him. "I don't know what else to say, Katy."

She got up and went into the bedroom where she stood staring at the bed, her back to him. He went to her.

"It was never supposed to be like this," he said. He took her into his arms, her back still turned to him, and she laid her head back on his shoulder.

"Like what?" she asked. "With a grown daughter who idolizes you and an ex-wife who is still in love with you?" She turned in his arms, and raised her face to his to be kissed.

Her body seemed frail, and he could feel that she was shivering. For a long time she clung to him as if she were never going to let go, but then she stepped back, her face even more flushed than before.

"Can you stay tonight?"

"If it's what you want, Kathleen."

"Katy," she corrected. She opened her robe and let it fall to the floor. Her body was wonderful, not as tight and firm as it had been when they were young, but in McGarvey's eyes, even more wonderful than he remembered.

"Make love to me, my darling," she said, coming back into his arms. "No compromises this time. I want you. Plain and simple, no strings attached, no promises, no questions. Just us."

SEVEN

Seawolf

Thomas Harding cocked an ear to listen to the sounds of his boat. It was 0900 GMT, which put them three hours into the first morning watch, the time when the crew, the majority of whom had too little to do, began making mistakes. Twenty-four hours ago, after they had deployed listening sensors on a forty-mile track, he had ordered the *Seawolf* rigged for silent running, which meant no unnecessary noises. Their job was to make like a hole in the water and simply listen. So far he'd heard nothing inside his boat, nor had sonar heard anything outside. It couldn't last forever.

He stood at one of the plotting tables where their present position was marked twenty-five miles off the North Korean coast in relationship to the downed MSDF submarine and the tracks of the two P-3s that had overflown them yesterday. They'd expected to hear the splash of sonobuoys being dropped in the water, but it had never happened. If the Orions were looking for a submarine it wasn't them. At least not for the moment.

"Conn, sonar." Lieutenant Karl Trela, officer of the deck, answered it.

"Conn, aye."

"We have two possible targets, one submerged, but very faint."

Trela glanced over at Harding, who motioned that he would check it out. "Okay, good work. The captain's on his way."

Harding got a cup of coffee and went forward to the sonar compartment located starboard and below the weapons loading hatch. Chief sonar operator Seaman First Class Mel Fischer was studying displays on two consoles, the three other operators working as backup.

Fischer's division officer, Lieutenant Charles Pistole, stepped aside to give the captain some room. "We don't have an identification on either target yet, Skipper."

"Are they North Korean?"

"Probably not, they're well east of us, and possibly inbound. Maybe Japanese."

Fischer suddenly held his earphones tighter. He adjusted a control on his BSY-1 console. "Conn, sonar. Designate first target Sierra one-seven. Konga class destroyer. Target bearing zero-eight-seven, range twenty thousand yards plus, making screw sounds for twenty knots. I'm not sure of the course yet, but it's definitely closing."

A printer behind Fischer spit out two lines of data, and he reached back and pulled it off.

"Conn, sonar, I have a positive ID now. She's the *Kirishima*, DD174 from Sasebo." He adjusted his controls again. "Course steady on two-six-seven, speed steady at twenty knots."

Harding used a growler phone to call the conn. "Karl, start a fire control track."

"Already on it, Skipper."

Fischer had switched to another console. He made a grease pencil mark on the Busy-one display, adjusted the controls and made another mark. He looked over his shoulder at the captain. "It's a submarine, Skipper. Real faint, a few miles south of the *Kirishima*, but closer to us."

"What's your best guess, Mel? Japanese?"

Fischer stared at the display, tweaked the controls and made another grease pencil mark. "She's a Yuushio class, I've got that much, but coming up with a sail number is going to be dicey until she gets closer."

"Inbound?" Harding asked.

"Definitely, making eight knots, maybe a little better, but very quiet.

She's not advertising her presence, and the noise the *Kirishima* is making isn't helping."

"Are those the only two targets?"

"So far, Skipper."

"Don't lose them," Harding said, and he went back to the control room where Trela and Rod Paradise were hunched over one of the plotting tables. The computers would automatically plot the course, speed and position of the targets fed into the BSY-1 consoles, but paper tracks were kept manually as a backup.

"Unless the *Kirishima* changes heading, she's going to pass about twenty miles north of us," Paradise said. "Same for the submarine."

"They sent scouts yesterday, and now this," Trela observed. "What do you suppose they're up to, Skipper?"

"Good question, Karl, but I think this just may be the beginning."

"Conn, communications."

Harding answered it. "This is the captain."

"We just received a one-group ELF message from COMSUBPAC. Reads, AAA." ELF, or extremely long frequency, was the way in which U.S. submarines submerged at sea could be contacted anywhere in the world. The drawback was that the ELF bandwidth was so narrow that only extremely brief messages in one-time cipher codes could be transmitted, and even at that it took a minute and a half just to transmit one three-letter grouping. In this case AAA was the order for *Seawolf* to go to periscope depth for a longer message sent burst transmission via an SSIX satellite in geosynchronous orbit. There was little danger that the approaching Japanese destroyer would pick up their burst transmission—it was still too far away—but it paid to be careful. They would only spend a minimum time near the surface with their masts up.

"Take us to periscope depth and prepare to dive on my order," he told Trela, then he turned back to the phone. "I'll have one to send as soon as we've received the incoming."

"Aye, Skipper."

As they headed up, Harding wrote the first part of his message for the commander of Pacific Fleet Submarine Operations at Pearl Harbor. He phoned sonar. "Have you identified that submarine yet?"

"Just came out of the computer, Captain. She's the *Sachishio* from Sasebo."

Harding added that bit of information to his message and sent it forward to the communications shack across the passageway from sonar for encryption and preparation for transmission. The radio operator would add the proper headings.

When they were settled at sixty feet, Harding called ESMs. "This is the captain. I want to know if those Orions are still around."

"Standing by."

"Prepare to dive," he told Trela, then raised the search periscope, ESM antenna and the UHF antenna which would link them with Pearl via the satellite.

It was late afternoon on the surface, and although the sky was still somewhat overcast, the seas had dropped considerably. He made a quick 360-degree sweep but saw nothing.

"Conn, ESMs. We're showing a faint radar signal to the southeast, but nothing else. The P-3s are gone."

"Good."

"We have the incoming," the radio operator called.

"Send our message."

A few seconds later the radioman was back. "Message sent and confirmed, sir."

"Very well." Harding lowered the periscope and masts. "Karl, take us to three hundred feet and move us about ten miles north. I want to be a little closer to the action when these guys pass us."

"Aye, aye, Captain."

Paradise brought the message back from the radio shack. "The ante has just been raised a notch," he said, handing it to Harding.

Z090712ZAUG

TOP SECRET

FM: COMSUBPAC

TO: USS SEAWOLF

INFO: CINC7THFLEET

A. USS SEAWOLF Z172111ZAUG

CHINESE FLEET OPS

1. NRO ADVISES CHINESE NORTHERN FLEET DEPLOYMENT, FROM BASES AT QINGDAO, LUSHUN AND XIAOPINGDAO XX POSSIBILITY THIS DEPLOYMENT IN RESPONSE TO REF A XX INTENT UNKNOWN.

2. A TOTAL OF EIGHT VESSELS HAVE BEEN DEPLOYED TO THIS TIME/DATE, AS FOLLOWS: SUBMARINES: IMPROVED 5 HAN CLASS TISING 404, BAOJI 405. DESTROYERS: SOVREMENNY CLASS TIANJIN 168, FUZHOU, 169, 15 LUDA/TYPE II CLASS JINAN 105, XIAN 106. FRIGATES: 252 JIANGHU CLASS NANTONG 511, YIBIN 552.

3. PRESENT COURSES AND SPEEDS INDICATE THESE VESSELS MAY RENDEZVOUS AT GRID REF21A/13Z WITHIN 72 HOURS XX NO PREVIOUS ANNOUNCEMENTS WERE MADE XX NO UNUSUAL SIG TRAFFIC MONITORED.

4. REMAIN AT OR NEAR STATION DESIGNATED ROUND ROBIN, AND CONTINUE TO MONITOR SITUATION XX REPORT AS NECESSARY XX UNRESTRICTED OPS ARE AUTHORIZED XX RPT XX UNRESTRICTED OPS ARE AUTHORIZED XX HOWEVER TAKE ALL PRECAUTIONS TO MAINTAIN STEALTH OPS.

GOOD LUCK
END MESSAGE
BREAKBREAK

"If we're going to get some help out here, Seventh is going to have to get out of the barn right now," Harding said.

"This ought to be their wake-up call," Paradise agreed. "One thing for sure, it's going to get interesting around here real soon."

"That it is, Rod." Harding glanced at the ship control station from where the submarine was actually driven. "Soon as we're in position I want all the senior officers in the wardroom. It's not only going to get interesting, it's going to get dicey, and I want everyone to know what we're facing."

The White House

The same crisis team as yesterday was already gathered in the situation room a couple of minutes after nine in the morning when Roland Murphy showed up and sat down next to Roswell.

"Good morning, Mr. President," he said, and he nodded to the other men around the table. It was Sunday, and none of them wanted to be here. It showed on their faces.

"Good morning, Roland. I think by now that everyone here knows about the Chinese naval deployment and the increased readiness of all Japanese forces. Has there been anything new from the NRO overnight?"

"Only that the six surface ships and two submarines have not altered their course or speed. They're still heading for the Sea of Japan through the slot between the Korean mainland and the island of Cheju."

"Their submarines have not submerged?"

"No, sir. The surface ships should catch up with them sometime tonight, and the entire flotilla will be in position off the North Korean coast by Friday night or sometime Saturday. They've slowed way down, for some reason."

"Have we shared this information with the Japanese?"

"There's no need for it. They have their own satellites monitoring the region. They knew the same time we did."

"I ordered Seventh Fleet to sail this morning right after we received the message from *Seawolf* about the two Japanese warships he detected."

"We'll be in position about the same time the Chinese show up," Admiral Mann said. "But it's going to be damned dangerous out there. Especially if the Japanese decide to throw more assets into the mix, which we think they will."

"Has the CIA gotten anything new from the South Korean team that was supposed to check out Kimch'aek?" the President asked.

"Unfortunately not, Mr. President. As of midnight no one had heard from the team. Could be nothing more than a communications problem, but no one in Seoul is sure. They're going to sit tight for another twenty-four hours before they send a second team in."

"What about the special operation to kidnap Kabayashi and Hironaka?"

"We're still working out scenarios," Murphy said. "But McGarvey thinks we should hold off for the moment. They might not tell us anything we don't already know, or at least nothing significant enough to justify the risk if the operation should go bad. At this point he thinks we should concentrate on the political solutions."

"Under the latest circumstances, I have to agree with him."

"What circumstances, Mr. President?"

"Seoul and Pyongyang will issue statements this morning. They'll be breaking on all the networks in another hour, but we were advised of the content overnight. They were looking for a reaction."

Secretary of State Carter handed copies around the table. "These came to us on the back burner, which I think was damned wise of both countries. Finally shows some restraint. The gist of Kim Jong-Il's statement is that there was a nuclear accident at Kimch'aek with the loss of at least one hundred and fifty lives, which he says was caused by outside pressures forcing them to cut corners in closing down their old nuclear facilities. The heart of the matter is that he's issuing a warning that should anyone take this as a sign that he is weak, or that should anyone try to take advantage of the situation, an appropriate response will be forthcoming."

"It's probably why the Chinese navy is on the way," the President's national security adviser Harold Secor observed. "He's asked for their help."

"The Japanese showing up in force won't do much to stabilize the situation."

"No, it won't."

"Apparently Kim Jong-Il hasn't seen the latest from Seoul," Carter said. "They've trotted out Hwang Jang Yop again, and this time he's out-done himself. The short version is that he claims North Korea engineered the accident themselves as an excuse to prepare for an all-out war. Scorched earth. Yop is warning that North Korea is planning to launch its nuclear arsenal at any moment."

Murphy could scarcely believe what he was hearing. "Is this the government's official position?"

"All South Korean forces have gone to DEFCON Two," General Podvin said unhappily. "Came out of the blue at 0600. Ken Addison is scrambling to play catch up. Caught him completely off guard." General Addison was commander in chief of all forces in South Korea.

Murphy sat back in his chair as he tried to work it out. "This could mean that the South Koreans heard something from their Kimch'aek team that they're not telling us," he said. "Wouldn't be the first time they held out."

"They're playing a dangerous game," Secor said.

"That they are," Murphy agreed.

"All right, gentlemen," the President said. "North Korea and South Korea are both rattling their sabers. In the meantime the Chinese are sending warships into a region where Japan already has deployed two ships of its own, not including the submarine of theirs that sank. What do we do about it?"

"We put Seventh Fleet between them," General Podvin said. "The Chinese backed down before over Taiwan, and they have a much greater interest there than they do in North Korea."

"What orders do we give Hamilton?" the President asked pointedly. Admiral James Hamilton was CINC of Seventh Fleet.

"To defend himself," Podvin said. "But nobody's going to shoot at us."

"They have before."

"Not the Chinese, Mr. President," Podvin said. "And the incident two years ago between us and Japan was an accident they're not going to repeat."

The President was troubled, but he nodded. "I tend to agree with you," he said. "Which is why I ordered the Seventh out of Tokyo Bay. But we have another kettle of fish to deal with. The Japanese embassy hand-delivered a letter from Prime Minister Enchi to me forty-five minutes ago."

Harold Secor was the only man around the table who didn't seem surprised.

"He's asked for our help," the President said.

"Did he admit they sabotaged Kimch'aek?" Murphy asked.

"No. But he's taking Kim Jong-Il's threats seriously enough to tell me that if the North Koreans so much as twitch he'll order an all-out offensive against them and expect our support."

"Then it's up to us to prevent Kim Jong-Il from twitching," Murphy said. "We do exactly what we've set out to do, because the North Koreans aren't going to do a thing without the support of the Chinese. If we make them back down, Kim Jong-Il will back down."

"What if the Japanese navy gets into it with the Chinese?" Podvin asked.

"Won't happen unless they know something that we don't," Murphy said, but even as the words came out of his mouth he wasn't so sure. In the past few years the Japanese had done some surprising things. Their economy was going down the drain, and yet they continued to build up their military and even continue with the space program. They'd taken up slack left by Russia's inability to keep pace with the *Freedom* space station, even though the cost to them was so enormous it was straining their budget at the seams.

"What do you mean?" President Lindsay asked.

"Japan going up against North Korea is one thing. They've been enemies for five hundred years, and the North Koreans are technologically no match for them, even with their four nuclear weapons and million-man army. But going up against China is another matter entirely. It'd be a war Japan couldn't possibly win."

"What could they know that we don't that would make the difference?" the President pressed.

"I was just thinking out loud," Murphy said. "The Japanese took the North Korean threat seriously enough to try to sabotage it, and Prime Minister Enchi sent a letter to you this morning knowing that the Chinese were sending a naval force. Makes me wonder if something else is happening that we're not aware of."

"It might be a good idea if I fly out to Tokyo this morning after all," Carter said. "Maybe a face-to-face meeting might slow things down a bit. Give us a chance to work something out."

"We owe them at least that much," Tony Croft, the President's adviser on foreign affairs, put in.

"I agree," the President said. "But we're going to keep the trip out of the media."

"They'll have to be told something," Secor said.

"I'll hold a news conference this afternoon to deal with Pyongyang's and Seoul's statements, but beyond that there will be no leaks."

Everyone around the table nodded. This was one president who did not enjoy being second-guessed by the media.

"In the meantime I want no slipups. As soon as the Seventh Fleet shows up, there are going to be a lot of tense trigger fingers. I'm going to need every piece of hard information that the CIA and NSA can provide me as soon as it occurs. Are we clear on that?"

"Yes, sir," said Murphy and Roswell.

"Then, let's get to it, gentlemen. I want a diplomatic solution this time. No shots fired."

After the meeting, Murphy went with Secor and Croft upstairs to Secor's office, where CIA General Counsel Paterson had just arrived. Paterson, a look of exasperation on his long face, was dressed as usual in a dark three-piece business suit.

"Sorry to disturb your Sunday morning," Murphy told him as they went inside.

"Comes with the territory, General," he said briskly. "Nothing more than I expected when I signed on." He shook hands with Secor and Croft. "We have our work cut out for us if we expect to get McGarvey confirmed by the Senate."

"The President doesn't want to take a hit, so we can't drop the ball," Secor said. "But I have to agree with you, it's going to be tough, if not impossible. I don't know what he's thinking."

"Wouldn't it be easier to convince the President to pick someone else?" Croft asked. He was scowling, as if he had a toothache, none of his usual good cheer showing. "There has to be somebody else over there who can do the job."

"Not as good as McGarvey," Murphy said. "You've looked at his record, you know what he's done for us."

"From what I've seen he's a one-man killing machine, and a maverick to boot," Croft said. "Is he the one you want for the job, General?"

"Frankly I wouldn't have picked him, but only because I never thought he'd accept the offer. And I'm even more surprised that the President wants him."

"Has he accepted?" Secor asked.

"He's been acting DDO as of yesterday."

Secor and Croft exchanged a worried glance. "That's not so good. You should have waited," Croft said.

Paterson took several files out of his briefcase and handed them around. "Our battle plan," he said. "And believe me we're going to need it because this is going to set a record for the all-time toughest appointment in our history."

Paterson, a New York lawyer like Ryan, had many of the same pretentious attitudes as his predecessor, but although he wasn't quite as effective on the Hill yet, he had none of Ryan's ambitions to become a spy. When Murphy had hired him he'd done so with the warning that people in the business tended to be odd ducks, hard to figure by an outsider and even harder to control.

"As I see it, we have four major concerns to deal with if we're going to make this fly, the first of which is McGarvey's past. It's going to have to be sanitized, which means we're going to end up lying through our teeth to Congress." Paterson looked over the rim of his reading glasses at Secor. "Does the President understand this?"

"Let's sidestep that part for the moment, Carleton, because we're not going to back the President into any corners. If there's any heat, we're going to take it. So I think we'd better find a way through this that we can all live with."

"McGarvey's official record with the CIA is actually quite brief," Murphy said. "And his special operations for us have all been black, so I don't know how much of that will have to come out."

"It's all grist for their mill," Paterson said. "And don't think otherwise. If something comes up that's too secret to share with the public, the subcommittee will meet in camera. What I'm telling you is that if McGarvey's full record comes out he'll never be confirmed, not in a thousand years." Paterson shook his head. "Just the Russian operation four months ago would be enough to sink him. What he did was illegal. Plain and simple. So what do we do about it?" he asked them all. He put his file folder down. "Because if we can't overcome this first stumbling block then we might just as well give it up here and now. Save us all the work and save the CIA a black eye."

"We lie to Congress," Murphy said it for the others.

"Just the high points," Secor said.

Paterson looked pointedly at Murphy. "I will not be a party to changing the actual record in CIA archives."

"Nor will it be changed," Murphy said. "We'll sanitize McGarvey's past as needed and present his record entirely in closed session."

"Very well," Paterson said. He picked up his folder. "The next two issues concern the terrorist attack against him in Georgetown and his response. I think we're all in agreement that the incident probably had something to do with proposing McGarvey as DDO. And it's now a matter of FBI record that McGarvey single-handedly killed the three alleged terrorists. Violence does surround the man. The question will be asked, then, if he is actually confirmed as DDO how many similar incidents will occur and how many other innocent civilians will be hurt?"

Croft slumped back in his chair, a dour I-told-you-so look on his pudgy features. "Tell us something to cheer us up."

"Americans don't like to be pushed around. If some outside interest is, in actuality, trying to block this nomination it could work as a plus for us, providing the FBI can find out who they are." He turned to Murphy. "I think this has to become a priority for us on top of everything else that's happening."

"McGarvey is working on it because it involved his daughter and his friend."

"How have the French reacted?" Secor asked with interest.

"The DGSE is sending someone over to help with the investigation."

"We're allowing that?" Croft asked, interested too.

"Under the circumstance, of course. There's no reason to tell them no."

"Six weeks," Paterson said. "That's the timetable we're working with. We need to develop plausible answers for his background and come up with the people and the reason behind the Georgetown attack to justify McGarvey's violent reaction."

"And the fourth hurdle?" Croft asked.

Paterson had to smile. "Maybe the toughest nut to crack of all. McGarvey himself. I've only met him a couple of times but it's quite obvious that he has, shall we say, a forceful personality."

"He calls them like he sees them," Murphy said, understanding exactly where Paterson was taking this. "Won't set well with the committee if he tells a couple of those senators what he actually thinks. Is that what you're getting at?"

"He's not a stupid man," Paterson said. "Even though the CIA has treated him that way at times. If he wants the job he'll have to play the game, and I don't think it's beyond him. It'll simply be a matter of motivation. That too will have to be worked out over the next six weeks."

"That's my job," Murphy said, and it would not be an easy one.

"Yes," Paterson said. "Because he won't listen to me; he doesn't especially care for me."

"He didn't like Ryan, he's indifferent to you," Murphy said.

Paterson laughed again. His skin wasn't as thin as Ryan's had been. "Those are the problem issues, and now we have to come up with a plan to deal with them."

FBI Headquarters
J. Edgar Hoover Building

McGarvey entered the fourth-floor conference room a couple of minutes after 10:00 A.M. Fred Rudolph had been surprised to hear from him so soon, but had agreed without hesitation to the unusual Sunday morning meeting. A couple of stacks of file folders were laid out on the table along with a carafe of coffee and a couple of cups.

"Good morning, Mr. McGarvey. Coffee?" Rudolph said. He was dressed in jeans, a short-sleeve yellow Izod and deck shoes. With his short hair and earnest attitude he looked preppy.

"No thanks." Before McGarvey called for this meeting, he'd telephoned the CIA's records section from Kathleen's house for some background on the FBI Special Investigative Division's assistant director. Rudolph had graduated from Fordham University with a law degree in 1982, summa cum laude, had joined the army's Staff Judge Advocate's office as a captain, rising to the rank of lieutenant colonel in a short seven years. He worked briefly for the U.S. Supreme Court and the Department of Justice until signing on with the FBI five years ago. Although he'd had no direct experience in law enforcement, his specialty had been criminal law and he had headed a number of special investigative efforts for the military and Justice, so he was well qualified for his present position. The recommendations in his file all indicated that he was a straight shooter who might never head the Bureau but would almost certainly be its assistant director one day.

"I understand that congratulations are in order. Dr. Pierone said you've been appointed as deputy director of Operations. It's an important position."

"Yes it is, thank you. It's one of the reasons I wanted to talk to you this morning."

"We got off on the wrong foot Friday, but I was coming up short on a bunch of serious questions."

"Forget it," McGarvey said. "The attack was meant for me because someone doesn't want me to take over the DO. It's up to us to find out who it was and exactly what they have to lose."

"Or hide," Rudolph said. "Do you have any ideas?"

"A few. But first I want to get something straight between us, all bullshit aside. If there's been trouble in the past between the CIA and the Bureau it stops now."

"Fair enough."

"That means I'm accessible twenty-four hours a day with one provision. You talk to me and you tell me the truth, all of it. Nothing held back, nothing classified for Bureau reasons. And if you have a problem with that, take it up with your boss."

"I can envision some exceptions, but we'll deal with them as and when they arise," Rudolph said seriously. "It's a two-way street."

"Yes, it is," McGarvey replied. "Tell me about the Bureau's investigation of Joseph Lee."

A flinty look came into Rudolph's eyes. "Where did you hear that name?"

"Lee's name was mentioned in a roundabout way by my predecessor, Howard Ryan, who knows Blair."

Rudolph took a moment to answer. "Joseph Lee is very close to the President, so I'm going to have to ask you why you want to know about him. Where's the connection?"

"It's a tenuous one at best, but I was involved in a couple of operations that dealt directly with the Japanese. Could be there is something else going on out there that might involve some of the same people I came up against."

"Two years ago, the airline disasters?"

McGarvey nodded. "I was told that Lee may have some connection with the Japanese, could be one of the groups I was involved with. He has a think tank in Tokyo which could be a front for something. If there's a connection between that operation and the group that sabotaged our Air Traffic Control system it might provide a bridge back to me."

"It's all over, why come after you now?"

"I don't know. Maybe I missed something last time, maybe, like I said, something else is going on. Two of the men involved who were sent to jail are out. In fact they were seen together a couple of weeks ago in Nagasaki."

"Are you sending someone to interview them?"

"We're working on it, but something is going on right now over there that might make that too politically risky for us to take the chance."

"Are you going to tell me about it?" Rudolph said. "Because there are a lot of coincidences piling up here, all leading back to the White House. Lee spent Friday night in the Lincoln bedroom."

"If I come up with a connection, I'll brief you, but right now you don't want to know."

Rudolph was trying to come to a decision. It was obvious he was troubled. "Wait here," he said. He got up and left, returning a minute later with a thick file folder bordered by orange stripes.

"Have you ever heard of Joseph Lee in any other connection, at any other time?" he asked, searching for something in the folder.

"First time I ever heard the name was from Ryan yesterday."

"Shit," Rudolph said. He looked up and stared at McGarvey for a long moment, then took a photograph from one of the other file folders and passed it across the table. It showed a young man wearing some kind of a uniform, a handgun at his hip. He looked like a cop.

"He was the one driving the car," McGarvey said.

"His name is Akira Nishimura. Hong Kong police provided us with a fingerprint match. He's Japanese, born in Kobe, but raised in Tokyo. Two years ago he was fired from his job as a security guard in Hong Kong at a place called Pacific Rim Development Institute."

"What about the other two?"

"Nothing on them yet," Rudolph said. He looked again at something in the thick folder. "Pacific Rim is a Joseph Lee operation."

"Bingo," McGarvey said, but for some reason he wasn't really surprised. He did not believe in coincidences.

"The Hong Kong police report came in yesterday afternoon, but there was no reason for us to connect the two investigations." Rudolph shook his head in amazement.

"Where is he now?"

"On his way back to Taiwan, but his wife didn't go with him. Looked as if he was in a big hurry to get out, and it came right after he was briefed at the White House."

"Who gave the briefing?"

"Tony Croft, the President's adviser on foreign affairs. That's all we were able to come up with. No telling what they gave him." Rudolph looked cornered. "The problem is, if you're suggesting that Lee was involved in the attempt on your life it's going to take us to some places I don't know if I'd care to go. Do you know what I mean?"

"Comes with the job," McGarvey said.

"Don't I know it." Rudolph glanced at the files spread out on the table. "Will the CIA give us a hand with this? We're going to need someone watching him in Taiwan, and we're going to need more background information on his other operations because right now it looks as if we're going to have to combine both investigations, and I'm going to need something solid to bring to Dr. Pierone."

"There might be no connection after all," McGarvey said, though he didn't believe it. "Nishimura was fired two years ago."

"You have to ask yourself what else a man like Lee has to hide, I mean in addition to funneling money into the White House? What does he have to fear from you?"

"We're going to find out."

Rudolph's expression softened momentarily. "How is your daughter?"

"She'll be getting out of the hospital in a couple of days. I'm putting her in a safehouse until this is all over."

"The sonofabitch," Rudolph said. "For money and power."

Maybe something else too. McGarvey told himself. Something none of them had thought about yet.

EIGHT

Georgetown

McGarvey was still beating himself up over Jacqueline's death. He knew he had to stop it if he was to do his job, but last night with Kathleen had only confused him more, deepened his dark mood. He stood at the end of Canal Street looking toward the bombed-out ruins of Jake's restaurant reliving every moment from the time he and Liz had arrived until the bomb exploded, trying to work out in his mind what he could have done differently to save Jacqueline's life.

Tourist season was in full swing and traffic was heavy. The street had been cleaned up, but nothing had been done to start rebuilding the shattered restaurant blocked off now by yellow crime scene tape. A police car and two BCI vans were parked in front, and several men were carefully sifting through the rubble looking for clues, bits of bomb fragments, anything that could help them pinpoint what kind of explosive was used and where it was manufactured. The investigation would drag on here for weeks, and in the meantime whoever had targeted him would try again.

A few gawkers lingered as they passed the scene of destruction. The number of deaths had risen to twenty-two, and although this place was not as famous as the Murrah Federal Building in Oklahoma City, people had died violent deaths here; terrorism on American soil, and people were frightened and curious.

The bombing was still the main story in all the newspapers and on the networks, but so far no solid connection had been made between the attack and the shootout on the Canal Street bridge a couple of blocks away. Washington was a violent city, and life went on, the shooting might have been drug related. It was a story the FBI and Metropolitan Police were doing nothing to dispute.

Sooner or later he was going to have to return to his apartment and face Jacqueline's things. He'd have to pack them up and send them to her parents in Aix en Provence. He'd never met them, but Jacqueline had spoken fondly about her folks often enough that he felt as if he knew them well. They would be confused and hurting now, and deserved something from the man she'd wanted to marry. But not yet. He couldn't face that task now.

A lot of flowers had been placed on the sidewalk in front of the restaurant, and McGarvey looked at them for a long time before he flipped his cigarette away and got back in his car. Twenty-one people besides Jacqueline had lost their lives, and their friends and family were grieving, as he was, trying to find answers, trying to find a rhyme or reason, paying their last respects, doing something, anything to help them over this tremendous psychological hurdle. Something. They were doing something.

Time now, he thought, for him to do his thing. The grieving could come later. Like Doyle had said, he'd been running away from commitments all of his life. Time to stop.

Merging with traffic, he called the duty officer at Langley to find out where Dick Adkins was. The former acting DDO was in his office, and the call was rolled over to him.

"Are you coming in today?" Adkins asked. He sounded harried.

"I'm on my way to the hospital now. I'll see you about noon."

"How's your daughter?"

"Better," McGarvey said. "How's everything there?"

"Busy," Adkins said tersely. "See you when you get here." He broke the connection.

The whole Agency was under pressure, and until McGarvey showed up, Adkins was in the hot seat. But if Dick thought he was going to be able to sit back and take it easy, he was mistaken.

Georgetown Hospital

A young, good-looking, athletically built man was seated on a chair next to the bed in Liz's room when McGarvey showed up. He and Liz were deep in conversation and it took a moment before they realized they were no longer alone and the man jumped up.

"Good morning, sir," he said. "I'm Todd Van Buren. I have this shift."

McGarvey recognized him from the Farm. He was one of Paul Isaacson's people. "Are you a student?"

"No, sir, I'm an instructor. Special weapons, PT and hand-to-hand combat."

Liz was beaming. Although the left side of her face was almost completely covered in bandages, she had managed to put on some makeup and fix her hair, and she was sitting up in bed. "Good morning, Father," she said.

McGarvey, amused, gave her a peck on the cheek. "How are you feeling, sweetheart?"

"A lot better. Todd has been telling me about my class. They wanted to know if they could come for a visit later today."

"Are you up to it?"

"Definitely. It's been kinda boring around here."

"They won't stay long, Mr. McGarvey. I'll make sure of it," Van Buren said. "But they've been asking about her."

"I want them screened."

"Don't worry, sir, nobody's getting in here who doesn't belong." Van Buren gave Liz a warm, interested look. "They'd have to deal with me first."

"That's good to know," McGarvey said. "Why don't you get a cup of coffee, give us ten minutes."

"Yes, sir," Van Buren said, practically falling over himself to get out of the room, but not before giving Liz another warm look.

Liz was grinning. "Don't you think he's beautiful, Daddy?"

McGarvey laughed. "You might embarrass him if you tell him that."

Liz caught herself and looked sheepish. "I never noticed him before, but he asked for this detail, and he seems competent enough."

"Good, maybe he can help keep you out of trouble."

"Okay," she said demurely.

Kathleen breezed in and gave her ex-husband a kiss. "I thought I'd find you here." She gave her daughter a kiss. "Good morning, Elizabeth, how are you feeling?"

Liz's gaze went from her mother to her father and back again, her smile widening. "A lot better, Mother, I mean it."

"Good," Kathleen said. "I spoke with your doctor just now and he said you're about ready to leave the hospital." She turned back to McGarvey. "This business about our staying in the safe house could last indefinitely, is that right?"

"I don't know how long it'll be."

"We're not going to sit out there doing nothing, Kirk. Elizabeth is a translator and trained analyst. You'll get her a computer so that she can do some work. I'll help." She hadn't put it in the form of a request.

"I'll see what I can do."

"We're involved now, whether you like it or not. You're going to have two extra troops in your platoon. We'll stay behind the front lines, but we won't be idle." She glanced at her daughter. "Close your mouth, Elizabeth," she said, and McGarvey had to shake his head.

"Who's supposed to be the boss around here?"

"You are," Kathleen said seriously. "So get the people who ordered this done to us, and let us get on with our lives."

"I want you to stick with Dick Yemm and the other guards, do what they tell you to do, okay?"

"Yes. But now get out of here and close the door on the way out. Elizabeth and I have some things to work out."

Van Buren was coming down the hall. "I wouldn't go in there right now," McGarvey told him. "She's with her mother, and if you interrupt they'd probably eat you alive."

CIA Headquarters

The guards were expecting him, and he was passed through the gate after his ID was checked. The main parking lot was nearly full even though it was a Sunday. Because of the developing crisis in the Sea of Japan the agency was on emergency twenty-four-hour-per-day footing and would stay that way until the situation was fully resolved.

Inside the lobby he was handed a security badge. All the red tabs were filled in, indicating he had access to every section of the vast facility. The plastic pass also allowed him to use the executive elevators, which went directly up to the seventh floor.

"Good morning, Mr. McGarvey," one of the guards at the security arches said. "Are you armed?"

"Yes, I am."

"May I see your weapon? I need to log the serial number."

McGarvey took out his Walther PPK, removed the magazine, cycled the round out of the chamber and handed the pistol to the guard, who logged the serial number then handed it back.

"After this you can use the executive entrance. Your driver will know where to drop you off." The guard's name tag read Scrignolli. "Welcome aboard, sir."

"Thanks," McGarvey said. He reloaded and holstered his gun, and took one of the elevators upstairs where he had to go through a similar security procedure before he was allowed to continue. Security was tight, but the guards seemed genuinely pleased to see him.

The deputy director of Operations's office wing occupied the entire east corner of the top floor, adjoined by a conference room, the offices of the deputy director of Central Intelligence and the director and their staffs, including the general counsel. Beyond that was another conference room and finally the deputy director of Intelligence's wing in the west corner.

Ms. Dahlia Swanfeld, a dowdy old woman with silver-gray hair up in a bun, who had been the private secretary to Howard Ryan and Phil Carrara before him, got to her feet when McGarvey walked through the door. Beyond her the door to the DDO's office was open, and McGarvey could see that no one was inside.

"Good morning, Mr. McGarvey," she said, a tight expression on her face, as if she were expecting trouble.

"Did Dick Adkins ask you to come in this morning?"

"No, sir. But I thought I should be here for your first day, and at least until you hire my replacement."

"Are you leaving the CIA?"

"Not unless I'm asked to leave. You know that I was Mr. Ryan's secretary during his tenure as DDO."

"But you also worked for Phil Carrara."

"Yes, sir."

McGarvey smiled. "Everyone's allowed at least one mistake. Are you ready to go to work?"

Her round, pleasant face broke out into a big grin. "Yes, sir."

"Good, then get me a cup of coffee, strong and black, and bring your notebook, I have a lot of catching up to do."

"Shall I call Mr. Adkins?"

"Not yet." McGarvey went into his huge office that looked out over the trees and rolling hills behind the second wing. The weather was absolutely beautiful, the foliage in full bloom, but he didn't think he would spend much time appreciating the scenery, not from this office.

All of Ryan's and Dick Adkins's personal belongings had been cleared out, leaving the desk blank. One door led to a conference room while another led to a good-sized, well-equipped bathroom that included a shower. Bookcases dominated one wall, and a number of file cabinets and a built-in safe for sensitive documents, another. A painting of skipjacks on Chesapeake Bay was hung on the wall above a couch, two chairs and a coffee table.

A lot of history had been made from here, some of it his own personal history, much of it not so pleasant to remember, though now that he was here like this, he harbored no grudges, held no resentment; too much was happening for that.

Ms. Swanfeld came in and set the coffee on the desk. "I took the liberty of stocking your bathroom. There's an electric razor, toothbrush and a few other things. The way this job sometimes goes, I suggest that you bring a change of clothes, maybe a couple of shirts, ties, a spare jacket, things like that." She opened one of the locked file cabinets and pulled out several thick file folders and books, which she placed at his elbow. "These are your computer access codes, safe combinations, Agency telephone directory, National Reconnaissance Office, National Security Agency and Federal Bureau of Investigation locator numbers and emergency contact procedures, as well as a White House staff directory of private numbers.

"I assume that you're going to want to meet with Mr. Adkins and your staff as soon as possible. They're all here today because of the crisis and because they knew that you were coming in. The only thing on your schedule so far is a three o'clock in the general's office with Mr. Danielle and Mr. Paterson.

"The General and Mr. Paterson are at the White House, and Mr. Danielle is having lunch with Senator Thomson in town. But the general was keen that you see him at three." She laid another file folder on the desk. "These are the pool drivers and bodyguards. They're all good men, but if you have someone else in mind, that's your prerogative, of course."

McGarvey set the folder aside. "We'll put that on hold for the moment. For now I prefer to take care of myself."

"Not a wise decision, Mr. McGarvey, but it's your call," Ms. Swanfeld said. Ryan had wanted to fire her because she wasn't afraid to speak her mind, but Murphy had not allowed it. She'd been with the CIA for a long time, and she was very good at what she did, taking care of DDOs and keeping them out of trouble.

"How much of my background were you given?"

She smiled faintly. "Enough to tell you that I'm happy you're here. And I can speak for the rest of the DO as well. It's about time."

"You might not be so happy three months from now."

Her smile broadened. "We'll just have to see, Mr. McGarvey." She flipped open her notebook. "How is Elizabeth coming along?"

"She'll be out of the hospital in a day or two. I want a safe house set up for her and her mother as soon as possible."

"Mr. Adkins took care of that. He has the file." Miss Swanfeld handed him a phone memo. "Colonel Guy de Galan from the DGSE would like to speak to you as soon as possible. He's sent two of his people over to help with the investigation. Mr. Adkins has that file as well. But Colonel Galan wants to speak to you personally."

"What can you tell me about Dick Adkins?" McGarvey said. Ms. Swanfeld's nostrils flared.

"If part of my job is telling you tales out of school, you may have my resignation now," she said.

McGarvey shook his head. "I think you and I are going to get along just fine."

"I never had any doubt of it, sir," she said. "I can tell you that Phil Carrara thought highly of Mr. Adkins."

"I know. And I'm going to count on you and Dick to keep me out of trouble, because I'm no administrator."

"We'll do our best."

"That's all I can ask. But it's going to make for some long hours."

"Whatever it takes."

"Very well. I want a staff meeting in my conference room in fifteen minutes. And dig out all their personnel files. In the meantime get me Colonel Galan on the phone."

"Do you wish to see Mr. Adkins first?"

"No," McGarvey said.

It was coming up on six in the evening in Paris when McGarvey's call went through. Galan, who headed the French Secret Intelligence Service's American and Western Hemisphere Division, had been Jacqueline

Belleau's boss and had taken her involvement with McGarvey very personally. Her death had deeply affected him.

"Thank you for returning my call, Monsieur McGarvey," Galan said. "May I offer my congratulations on your appointment."

"Thank you, Colonel," McGarvey said. He could hear the barely suppressed anger in the French intelligence officer's voice. "I assume you've seen the report of the incident."

"*Oui*, and it seems as if you did all that could have been done. Are there any further leads on who ordered the bombing?"

"We're working on it with the FBI. I'm told that you're sending two of your people over to help."

"There has been a delay, but they will arrive at our embassy tomorrow afternoon. Will they have your cooperation?"

"Naturally. We can use all the help we can get."

"Then we will find the bastards, *hein?*"

"Definitely."

Galan hesitated a moment. "The report placed Jacqueline at the exit from the restaurant when the bomb exploded. Was she coming or going?"

"She was leaving," McGarvey said. "I was sending her back to Paris."

Again Galan hesitated, evidently struggling with what he wanted to say next. His voice was thick. "Better to have sent her home sooner, or perhaps never to have brought her to Washington in the first place."

"Yes," McGarvey said. "It would have been better."

"*Tant pis*," Galan said sadly. "Will you write to her parents? They have asked about you."

"I will."

"*Bon.* Then that is all I can ask of you for the moment. Good hunting, monsieur. Get the men who were ultimately responsible for this terrible act."

"I will, Colonel, you can count on it."

The Directorate of Operations, which used to be called clandestine services was, with a staff of more than ten thousand professionals and clerical types, the largest of the CIA's four divisions. The DDO's conference room, laid out much like the President's situation room beneath the White House, was a long narrow, windowless space dominated by a large conference table that could easily seat twenty people. A large rear projection television monitor was built into the wall at one end of the room, a technician from Technical Services operated the display and projection equipment from a console at the other side. When McGarvey walked in five minutes before noon and took his position at the head of the table, Adkins and six other men were already seated. Each of them had a stack of file folders and other materials in front of them. Miss Swanfeld sat directly behind her boss at a small table equipped with a telephone and recording equipment. She would take the minutes.

"Good morning, gentlemen. Sorry to have interfered with your lunch hour, but we're under the gun here, and I have a lot of catching up to do. Dick, could you make the introductions?"

"Yes, sir, congratulations on your appointment," Adkins said. He was a short, husky man with light wavy hair and a pale complexion. He looked as if he hadn't seen the sun in six months. He sat on McGarvey's left, and he introduced the other six around the table, starting with Randy Bock, who headed the DO's Foreign Intelligence staff which was responsible for espionage activities. Beside him was Jared Kraus, the heavyset and sometimes ponderous director of the Technical Services Division, which designed and built the secret equipment field officers used: miniature cameras, disguises, special weapons. Next to him was Scott Graves, chief of Counter Intelligence and then Arthur Hendrickson, head of the Covert Action staff whose job, among others, was propaganda and disinformation. Seated near the end of the table was Raife Melloch, who headed up the DO's Missions and Programs Division which was responsible for bureaucratic planning and budgeting. Finally, next to him, was David Whittaker, Area Divisions chief, responsible for the stations and bases around the world and the area desks for Russia and former Soviet bloc nations, Europe, the Western Hemisphere, the Far East, Near East, Africa and domestic and special operations. His was the largest of the DO's division, and he'd been running his shop for ten years with such an efficiency that most of his staff thought he was a magician or at the very least a genius.

McGarvey looked around the table. "We're missing Tyron. Where is he?" Alfred Tyron was the head of Operational Services, which set up cover stories and legends for field officers on clandestine missions.

"He asked that we start the meeting without him," Kraus said. "He was going to stop by the cafeteria to grab something to eat."

McGarvey had had a chance to briefly look over all of their dossiers and division personnel rosters before the meeting. Tyron had been one of Ryan's handpicked men, with a special note attached to his file that he was someone to be watched for possible advancement. He knew his place.

"Mr. Tyron is relieved of his present duties," McGarvey said. He turned to his secretary. "Have Ms. Jordan join us with the division reports." Brenda Jordan was Tyron's assistant division head. "She'll be our new chief of Operational Services."

"What do you want done with Tyron?" Adkins asked.

"That'll be up to his new boss," McGarvey said. He looked around the table again. "Gentlemen, whatever you've heard about me is probably all true. I'm going to make a lousy boss because I don't accept excuses or apologies, nor will you have to accept them from me. I want straight answers to straight questions. If you don't know something, admit it, don't try to blow smoke up my ass." A few around the table chuckled. "I'm not much of an administrator, which means I'm likely to be in the field more than any other DDO ever was. So as of this moment Dick is no longer my assistant DDO, he's my chief of staff. Whatever he says, goes, and when I'm out of the office this directorate will not shut down; he'll make the decisions. Anybody have a problem with that?"

"What if I don't want the job?" Adkins said evenly.

"That's not an option, Dick. In the meantime we have work to do, so let's get going."

Adkins looked down at the stack of thick file folders in front of him. Each of them was marked with a code name and was color coded to indicate the degree of classification of the material it contained.

"Getting you up to date any time soon is going to require some serious homework on your part, Mr. Director."

"Mac."

Adkins looked up. "Okay, Mac." He handed McGarvey two fat file folders. "There's no doubt that the top of the agenda today is the developing situation in the Sea of Japan between our forces and those of Japan, China and North Korea. In the meantime you can look through the National Intelligence Estimate and the current Watch Report. There are some points of interest in Iraq, Bosnia, Greece, Columbia, Cuba and of course the current extremely unstable situation in Russia, especially in Moscow and along the border with Iran, as well as India and Pakistan."

Both documents were produced on a weekly basis by the U.S. Intelligence Board made up of the director of Central Intelligence and the heads of the other intelligence agencies, including the National Security Agency, Defense Intelligence Agency, the military intelligence branches, the State Department, FBI, Nuclear Regulatory Commission and Treasury Department. The National Intelligence Estimate listed targets for the U.S. intelligence community, estimates of future international events and enemy strengths, a technical intelligence review and decisions on which product was to be shared with which allies. A separate document, the Watch Report, indicated trouble spots where armed conflict was possible or even likely. The two reports were issued each Thursday, after the USIB meeting at the CIA, and were delivered to the President and all the top policymakers in the government.

"Okay, I'll wade through this stuff this afternoon, unless there's something that needs our attention right now."

"It'll wait," Adkins said. He passed two more thick files to McGarvey both marked Top Secret. "These are the suggested current updates to the National Intelligence Estimate and Watch Reports on the Sea of Japan situation, which for the moment we've code named *Watchful Thunder*. I'm told that you know some of this, but if you'll give me a couple of minutes I'll give you a précis of everything we have so far." The room lights dimmed and a satellite image of what appeared to be a major seaside industrial installation appeared on the monitor.

"This photograph was taken by one of our Keyhole satellites, six days ago," Adkins said. "It's the partially dismantled nuclear-powered electrical generating plant at Kimch'aek on North Korea's east coast. It's hard to tell from this shot, but NRO and NSA analysts reported seeing a good deal of activity here during the past week. Apparently the North Koreans were moving something out of the facility in great secrecy. It's now believed that the object of all this activity was the removal of four of their five operational-ready nuclear devices. Over the next several days heavy cloud cover in the region rendered our photographic capabilities useless."

Another satellite image came up on the screen, this one showing a huge depression in the ground. Nothing of the power plant, its cooling towers, twin reactor containment domes or the distribution yards was left. "Seventy-two hours ago we recorded an underground nuclear event in the range of twenty kilotons directly beneath the installation, which, as you can see, was totally destroyed. The actual event was witnessed by one of our nuclear patrol submarines, the *Seawolf* which had detected the presence of a Japanese submarine just off shore. It's believed that this submarine, the *Hayshio*, home ported at Sasebo, may have sent a party of commandos ashore either to gather intelligence on the nuclear weapons stockpile, or to commit an act of sabotage. The shore party did not return to the *Hayshio*, which was apparently heavily damaged in the explosion. Twelve hours later, in response to a Mayday, an MSDF rescue vessel showed up and recovered the submarine's crew." Adkins looked up. "This was without interference from the North Koreans and apparently without detection of the *Seawolf*, which has been ordered to stand by and monitor the situation."

A series of four images came up one after the other. "Since then a number of interesting developments have occurred. The Chinese navy has deployed eight warships, two of them Han class nuclear attack submarines, from their Northern Fleet bases at Qingdao, Lushun and Xiaopingdao. Best estimates place them off North Korea's coast no later than Friday or Saturday."

Another series of satellite images flashed across the screen. "These are Japanese military installations across the three main islands, among them air force regional headquarters bases at Misawa, Iruma and Kasuga, as well as navy bases at Yokosuka, Kure, Sasebo, Maisura and Oominato. All of them have gone to a high state of alert without the proper notification to our command structure either in Japan or at the Pentagon. In addition, the MSDF has begun to deploy a number of warships into the area." Adkins looked at McGarvey. "The actual details are listed in the NIE update, but the situation is extremely fluid at the moment so we're getting new information hourly."

"Has the President deployed the Seventh Fleet?" McGarvey asked.

"Yes. They should be in striking range about the same time the Chinese fleet shows up," Adkins said. "Maybe sooner."

Brenda Jordan, an earnest-looking woman in her late thirties with flaming red hair, had slipped in and quietly taken her place. She'd brought the Operational Services division files with her.

"Okay, what do we have on the ground at Kimch'aek?" McGarvey asked.

"Not a thing, sir," Jordan said. "The South Koreans sent one unit up there but they lost contact, so they're sending another, although they're not sharing any of the operational details with us."

"We do have confirmation that there was probably a considerable loss of life in the incident," Whittaker said. "Pyongyang is saying that it was an accident brought on because we forced them to cut corners in closing the facility. Which of course nobody believes."

"Is such an accident possible?"

"A meltdown, yes," Kraus said. "But not an explosion of that magnitude. It was definitely a nuclear device."

"Have the North Koreans made any military response yet?" McGarvey asked. "Other than calling for help from the Chinese?"

"None, at this point. But all of their military installations are always at a high state of readiness," Adkins said.

"Has Seoul or Tokyo made statements?" McGarvey asked. The more he was hearing the more the situation became surreal to him. It was as if everyone out there had suddenly gone crazy.

"Kim Jong-Il is warning that if he is pushed too far he'll strike back.

So the South Koreans brought out Hwang Jang Yop, who says that North Korea is getting ready to launch an all-out nuclear attack on Seoul and Tokyo. Scorched earth, he said. Prime Minister Enchi responded that if Kim Jong-Il so much as twitches they'll mount an all-out offensive against North Korea. Secretary of State Carter is on his way to Tokyo to see if he can talk some sense into them, and the President has scheduled a news conference for two this afternoon."

"What else?"

Adkins glanced at the others. "That's about it, except for the details which you have in front on you. The question is what the hell does the CIA do about it?"

"Nothing other than what we're already doing, only more of it," McGarvey said. "This is going to have to be worked out politically, because nobody wants to start a shooting war over there. So we have to provide the White House with everything they need. And I don't mean by that another series of Howard Ryan reports. Only the facts. Right now what we're short of is human intelligence. I want our chiefs of Seoul and Tokyo stations to lean hard on all of their networks, active or not, to find out what the hell is really happening, and who is directing it."

"That could ruin a lot of assets," Whittaker warned.

"I don't care. We'll bring them in if need be once they're blown, but as of this moment this operation is our number-one priority."

"There is one other operation," Adkins said. "The general asked me to put something together, but perhaps we don't need to bring it up here."

"The kidnapping of Kabayashi and Hironaka," McGarvey said. "Have you worked out a scenario?"

"Yes." Adkins handed across a file folder.

"I'm putting this one on hold for the moment, but I want our Tokyo COS to be made aware of what might be coming his way."

Adkins looked relieved. "Okay."

"Anything else, even of a peripheral nature in the region that we should know about?"

Adkins shrugged. "Just the upcoming space launch from Tanegashima."

McGarvey zeroed in on him. "The launch of what?"

"They're putting up a component for the international space station. Should be launching in four days unless there's a delay. NASA has a team of inspectors over there helping out."

"Has the countdown been delayed because of the North Korean situation?"

Adkins spread his hands. "Unknown."

"Find out," McGarvey said. "And I want to see the file on it, including dossiers on the NASA team as well as the Japanese launch director and his staff."

"I'll get on it as soon as possible—"

"Now," McGarvey said. "Anything having to do with Japan, China or North or South Korea is priority one. I want everything, no matter how insignificant or off the wall it might seem. Clear?"

Everyone around the table nodded.

"All right, we have another investigation I'm throwing into the mix. Dick will have someone liaise with Fred Rudolph's staff over at the FBI. We're going to look into the background of a Taiwanese businessman by the name of Joseph Lee."

"We're already on that," Whittaker said. "Dennis Ford, my Taipei COS, has his people digging around at the Bureau's request, but we weren't giving it a very high priority."

McGarvey eyed him. "Does that have anything to do with the fact that Lee is a personal friend of Jim Lindsay?"

"Hell no. I'm a born and raised Republican," Whittaker said. He was a large man with a square, honest face. "I didn't think the CIA needed to get involved with another investigation of this nature. We could spend all of our time doing them."

"I agree, but this time it's different," McGarvey said. "There may be a connection between Lee and the Georgetown bombing to stop me from becoming DDO. The Bureau identified one of the shooters as Akira Nishimura, a Japanese who was fired two years ago as a security guard at the Pacific Rim Development Institute in Hong Kong. Pacific Rim is a Joseph Lee enterprise."

Whittaker whistled long and low. "I'll be a sonofabitch. I'll light a fire under Dennis and have Hong Kong station get on it too."

"Make it an all stations flash bulletin. Lee has similar operations in Seoul, Bejing and Tokyo."

"Where are we going with this, Mac?" Adkins asked. "Let's say for some reason Lee wants you dead. Are you looking for a connection between him and the military situation out there?"

"I don't know, Dick. But I don't like coincidences, and right now Joseph Lee's name keeps popping up all over the place."

"Could be a connection between him and Kamiya's old *zaibatsu*."

"That's a start. Lee's supposedly in Taipei right now, so we're going to keep him on a tight rein until he comes back here where Fred

Rudolph's people can take over. Do we have the manpower to do that?"

"No problem," Whittaker said. "I'll get the word out as soon as we're finished here."

"Okay, is that it for now?" McGarvey asked, looking around the table. Everyone nodded. "I have a three o'clock with the general. I want you there, Dick."

"I'll be there."

Taipei, Taiwan

Taipei, sparkling like a million diamonds scattered across a black velvet cloth, was spread out below Joseph Lee's sprawling Japanese-style house on Grass Mountain. It was two in the morning, the night air warm and soft with humidity and the odors of night-blooming flowers. He stood deep in thought sipping jasmine tea from a delicate porcelain cup on one of the balconies when Bruce Kondo, his chief of staff, joined him. They had been together for ten years now. Lee had hired him from the Japanese Ministry of International Trade and Industry with the blessings of Tokyo because of certain financial considerations. Japan was also more than happy to be rid of Kondo, who had been one of the men instrumental in the debacle at Yokosuka. He'd become something of an embarrassment. Since that time Lee had never had reason to doubt the man's loyalties or abilities until now.

"The last of your board of directors has gone," Kondo said, his voice cultured. He'd received his education at Oxford.

"It went well," Lee said coolly, not turning to the man.

"As it should have. You've done a magnificent job, and they're happy with the results. They'd be fools to feel otherwise."

"But they also understand the problems we're facing."

"I believe you made that quite clear," Kondo said. "But they still have complete faith in you. Nine U.S. senators, nineteen representatives and the ear of President Lindsay and much of his staff, all in less than six years. Stunning."

Lee finally turned to face him. Kondo, like many Japanese, was short of stature, but wiry, with a round face that was almost always devoid of any expression. Lee, whose father had been Japanese, still harbored a deep-seated dislike of the arrogant home island Japanese, which was why he had changed his last name as a young man, but he was pragmatic enough to make use of talent no matter what disagreeable package it might come in. "Do you still have complete faith in me?"

"As always," Kondo said. "But I think that your trust in me has wavered because of my failure in Georgetown."

"I've learned that McGarvey has finally accepted the post as deputy director of Operations, and may in fact already be busy at work. Now with a clear purpose in his heart because of the injuries to his daughter and the death of his French whore."

"He cannot work miracles," Kondo said indifferently.

"I wouldn't be so certain of that. But it has become a delicate matter of timing. Everything we have worked for is finally coming to fruition. All the chess pieces are in play, and it will be only a matter of days before the end game begins."

Kondo shrugged. "Killing McGarvey now would create an even bigger storm. He's no longer a maverick; he is the third most powerful man in U.S. intelligence. There would be repercussions."

"Are you telling me that you are no longer capable of fulfilling your responsibilities?" Lee demanded harshly.

"Not at all. But the stakes have increased by a quantum jump. There will be a backlash, killing someone so highly placed."

"Nonetheless it must be accomplished, and within the next three days."

"With such a deadline the job becomes even more difficult."

"Impossible?"

"No," Kondo said looking Lee directly in the eye. "Merely more difficult than before."

"Then it's settled. You will personally see to McGarvey's death and the elimination of another, potentially even more harmful person. A man who has the President's ear and who may just have stumbled on the key that could unlock all our work, making Morning Sun impossible."

Kondo's eyes narrowed for the first time. "Who is this second target?"

Lee took Kondo's arm. "It's more secure in my study, less chance of us being heard. It's time that you were told about the next step and the reasons why both of these men must be eliminated."

Seawolf

"Skipper?"

"Come," Captain Harding said, looking up from the letter to his wife he was still trying to finish. It was coming up on 1900 GMT.

His XO, Rod Paradise, came in and handed him a message flimsy. "This just came in on ELF."

| PSU | | LTT | | |
| FROM COMSUBPAC | | TO SSN21SEAWOLF | | |

| NIG | OES | GDQ |
| SEVENTH FLEET | ENROUTE | YOUR POSITION |

| CHF | QVW | EFM |
| FURTHER | MSDF FLEET | DEPLOYED |

| GDQ | PPP | YNJ |
| YOUR POSITION | STANDBY | CONTINUE OPERATIONS |

| QPR | DMN | HIK |
| CONTACT VIA SSIX | IF POSSIBLE | 2400Z |

Harding looked up. The SSIX was a military communications satellite system. "They want us to call home about three hours from now. Have sonar keep a sharp watch. If need be we'll move south; this is one message we have to get."

"Good news about Seventh," Paradise said.

"Is it?" Harding asked. "I wonder."

NINE

Great Falls, Virginia

The surveillance position was at the edge of a gravel pit across Highway 193 from the long driveway to the Lee mansion on the Potomac. Parking was fifty feet below, but from the crest of the hill they had an unobstructed view of the expansive house and grounds. Morgan was having a sandwich and a cup of coffee in the van when Kuchvera came running down the path, the powerful binoculars banging against his chest. Morgan pulled off the earphones he was using to monitor the radio link to the four telephone lines into the house.

"His driver just pulled out," said Kuchvera, out of breath. He tossed the binoculars inside, climbed behind the wheel and started the engine as Morgan slammed the side door and climbed up front.

"Has he got the limo?"

"No, he took the Jeep," Kuchvera said, heading through the woods to the highway slowly, to give Lee's chauffeur time to reach the end of the driveway. "He's on his own this afternoon, so I thought maybe we could have a little chat with him. Just one-on-one."

Morgan grinned wickedly. They weren't accomplishing much by merely watching Lee's staff who knew they were being watched. Rudolph said step it up a notch, which is exactly what they were going to do, starting with Lee's chauffeur, Arnold Toy, a Taiwanese national working in the U.S. on a green card. Morgan keyed the radio. "PARA/MEDIC driver is on the move. We're going to tag along."

The Jeep pulled onto the highway and headed toward Washington. "Is he alone?"

"Affirmative. He's in the Jeep, Virginia three-two-baker-one-seven-seven. Southbound on one-nine-three."

"Roger, one. Do you want backup?"

"Negative," Morgan said.·

Tactical command for the PARA/MEDIC surveillance operation was located downtown, but the watch commander this afternoon had either stepped out or didn't care that they had left their post. Since Lee was out of the country, the operation was somewhat lax, giving the special agents more freedom to act independently.

Two miles later the highway crossed under Interstate 495, and the Jeep pulled into a Texaco station and parked around the side by a pay phone. Toy, dressed in a pair of slacks and a light short-sleeved shirt, was making a call when Kuchvera pulled in out of sight on the other side of the station, and he and Morgan went in one door and came out the other. When Toy saw them, he hung up and started for his Jeep.

"Mr. Toy, could we have a word with you?" Morgan said, pulling out his ID. "FBI."

Toy stopped, the expression on his face wary but not concerned. "I have to get back to work."

"We'll just take a minute of your time, sir," Kuchvera said.

"Actually, we need your help," Morgan said. "We're trying to find one of your friends. He didn't show up for an appointment yesterday and we're a little worried." Morgan watched him closely.

Toy shrugged. "I don't know what you're talking about."

"His name is Akira Nishimura. He said he might have something for us."

All expression left Toy's face. "I don't know anybody by that name."

"He mentioned you. Said he'd worked with you a couple of years ago in Hong Kong. Pacific Rim Development Institute."

Toy forced a laugh. "This is a joke, right? I've never been to Hong Kong in my life, and I've never heard of this company."

"It's an institute, actually, one of Mr. Lee's operations, according to what Akira was telling us. He was here with a couple of his friends, but like I said they just disappeared."

"Hey, I'm just a chauffeur, I don't know anything. You want to talk to somebody, talk to my boss when he gets back."

"When might that be?" Morgan asked.

Toy shrugged.

Kuchvera glanced at the pay phone. "Having trouble with the phones at the house?"

"That's right. I was reporting the trouble to the phone company."

Morgan smiled and nodded. "Hope you get it fixed. I'm sure that Mrs. Lee wouldn't want to miss a call, especially if it was from her husband."

Toy looked at them, his gaze unblinking. It was impossible to tell what he was thinking.

"That's it," Morgan said. "Appreciate your help. We'll mention your name in our report."

When Toy was gone, Kuchvera wrote down the pay phone's number and back at the van called it in to tactical command. If the call had been long distance it would show up in phone company records. It took less than five minutes to come up with the answer. Toy had called the Japanese embassy in Washington. "The plot thickens."

"Better tell them to flag it for Mr. Rudolph. He'll want to know about this," Morgan said, as they headed back to the gravel pit.

CIA Headquarters

McGarvey and Adkins walked down the hall to the DCI's office a minute before three. He'd spent the afternoon at his desk wading through the National Intelligence Estimates and Watch Reports, as well as the updated material on Watchful Thunder. Although he was a speed reader, he managed only to skim through the material, which ran to five thousand pages, plus five dozen satellite photographs and infrared images. The CIA's problem was hardly ever a lack of information. In fact in the past ten years the amount of data coming in had risen at such an exponential rate they were having a hard time collating it into manageable chunks, pieces that were recognizable as meaningful.

"I just got a call from Fred Rudolph's office," Adkins said.

"Have you set up the liaison already?" McGarvey asked.

"Yeah, and it's already starting to pay off. The guys watching Lee's house up in Great Falls followed his chauffeur to a pay phone. You'll never guess who he called."

"Who?"

"The Japanese embassy."

"How about that," McGarvey said, not really surprised. "Were they able to listen in?"

"No. But when they asked him who he'd called, he said it was the phone company to report something wrong with the phones at the house." They stopped at the DCI's door. "I think I'm starting to dislike coincidences as much as you do."

"Doesn't take a lot of practice."

Carleton Paterson and Lawrence Danielle were with the general in his office, sun streaming through the floor-to-ceiling windows doing little to dispel the gloomy mood.

"Good afternoon, gentlemen," McGarvey said.

"Are you settling in?" Murphy asked.

"If you can call it that. I met with my staff, and I've gone through the last NIEs, Watch Reports and the updates on Watchful Thunder. It's mostly a mess, but it looks as if we're getting some reliable intel. Oh, and I've made Dick my chief of staff, so when I'm out of the office his word will carry the same weight as mine."

"Good idea," Murphy said. "How is Elizabeth coming along?"

"She's on the mend."

"What conclusions have you drawn?" Danielle asked. He looked tired. Word was out that he'd be retiring in a few months. He was one of the only people left in the building who actually remembered the old days before the Langley facility was built, when the CIA's offices were spread all over Washington. A legacy from the OSS days.

"Nobody knows what's going on out there or why. All we can do for now is give the White House as much information as we can get. No speculation or guesswork."

"Lindsay will appreciate that," Murphy said. "Did you see his news conference?"

"I was too busy. What'd he say?"

"He called Kimch'aek an accident and said that we were going to cooperate with the North Korean government to find out what happened. About what we expected."

"Did the media buy it?"

"There were a couple of tough questions, but since there were no Americans on the ground, Lindsay downplayed it as much as possible. The winds out there are blowing the radioactive dust inland over North Korea and into the Gobi Desert, so the impact to human lives will be minimal."

"What he did was buy us some time," Danielle said, "which is exactly what we need.

"It's coming down to a standoff between Japanese and Chinese forces with us in the middle, which makes it political. Secretary Carter is on his way over to Tokyo to see if he can talk some sense into them, and as long as the lines of communications remain open out there, the situation might stabilize."

"Unless it's given a nudge," Murphy said shrewdly.

McGarvey laid a file on the general's desk. "Joseph Lee, a friend of Lindsay's. He's in Taiwan now, so I've issued a worldwide bulletin to find out everything we can about him. And I've activated all of our in-place networks in Japan, China, Taiwan and North and South Korea."

"A lot of resources," Danielle observed.

"One of the terrorists has been identified. He was Japanese, and until a couple of years ago worked for Lee in Hong Kong."

"Do you think Lee may try to provide the nudge?" Murphy asked.

"I'm going to look for the connections," McGarvey said. "Coming after me was just too coincidental. Could be something out of my past."

"What's your best guess, Mac?" Danielle asked. "What's your gut telling you?"

McGarvey took a moment to answer. "I don't know," he said. "It's the timing that has me wondering. If there's a connection between Lee and something in my past, why did he wait until I was put up for DDO to act on it? Why right now in the middle of some Japanese operation against North Korea? If there's a connection, I don't see it yet." He looked at the general. "But if it's there, I'll find it."

"Not much time to do it in," Murphy said.

"In the meantime we have to get you ready for your confirmation hearings," Paterson broke in.

"Later," McGarvey said, barely looking at the general counsel.

Paterson started to object, but Murphy held him off. "All right, it's your call, but since this involves Joseph Lee, with his ties to the White House, I don't want to be kept in the dark. You have a habit of stepping on toes, and this time the toes are big ones, so watch your step."

"General, that's what I intend doing."

*   *   *

With the DO off and running for the moment under Dick Adkins's capable direction, McGarvey began his search through his past looking for connections between him, Joseph Lee and the recent events in the Sea of Japan. Less than one-tenth of one percent of the CIA's vast repository of files, stored in the vast underground caverns of an abandoned salt mine sixty miles outside of Washington, was accessible by computer. Indexes and précis of files, however, along with the current and most recent case histories, were kept in the Directorate of Intelligence's Central Reference Service in a subbasement at Langley. Because of his position he was given immediate and unlimited access to the system. By four-thirty he was set up in a small cubicle furnished with a long table, a blackboard and a computer terminal where he started with the files on the FBI's deep background investigation of him when he was first issued a secret clearance in the air force, through his top secret and cryptographic access clearances when he was hired by the Company and trained as a black operations field officer. All he was coming up with, however, were references to paper files with addresses at the Fort A.P. Hill Military Reservation near Bowling Green. A few minutes after seven his phone rang. It was Otto Rencke.

"Hi ya, Mac, burning the midnight oil?"

"How the hell did you find me?"

"Dumb question," Rencke said laughing. "You're leaving a computer track a mile wide." His voice was suddenly serious. "How's Elizabeth? I just found out."

"She'll be okay, but she was banged up pretty badly."

"You're not shitting an old shitter, are you?"

"It was close, but she'll recover. Anyway, where are you?"

"I'm on the Parkway about two miles out. Can I come in?"

"I'll leave word at the gate, and I'll meet you at the main entrance."

"This is another big one, isn't it, Mac?" Rencke said. "I mean Murphy finally pulled his head out and made you DO, and just in time if what I'm reading between the lines isn't a bunch of Beltway bullshit."

"This is a big one, and I need you, Otto."

"Oh, boy, I knew it!" Rencke said excitedly and the connection was broken.

McGarvey phoned the front gate, then took the elevator up to the ground floor and walked out to the main entry hall, quiet at this hour even though most of the building was busy.

He'd known Rencke for a long time, and over the years they'd developed a close, almost familial bond. Otto had been trained as a Jesuit priest and professor of computer science and mathematics, but he'd been kicked out of the church when he'd been caught having sex with the dean's female secretary. He enlisted in the army, but had been kicked out six months later for having sex with a young staff sergeant—a male. And a year later he'd shown up at the CIA, his record mysteriously blemish free.

But he was a genius, and nobody looked too hard at his past, or wanted to, because he got the job done. It was Otto who'd brought the Company into the computer age, updating its entire communications system and standardizing its spy satellite analytical section so that everyone's satellites could cross talk and share information on real-time basis with everyone else's. He'd also come up with an online system so that field officers on assignment could be fed updated material the instant it became available no matter where in the world they were located.

His past had finally caught up with him, though, in part because he was a maverick and men like Ryan were coming into power within the agency, so he'd been dumped. He'd moved to France a couple of years ago.

More than once he'd backstopped McGarvey, most recently in Russia where without him the operation would have been a total disaster. McGarvey and his daughter both would have been killed were it not for Otto. It was a debt of gratitude that would never be called, and could never be repaid.

McGarvey had arranged for an all-sections pass, and he picked it up at the counter just as Rencke came through the automatic doors. He hadn't seen his friend in four months, but it could have been four hours ago. Nothing had changed. Rencke's long, out-of-control fuzzy red hair still stuck out in all directions as if he'd never combed it, and he wore the same faded blue jeans, tattered MIT sweatshirt and unlaced high-top sneakers. He carried a satchel slung over his shoulder which he laid on the floor by the security arches before giving McGarvey a huge bear hug.

"Oh, boy, am I glad to see you. You can't even imagine what a lonely bitch Rio is, especially this time of year."

"I figured that's where you went," McGarvey said.

"It was getting squirrelly in France. The service wasn't exactly in love with me." Rencke was hopping from one foot to the other, which he did when he was happy or excited. "Once I was sure that you and yours were okey-dokey I lit out. Retreat's the better part of valor and all that happy crappy." His expression suddenly darkened. "Jackie didn't make it, but you're sure about Elizabeth? I mean she's going to be okay, Mac? You weren't just saying that to make me feel better? Honest injun?"

McGarvey had to smile. Being around Rencke for more than thirty seconds was like jumping onto an out-of-control carnival ride. "We'll go over to the hospital and you can see for yourself. She'll want to see you."

Rencke cocked his head. "I know just what she's needing right now." Rencke turned to the guards who were eyeing the satchel. He opened it for them. "My laptop, passport and a few goodies."

One of the guards pulled out a package of Twinkies.

"He never leaves home without them," McGarvey said.

"Yes, sir."

Rencke signed in, McGarvey gave him the pass, which he hung around his neck, and they took the elevator down to the cubicle in Central Reference Service. Rencke glanced at the computer screen.

"Something out of your past gaining on you?"

"I'm looking for the connections, and we don't have a lot of time," McGarvey said.

"Deep past?"

"I just don't know. But it's a possibility."

"Well, we're not going to find it here. If it's answers you're looking for, they'll be out at Bowling Green."

"This is a start—"

"I can access this shit from out there," Rencke said. He looked closely at McGarvey. "This one was even closer than Moscow or Santorini, wasn't it? Are they after Kathleen as well?"

"A couple of phone calls and a virus to her PC at home."

"That's a break. Viruses leave calling cards, and I've either invented all the major ones, or know about them. This about North Korea and Japan?"

McGarvey nodded. "The Chinese are getting into it now, and there could be a tie to the White House through a Taiwanese billionaire by the name of Joseph Lee."

All expression left Rencke's face for a moment. At forty-one he still looked like a kid in his twenties with a wide-eyed innocence, but behind the facade was a shrewd man, wise well beyond his years in some things.

"Timing," he said almost dreamily. Then he blinked, and his face became animated again. "Did you know that Japan is launching a module for *Freedom* in a few days?"

"Yes."

"Puzzles, Mac. Don't you see, it's a big puzzle, and I've still got the magic to put it together, because this time chartreuse is the color."

Taipei, Taiwan

Bruce Kondo put down the telephone, hesitated a moment, then walked out to the balcony of his penthouse apartment at the base of Grass Mountain. His number two, Shiro Kajiyama, was studying Lee's mansion, higher up on the mountain, through a powerful pair of tripod-mounted U.S. Navy binoculars. The morning was warm and humid, and a haze had settled over the city and its environs, making viewing difficult.

"Are you able to penetrate the fog?" Kondo asked.

Kajiyama looked up, his lips curled into a cruel grin. "This fog is easy by comparison to the real veil."

"Has Mr. Lee left?" Kondo asked ignoring the jibe. Kajiyama was number two on the security team, but only Kondo knew the entire picture.

"Ten minutes ago."

"It's up to him now to lose his tail, and it's up to us to get on with our assignment."

"Then the decision is final?" Kajiyama asked coolly. There was no love between these two men. But Kajiyama was good at what he did, coming out of Japanese intelligence six years ago, and both men respected each other's abilities.

"Mr. Lee has ordered it," Kondo said, studying the other man for a hint of uncertainty. "Of course if you do not wish to participate . . ."

"Your contacts in Washington are ready for us? For both missions?"

"I just spoke with them."

Kajiyama nodded. "*Hai*. Then let us hope there will be no dog's death for us." It was an allusion to the old Japanese warrior's code that death for an unworthy cause was a dog's death. The allusion was not lost on Kondo.

"This is for the most worthy of causes. Honor." Kondo glanced at his watch. It was a few minutes after nine. "Have the others already gone?"

"Last night and this morning, as you ordered."

"Good. Then it's time for us to leave. We'll be in Vancouver for breakfast and Washington for lunch."

Georgetown Hospital

McGarvey hadn't gotten much sleep in the past forty-eight hours since the bombing, and he knew that he had to go down soon or he wouldn't be worth a damn to anybody. But now that Rencke had finally shown up, he felt as if they would begin to make some real progress. Otto would help unravel the puzzle and McGarvey would act on it. They were a team again.

They parked in the garage across the street and walked through the tunnel. Todd Van Buren was stationed in the corridor outside Elizabeth's room, and he did a double take when he spotted Otto, who was carrying a McDonald's bag.

"Did they kick you out again?" McGarvey asked.

"Yes, sir. Mrs. McGarvey is with her." He looked forlorn, and McGarvey almost felt sorry for him.

McGarvey introduced him to Rencke. "Otto is a friend of the family, and he works for me."

Van Buren nodded uncertainly.

McGarvey knocked once and stuck his head in the door. Elizabeth was propped up in bed, and Kathleen was saying something to her. They looked up.

"Daddy," Elizabeth said, her face lighting up with pleasure.

"Is this women's only night, or are you up for a visitor?"

"Who is it?" Elizabeth asked, interested.

McGarvey stepped aside to let Rencke into the room. Kathleen's mouth dropped open in surprise, but she recovered quickly. For a second Elizabeth was puzzled but then a big grin broke out on her face. She'd never met him face-to-face.

"Twinkie?"

"Oh, wow, Liz," Otto gushed, grinning from ear to ear. He approached the bed, but then stopped, suddenly unsure of himself.

"Come here," Liz said, her eyes beginning to fill.

Rencke went to her side, and Liz reached out for his hand, drew him close and kissed him.

"You're the greatest thing since sliced bread," she whispered. "I've been wanting to tell you that since Paris. You saved my life."

Rencke drew back and hopped from one foot to the other. "Wonder bread," he said gleefully, awkwardly clapping his hands. "Oh, wow." He looked back at McGarvey for reassurance, then gave the bag to Elizabeth. "I thought maybe you could use a Big Mac and some fries. I got you a Coke too, I hope it's okay."

"Thank God. You can't imagine how bad the food is here," Liz said enthusiastically.

Otto took a package of Twinkies out of his pocket and held it out to her. "I don't know anybody who likes these things, but sometimes they're pretty good for desert."

Elizabeth's eyes filled again, and she took the package. "They're a major food group in my book," she said. She shook her head. "What a lovely man you are."

Kathleen came around the bed and offered her hand. "I'm Kathleen McGarvey."

Rencke wiped his hand on his pant leg and shook hers. "You're beautiful," he said simply.

Kathleen smiled. "I want to thank you for what you've done for my daughter, and for my husband."

Otto lowered his head.

"Please look at me when I'm speaking," she said, and Otto looked up. She smiled warmly. "You're a little old to be my son. But from this moment you're to consider yourself a part of this family. Wherever you go, whatever you do, we will always be here for you."

"Oh, wow," Otto said, hopping from foot to foot again. But then he stopped, and a serious expression came over his face. "We'll get them, Mrs. M., the people who did this to Elizabeth. I promise you with everything in my soul, we'll get them."

Kathleen looked into his eyes for a long moment. "I know," she said softly. "But Twinkies? Ugh."

TEN

Cropley, Maryland

Elizabeth was released from the hospital at noon on Monday, a full day earlier than the doctors had forecast because she was healing quickly. McGarvey, after a twelve-hour sleep, was hung up with meetings at Langley so that he could not be there, but Paul Isaacson from the Farm had assured him that he was taking over, and it would take a regiment of marines to break through the security he was planning not only for the move but out at the safe house. Kathleen called around two to assure him that they were safe and sound and starting to settle in already. But McGarvey could hear the concern in his ex-wife's voice, and it did nothing to dispel his gloomy mood, so that he raced through his final meeting with Murphy over Watchful Thunder and was able to break away by three-thirty and head north on the Parkway, the weather glorious for the fourth day in a row.

The situation in the Sea of Japan would resolve itself either militarily or politically, and there wasn't much the CIA could do about that except to continue feeding the President accurate intelligence. Rencke was settled in at the CIA's Bowling Green records repository, and there wasn't much McGarvey could do to help him either. He would come up with something if it was there. And Adkins was running the DO with a steady hand, which for the moment had no need of McGarvey's input.

Traffic was light on the interstate—most of it out-of-state plates—when he crossed the Potomac and headed north the final couple of miles. This entire area along the river was federal park land right in the middle of dozens of important Civil War battle sites. The foliage was thick, and seemingly every hundred yards or so there were park entrances, scenic overlooks, historical markers or roadside rest areas with barbecue grills and picnic tables. Just before a curve on the secondary highway he turned right onto an unmarked gravel road that wound its way nearly a mile through a forest dense with undergrowth and marshy patches to a rambling Kentucky horse country house. Three years after the Aldrich Ames case had broken, another mole had been discovered. This one never hit the media because he'd not sold out to the Russians, he'd merely ripped the Agency off for nearly four million dollars. This house and the one hundred acres it sat on had been his, and now it belonged to the CIA. Since there'd been no publicity on the case, and since the thief had worked alone, the Cropley house was unknown and perfectly safe.

The road emerged from the forest to paddocks bordered by white fences, the horse barn and riding arena to the south and the house and five-car garage across a broad lawn, in the center of which was a circular manmade pond complete with a fountain that was lit at night.

There were no cars in sight, nor could he see any activity anywhere, as if the place were deserted, and as he approached the house all sorts of dark visions ran through his head. He parked his Nissan in front and got out. The afternoon was utterly silent. He thought he spotted a movement at the edge of the woods a hundred yards away, and then he caught another movement out of the corner of his eye and he reached for his gun as he turned. One of the instructors from the Farm had come around the corner of the house. He said something into a lapel mike.

"Good afternoon, Mr. McGarvey," he said, and McGarvey allowed himself to relax.

"I didn't spot anybody on the way up."

"No, sir," the young man said, smiling slightly. "We have a good perimeter."

Something wasn't adding up. McGarvey frowned. "How many people do we have out here?"

"Twelve, sir. Of course that's not counting Mr. Isaacson, Todd Van Buren and the two Frenchmen."

"Are you expecting trouble?"

The instructor shrugged. "That's unknown at this point. But we're ready for it."

McGarvey glanced again at the woods, but there was nothing to be seen. "Do you want my car in the garage?"

"I'll take care of it, sir. Mr. Isaacson and the others are waiting for you inside."

McGarvey got the laptop computer for Liz and went into the house. This place was supposed to be a safe haven where Katy and Liz could hide out. But Isaacson, who never overdid anything, had turned it into a fortress. He found the Camp Perry commandant with two of his people plus the two DGSE officers that Colonel de Galan had sent over in the formal dining room, which had been turned into a command center. Detailed topographic maps were spread out on the table. A powerful shortwave radio and three laptop computers were set up on the buffet and a side table.

"Here he is," Isaacson said looking up. "Did you spot my people in the woods?"

"Not until I got to the house."

"Good." Isaacson introduced the others. Jeff Stromquist and Pat Dyer from the Office of Security, and the two French intelligence officers, Albert Level and Louis Maurois, who were built like Sherman tanks. No one seemed happy.

"What's going on, Paul?" McGarvey asked. "Why all the muscle?"

"You're not going to like this," Isaacson said. He went over to one of the computers and brought up the FBI's Website. "This is supposed to be secure. But take a look." He brought up the FBI-CIA liaison page, which detailed not only the location of the Cropley safe house but its current occupants and the reasons they had been brought here.

"When did this show up?" McGarvey demanded, the vise clamped on his heart again.

"We didn't see it until we got out here, so I brought in some more people. We just finished deploying them."

"Where are Katy and Liz?"

"In the sitting room upstairs with Todd," Isaacson said. "And I know what you're going to say. You want to get them out of here. It was my first thought, but that would be exactly the wrong thing to do. Rudolph is tearing the Bureau apart to find out where the leak came from, but in the meantime there's no guarantee we wouldn't run into the same problem at the new place." Isaacson's expression softened. "They're safe here, Kirk."

"They could have got to them at the hospital," Level suggested.

"They didn't have time to plan a new operation," McGarvey countered.

"But if they are coming, *m'sieur*, then this is a good place to meet them." The Frenchman shrugged. "If that's what you want."

"It's my family we're talking about putting into jeopardy."

"Before Jacqueline changed her last name she was a Level. She was my sister."

McGarvey looked at him, but he could detect no anger or resentment, only grim determination. "I'm sorry. She told me that she had a family, but she never mentioned a brother."

"She would have, eventually. She wanted me to come over to meet you."

"I was sending her home."

"*Oui*," Level said tightly. "Colonel de Galan told me. The timing was bad." He held McGarvey off. "That is behind us now. Let's catch the bastards who did this thing. Is it the Russians?"

"I don't think so."

Level shrugged. "Too bad. It would have made things simpler."

"This attack had nothing to do with Jacqueline?" Maurois asked. "She was merely in the wrong place?"

"That's right," McGarvey said.

"Then she was an innocent bystander, which makes it all the more important for us to punish the people behind this act."

"That might not happen," Isaacson said, once again taking charge. "But if it does we want to be ready for it. And this is the ideal place, because we've had the property long enough to know every possible approach. We've even run exercises out here."

"Okay, let's see what we've got." McGarvey hunched over the topo map which showed the highway, the entire hillside to a mile on either side of the driveway and a mile to a hiking path behind the house. A creek ran from a gathering pond, crossed beneath the highway and emptied eventually into the Potomac. In the summer Isaacson and some of the other instructors from the Farm came out from time to time to fish for trout. Last year they'd taken a class of eight students along the trail all the way up to the Watts Canal on the northwest side of Highway 189, which led to Rockville. They'd not seen another living soul in the woods the entire weekend.

"It wasn't just a camp out for the boys and girls, Kirk," Isaacson said. "We spent most of the weekend installing sound and motion detectors along the path and around the entire perimeter of the property. Since then we've run a couple of penetration exercises. We learned that trick from the Mossad, and not even the students who were given a map pinpointing the detectors got through. They're equipped with fail-safe alarms. If any one of them fails for any reason—malfunction or tampering—an alarm goes off here. So we know someone is coming."

McGarvey studied the map. "What about the driveway? They could fight their way up to the house with an armored car."

Isaacson pointed out several asterisks spaced at twenty-five-yard intervals up the road. "Explosive charges. We can set them off in sequence, or set them to explode by pressure switches." He looked up. "We can kill anything coming from the highway."

"How about the house itself?" McGarvey asked.

"Bullet-proof windows, steel shutters on the doors and windows and as a last resort a bomb-proof shelter in the basement."

"Providing someone inside the house knew that they were under attack."

Isaacson conceded the point. "But it's hard to imagine them not knowing with all the alarms and detectors."

"Power lines?"

"Buried, along with the phone lines. In addition there is a generator in the basement and nonjammable cell phones throughout the house."

McGarvey went to the large bowed windows that looked out across the lawn past the fountain toward the woods. Isaacson was the best. Everything had been covered. This place was like Fort Knox, and yet a lot of dark thoughts nagged at the back of his head. The best brains in the country, the finest scientists and engineers, had designed and built the space shuttle. Yet in the end it was just a man-made machine, and even *Challenger* had not been immune to glitches. If a man designed and built it, no matter how cleverly, it was possible that another man could find a way to defeat it. Nothing was immune, nothing or nobody was one hundred percent safe. Yet he had to admit that Katy and Liz were probably much safer from attack here than they had been from a car accident on the drive out from the city. And it wouldn't be forever, just until the bad guys were caught.

"You can stay if you want to, Kirk, but you'll be more effective at Langley running the show," Isaacson said from behind him, and McGarvey turned back. "We're running triple shifts at the Farm. One for the program, one for sleep and the third out here. We've got the manpower willing and able to cover this operation twenty-four hours a day. No one is going to sleep on their posts."

"Students."

"Instructors, augmented by motivated students." Isaacson smiled. "Elizabeth made quite an impression on everyone. She has a lot of friends. Just like you do."

McGarvey had been a loner most of his life, so it was hard for him now to accept help. Maybe this was part of what Tommy Doyle had tried to tell him. He nodded. "I owe you one."

"Yes, you do," Isaacson said quietly. "Why don't you say hi to your wife and daughter, and then get the hell out of here so we can button the place up for the night."

"Keep me in the loop."

"Just get the bad guys. I don't want to retire out here."

Todd Van Buren, wearing a 10mm Colt automatic in a shoulder holster over a military-style short-sleeve khaki shirt, was just coming out of the sitting room when McGarvey got upstairs. He looked irritated.

"Afternoon, Mr. McGarvey," he grumbled.

"Trouble?"

Van Buren shook his head. "If you don't mind me saying so, sir, your daughter is one frustrating woman."

"That she is. What'd she do this time?"

"The docs told her to take it easy. But she's not doing it. Even her mother can't talk sense into her." Van Buren glanced back at the door. "She found a gun somewhere. She's in there now standing lookout at the window, and she kicked me out 'cause I wouldn't keep my mouth shut."

"I brought some work for her, maybe that'll take her mind off things."

"I wouldn't count on it, sir. But it would make my job easier. Paul wants me to stick with her, but it's going to be tough."

McGarvey knew what the problem was. Liz wanted to appear independent and capable to a man she found attractive, and Van Buren wanted to play the role of big bad bodyguard. If the situation weren't so dangerous he would have found their dilemma amusing. Once the operation was resolved it was going to be interesting to watch them work out their differences. The CIA encouraged husband-and-wife teams. They could be posted to a relatively safe station like London or Paris or Bonn. Wishful thinking at this stage, but it was comforting.

Liz was perched on the window seat, a Walther PPK, spare magazine, ashtray and cigarettes next to her, and Kathleen was in the adjoining bedroom, the connecting door open, unpacking a suitcase.

"You make a good target sitting there," McGarvey said.

Liz lit up in a bright smile. "I told them you'd show up." Most of the bandages had been removed from her head, but her face was a mass of cuts and bruises. She was dressed in blue jeans, a Snoopy T-shirt and low-top sneakers. She still looked a little weak, but definitely much better than she had in the hospital.

"See if you can talk some sense into her," Kathleen said from the bedroom. "I certainly cannot."

McGarvey laid the laptop on a table. "An RKG would take out the entire room, you with it."

"They'd have to get pretty close to fire a rifle-launched grenade, and in the meantime we'd have plenty of warning." She glanced at the pistol beside her. "But if someone makes it this far, I want to be ready for them when they come through the door."

"Where'd you get the gun?"

"I've been carrying it ever since Paris," she said defensively. "And, no, I don't have a permit yet. The Company hasn't seen fit to give me one. Maybe you can say something to someone."

"I want you to get away from the window and stay away from it. I brought some work for you to do, unless you're ready to quit."

"Baiting me isn't going to work, Daddy," Liz flared.

"I've brought you a laptop with a built-in modem and cell phone. I want you to connect with your old boss Toivich in the DI."

Elizabeth's brow furrowed. "That's the Russians. I thought we were dealing with the Japanese."

"We're not a hundred percent sure. Could be someone from Moscow, maybe Tarankov's old crowd. They might figure that they have a score to settle."

"It's a dead-end job, a waste of effort."

"I'm not willing to bet your life, or mine, on it," McGarvey said harshly. "Either you'll do this for me, or I'll have to take someone with more training and experience than you off something vital to run it down. But if you truly want to work in the DO you're going to have to learn to take orders sooner or later."

"You're not going to make me give up my gun?"

McGarvey glanced at his ex-wife and shook his head. "You can keep it. I just don't want you shooting Van Buren by mistake. It'd make him even less happy with you than he is right now."

"He's a strutting shit."

"Who's trying to do the job he was ordered to do," McGarvey told his daughter. "Of course he could be replaced with Don Billings," he said slyly.

"Yes, sir," Liz said. "I get the point."

McGarvey went into the bedroom as Liz hopped stiffly off the window seat and started setting up the laptop.

"Paul Isaacson seems competent," Kathleen said, lowering her voice.

"It's a good setup here. You and Liz will be safe."

Kathleen looked into her ex-husband's eyes. "I'm not blind, Kirk. Ten minutes after we got here, he called out the cavalry, and most of them are hidden in the woods. What's going on?"

"The fact that you're here has shown up on a nonsecure Website. We're trying to figure out where it came from, but in the meantime since it's now public knowledge, Paul figured he'd step security up a notch."

"That should provide a clue as to who's behind this," Kathleen said shrewdly.

"It's possible. We're looking into it. In the meantime this is still the best bet for you and Liz. If they could get to you here, which they can't, they'd be able to get to you anywhere. At least here we're ready for them. No surprises."

Kathleen touched her husband's face. "Life is full of surprises, haven't you learned that yet?"

McGarvey took her in his arms and held her close. "You'll be fine here."

"Get the bastards, my darling. I don't want to live in fear anymore."

"Guaranteed," McGarvey said, unaware that their daughter was watching them from the sitting room door, a happy glow on her battered face.

Morningside, Maryland

The facility was perfect. Kondo and Kajiyama made a quick inspection tour of the building that had once housed a Kmart store and was now supposedly leased to the government as a surplus office equipment storage center. No one would bother them here, nor would the neighbors in what had become an industrial park take any special notice of the two plain gray vans and gray Ford Taurus with government plates that they would be using.

Sandy Patterson, executive director of the Far East Trade Association, met them in an upstairs office at the back of the building. A small, vivacious woman of fifty with a small round face and pixie hairstyle, she had once been Joseph Lee's mistress in Hong Kong, and she now oversaw some of his more shadowy, arm's-length endeavors here in the States. She was totally dedicated to Lee, and if he had taught her nothing else, he had instilled in her the value of ruthlessness.

"Is this place to your liking, Mr. Kondo?" she asked coolly.

"You have done a good job as usual," Kondo said. "Where are the rest of my people?"

"I put them up in three motels nearby until you arrived and approved the arrangements. I'll bring them here later this evening." She pursed her lips. "This time I was given sufficient notice to do it right. I apologize for the last fiasco."

"There were unforeseen circumstances beyond your control."

"Yes," she said dryly.

Kondo turned and looked through the one-way glass at the piles of desks, chairs and file cabinets on the main floor. "The equipment I requested is here?"

"Yes," the woman answered. "May I ask where you gentlemen will be staying?"

"Mr. Kajiyama will remain here with the others, and I have taken a room at the Hay Adams."

Sandy Patterson's left eyebrow rose. "If you'll be using the car, I suggest you park it someplace inconspicuous and take a cab to and from the hotel."

"A good suggestion." Kondo looked at his watch. "Now, if there is nothing else, I have an appointment in town." He looked at Kajiyama. "Get the men settled in, then inspect the equipment that Ms. Patterson was so kind to arrange for us. I'll be back no later than nine."

Kajiyama nodded.

"There is one thing," Sandy Patterson said, and Kondo turned his expressionless gaze to her. "Arnold Toy and the others at the house are keeping the FBI's surveillance teams busy, but something did come up that you may not have been told about yet. Unfortunately you were already in transit."

"What is it?"

"One of the FBI teams stopped Toy and asked if he knew anything about Pacific Rim, or Akira Nishimura."

Kondo thought about it for a moment. "Is there any way that the FBI could link Nishimura or the others to you?"

"No. But the fool telephoned the embassy for instructions. It's possible that his call was traced."

"That won't present a problem," Kajiyama said.

Kondo nodded. "Anything else?"

"No," Sandy Patterson said.

Fort A.P. Hill, Virginia

Aside from a couple of CIA historians and a half-dozen file clerks, the vast underground records storage facility was devoid of life and activity. The abandoned salt mine had been fitted out with acoustical tile ceilings, proper walls, painted concrete floors and climate controls. There was absolutely no dust, nor was there any odor. All the old files were in the same condition they'd been in the day they were brought here, and would remain so presumably far into the foreseeable future.

Rencke installed himself in one of the map rooms furnished with a large table so that he had plenty of room to lay out the documents and files he intended retrieving. He hooked up his powerful laptop computer to a printer and to one of the phone lines so that he could connect with the Central Reference Section at Langley, as well as the mainframe here. And, declining the services of a clerk, he was assigned an electric golf cart so that he could get around the miles of eighteen-foot-tall stacks.

He took a package of Twinkies from his canvas bag and a quart of heavy cream from the cooler he'd brought with him, then connected with Langley, bringing up McGarvey's personnel file, and dumping it across to the printer. If he was going to have any success finding the bad guy or guys out of Mac's past who might be gunning for him now, and the reasons they were doing it, Rencke figured he first needed to know how accurate the files were. It was possible that someone had come through and sanitized the record, or worse, erased it. If that were the case he would have to direct his efforts toward looking for who did that, instead of looking for the clues in the records.

The watershed at both ends of McGarvey's career was his parents, who at the end of the second World War were engineers on the Manhattan District Project to build the atomic bomb at Los Alamos, New Mexico. McGarvey had been very close to them, so that in the mid-seventies when he was already working for the CIA and they were killed in a car accident, he was devastated. He went back to their ranch in southwestern Kansas to close out their house, and close out their papers when he made a discovery that was even more devastating to him than losing them. From what he found in Kansas and later in CIA records, he pieced together that his parents had been spies for the Soviet Union. A part of the network that, along with Klaus Fuchs, had sold atomic secrets. From that moment he was a changed man. Except that his parents never were spies. The records had been planted by Valentin Illen Baranov, possibly the most effective spy master ever to work for the KGB. It was an operation designed to ruin McGarvey, whom the Russians were seeing as a serious threat. But it wasn't until six months ago when the truth finally came out, and again the news had profoundly affected McGarvey, changed him for the second time in his life. He was a man who didn't know what to believe in or whom to trust. A killing machine, a loner and a lonely man.

The two events—the falsifying of his parents' records and the subsequent revelation of the truth—were so central to McGarvey's core that they would make a test of the validity of the records here.

Under McGarvey's biographical record at Langley there was a reference from this spring of an internal investigation, with a subsequent amendment to his deep background. Rencke retrieved that file and dumped it into the printer. The signatory on the order for the reinvestigation was Howard Ryan, McGarvey's predecessor as director of Operations. In Rencke's estimation the man was a jerk and a dangerous fool, but not a traitor.

Bringing up the file address, Rencke drove the golf cart back into the stacks. Avenues were alphabetic A through Z then AA through ZZ, and so on. Streets were numeric beginning with 000. Each stack was divided L, left, and R, right, alphabetized by shelves, and numbered by bins. Nonetheless, because of the vastness of the facility, it took Rencke nearly a half hour to find the bin near the middle of one of the stacks, load the file contained in a drawer-sized plastic container on the cart and make it back to the map room.

The bin contained a dozen or more thick envelopes, each marked with codes that could be cross-referenced to other files and laid out in reverse chronological order, the most recent information at the front. The first file contained the Ryan-instigated investigation and was marked Secret. Otis Brenner, the chief internal security investigator on the case, began with the conclusion that Herbert and Claire McGarvey had never spied for the Soviet Union. The allegations were false and had been planted in CIA records by an unknown party or parties at some unknown time for some unknown purpose. But that was a crock of shit as far as

Rencke was concerned. The date on the file was in April this year, and by
that time the Russians had already confirmed that the disinformation plot
had been engineered by Baranov to discredit McGarvey. The KGB was
getting worried that McGarvey would become an even more effective
agent than he already was, and that he would possibly rise to some position of considerable power in the CIA. It was something Baranov didn't
want, which gave Rencke pause to wonder if it wasn't the Russians after
all who wanted to stop Mac from becoming deputy director of Operations.
But Baranov was long gone, the KGB had been broken into two parts—
one for internal security and the other for external operations—and no
one was left who cared anymore. Russia's political agenda had changed
since Glasnost and Perestroika, and Baranov's old circles of influence were
either dead or very old men retired to their dachas.

Brenner even lamented at one point in his report that finding anyone
who'd been alive at the time was a major problem. It was a dead issue as
far as the CIA was concerned, except that it was necessary to set the
record straight for the sake of the principal target of the KGB plot, namely,
Kirk McGarvey.

The file outlined in fairly precise detail the bits and pieces that in
the seventies brought the CIA to believe that the McGarveys were spies.
Most of it was circumstantial, such as Russian paymaster decoded transmissions which gave a series of dates and payment amounts. Their dates
and dollar amounts matched deposits made in the McGarvey's checking
and savings accounts in the First National Bank of Garden City, the small
town in southwestern Kansas where their ranch was located. But there
was an alternative explanation, of course, which Rencke spotted immediately. The deposits were money that the McGarvey ranch had earned,
and the Russians had lifted the deposit records *after the fact* to create a
backtrack. The dates and payment amounts matched too precisely to bank
records, which almost never occurred in real life. But no one at the time
bothered to check it out, though why the CIA had investigated the
McGarveys' bank records in the first place was something of a mystery.

An addendum to the first report indicated that after the McGarveys'
death in an automobile accident, Kirk had discovered payment records
and a Russian code book hidden in his parents' personal effects. (See
additional files, ref #2237-QQ-CKDONNER.) The addendum also reported that the Kansas Highway Patrol had interviewed one eye witness
to the tragic accident in which the McGarveys' car swerved off the highway one evening and smashed into a power pole, killing them instantly,
who said it looked to her as if they'd "been run off the road" by a large
dark car, possibly a Cadillac or Chrysler, possibly with out-of-state license

plates. But the car was never found, nor did any other witness come forward to corroborate the story. (See additional files ref #2239-QS-CKDONNER.)

Rencke turned next to the reference 2237 file, which outlined Kirk's discoveries at his parents' ranch. That had been in the midseventies. But one of the signatories on the final investigation was John Lyman Trotter, a friend of Kirk's who had eventually become deputy director of Operations and who subsequently had been found out to be a traitor. McGarvey had killed his old friend in a shootout in Germany. But the most interesting aspect of the file, in Rencke's mind, was that Trotter didn't sign the file until 1992, only nine months before his death, and a very long time after the car accident. It didn't make sense, except that Trotter had been working for Baranov. But again no one in the CIA at the time bothered to question the dates.

Sloppy work, Rencke wondered, or had it been a carefully crafted oversight? Trotter certainly had the influence at the time, and in those days proper records were not yet so fully backed up or cross-referenced on computer as they were these days. To this point, however, he was not seeing any indications that the records had been tampered with recently.

The next file was the accident report, complete with copies of the Kansas Highway Patrol's photographs of the scene. Some of the grainy black-and-white pictures were so graphic that Rencke had to put the file down, get up and leave the room. He drove the golf cart around the vast repository for nearly a half hour, trying without much success to blot the gruesome images out of his head. He hoped to God that Mac had never seen the pictures, or ever would. It wasn't something a family member should be subjected to. The pain it would cause would be immense and of no use. Rencke figured that his own problem was his overactive imagination. Riding around in the cart he found himself reliving the terrible last moments leading up to the crash. The fear, the momentary flash of pain as the car was destroyed and the light went out for them. Not a scene to remember for long, though he knew the pictures would stay in his head for the rest of his life. At that moment he felt closer to Mac and his ex-wife and daughter than he'd ever felt to anyone else. He felt a kinship now that he had shared a family tragedy. He felt part of them, and at this moment the feeling was bittersweet.

Rencke drove back to the map room, where he put away the accident file and opened the first envelope, therefore the oldest, in the bin. The two photographs staring up at him were of Herbert Cullough McGarvey, and his wife Claire Elizabeth (née Leesam) McGarvey, taken when they were in their twenties at Los Alamos. The resemblance of Kirk to his father and Liz to her grandmother was so startling that for an instant Rencke could fully understand one aspect of Kirk's love for his daughter. Every day he saw her, he had to be reminded of his mother, a woman he'd loved with all his heart and soul. And every time Kirk looked into a mirror, he had to see bits of his father staring back at him. It would be wonderful, Rencke decided, to live with such memories. He didn't have them himself, so he could envy his friend's.

Rencke opened another package of Twinkies. Nothing in those files had been tampered with recently, except for the Ryan investigation in the spring. At least this part of Mac's record seemed clean. Although what it represented in terms of suffering was horrible, nothing new had been added.

Time to start from square one, Rencke told himself, replacing the envelopes in the bin. Mac's past, from the day he was born up until his last operation in Moscow. If there was something there, Rencke would find it.

Morningside, Maryland

Kondo was a happy man. He had gotten the information he needed to accomplish the first of their objectives and had planted the seeds that would likely help accomplish his second. And all of that from two meetings that had lasted less than one hour. There'd been only one glitch, but he'd even worked that one out on the way back to the storage center. All it would take was some special equipment.

"Ingenious," Sandy Patterson said. She was gathered with Kondo, Kajiyama and the other six men, all of them highly trained Japanese commandos and former soldiers of fortune, on the floor of the warehouse.

"Can you get what we need without arousing any suspicion?" Kondo asked. They'd inspected their weapons and night vision oculars and were studying the topographic maps of the area around the Cropley safe house.

"No problem whatsoever," she said. "But if I can make one suggestion, it'd be better to come in from the river." She pulled out a highway map of Maryland. "We could rendezvous at Whites Ferry. There's a marina there and it'll be no problem to rent the proper boat. Nobody will think twice about it at this time of year." She looked up "The problem will be getting you out."

"Helicopter."

She nodded. "I can arrange that too." She looked frankly at Kondo. "You're certain about the security precautions at the safe house?"

Kondo nodded. "My source is reliable," he said. "But the helicopter will have to be capable of carrying us, plus the two women."

"I thought we were going to kill them," Kajiyama said sharply.

"It's simply a contingency. Our main target is McGarvey. If he's not out there, we'll take his ex-wife and daughter with us."

"He'll come after us. The CIA, the FBI and every law enforcement agency in the region will be fully mobilized."

"That's right," Kondo said with a look of satisfaction on his round face. "While that's going on McGarvey will be distracted from doing his real job." He looked at his people. "We'll kill him if we can. But our primary objective is to buy some time. Four or five days at the most."

"Why?" Kajiyama asked.

"You don't need to know that yet," Kondo told him. He turned back to Sandy Patterson. "I'll need a light plane as soon as possible. I want to fly over the house."

"Pick an airport, and by the time you drive out to it, your airplane and pilot will be waiting for you."

"I'll let you know when," Kondo said. "In the meantime everybody get some rest. Inspect your weapons and equipment and familiarize yourself with the maps. All of them."

"What about afterwards?" Kajiyama asked.

"We'll leave the same way we came."

"I mean about the women."

"Kill them, of course."

ELEVEN

SS584 Natsushio

The MSDF Improved Harushio class attack submarine *Natsushio* slowly rose to periscope depth forty miles off the North Korean coast. She'd run all night three hundred feet beneath the surface at her top speed of twenty-four knots on a northeasterly course from her home port at Maizuru, and everyone aboard was keyed up. All of Japan's military forces were at a heightened state of alert since the nuclear event at Kimch'aek, but the sealed orders that Captain Akira Tomita had opened once they'd cleared the sea buoy were in his estimation lunacy. He did not share his views with his crew, not even with his XO, except to tell them that this was not an exercise and that all tactical situations would be met with weapons hot. He was a compact man who was an expert in kendo and a half-dozen martial arts, which had taught him, above all else, the ability to remain calm in all circumstances.

They were to look for targets, surface or submerged, attempting to approach either the downed submarine or heading for the Japanese home islands, and stop them with whatever force the captain deemed necessary. Stopping the North Korean navy was one thing, but the Chinese had deployed at least eight ships which were on their way, and in these waters it was assumed that the Americans had patrol submarines on station. In addition, the Seventh Fleet had been deployed from Yokosuka. He did not want to tangle with them, yet his orders were clear in that MSDF command was making no exceptions.

The only leeway Tomita had was identifying the target's intent. The Sea of Japan was a large area, most of it international waters, in which ships of any nation had a perfect right to sail. On top of that, the *Hayshio* had gone down only ten kilometers off the North Korean coast, well within their territorial waters, which gave them the perfect right to conduct exercises there. Orders were orders, but before he set about to kill a ship and her crew he was going to make certain its action fell under the parameters of his orders.

"Sonar, what are you showing besides our ships?" Tomita had been advised of the five MSDF warships that were in the area, including the submarines *Sachishio* and *Fuyushio*, the skippers of which he knew.

"Nothing ahead of us, *kan-cho*," Seaman Tomifumi Mizutami reported.

"We're now on station," his executive officer Lieutenant Nobuyaki Uesugi reported softly from the plotting table. He was a delicately built man whose only passion was training bonsai trees.

"Very well, commence your pattern," Tomita said. "Sonar, we're ready to deploy the ZOR-one." Similar to the American BQR-15, it was a low-frequency passive search sonar deployed at the end of a very long cable. Extremely sensitive, it would pick up more than the hull-mounted sensors could. If anything was moving within twenty miles anywhere except directly aft, they would hear it.

Tomita glanced over at his XO, who looked excited. Now the real battle began.

Seawolf

Seaman Fischer had been tracking a very quiet subsurface target picked up by one of the sea floor sensors they'd dropped yesterday, when he suddenly sat forward. He flipped on the tape recorders and held the earphones tighter. He was hearing a low-pitched, grinding sound that for the first few moments he could not identify, but then a big smile creased his features.

"Conn, sonar. Possible target designated Sierra nine, bearing one-nine-five, indeterminate range."

"What've you got, Mel?" the XO, Lt. Cr. Rod Paradise, asked from the conn. He and the captain were splitting the watches, twelve on and twelve off. It was 0500 GMT, and the captain was in his quarters.

"Somebody down south is deploying a towed array. Sounds like a ZOR-one to me."

"Stand by," Paradise said, and he came forward to the sonar compartment.

Fischer switched the signal to the speaker so they could all hear the grinding noise. Moments later an analysis spit out of the computer. "ZOR-one," Fischer said. "Probably being deployed from one of their new Harushios, but we're too far out to tell for sure. That sub is a hell of a lot quieter than its towed array cable reel system."

"Okay, they're looking for something, which means they'll be running a pattern. See if you can establish the time intervals between aspect changes. I'd like to get down there without them knowing about it, which we can do if we make our runs when we're end-on to the array."

Fischer's eyes widened a bit. "Tricky," he muttered. "I'll see what I can do, sir."

"Are we far enough away right now to avoid detection?"

Fischer studied his display. "Definitely."

"You're calling the shots, Mel. When you think we're getting too close, let us know and we'll shut it down."

"I see what you're getting at, sir," Fischer said straightening up. "But I'm going to be real conservative."

"Good." Paradise called the order to the deck officer to start south, dead slow, then headed aft to get the captain.

An Orion P-3C

The MSDF Lockheed/Kawasaki P-3C sub-hunter/killer, tail number 3311, arrived on station at 1422 local, the skies partly cloudy, the wind gusting to thirty knots, the seas five hundred feet below them running to ten feet.

"On station now, *kan-cho*," the navigation officer radioed the pilot.

"Okay," Lieutenant Hitoshi Kuroda acknowledged. On the flight out from the naval air station at Komatsujima on Honshu's west coast, they had passed a half-dozen MSDF warships. Their orders were to rendezvous with the submarine *Natsushio* and help hunt for Chinese submarines.

He eased back on the throttles, and when the aircraft began to slow down, added ten degrees of flaps so that they were mushing along in a circular pattern just shy of 150 knots.

"Comms, release the dipping buoy."

"Hai, *kan-cho*," the communications officer responded crisply. Everyone aboard was hyper. "Buoy is deployed."

Seawolf

They were in the silent mode. The Japanese submarine had turned to port once again, presenting the ZOR-one's sensors at a right angle to the *Seawolf*'s path. Captain Harding watched the sonar display over Fischer's shoulder, the extremely thin line on the waterfall showing the slowly changing aspect.

Fischer held up a hand. "Wait," he said, his head cocked as he strained to listen to something in his headphones. He made a grease pencil mark on a minuscule spike on the display, then looked up at the captain. "That's a dipping buoy, Skipper."

"An Orion?"

"Be my guess they're out here looking for those Chinese submarines, and the Orion driver just told the submarine that he was here."

"Do we have an ID on the sub?"

"We're still too far, sir, but the next pass should do it. I almost had him the last time."

Natsushio

"Conn sonar, I have a target designated Sierra three, at eight thousand meters, bearing two-eight-five, heading toward us."

"This is the captain. Can you identify the target?"

"*Hai, kan-cho*. She's Han-four, from Qingdao. The computer agrees."

"Have they detected us?"

"No, sir."

"Are there any other targets?"

"*Iie, kan-cho*." No, the sonar operator assured him.

"Reel in the ZOR-one, we'll start a TMA," Captain Tomita said. He went to the plotting table where his deck officer Lieutenant Hiroshi Kubuzono had already begun the paper plot of the Target Motion Analysis from which shooting solutions could be developed. Sonar information would now be fed automatically into the BSY-1 combat system's computers.

Kubuzono looked up. "His track will take him directly to the *Hayshio, kan-cho*," he said. "But he's at least twenty-four hours early. And where is the second Chinese submarine?"

"Neither of them are here yet. This is a third boat, one that no one expected."

"Except for you, *kan-cho*," the young lieutenant said with sudden pride.

Tomita walked back to the command consoles above the periscopes. "Sound battle stations, torpedo," he told his XO Lieutenant Uesugi. "This is not a drill."

"*Hai, kan-cho.*"

"Load tubes one and two, and stand by to flood on my orders." Tomita pulled down the growler phone as the battle stations announcement was broadcast over the boat's PA system. "Communications, this is the captain. Send a SLOT buoy up, zero delay to transmit, and inform thirty-three-eleven of the approximate position of our target. This is a live exercise."

"*Hai, kan-cho.*"

The SLOT was a communications buoy that would radio the information to the circling Orion in a burst transmission, not easily detectable by anyone else. He was asking the Orion to help with the battle. Although the nuclear-powered Han class Chinese submarines were thirty years old, they'd been recently refitted with advanced electronic suites, and they carried a lethal sting. Tomita wanted to be a live victor, not a dead fool. He would take all the help he could get.

Orion 3311

The pilot, Lieutenant Kuroda, increased power, retracted the flaps and hauled the big four-engine turboprop ASW airplane in a tight turn to the southwest, directly toward the position of the Chinese submarine that the *Natsushio* had radioed them.

Three minutes later an excited ELINT officer, Ensign Kuminori Godai, was on the aircraft intercom. "I'm recording a positive MAD contact, designated Mike one." MAD was the Magnetic Anomaly Detector, which could pick up interferences in the Earth's magnetic field caused by the ferrous mass of a submerged submarine as long as it was moving and wasn't much deeper than one thousand feet. "She's at three hundred feet and slowly rising."

"Is there any indication that she's detected *Natsushio?*"

"*Iie, kan-cho.*"

"Weapons, this is the pilot. Prep two Mark fifties, and stand by to launch on my order."

"*Hai, kan-cho.*"

"Do you have any idea what's going on, Hitoshi?" his co-pilot Takaji Murayama asked.

"Looks like we're going to war with China," Kuroda quipped nervously, half wondering if he wasn't witnessing the beginning of just that. "But we'll give *Natsushio* the first shot."

Seawolf

"Skipper, that's definitely a Han class Chicom submarine, bearing three-one-zero, nineteen thousand meters," Seaman Fischer said. "Target designated Sierra ten." The printer spit out a one-liner. "The Japanese sub is the *Natsushio*, home port Maizuru, Improved Harushio class," he said.

Harding turned back to tell Paradise to start a track on the Chinese submarine, when Fischer practically jumped out of his skin.

"Holy shit! Skipper, the *Natsushio* just flooded two forward tubes."

"What's the Chinese submarine doing?"

"Same course and speed as before," Fischer said. "But they must've heard the flooding."

Harding went back to the conn, plotted the position, course and speed of the Chinese submarine and then extended its track. "The crazy bastard is going to shoot," Harding said.

Paradise came over. "Sir?"

Harding looked up. "The Chinese are heading right for the downed MSDF submarine, and the Japanese sub driver is going to stop him."

Paradise looked at the chart. "What're we going to do about it?"

"Nothing, Rod," Harding said frustrated. "Not a damn thing except watch."

Natsushio

"Sonar, conn. This is the captain. Give me one ping to verify the bearing and range to target."

"*Hai, kan-cho,*" Seaman Mizutami said. He was impressed.

The problem was that Tomita could see both sides of the issue with equal clarity. The North Koreans had every right to defend their home waters using any means at their disposal, including allies. On the other hand, the Sea of Japan was in reality so small that Japan had a legitimate reason to control what happened here. Especially anything that threatened the safety of the home islands. And a North Korea with nuclear weapons and the means to deliver them to Tokyo or anywhere in Japan was a genuine threat.

The single ping from the active sonar reverberated through the boat, and a split second later the final range and bearing to the target showed up on the BSY-1 combat system. An instant later the firing solution came up.

"Weapons presets completed," the fire control technician reported.

"Fire one, fire two," Tomita ordered.

Seawolf

"I have two torpedoes in the water," Fischer called out. He eased the headphones off his ears and looked up.

"How long 'til impact?" Harding asked.

"Twelve seconds."

Harding glanced at his watch, then reached up with his left hand to brace himself against the overhead. At twelve seconds one explosion, followed almost immediately by a second, hammered the *Seawolf*'s hull.

Fischer turned back to his sonar set, pulling the earphones back over his ears. After a few seconds he adjusted a control. "I'm getting breakup noises. The Han is on her way down." He listened a half minute longer, then nodded. "She's definitely dead."

"What's the *Natsushio* doing?" Harding asked.

"She's turning to port, sir, and diving."

"Keep a close watch on her, Mel," Harding said, and he went back to the conn. "Hard over to starboard and get us out of here." He went to the plotting table as the *Seawolf* banked to the right. "New course one-three-zero, all ahead one-third."

The officer of the deck was relaying the orders, and Paradise came over. "We have to call this one home, Tom."

"As soon as we're in the clear," Harding said. "I don't want to get into a pissing contest with the Japanese until somebody tells me what the hell is going on."

TWELVE

The White House

It was a few minutes after 9:00 A.M. when Tony Croft, his letter of resignation in his pocket, shambled down the corridor from the Executive Office Building to the Oval Office. The President's appointments secretary Dale Nance had called and told him to come over on the double, and in Croft's present state of mind he had to wonder if his secret had gotten out. He was a traitor, and he didn't know how he could face the President at this moment. Or how he was going to face his wife and children and his friends and colleagues. He didn't know how he could explain himself, because even now he didn't know how it had happened, except that at the time he thought he was protecting the President and the nation.

At the very least he would be severely criticized for walking out at this most difficult of times, but he was part of the problem, and therefore he could not be part of the solution. At the worst, and that's how he was thinking this morning, he was going to federal prison for a very long time. That possibility was terrifying, because he was sure he would be doing hard time at some institution like Leavenworth, and not one of the country club lockups that the media loved to poke fun at. He was sure that he wouldn't be able to hack it, and that made his present state of depression even worse. Where had it all gone wrong for him?

Roland Murphy came down the corridor in a big hurry from the opposite direction, a tight scowl on his bulldog features. "What a goddamn mess," he said.

"What's happened?" Croft asked, his gut tightening.

"It's the goddamned Japanese. One of their subs destroyed a Chinese submarine last night. Haven't you heard?"

"No."

The Oval Office was filled with people, telephones rang, the television was tuned to CNN, the sound low, and Croft noticed gratefully that they were doing a report from what looked like Havana, so at least for the moment this incident hadn't hit the news. But he briefly wondered why they weren't meeting downstairs in the crisis room. The President and Howard Secor were in deep discussion by the bowed windows, while Secretary of Defense Landry and General Podvin were speaking on telephones. Thomas Roswell came in right behind them. Like Murphy, he carried a bulging briefcase, which he opened. He spread several satellite photographs, some of them in infrared, on the President's desk.

"These came in from the NRO early this morning," he told Murphy.

The President looked up, clearly angry. "Not such a good morning, gentlemen. Roland, can you fill us in on the latest?"

"Perhaps we should go downstairs, Mr. President," Croft said. He was seething with a mix of emotions, guilt and fear.

"No time, Tony. I'm going to call the Japanese ambassador over here, and I want to know what to say to the bastard."

The President rarely spoke that way, and it got their attention.

"Tom's brought over the NRO shots taken overnight. And we got a break with the weather this time," Murphy said. "The battle took place three hundred feet beneath the ocean, but you can see that something definitely blew up."

They gathered around the desk to look at the pictures. "There's absolutely no doubt what happened?" President Lindsay asked.

"We got it direct from the *Seawolf*," Landry assured him.

"What did we miss?" the President asked.

"Sir?"

"The two submarines China sent weren't due to show up so soon. Which means we missed this submarine. What else have we missed?"

"There's no way of telling for the moment," Roswell had to admit, and it didn't make the President happy.

"Roland?"

"In a nutshell, a Japanese submarine, the *Natsushio* out of the MSDF base at Maizuru, showed up last night, started a search pattern and discovered the Chinese submarine. For whatever reason, the Japanese submarine fired two torpedoes, both of which hit the target, and the Chinese submarine was destroyed."

"Did they give any warnings?"

"There's no way of knowing that," Murphy said. "But Harding, the *Seawolf's* skipper, said it had to have come as a surprise to the Chinese captain because he didn't try to evade, nor did he try to fight back."

"Then what happened?"

"The *Natsushio* bugged out, and Harding retired to a safe distance and radioed in his report. He's standing by out there for now."

"One confused captain, I would suspect," Landry said.

"What did we tell him?" the President asked.

"To stay put and continue to monitor the situation," Landry said. "Admiral Mann wants to pull him out of there. He can head north and join up with the Seventh Fleet."

"I want him to follow the Japanese submarine," the President said. "For now he's the only one with the capability of telling us what's going on."

"If I may make a suggestion, Mr. President, why not have John put some pressure on Enchi," Croft said. This situation was getting way out of hand, and he felt partly responsible.

"They're giving him the runaround," the President said.

"Does he have this latest information?"

"It's on the way, but it's not going to make any difference," Landry said. "They've stonewalled him this far, they're not going to suddenly open up because of this."

"Maybe he should go to Beijing," General Podvin said. "I was wrong about the Japanese not tangling with the Chinese navy, so the Seventh Fleet might be sailing into the middle of a mess a lot bigger than we think."

"I agree," Croft said. "There's not going to be a military solution out there. The first thing we have to do is get them talking so this doesn't escalate."

"The problem of North Korea's nuclear weapons and missiles still exist," Murphy pointed out. "Telling Japan to back off won't make any sense to them. They're protecting their country."

"I seem to remember that you said the Japanese wouldn't get into it with the Chinese over this unless they knew something that we didn't," Croft said. He felt like he was the only one fighting a developing forest fire, and all he had were a bucket of sand and one shovel.

"That's right, but we're still no closer to finding out what that might be than we were two days ago."

"Then what do you suggest?" Croft demanded.

"Tell the governments of Japan and China to back off, and tell Admiral Hamilton to enforce it."

"We're going to have to offer them something in return," Secor said.

"We'll find and destroy North Korea's nuclear weapons and weapons program."

"Is that Kirk McGarvey's shoot-'em-up suggestion?" Secor asked sarcastically.

Murphy eyed him coolly. "It's my suggestion, Harold. Anything short of that and we may be facing a full-scale war out there."

"Very well," President Lindsay said. "Bob, how soon before Hamilton has the fleet in position?"

"Another twelve hours," Landry said.

"How about John?"

"I'll get on the phone and tell him what's going on," Secor said. "If he doesn't get anywhere in the morning in Tokyo, he can head over to Beijing."

"Tony?"

Croft tightened up. "I wouldn't recommend this course of action, Mr. President."

"What do you think we should do?"

"Hold the Seventh in reserve, somewhere up north, until we can open a dialogue between Tokyo and Beijing."

"What about the North Koreans?"

"It'll be tough, but if the CIA can give us some accurate information this time and we can take out their nuclear weapons, and at least damage their missile launch sites and maintenance depots, it'd be our best bet."

"I'll call both ambassadors in, set them down face-to-face and let them hash it out," the President said. He turned to General Podvin. "Get word to Hamilton that I want his fleet right in the middle of the Sea of Japan, with all possible speed. And bring him up to date on what we've decided here."

"What defense posture can he take?"

"If someone shoots at him, he can shoot back."

"What if the Japanese try another stunt like last night, or the Chinese decide to retaliate?"

"I'll have to get back to him on that one," the President said. "But assure him that he will not be left hanging. Better yet, tell him that *I'll* not leave him hanging."

"Yes, sir," Podvin said.

"We all have work to do, let's get to it."

Croft walked out of the office, and resisting the urge to stick around for a final word with Murphy, went back to his office.

He told his secretary that he was going out to the CIA and to cancel all his appointments and hold all his calls until he got back. He unlocked his secured file cabinet and removed five files that he'd packed in a big manila envelope this morning and stuffed them into his briefcase.

Hesitating for just a moment, he glanced out the window toward the White House front lawn and the pedestrian traffic along Pennsylvania Avenue and Lafayette Square. The weather was magnificent. Tourist season was in full swing. The problem was that he couldn't remember the last time he'd taken a vacation with Beth Ann and the kids. It was something he'd been meaning to do, but ever since Lindsay had pulled him from Yale, he'd been on a merry-go-round with no way off.

He took a leather case about the size of a small toiletries kit from the bottom drawer of the file cabinet, put it in his briefcase, then locked up and walked outside to get his car. He was senior staff so no one would check him.

Hay Adams Hotel

Croft drove around the corner to the Hay Adams Hotel across from Lafayette Square and the White House. He maintained a room there for the times when he worked late and couldn't face the thirty miles of traffic to his home in Edgewater on the South River near Annapolis. The media hadn't gotten onto the arrangement because it was nothing unusual, and he was careful. He stood looking out the window toward the White House, sipping a brandy, his stomach tied up in knots, when the door opened and Judith Kline came in, a bright smile on her pretty oval face. This place was his crisis center, and Judith was his extracurricular crisis team.

"Anybody see you coming up?" he asked.

"You ask the same thing every time. Don't be such a worrywart," said the high-priced call girl. The service she worked for was very discreet, and over the past six months in fact, Croft had been only one of three regular johns for her.

"You're right," Croft said, his heart swelling as it did each time he laid eyes on her. She was twenty-four and stunningly gorgeous. She did not look like a prostitute. The way she dressed and comported herself, she could have been mistaken for a White House staffer. She had real class.

She dropped her big bag and the room key on the couch, languidly glided over to him as she slipped out of her high heels and came into his arms. Her slight body was dwarfed by his bulk, but she'd never seemed to mind the fact he was overweight.

Croft let out a pent-up sigh. "Just what the doctor ordered," he said softly in her ear. "Did I wake you when I called?"

She laughed. "As a matter of fact I was half expecting it. You've been really uptight. After the other day I figured you'd be needing a little more TLC." She looked up at him sweetly. "Am I right?"

He smiled. "I have all afternoon."

She cocked her head. "Well, I don't," she said, and he started to object but she raised a finger to his lips. "We've gone over this before, Tony. We both have lives to maintain, and I don't object when you have to go home." She shrugged. "It's better this way. You'd just get tired of me."

A blind, unreasoning panic rose up. "Don't you desert me too."

She looked at him critically. "You really do have it bad, don't you?"

"It's the White House," Croft mumbled, his thoughts drifting for just a moment.

"Trouble in Camelot?" she asked.

His breath caught in his throat. "I didn't mean that," he blurted. "That White House. I meant—"

Judith held a finger to his lips again. "Doesn't matter, Tony," she cooed. "We both know what you need. Come on."

He dutifully went to the big king-sized bed where he helped her turn down the covers. Like an old married couple, he thought, watching her every move. She was dressed in a lightweight summer suit and silk blouse. She got undressed slowly, not turning away from him like Beth Ann always did, and when she was naked he drank in the sight of her translucent skin and perfect body. Her breasts were small, the nipples already erect. Beneath the slight curve of her tummy, the hair at her pubis had been completely removed, and seeing the bare mound of her vagina was the most exotic sight he'd ever imagined, and he could never get tired of it.

Her eyes never leaving his, her lips curved in a slight, lascivious smile, she propped up the pillows, got into the bed, spread her legs and moistening her forefinger in her mouth, slowly began to masturbate.

"Am I going to have to do this all by myself?" she asked huskily. She caressed the nipples of her breasts with her other hand, and half closed her eyes. "Tony?"

All other thoughts driven out of his mind, Croft got undressed, leaving his clothes where they fell and climbed into bed with her. Clumsily he kissed her breasts, sucking her nipples as he reached for her vagina with his left hand. But she pushed him away, gently forcing him on his back.

"First things first," she said softly. She kissed his lips, then his nipples, the tips of her fingers tracing patterns along the stretch marks on his distended belly.

He used to be embarrassed when she played with him like that, ashamed of his gross body next to the sleekness of hers. But after the first few times when he couldn't see the slightest hint of distaste in her eyes, he lay back and went with her.

She spread his legs, then pushing her hair back, took his flaccid penis in her mouth, and he almost came, his entire body twitching as if he'd received an electric shock.

Pulling away, she turned around and straddled his chest, presenting her bottom to him, took him in her mouth again and lowered her vagina to his mouth.

She was sweet-smelling and sweet-tasting, and Croft reveled in her body, her moisture, the tastes and sensations, and finally he could feel himself stiffening in her mouth, the distraction of ministering to her needs taking his mind off his own body long enough so that he wouldn't prematurely ejaculate as he'd done all of his life. A little diversion, she called it.

A minute later he felt and tasted her climax the same moment as he came, and just like he did every time, he thanked God for a friend who'd told him about the service Judith worked for.

"There now, all better?" Judith said sweetly. She gave his penis a playful nip, then climbed off him and got out of bed.

"Don't go," Croft said.

She came around to his side of the bed, pulled the sheet over him and kissed him lightly on the lips. "I told you I couldn't stay long. But if you're going to be in town Friday I'll see you."

"I'll call," he said softly.

She gave him another kiss, then gathered her clothes, went into the bathroom and closed the door. It was funny because she always undressed in front of him, but she never let him watch her get dressed.

He let his thoughts drift, except for a light aftermath of guilt as usual, back to the impossible situation at the White House. He'd screwed up, and there was no way out of it for him. That had been made painfully clear to him last night. The forces of darkness were closing in, he thought melodramatically. He had tried to put out the fires, he had tried to divert their attention to the real problems at hand, but it had somehow gotten away from him.

If he'd only been told the entire story, if they'd only confided in him, he thought bitterly, perhaps he could have done a better job.

Judith came out of the bathroom, and he feigned sleep. Through half-closed eyes he watched her looking at him. Then she put on her jacket, checked her hair once again in the dresser mirror and without a backward glance got her purse and key and left.

It occurred to Croft that he would never see her again, and in a way he was almost relieved. She'd been one of the attractions on the one-way merry-go-round. A Beltway perk, every bit as dangerous and expensive as all the other perks that came with power. Be careful you don't get burned down there, his friends at Yale had cautioned.

A half hour later Croft got out of bed, and in the bathroom, avoiding his own reflection in the mirror, closed the tub drain and started the water running.

Back in the room he sat down by the desk at the window, took a piece of hotel stationery from the drawer and wrote a brief note apologizing to his wife and children and to the President for letting them down.

What else to tell them, he wondered as he idly stared out the window at the beautiful summer day. About the things he'd learned in college or about the contradictions he'd found in the last six years working at the White House? About his principles or about the lack of principles of the sharks around him? About his vision for the future and his devotion to a few basic ideals or about the distortions and cynicisms he saw all around him?

He looked again at the letter, hesitated a moment longer, then signed it. Let the facts speak for themselves, he assured himself.

Unlocking his briefcase he took the thick manila envelope out, laid it on the desk, placed the note on top of it, then took the toiletries kit into the bathroom.

Beth Ann had pleaded with him not to take the White House job when President-elect Lindsay had offered it to him. They were settled in at Yale for the long haul. They had a beautiful old home, they took summer vacations, and besides teaching political history he had plans for at least six major books, two of them textbooks. He had a lot to say and the time in which to say it.

He shut off the water and took the .38 Smith & Wesson snub-nosed pistol from the kit, loaded it and climbed in the tub. He didn't want to make a mess.

God forgive me, he thought, because he didn't believe his colleagues would. He wrapped a towel around the gun, placed the barrel against his right temple and without hesitation pulled the trigger.

Croft had done a number on himself. Bruce Kondo stood in the doorway to the bathroom studying the lifeless remains of the foreign affairs adviser to the President of the United States, the room utterly silent. He'd waited a full ten minutes to make sure that no one had heard the gunshot and was coming to investigate. Lee had predicted Croft's instability. Sane men did not take their own lives because of nothing more than a warning from their spymasters. But then, Kondo supposed, traitors were by definition unbalanced individuals.

Donning a pair of latex gloves, Kondo methodically searched the bathroom and bedroom, including Croft's clothing, before turning his attention to the desk, where he retrieved the bug he'd placed yesterday.

The suicide note was straightforward and revealed nothing of any importance, which was a break. It could be left as is. But the thick manila envelope contained about what Kondo expected it would. He took only a minute to look through the files, which outlined the details of Croft's work for Joseph Lee, the Far East Trade Association and the Japanese Ministry of International Trade and Industry, through his contacts inside not only the White House, but the FBI, CIA and State Department. Croft had been convinced that a war in the Far East would of necessity expand to include the United States. And it was a war that in his estimation the U.S. could not possibly win. He viewed himself as an American patriot.

As an intelligence resource he would be missed. But the countdown clock had begun, and with or without Croft, Morning Sun was a fait accompli. Nobody could stop it now, Kondo thought, letting himself out of the room, not even Kirk McGarvey.

CIA Headquarters

"Okay, the President's taking your advice; he's moving the Seventh Fleet into the middle of it," Murphy said.

McGarvey looked up from the NRO photographs and the analysis that Tommy Doyle's shop had come up with. "I hope he's doing some serious talking with Japan and China, because this is getting out of hand a lot sooner than we thought it would."

"Secretary of State Carter is in Tokyo now, and he'll be flying to Beijing later today. It's nighttime over there right now, and he wants to wait until morning to have one more shot with Enchi."

"That'll take too much time. How about their ambassadors?"

Murphy nodded. "You don't miss a trick, do you? Lindsay is meeting with them later today or tonight, as soon as it can be set up. They're probably going to be reluctant to see him, let alone make any commitments."

"At least they'll be talking, and if Lindsay is straight with them, they'll know what we know and what we intend doing about it. No bullshit. No misunderstandings."

Murphy eyed him. "But?"

It was a few minutes past two-thirty and they were alone in the DCI's office. "Our networks in Japan are coming up empty-handed. Some of them aren't even responding which could mean they've been blown. It also means that this incident has the government's backing."

"It'd have to, otherwise the MSDF wouldn't be out there in force. What are you getting at?"

"Tokyo was in it from the start. It's almost as if they set out to provoke the North Koreans into demanding help from Beijing."

"I'm with you so far, Mac. And I can't say as I blame them. As soon as they found out about the nuclear weapons at Kimch'aek they went after them. We could have done the same thing in Cuba in the sixties."

"But we didn't because Kennedy was worried about touching off a nuclear war between us and the Soviet Union."

"A war we couldn't have won. Or at least it would have been a draw, and we would have all been back in the horse and buggy era."

"But that's not what the Japanese think," McGarvey said. "They're pushing the Chinese to the wall. Why?"

"I see what you're getting at."

Danielle came in from his connecting office without knocking. He looked as if he'd just gotten some bad news. "You'd better see this. Turn on CNN."

"What happened?" Murphy asked, switching on the television.

"They found Tony Croft dead at the Hay Adams. He was shot in the head."

As the television came on, Murphy's phone rang.

McGarvey sat back. "Shit," he said softly, and Danielle caught it.

"What nasty thought just occurred to you, Mac?"

"Croft briefed Joseph Lee on Saturday, and the next day Lee left the country." He shook his head. "His death is no coincidence."

"They're calling it suicide."

"It's no coincidence, Larry, I'd bet my life on it."

THIRTEEN

FBI Headquarters
J. Edgar Hoover Building

Jack Hailey is a good man, and if Croft didn't kill himself, he'll find out," FBI Director Dr. Gerald Pierone Jr. said. "He's moving fast on this one. I have his assurances."

"I have no doubt," Fred Rudolph said carefully. "But he's working under a handicap, because he doesn't know all the facts. He might stumble across something that will make no sense to him, and we'll miss an opportunity."

"Facts that you have," Pierone said. They were in his office.

Rudolph nodded glumly. "I'm going to need your okay to proceed."

He had been at a meeting with the antiterrorism division until an hour ago and hadn't heard about Croft until then. Hailey, who was the Bureau's special agent in charge of the District of Columbia, had taken over the investigation from the Metropolitan Police as soon as the call had come in. He had immediately sent a team of forensics specialists and special agents to the Hay Adams. Croft's body had been discovered by a maid apparently within a half hour of his death. The medical examiner's snap judgement was that Croft had killed himself with a single .38 caliber bullet to the brain within an hour of having sex. The hotel staff remembered seeing a young, good-looking woman coming and going from Croft's room on several occasions over the past six months, but she'd never been a registered guest of the hotel. She was obviously a prostitute, she had the look, but she'd never been blatant and the Hay Adams was a discreet establishment. The staff had also seen Croft in the company of a slightly built Asian man in the lobby bar and across the street from the hotel at the entrance to Lafayette Square at least twice in the last twenty-four hours. He was registered in the hotel under the name Thomas Wang, a South Korean businessman. He'd not checked out, but his room was empty of any personal belongings, nor had the bed been slept in or the bathroom used. Hailey's people were checking now for fingerprints. Rudolph had got all that from Hailey's operations officer twenty minutes ago.

"This is a high-profile case, and before I take it out of Jack's hands and give it to you, I'm going to have to be convinced it's the right move." Pierone wasn't happy.

"At this point it's the only move. A lot of stuff has started to pile up since Friday. Most of it circumstantial, but everywhere I turn I come back to the same starting point."

Pierone knew what Rudolph had been working on, and he was beginning to draw the same conclusions, it was obvious from his suddenly dour mood. "What starting point is that, Fred? Exactly where are you taking this?"

"The White House."

"The comparison with the Vince Foster thing is already being made."

"This time we have some better leads," Rudolph said. "One of the Georgetown terrorists that Kirk McGarvey took out was a Japanese named Akira Nishimura. Two years ago he was fired from his job at the Pacific Rim Development Institute in Hong Kong. The President's friend Joseph Lee owns the institute. In fact, Lee and his wife were staying at the White House that night. The next morning Lee was given a private briefing by Tony Croft, and the next day he went back to Taiwan in such a hurry that he didn't wait for his private jet to pick him up; he flew commercial, something he never does."

Pierone shook his head. "Okay, I don't like this, but you have my attention. What else do you have?"

"Kirk McGarvey has come to the same conclusions as I have and the CIA is helping out on this one. Lee showed up at his home in Taiwan, met with some of his directors and then disappeared. They've issued a world-wide alert to all their stations to be on the look out for him."

"That's one," Pierone said. He had a doctor's mentality; the logical, scientific approach was the only way.

"Croft left a brief suicide note apologizing not only to his wife but to the President."

"For his suicide?"

"Maybe. But he'd apparently been screwing a high-priced call girl for the past six months. Why pick right now of all times to kill himself?"

"That's fitting the timing with the facts after they've happened. You can do that with anything. Monday morning quarterbacking."

"He was spotted by the hotel staff twice in the last twenty-four hours meeting with a man by the name of Thomas Wang, a South Korean businessman, who has also disappeared."

"Any connection with Lee?"

"That's one of the leads I want to work on," Rudolph said. "I could turn my files over to Jack, but I'd like to keep the need-to-know list as short as possible. At least for the time being."

"You have three leads: Lee, a prostitute and a South Korean businessman. What else?"

"That's it for now, but something's going on here. The minute McGarvey is put up for DDO, somebody tries to take him out, and they don't care how many other people they kill trying to do it. At least one of the shooters had a connection to Lee. Then Tony Croft gives Lee a briefing and a couple of days later he blows his brains out."

"If you can connect Thomas Wang to Lee you might have something."

"It's a fictitious name," Rudolph said dismissing the director's suggestion. "The real point is if the two incidents are connected, whoever is behind this hasn't given up. They'll try again."

"You're suggesting that Croft was murdered?"

That was a stumbling block for Rudolph too, because the only conclusion that seemed to fit—a suicide rather than a murder—was even more frightening. He shook his head. "I think he killed himself."

"Why?"

Rudolph, who'd been looking inward, focused on the director. "Because I think Tony Croft was feeding Lee information. He had almost total access to us and the CIA and every other agency in Washington. I think it finally got to him that he was committing treason, so he blew his brains out."

"He would have left more than a note," Pierone suggested.

"Maybe he did and someone got in and out before the maid discovered the body."

"The prostitute?"

"Or Thomas Wang."

Pierone smiled wryly and shook his head. "I met Joseph Lee and his wife, Miriam. Did you know that she was born and raised in San Francisco? Charming people, witty, gracious, pleasant. They've been friends with the Lindsays for at least five years. Close friends, which is why Sam Blair was appointed special prosecutor—he's tough but nonpartisan—and why you were assigned to find out about his campaign contributions."

"We're drawing blanks for the moment," Rudolph admitted.

"I know. Point is that if Joseph Lee was behind the Georgetown bombing and somehow involved in Tony Croft's suicide, this won't simply land in the backyard of the White House. It'll end up in the President's lap, and where would that put us?"

"In the middle of a criminal investigation," Rudolph said, acutely aware that he had probably uttered the biggest understatement of his life.

"Have you discussed any of this with Sam?"

"No."

"Don't, without talking to me first," Pierone said. He called his secretary. "Get Jack Hailey up here as soon as possible, would you?"

On the way back to his own office, Rudolph tried to remember why he had ever left his job with the Supreme Court. For the life of him he couldn't, and for the first time he knew that he would give serious consideration to leaving once this investigation was over.

Tokyo

Traffic was a bitch on Sakurada-Dori Avenue as it always was Monday through Friday. Peter Rivas, parked in a bright green Honda Prelude across the street from the Metropolitan Police Headquarters, raised his motorized Nikon and took three rapid-fire shots of the exit from the police garage as a Mercedes limousine emerged. He got at least one good picture of the lone passenger in the backseat, the image through the 200mm telephoto lens clear enough so that he was sure the passenger wasn't Joseph Lee.

Tokyo was a huge city of eight and a half million people living and working in twenty-three wards, twenty-six small cities, seven towns and eight villages spread out over 227 square miles. As far as the young CIA officer was concerned, trying to find one person in the middle of all that was worse than looking for a needle in a haystack, it was a gross waste of time. But orders were orders. And Lee was a top priority.

Rivas laid the camera on the passenger seat and lit a cigarette. He'd been here two hours already, since eight-thirty this morning, and had six to go. The COS had spread his twenty-three available personnel at the airport and through the city, eight hours on, eight hours off. Places where Lee, if he showed up in Tokyo, might logically be spotted.

Another Mercedes limo came up the ramp and waited for a break in traffic. Rivas flipped his cigarette away, raised the camera and focused on the two men in the backseat. The man on the right, behind the driver, had a narrow, pinched face, short-cropped gray hair and a round nose. He was Joseph Lee, there was no doubt of it.

Rivas snapped a half-dozen photographs as the car pulled out into traffic and headed south. He started his car, waited for a taxi to pass, then shot out behind it. He snatched the microphone.

"Control, seven. Red-one is on the move, south from my QTH. I'm in pursuit."

"Don't crowd him."

Crowd him, hell, Rivas thought, just keeping up with the bastard was going to be a trick all in itself. This was the big one and he didn't want to blow it.

The limo and cab shot through the light at Sotobori-Dori Avenue as it was turning yellow, and Rivas had to floor it to get through. His apartment was nearby so he was reasonably familiar with this section of Tokyo. But in another mile Sakurada-Dori branched off, to the right toward Roppongi, Akasaka and Aoyama, and left toward Hamamatsucho Rail Station, Shiba Rikyu Garden and the port of Tokyo. Either way the limo turned there would be dozens of opportunities for Rivas to lose it.

"Control, seven, I'm going to need some help."

"Has he come to the turn yet?"

"Another couple of blocks."

"If he turns toward the port, follow him, otherwise back off. Nine is in Akasaka."

The radio transmissions were encrypted and sent in one-millisecond compressed bursts, but Rivas was still nervous. The Japanese may not have invented modern technology, but they sure as hell were masters at it.

"Okay, he's in a black Mercedes 600, license seven-one-seven, governmental."

"Stand by."

The limo moved over to the center lane and the taxi switched lanes with it. Before Rivas could follow suit a pair of white Toyota vans pulled up on either side of him, boxing him in.

"Seven, the limo belongs to Shimoyama, so watch yourself." Shiego Shimoyama was chief of Tokyo police. He had a reputation for hating Americans.

Rivas tried to speed up, but a third white Toyota van, which had been in front of the limo, switched lanes directly in front of him and dropped back.

"Control, seven, I've got trouble here," Rivas radioed, but there was no reply.

The limo suddenly shot across three lanes and made the left turn toward the port, but Rivas, still boxed in, was forced to turn right through the intersection, toward Rappongi.

"Control, seven, you copy?"

The radio was silent.

"Shit," Rivas said, looking for a way out, but the three vans refused to get out of the way, and a fourth suddenly appeared in his rearview mirror.

"Control, seven," he radioed.

When there was no answer, he dropped the microphone. Like taking candy from a baby, he thought. But then it was their city, where a Westerner stood out like a sore thumb. The real trouble would come when he had to write his report. This was hot, and he'd blown it.

A few blocks later the white vans turned off, which came as no surprise, and his radio started to work again.

"Seven, this is control, do you read?"

"Control, seven, I copy. I lost him."

Tanegashima Space Center

Joseph Lee gazed out the floor-to-ceiling windows toward the powerful H2C rocket on its launchpad five miles away, only a few puffy clouds marring an otherwise perfectly blue sky. Except for the incident this morning with the CIA officer in Tokyo, he was certain that the Americans had no idea he'd flown down here for the launch. Everything that he'd put in place for Morning Sun was developing as planned, in Taiwan, in Tokyo, in Washington and especially here at the space center. Nothing would go wrong.

"Joseph, I came as soon as I heard that you had arrived," Tomichi Kunimatsu said.

Lee turned as the slightly built Tanegashima Space Center director came across the palatial great room, his hand outstretched.

They shook hands. "I'm happy to be here at least," Lee said. "How is the countdown coming?"

"We're at seventy-two hours, and I'm happy to say that so far there have been no major holds." Kunimatsu, whose quarters these were behind the launch control complex, frowned. "I understand that you ran into some trouble in Tokyo?"

"Nothing serious," Lee said. "How about the American Tiger team, are they behaving themselves?"

"No, but we're taking care of them. Kimura wants to send them home now, and I agree."

"Not until the launch. Otherwise there might be questions. That is, of course, if you can keep them out of mischief."

"This close to launch, frankly they make me nervous, but I can see the wisdom in what you advise." Kunimatsu looked out the windows. "Nine minutes after launch we will lose contact with the spaceship. And by the time Norad's space command finds our wayward satellite, if they do, we will already have made the announcement." He turned back to Lee. "Everyone will know the true meaning of Hagoromo."

Kunimatsu was more of an engineer than a politician. But it wasn't votes that raised a rocket, it was science, and he'd done an excellent job, though of course even he didn't know the full story. Only a handful of men knew everything, and for the next seventy-two hours all of them would be incommunicado to the outside. Only afterward when the storm started to develop would they make their assurances to a stunned world.

"Is there any possibility of a leak from here?" Lee asked. Tanegashima security had always been very good, but this time it had to be perfect.

"The Americans are the weak link, of course, as we knew they would be. But we're monitoring their every move."

Lee gave the launch center director a pointed look. "Don't underestimate them. If they get wind that something isn't as it should be they could make trouble. Something we cannot afford at this late date."

Kunimatsu chose his words with care. "They know that something out of the ordinary is going on. But so does everybody else because of the incident in the Sea of Japan. Our navy has been deployed and all of our military installations are at a high state of alert. But nobody has made the connection to us."

"Yet."

"Seventy-two hours, Joseph. Not so long a time to keep it together. We'll hold up our end."

"See that you do," Lee said, turning again to the awe-inspiring sight out the windows. No one was going to guess until it was too late.

"I assume that you're going to remain here until after the launch?" Kunimatsu said.

"Of course. But I've left Miriam at our Washington house to allay any suspicions that the FBI has. She'll leave the morning of the launch."

Kunimatsu's normally bland expression changed to one of pensiveness. "I've learned only now something of the happenings in Washington, and frankly, Joseph, I'm a little confused."

"Quid pro quo, do you understand?"

"No," Kunimatsu said shaking his head.

"You will," Lee said, smiling.

Cropley, Maryland

They followed the Potomac southeast from White's Ferry at an altitude of five hundred feet, Sandy Patterson in the front seat. Bruce Kondo, in the backseat of the Beach Bonanza, took pictures using a Haselblad camera with a wide-angle lens of the rolling hills, park lands and the occasional farm or mansion. Although the Capital City Aviation pilot had done contract work for the Far East Trade Association in the past, Kondo's cover story was that he was looking for riverside property to buy.

"There are some pretty spots down there," Sandy Patterson said as the CIA safe house came into view.

"Yes, thank you, I can see that."

"Would you like me to come in a little lower and circle, Mr. Thomas?" the pilot asked.

"That's not necessary," Kondo said, snapping pictures as fast as the motorized drive would work. There were no surprises in the layout from what he'd been told, or from what he'd been able to glean from the topographic maps. But seeing it from the air like this gave him a much clearer perspective of what they would be facing. Just on the one pass he'd picked out at least three spots where he and his men could come in.

As he suspected would be the case, however, he was unable to spot any activity on the ground. The foliage was so thick that an entire army could be hidden down there and still be invisible to the human eye. But the camera, with its special film, might pick something up.

"There's property closer to the city, if you would like to look at it as well," Sandy Patterson prompted. A couple of miles ahead was a busy interstate highway. "But that's four ninety-five down there, I don't think you want to be that close."

"I think I've seen all I need to see for now. Perhaps next week we can try south of the city. It'll give me time to do my homework."

"It's only six-thirty, there's still plenty of light to take a pass that way now," the pilot suggested.

"Next week," Sandy Patterson said sharply.

Grand Hyatt Washington

Judith Kline was a young woman who until today had thought she knew exactly where she was going, and how she was going to get there. But sitting at the Atrium Bar a few minutes after 6:30 P.M., she understood that Tony Croft's death, which she'd just heard about, had changed all of that for her, and she had a sick feeling at the pit of her stomach.

Tony was going to be her meal ticket, her way out from being an escort, and her way into a cushy job in the White House, or at least some government agency. Tony had been mentioning the Pentagon lately and the State Department, and she'd hung on his every word. She'd done exactly what he'd told her to do. She was not a stupid girl; although she'd finished only two and a half years of college, she was merely impatient. She'd seen how the other half lived, and coming from Des Moines, Iowa, to Washington was a real eye-opener for her. She wanted to be one of them, and she wanted it soon.

At Tony's suggestion, she'd taken several crash courses on the computer, read a half-dozen newspapers each day including the *Washington Post* and *New York Times*, read all the news and business magazines, and she'd even begun reading *Aviation Week & Space Technology* in case the Pentagon job materialized first. It was all a matter of timing, Tony assured her. And he might have gotten her a position and she might have been able to hold it for a little while on her looks alone, but over the long haul she was going to have to be good at her job.

Tony had also made another suggestion, which she'd taken to heart. If you wanted to get ahead in this town you had to watch your back at all times. His philosophy was to do the best job you could and keep an insurance policy in case the bottom fell out. Keep notes, he told her. Tape recordings. A diary.

"Present company excluded," he told her and they'd laughed about it.

That was why she'd been watching him lately. Over the past few weeks he had changed, he'd become moody and nervous and sometimes even frightened. Sometimes after they made love he would sleep for a half hour or so, and he talked in his sleep. It was mostly incomprehensible gibberish, but in the last few days he repeated the same thing over and over, "the White House." No other references, just the three words. The same three words he'd said today.

Since July each time he'd called her and set up a time to meet at the Hay Adams, she showed up an hour early. On three occasions she'd seen him with an older woman, short, mousy, across the street in Lafayette Square. There'd been something vaguely familiar about the woman, but the distance had been too great, and Judith's vanity would not allow her to wear her glasses in public. Then yesterday she'd seen him meeting with a Chinese guy in front of the hotel. A sharp dresser, and she'd taken several photographs of them from the lobby with a disposable camera. She didn't know how the shots would turn out, but she figured that if need be someone who knew their stuff would be able to do it.

Now she was faced with the choice of ignoring the situation, maybe head back home until it all blew over. It was a safe bet that someone in the hotel had noticed her hanging around and given the FBI her description. Better to leave while she could, especially after what she'd seen today.

She motioned to the bartender for another glass of chardonnay, then lit a cigarette. She would fit back in Des Moines like a square peg in a round hole. All her life she had worked to get away from the Midwest, and here she was faced with the choice of going back.

Her drink came and she paid for it with cash, as she did everything. The bartender gave her a stern look, as if to say: Go ahead and have your drink, sweetheart, but don't look for any action in my establishment. She'd seen the same thing before and she was getting tired of it.

She shook her head, more in frustration with the situation she'd gotten herself into than fear, although she was plenty frightened. Fact was she couldn't simply walk away from her life this time the way she had left Des Moines.

She signaled to the bartender that she would be right back, and walked around the corner toward the restrooms. A bank of pay phones lined the wall of the corridor. She called a number she'd memorized and it was answered on the second ring.

"You have reached the Federal Bureau of Investigation. If this is an emergency please press one. If you know the extension of your party please enter it now. For all other calls please press two."

Judith pressed one. A moment later a man came on.

"FBI hotline."

"I need to talk to whoever is in charge of the Tony Croft investigation. I have some information for you."

"Yes, ma'am. Can you give me your name please."

"Transfer me now, or I'll hang up," Judith said. "I'm not screwing around."

"One moment please."

Judith lit a cigarette with shaking hands. What the hell was she doing? What the hell had she gotten herself into?"

"Hello, this is Fred Rudolph, who am I talking to?"

"Never mind that for now," Judith said. "I think Tony Croft was murdered, and I think I know who did it."

FOURTEEN

National Reconnaissance Office

A heat bloom suddenly showed up where it didn't belong on the Whiskey Clipper Four satellite console, and Louise Horn sat forward so fast she spilled some of her coffee. "Damn."

She brought up another infrared sensor to confirm what she thought she was seeing and fed both inputs into her computer. A second later the machine answered, "*Natsushio.*"

Louise looked up at the big board as she pulled out a cigarette and lit it. The tactical display showed the entire Sea of Japan and all the warships converging on a point southeast of Kimch'aek that they designated P1. Each time a satellite passed overhead the information on the screen was updated, showing the new position for each ship, the tracks they had taken since the last pass and their projected courses.

A small red circle showed the position where the *Natsushio* had attacked and killed the Chinese submarine, with two tracks leading away from it—one for the Japanese submarine and the other for the *Seawolf*. The problem was that the *Natsushio* had changed course. She was not heading, as they assumed she would, back to her base at Maizuru. She had turned southwest, directly toward the oncoming Chinese fleet, or even a little south of it, perhaps trying to make an end run and sneak up on them as they passed. If that was his plan, Louise thought, he was one gutsy submarine commander. Or crazy.

She dialed up one of the high-resolution cameras aboard Whiskey Clipper Four, enhanced the image and zeroed in on the exact position of the diesel exhaust heat bloom.

It was morning out there, and except for a few puffy clouds viewing was nearly perfect. At first she saw nothing. She dialed up the highest magnification and image enhancement, which actually degraded the picture somewhat, and she spotted a tiny white wake, at the head of which was obviously a masthead sticking out of the water. It was the *Natsushio's* periscope and radio antennae. The Japanese were talking to someone.

The information was already being transferred to photo interp upstairs. She called the night duty officer.

"I see it, Louise," Major Wight said. "But hold a moment, I'm on the line with Fort Meade."

The National Security Agency, headquartered at Fort Meade, Maryland, monitored electronic emissions all over the world. Like the NRO they were focused on the situation in the Sea of Japan. If the Japanese submarine was communicating with her home port, the NSA would be listening in right now.

While she waited for Major Wight to come back, she brought up control of the main tactical display on one of her consoles and asked the computer to extend the submarine's track for the next twenty-four hours, juxtaposed against the tracks of the Chinese fleet.

"Okay, NSA says the *Natsushio* sent out a directed burst transmission, duration two hundred and ten milliseconds, which means it was a long message."

"Was it sent to Maizuru?"

"Apparently not, but they can't say where, and they haven't decrypted it yet, but they're working on it."

"Well, she's not heading back to the barn, Bert. From what I'm looking at on the board, she's heading directly for the eastern channel south of Tsu Island. The Chinese fleet is using the western channel."

"The skipper got smart, he doesn't want to get into another fight. Especially now with those odds."

"So where's he going?" Louise asked.

"Maybe he plans on sneaking up behind them."

"Once they've passed each other, he'd never be able to catch up." Louise's first cigarette was still burning in the overflowing ashtray. She lit another. "Could be he's heading for Tokyo the long way around. That way he'd not only avoid the Chinese fleet, he wouldn't have to deal with Seventh."

"What are you getting at?" Major Wight asked carefully.

"Tokyo Bay is pretty empty right now. Maybe we should take a closer look at what's happened over there since our fleet cleared out."

"Are your projected tracks in the computer?"

"I'm looking at them right now."

"Okay, good job again, Louise," Major Wight said. "I'll get this next door, but I want you to stick with this one for the duration. Can you handle that?"

Louise had to laugh. "The overtime pay sucks, but I can manage."

Major Wight disconnected. Louise put down her cigarette, took a drink of coffee, then lit another cigarette as she stared up at the big board. This was how wars started, she had the unhappy thought.

The White House

FBI Director Gerald Pierone was shown into the Oval Office at 7:00 P.M. by the President's appointments secretary Dale Nance. President Lindsay and Harold Secor were going over some information contained in a file open on the President's desk. Lindsay closed it.

"The Japanese and Chinese ambassadors are coming over in a half hour, so I can't give you much time, Gerald," the President said. "You have some new information about Tony?"

Pierone had agonized all afternoon over what the Bureau's role was in the investigation and exactly what position he should take personally. But he didn't have any choice in the matter, as he saw it. He was the nation's top cop, and if a law had been broken, it was his job to investigate it.

"There's an outside chance that Tony Croft was murdered. We received a call on our hotline from a woman who claims that she knows who murdered him. The partial description she gave us fits a man by the name of Thomas Wang, a South Korean businessman. He was registered at the Hay Adams but apparently he never used his room, and he's disappeared."

The President was shaken. He sat down. "Do you know who the woman is?"

"We don't have her name, but she claimed to be Croft's mistress. They'd been meeting once or twice a week at the Hay Adams over the past six months. The hotel staff think she was probably a prostitute."

The President and Secor exchanged a glance. "Did you know anything about this, Harold?" Lindsay asked.

"Tony's been under a lot of pressure lately, like we all have been, but this is the first I heard anything like that."

"Terrible," Lindsay said, moved. He shook his head. "Do you have the woman in custody?"

"We don't even have her name yet," Pierone said. "But she promised that she would call back with more information. She told us that she had to take care of something first, for her own protection."

"Who would want to kill·him, and why?" the President asked.

Pierone girded himself for what he was going to have to say next. He laid a leather-bound folder on the President's desk. Neither the President or Secor reached for it. "I don't know how to give this to you, Mr. President, except straight. It's very likely that I'm going to be subpoenaed by Sam Blair to turn over what we've come up with in the Joseph Lee investigation."

"What are you talking about?" Secor demanded. "What information?"

"It looks fairly certain that the bombing in Georgetown on Friday was aimed at Kirk McGarvey by someone who not only knew he was being proposed as the CIA's new deputy directory of Operations, but who wanted for some reason to stop him. At any cost. One of the terrorists was identified as a former employee of an operation in Hong Kong owned by Lee."

"A former employee?" Secor said.

Pierone nodded. "He was fired two years ago."

"What does this have to do with Tony Croft?"

"Saturday morning Tony held a private briefing here in the White House for Mr. Lee—"

"How do you know that?" the President demanded.

"One of Croft's staffers told us. We weren't given the substance of that briefing, except that it was extensive and dealt with a current hot-button topic. Twenty-four hours later Lee returned to his home in Taiwan. He stayed there overnight, then disappeared. The CIA spotted him in Tokyo this morning, but lost him again. Nobody knows where he is now."

Pierone was speaking like a prosecutor, he could hear himself, but he didn't know any other way to lay this on the President's doorstep.

"Mr. Lee is under investigation for a possible connection to illegal campaign funding, and there've been a lot of leaks from Sam Blair's office and from the grand jury. If I'm forced to give him this information, the media will have it within twenty-four hours and there'll be a lot of questions." Pierone felt like hell. He admired this President for the good job he was doing. Lindsay had only two years left in his second term, and he didn't need something like this to mar his record.

"I thought you should get a chance to see this first."

"I appreciate it, Jerry," the President said tightly. He looked angry, but he was holding it in check.

"You don't have to turn any of this over to Blair," Secor said.

"I'm not going to volunteer it," Pierone said. "But I have a job to do, and I'll do it. My hands may be tied."

"Bullshit—" Secor exploded, but Lindsay held him off.

"Nobody will interfere with your job, Gerald," the President said. "You have my word on that. And I want to thank you for coming over here like this. Can I ask a favor?"

"Of course, sir."

"Keep me abreast of what you come up with."

"Naturally," Pierone said. "After all I am working for you."

"Yes, you are," the President said, and something about the way he said it troubled Pierone.

Harold Secor had not recovered from the stunning news Gerald Pierone had handed them by the time the Chinese and Japanese ambassadors arrived at 7:30 P.M. Neither had the President, but this was a meeting that simply could not be delayed and one that would have to be played straight from the hip if they expected to somehow calm the Sea of Japan situation before more lives were lost.

Both ambassadors were similar men in that they were career diplomats with more than sixty years of foreign service between them and each was a soft-spoken, brilliant, tough negotiator. Jun Zheng, the Chinese ambassador, worked under a handicap in that he did not have the negotiating freedom that his Japanese counterpart, Ryutaro Mitsui, enjoyed—it was a manifestation of the differences between totalitarian and democratic regimes—but he was every bit as capable despite it.

If there was any tension or hard feelings between them, Secor could not detect it. They were consummate diplomats.

"Good evening, Mr. President, Mr. Secor," Zheng said, bowing slightly.

"Mr. President," Mitsui said, his English even better than Zheng's.

"Gentlemen, thank you for coming over on such short notice," the President said. "But we've been monitoring an increasingly troubling situation in the Sea of Japan involving your two countries."

"I don't know what you're talking about, unless you're referring to the explosion at North Korea's nuclear power station," Zheng said blandly.

"I'm talking about the eight warships your country has sent into the region," the President said. "Our satellites are monitoring their progress right now. Along with the several warships Japan has dispatched. Are you going to tell me that you know nothing about that?"

"There was an accident with one of our submarines," Mitsui broke in smoothly. "We have mounted a recovery operation, nothing more."

"Can you tell us why all of your military bases have been put on alert?" Secor asked.

"Merely a precaution," the Japanese ambassador said. "I think the North Koreans made their position perfectly clear in the aftermath of their unfortunate accident at Kimch'aek. We would be reckless not to take certain steps to prepare for our defense should the unthinkable happen."

"Is that why China has sent its navy?" Secor asked. "Has Pyongyang asked for your help?"

"So far as I'm aware, no such request has been made of my government," Zheng replied. It was impossible for Secor to determine if he was lying. The ambassador's expression was perfectly neutral, as was Mitsui's. They could have been discussing the weather.

"Are you telling us that your navy is simply conducting an exercise?" Secor asked.

Zheng inclined his head slightly. "It's not uncommon."

"You can understand our concern, because very soon ships of both your navies will be in close proximity to each other," the President said. "Accidents have been known to happen in such situations."

"We are aware of such dangers," Mitsui agreed. "Our commanders have been given very specific orders to operate with extreme caution."

"I'm glad to hear that, because it will make it easy for you to take a message back to both of your governments."

"Yes, Mr. President?" Mitsui said.

"We would like to see the situation stabilized by an immediate withdrawal of your forces to a safe distance. A one-hundred-mile separation between your ships and the coast of North Korea would be reasonable. I have ordered the Seventh Fleet into the area as observers. Like both your governments, the United States is deeply concerned by the incident at Kimch'aek. In the morning I shall call for a UN investigation to make sure this doesn't go any further. Until we have all the facts, any military operation there would not only be foolish but would certainly be dangerous."

"We have the right to defend our homeland," Mitsui said.

"With the help of the United States through our Joint Forces agreement," the President said. "We intend honoring our responsibilities to Japan with the same vigor we have in the past. Believe me, we understand perfectly well the threat that Kim Jong-Il represents, and we won't allow him to take any action whatsoever against you. He understands the consequences."

Mitsui nodded. "I appreciate your candor, Mr. President, and I will pass your message back to Tokyo immediately."

"As I will to my government," Zheng said cautiously.

Both ambassadors rose to go, but Secor passed a file folder to the President. "There is one further matter of concern," Lindsay said.

The President opened the file folder, studied the photographs it contained, then passed two of them across the desk, one to each of the ambassadors. "These were taken from one of our satellites of what appears to be an underwater explosion."

The ambassadors glanced at the pictures, then handed them back without comment, no visible change in their expressions.

"Of course we have no way of knowing all the facts; even the best of satellites cannot show us everything. But my military advisers tell me that there is a great probability that what we picked up was the result of an underwater battle between two submarines. Considering what's going on out there, they think it's more than possible that a Japanese submarine may have fired on and destroyed a Chinese submarine. If that's the case the situation has already gotten out of hand."

"I know nothing about this, Mr. President," Zheng said.

Mitsui shook his head. "Nor have I heard anything," he said. "If indeed there was an explosion, it must have been an accident. Such things do happen. As I told you, our commanders have been issued very specific orders to use deadly force only if Japan is directly threatened."

"How do you explain the photographs?" Secor asked point blank.

"I cannot, Mr. Secor," Mitsui said, straight-faced.

"Nor can I," Zheng parroted. "But I will certainly pass this message on to my government as well."

"I want to make this perfectly clear," the President cautioned. "I have ordered the Seventh Fleet into the Sea of Japan for one reason only, that is to maintain the peace. At any cost."

"An admirable mission, Mr. President," Mitsui said without a trace of sarcasm.

"A view I certainly share," Zheng said.

"Then I won't keep you," the President said. "Thank you for coming. Good evening."

When they were gone Secor poured a cup of coffee. "You couldn't have made it any plainer for them."

"Now the ball's in their court," the President said. "Question is, what will they do with it?"

CIA Headquarters

McGarvey's secretary had gone home around 7:00 P.M., and by eight he was about ready to pull the pin himself. The day had somehow gotten away from him, one meeting piled on top of another, reams of files and documents and satellite shots updating the NIE and Watch Report, agent reports coming in from around the world turning up nothing new in their search for Joseph Lee and the disturbing suicide of Tony Croft at the Hay Adams all made him wonder why the hell he'd agreed to take this job. He was a field officer, not an administrator.

Through the day he felt as if he was spinning his wheels, or more accurately trying to run through thick molasses. He was getting nowhere. Coincidences were piling up all around them, but he couldn't see any pattern, he was not making the connections he thought he should be making and he was frustrated.

Tommy Doyle called it bureaucratic bullshit, but until today McGarvey never knew how true it could be.

The telephone rang on McGarvey's private number. It was Howard Ryan.

"I thought you might still be at your desk," Ryan said. "The trouble is that it never ends."

"I'm beginning to learn that."

"I think I may have come up with something for you. It might be nothing more than a coincidence, but in this business I guess you can't take anything for granted."

"What have you got?"

"There's an outfit here in town called the Far East Trade Association.

They're on Dupont Circle. They might have a connection with Joseph Lee, but I got that from only one source who admitted he was merely guessing, and I haven't been able to confirm it yet. In fact I wasn't even going to call you, except for what happened to Tony Croft."

McGarvey jotted the name of the association on a notepad. "What about him?"

"Far East's executive secretary is a woman named Sandy Patterson. She was friends with Tony. I don't know how far back they went or how close their relationship was, but they definitely knew each other."

"Are you sure about this?

"Sure enough that if I were sitting where you are I'd look into it. Could be nothing more than the mechanism Lee uses to funnel money into the White House, if that's what's been going on."

"Does Sam Blair know about this?"

"Not yet," Ryan said. "At least I don't think he does, otherwise he would have called the woman before the grand jury."

"Will it go public that you're feeding me information?" McGarvey asked.

"Not on your life," Ryan said. "Like I told you before, I've got my own reputation to consider. And whatever you think about me, I'm still doing some good things in this town."

"All right, Howard, I'll see what I can dig up. Thanks for your help. I won't forget it."

"Right," Ryan said. "If I find out anything else I'll give you a call."

"Do that." McGarvey was getting the ugly feeling that very soon he was going to be even more unpopular in Washington than he had ever been.

He caught Fred Rudolph at home, just getting ready to sit down to supper.

"Why is it that anytime the phone rings these days, I don't want to pick it up, because I know the news is going to be bad?"

"I just talked to Howard Ryan about Tony Croft and Joseph Lee," McGarvey said. He didn't think Rudolph was going to enjoy his dinner tonight. "There might be another connection between them through an organization called the Far East Trade Association on Dupont Circle. Croft and Far East's executive secretary, Sandy Patterson, were friends, and apparently Lee has some link to it."

"Where did Ryan pick that up?"

"He didn't say and I didn't ask. If we lean on him he'll back off. But I think we should at least take a look at Far East."

"I'll get a search warrant tonight. Do you want to tag along?"

"Not on the first pass. But if you find something let me know."

"Will do."

"For the time being I want Ryan's name kept out of this, okay?"

Rudolph hesitated a moment. "I don't know if that's possible. We're talking about a major criminal investigation here that could reach all the way to the President. Besides, from the way I read it you don't owe Ryan a thing."

"I gave him my word that I would protect him for as long as I could. It's the only reason he's cooperating with me."

"I'll see what I can do," Rudolph said, and it was clear he wasn't happy.

Another of McGarvey's phone lines began to blink. "Call me if you come up with anything."

"It's been a long week, and it's going to get even longer," Rudolph said.

"That it is," McGarvey replied. He broke the connection and picked up on the second call. It was Rencke.

"How're Mrs. M. and Liz?"

"They're fine, they're safe for now," McGarvey said. "Are you calling from Archives?"

"I'm still here," Rencke said. He sounded odd, as if he were out of breath.

"You okay, Otto?"

"I've gone through your record, Mac. The whole enchilada, you know. And, oh boy, you've been busy. A whole group of people out there have to be seriously pissed at you. Know what I mean?"

"I get that impression now and then," McGarvey said. "Have you come up with something?"

"Maybe," Rencke said vaguely. "Can you come down here tonight?"

"What is it?"

"I need to pick your brain. The records are here, but they're not complete. Like something's missing. Like impressions, maybe memories. Can you come?"

"I'll be there in an hour," McGarvey said, and Rencke hung up.

CVN 73 George Washington

CINC Seventh Fleet Rear Adm. James Hamilton, who had assumed command of the primary carrier group, was on the bridge with the *George*

Washington's skipper, Captain David Merkler, when a signals man came in and handed the admiral a message flimsy.

"What is it?" Merkler asked.

Hamilton looked up. "The President wants to talk to me," he said. "We'll take it in my quarters."

"Maybe now we can start to get some answers that make sense." Merkler looked like a heavyweight boxer and in fact had boxed for the navy when he was at Annapolis. There wasn't a man in the navy who had ever entertained the notion of crossing him. Even smiling he looked dangerous, exactly the opposite of Hamilton, who was short, slender and intellectual. Together they made a formidable team.

"Don't count on it, Dave," Hamilton said, as they left the bridge together.

In the distant haze off the port side of the mammoth nuclear-powered Nimitz class aircraft carrier, they could just make out Cape Tappi on the Honshu headland at the western end of Tsugaru Strait that opened to the Sea of Japan. In a matter of hours his battle group would be out of the confining waters of the strait and into waters where they would have some maneuvering room. It wouldn't be too soon for Hamilton, whose primary love was the sea, not some confining office in Yokosuka or Washington.

The marine guard followed them, and at the admiral's quarters, opened the door for them and saluted smartly.

It took a couple of minutes for the call from the White House to go through, time enough for Merkler to pour them some coffee. Hamilton put the call on the speakerphone.

"Good evening, Mr. President," Hamilton said. It was ten-thirty in the morning here, which made it 8:30 P.M. in Washington. "I have Dave Merkler with me."

"Good morning, Admiral," President Lindsay said. "I'm glad to hear it because this is for both of you. How is everything going out there?"

"We'll be in the Sea of Japan in a few hours, and so far nobody seems to be taking any notice of us."

"I'm glad to hear that too. But the situation might not hold together much longer, and it'll be up to you to make sure nothing gets out of hand."

"I'm not sure I understand, Mr. President," Hamilton said exchanging a glance of puzzlement with Merkler. "Could you be a little more specific?"

"There've been some new developments between the Japanese and

Chinese navies that you need to be aware of," the President said. For the next fifteen minutes he went into detail about the destruction of the Chinese Han class submarine, the reactions of the Chinese and Japanese ambassadors, the continued buildup of naval resources off the North Korean coast and his warning to both governments to keep a one-hundred-mile zone of separation between their ships and North Korea.

"Good lord," Hamilton said. "Mr. President, are you ordering me to place my carrier groups down there to enforce the separation zone?"

"That's exactly what I want you to do, Jim," Lindsay said. "With all possible speed."

"What if someone takes exception to our presence?"

"I'm giving you the authority to defend yourself at all times. Someone shoots at you, shoot back."

"No, Mr. President, that's not what I mean," Hamilton said. "What do you want us to do if they simply ignore us? These are international waters, but considering what happened at Kimch'aek and Pyongyang's warnings, the Japanese would be fools not to maintain a strong presence down there. Add to that the probability that the Chinese have gotten themselves in the middle of it because Pyongyang has asked for their help, and they might just start shooting at each other in earnest. We could hardly blame them for something like that."

The President had never served in the military. He hesitated a moment. "If you place your ships between them I don't think they'll be foolish enough to start anything."

"Yes, Mr. President. But what do I do if someone makes a mistake?" Hamilton said. Getting a politician to make a straight statement was usually impossible, so the President's next order came as a surprise.

"Stop them with whatever force you think is necessary, Jim."

"I see," Hamilton said quietly. "Can I assume that Tom Logan knows the score?" Air Force General Thomas Logan was in charge of all U.S. forces on Okinawa.

"He does," the President said. "But I want you to be perfectly clear on our intent here, and that's to prevent an all-out shooting war between Japan and North Korea and whoever Pyongyang has as its ally."

"Yes, sir." Hamilton figured that no matter how this turned out, relations between the U.S. and Japan would never be the same again.

"I won't leave you to hang out to dry, Jim," the President said. "I'll have my orders sent to you in writing within the hour." That came as another complete and somewhat welcome surprise to Hamilton.

"I appreciate that, sir. We'll do the very best we can."

"I know you will. Good luck."

Fort A.P. Hill, Virginia

McGarvey parked in the visitor's lot and took the elevator eight hundred feet down to the main records storage level. He'd called ahead so that the night security people were expecting him, and they let him inside without delay. He passed through a pair of heavy steel doors, his DDO pass keying the electronic locks. Rencke was waiting with a golf cart, his long fuzzy hair even wilder and more out of control than usual.

"Oh boy, Mac, thanks for comin'," Otto gushed as McGarvey climbed into the cart beside him. They took off immediately from the central square down a long, broad avenue that led through the tall stacks for as far as they could see.

"Are you okay?" McGarvey said. Rencke looked like he hadn't slept in a week. His clothing was dirty and rumpled, and the laces were loose on one of his sneakers and missing on the other. He didn't smell so good either.

"No time for that now," Rencke said. "There's bad shit lying around all over the place down here." He shook his head in wonder. "It's like looking for a word in a dictionary; you get sidetracked to some really weird shit sometimes." Tears suddenly came to his eyes and he glanced at McGarvey. "Your folks were good people, Mac. Top shelf, the best, really the best. It was that bastard Baranov and Trotter who did it to them, 'cause they were afraid of you."

"You saw the records?"

Rencke's lips compressed, and he nodded. "But you don't want to see them. Not ever."

"You're probably right," McGarvey said. But he'd already seen them. "What have you come up with? Anything we can use right now?"

"I don't know. I've been through your record, and I've even come up with a list of names. People still alive, with the position and power to come after you if they wanted to. You're going to have to consider them, but as far as I can tell that angle's not going to wash. Some of them, like a couple of Tarankov's people and a few Mafia guys from Moscow, hate your guts. But killing you wouldn't do them any good, not if you consider the kinds of risks they would have to take and compare them with what they have to lose if they fail. And none of them is going to get in much trouble just because you're the new DDO. No real gain for them if you were taken out."

"Just revenge," McGarvey said.

Rencke glanced at him again. "That might be the point after all. Revenge. It's worse than hunger or lust."

McGarvey figured they must have gone a half a mile or more into the underground installation when Rencke turned left down a narrower side avenue. They passed four intersections, and then he turned right and stopped fifty feet later. A tall ladder on wheels was drawn up to a eighteen-foot-high section of shelves. Several plastic bins had been brought down and set on the floor. File folders and envelopes were strewn around the base of the ladder. The light back here was barely good enough to read by.

"Midseventies," Rencke said, hopping out of the golf cart. "Your first CIA duty station, Berlin. Remember?" He rummaged through the loose file folders, finally coming up with the one he wanted.

"That was a long time ago. I was just a kid."

"A trained CIA field officer in the badlands, that's what you were," Rencke said. He was beat, his mood brittle, but a look of pride had come into his tired expression. "All your FITREPS gave you the highest marks. Dean Fields, the chief of Berlin station, made no bones how he felt about you. In his books you were the tops." Rencke looked a little sly. "If you had one fault, according to him, you were too brash, too quick to pass judgment. 'Just like a tent revival preacher,' he wrote in one of your fitness reports."

McGarvey chuckled. "He was right."

Rencke handed him the thin file folder, which contained a brief, three-page incident/encounter sheet. Most of it was typewritten, but McGarvey recognized the handwritten notes as his own, although at first he couldn't recall the incident.

"Does that bring back anything?" Rencke asked.

"Just a minute," McGarvey said, and he quickly read through the report. It was early in the morning, New Year's Day 1979, a hundred yards west of Checkpoint Charlie, near the Philharmonic Hall and National Gallery. McGarvey had been on his way back to his apartment off Pots-dammerstrasse after a party, when he spotted a group of a half-dozen people trying to climb over the wall.

He parked in the shadows and trotted around back, thinking at first that he was seeing a group of East Germans trying to escape over the wall to the West. Instead, he walked into the middle of what one of them called a prank. They were Americans, graduate students and postdocs on Christmas break; all of them drunk, out looking for a little fun. An adventure.

It was starting to come back to McGarvey now; vague memories of how cold it was and how the kids looked guilty, foolish (and they knew it), stupid, ashamed and finally angry that someone their same age was putting a stop to their lark.

All of them were dressed in tattered blue jeans, sandals and wool socks, hair down around their shoulders, and McGarvey remembered being mad as hell at them. They were college students, probably rich, who were trying to look like hippies. They were fucked up in the head, he remembered telling them that. And one of them had responded that he should mind his own fucking business.

McGarvey had zeroed in on that kid, who was much older than the others and who seemed to be the leader, or at least their spokesman, and reamed him out. Told him that he had been seconds away from getting himself and his friends shot to death, and that if he hadn't learned anything better than that in college, maybe he should go back to his mother's lap so that he could have a few more years to grow up.

There'd been more words, and the kids were going to simply ignore him, when he flashed his gun and his CIA identification. It had been a stupid move on his part, he knew that now. But it had worked. The kids, pissed off, left. Now McGarvey vaguely remembered the look of embarrassment and hate on the one kid's face, but nothing more.

He looked up. "I remember it, but that's about all."

"You made an enemy, Mac," Rencke said.

"He was just a kid, and that was a long time ago. He'd have to be a complete idiot to still harbor a grudge."

Rencke shrugged, conceding the point. "Did you get their names?"

"Evidently not, or I would have mentioned it in my report."

"Do you remember any of them? I mean can you remember what they looked like?"

"Hippies. College kids with long hair. It was party time for them. Lot of that going on over there in those days. What's your point, Otto?"

"I've worked out all the major shit in your background, all the obviously bad guys who might still hold a grudge, and now I'm working on the little shit. This one sorta stuck out."

McGarvey shook his head. "I think we should stick with trying to find the Japanese connections."

"I'm doing that, Mac," Otto said, the vagueness back in his voice. "There's just something about this." He looked up. "If I came up with some photographs, do you think you could pick any of them out?"

"Maybe," McGarvey said. "When have you slept last?"

"I don't keep track," Rencke said. "I'll take you back to the elevators."

"Listen, Otto, maybe you should come back to Washington with me.

You can stay at my place or out at the safe house. We'll have some dinner, a couple of beers and you can get a few hours sleep."

Rencke gave him a long, penetrating look. "You gave me a job to do, Mac, and I'm doin' it, you know." He shifted his weight to his left foot and raised his right a couple of inches off the floor, as if he were an ostrich. "They came after Liz, and Mrs. M. We can't let that happen again, so you gotta let me keep looking here. Okay?"

McGarvey had to shake his head again. "It's your call."

"Oh, boy. Great." Rencke said, without much enthusiasm and he gave McGarvey a hug. "We'll get the bastards, Mac. It's not chartreuse anymore, but we'll get the bastards."

FIFTEEN

Washington

Fred Rudolph met the District of Columbia SAC Jack Hailey in the parking lot of the new International Trade Association building off Dupont Circle a few minutes after ten.

"Thanks for coming out tonight, Jack. May be nothing, but I figured you wanted to be kept in the loop."

"I appreciate it," Hailey said. "Had to be some kind of world record, getting a search warrant that fast."

"Judge Miller is one of the good guys who still thinks we're doing an okay job," Rudolph said. The fact that he and the federal judge were next-door neighbors and belonged to the same country club hadn't hurt either. Over the past few years they had developed a mutual trust and respect on and off the golf course that sometimes paid off, like tonight.

A half-dozen FBI agents in blue windbreakers had secured the front and rear entrances to the twelve-story building, and while a nervous night watchman made two calls, one to the building's manager and the other to the office manager of the Far East Trade Association, Dan Parks and twenty special agents had gone up to the top floor to open the offices and begin their preliminary search.

He came back down on the elevator and trotted over to where Rudolph and Hailey were waiting at the desk in the lobby. He was a short, heavyset man with dark curly hair who had been a computer programmer by trade until he had signed on with the Bureau's Special Investigations Division. He could sniff out a hidden computer cache a mile away.

"Okay, we're in," he said. "Do you want us to get started now, or should we wait until Far East sends someone over?"

"Anybody up there?"

"No. The place was locked up for the night."

"Find anything interesting?" Rudolph asked.

"Computers on both floors, but it looks as if they're all tied to the same mainframe on eleven. Some locked file cabinets in the mail room and a couple of the offices and a big wall safe in one of the front offices. We can peel the safe."

"Stick to the computers for now. I want to see what kind of a reaction we get from their people when they show up and we ask for the combination. We'll be up when they get here."

Parks smiled humorlessly. "If there's a connection to Croft or Lee, we'll find it." He turned and took the elevator back up.

"I'll wait down here, if you want to go up," Hailey said.

"Won't be necessary," Rudolph replied, spotting two men at the front doors. "Looks like the opposition is about to storm the gates."

He and Hailey went over and let them in. The older of the men was dressed in a tuxedo, the other in a pair of blue jeans and a short-sleeved Izod. Neither of them looked happy.

Rudolph showed them his FBI identification. "I assume that you gentlemen work for the Far East Trade Association?"

"That's right," the man in the tuxedo said indignantly. "I'm Calvin Wirtz, the association's legal counsel. What's going on here?"

"Who are you, sir?" Rudolph asked the other man.

"He's Christopher Antus, the association's office manager," the attorney spoke for him.

"Will your executive director, Sandy Patterson, be showing up tonight?"

"She's unavailable."

"Where is she?" Rudolph asked.

"Out of the city, but I couldn't tell you where," Wirtz said. "Now that I've answered your questions, tell me what you're doing here."

Rudolph handed him the search warrant. "The association's records will be subpoenaed in the morning, for now we're conducting a search of the offices."

Antus looked guiltily toward the elevators. "No," he said, starting forward, but Wirtz put out a hand to stop him.

"They're within their rights, Chris," the attorney said. He glared at Rudolph. "But all they can do tonight is look. We'll just see about the subpoena in the morning."

"There's a safe in one of the offices. Would either of you gentlemen know the combination?" Rudolph asked.

"No," Antus said, and Rudolph was sure he was lying.

"That's okay, we'll get it open," Hailey said. It was obvious he'd taken an instant dislike to both men.

"You'll be liable for damages," Wirtz warned. "But if you'll tell me what you're looking for, we might be able to speed this up tonight. I'm sure we can work something out with Sam Blair, something to everybody's satisfaction."

Rudolph smiled inwardly, though he let nothing show in his expression. Blair's name wasn't mentioned on the search warrant.

"We'll just have to look around upstairs. You're certainly welcome to observe."

"Damn right we will," the attorney said.

Antus stepped back. "These guys are probably going to be here all night," he told Wirtz. "I think I'll go home and leave it to you."

"I think not," Rudolph said sternly. "Jack, do you want to read Mr. Antus his rights?"

"What's this?" Wirtz exploded.

"A criminal investigation, counselor," Hailey said. "You don't think we'd stay up all night for anything else, do you?"

Morningside, Maryland

They'd spread the topographic maps and aerial photographs of the Cropley safe house on a conference table on the main floor of the warehouse. Kondo, Kajiyama and their six commandos were gathered around the table shortly before midnight. It was to be their final briefing before the operation.

"I count at least eight warm bodies hidden in the trees," Kondo said.

He marked their exact locations on the map. "But there are probably more men on the grounds as well as in the house."

"They're taking security seriously," Kajiyama said dryly.

Kondo nodded in agreement. "But that's their biggest weakness." He drew sight lines from each man the special film had registered hidden in the woods—all of the lines converged on the driveway in front and toward a foot path at the rear of the property. They're watching for an attack from the ground. Not the air."

Kajiyama stabbed a delicate finger at the driveway. "The road is probably targeted. Video cameras perhaps. Tire shredders, maybe explosives."

"That makes sense," Kondo said. "The same for the path." He drew red arrows on two narrow openings on the east side of the property and one on the west, the woods between the clearings and the house.

"If there's any wind above eight or ten knots, making such a precise landing would be risky," one of the commandos pointed out. "If we miss and come in on top of them, our element of surprise will be gone."

The weather forecast is for calm to light winds from the southeast," Kondo said. "If the forecast is wrong, we'll delay the drop."

The others around the table nodded. Kondo had handpicked them all. Their courage was unquestionable, but like most professionals in the business, they were cautious, not foolhardy. They were willing to take risks, but not unnecessary chances.

"For the moment we can assume that they have double the men I was able to photograph," Kondo continued. "Three-quarters of their force outside, the remainder in the house. After the drop, the most critical phase will be taking down the outside guards in absolute silence, and quickly. They'll have radios, of course, but we can count on a ten-second threshold of delay. After that point, if someone doesn't answer their radio someone will be sent to investigate. That means we hit them all at once. One click on your comms unit means you're in position to take out one guard. Two clicks and you can take out two. When everyone is in position, you'll receive a tone in your headsets which means strike. One click and you've taken out your man, two and you've taken out the second. A tone and you're in trouble."

Kondo looked around the table at their faces to make certain each of them understood the orders.

"If anything goes wrong, you'll receive the warble tone and we'll rendezvous here." Kondo circled the helicopter's evacuation point a few meters from the highway. He looked up again, a stern expression in his eyes. "You will not carry out the wounded, nor will you leave anyone alive."

It was a hard world, Kondo thought. They would carry no identification, nor would their dental records, fingerprints or descriptions be accessible by anyone from the West. The mission was of primary importance, the commandos expendable. They understood this, and there were no objections now.

"We will take the house in the second phase," he continued. "Since no electrical or telephone lines show up on the photographs we can assume they are buried. We can also assume that once the people in the house realize they are under attack, they will call for help. I'm giving us a five-minute operational window. We'll divide our team in two units, one for the front, the other for the back. Blow the doors, kill the guards inside and kill McGarvey, if he's there. If not we take his wife and daughter and rendezvous here." He circled the helicopter's primary pickup point on the parking area directly in front of the house.

"Mr. Kondo," Sandy Patterson called from the corridor to the offices upstairs.

He turned around. She looked as if she had seen a ghost.

"Could you come upstairs?" she asked.

Kondo nodded tightly and turned back to Kajiyama. "Finish the briefing," he said, and he went upstairs to where the woman had gone back into the office.

She stood at the desk, her cell phone lying by her open purse. She was visibly trembling, and her complexion was very pale.

"What has happened?" Kondo asked.

She looked up, as if seeing him for the first time. "My sister called. The FBI has raided my office."

"When?" Kondo demanded.

"Right now—they're still there. Tina's travel agency is on the ground floor, and she was working late, so she saw them coming in and she checked on it. There's a federal warrant for my arrest."

"Okay, take it easy. Is there anything in your offices that could lead them here?"

Sandy Patterson was shaking her head. "No, nothing. They're probably after our financial records. And if they can break the encryption codes in our computers, they'll find out about Mr. Lee." Her eyes were wide. "But that's not all. They know about you."

"You said there were no records tying you to me," Kondo said, wanting to lash out at the stupid woman, break her neck, but he held his temper in check.

"Judith called right after my sister."

"The whore?"

Sandy Patterson nodded. "She said she was going to tell the FBI that

Tony Croft was murdered. She said she took your picture in front of the Hay Adams. She wanted to know if she was doing the right thing, and she didn't know who else to talk to."

"What did you tell her?"

"She said that she was calling from a pay phone in the Grand Hyatt, so I told her to stay there and not to call anyone, and I'd send someone over to take care of everything." Sandy Patterson shook her head again, as if she couldn't believe that this was happening. "I didn't know what else to say."

"Does she know about this place?" Kondo asked.

"No."

"Does anyone else know about it or about your connection here?"

"No. I rented the building through a triple blind. There's no way that anyone could trace it back to me. Not in a million years. It'd be impossible."

"Then nothing has changed," Kondo said. "This operation will continue as planned."

"What about Judith?"

Kondo looked at the woman with a mixture of anger and disgust. She had served them well to this point, but Lee would understand perfectly well when Kondo told him that she was dead. "There's nothing she can tell the FBI that would hurt us. Tony Croft killed himself and by now the FBI knows it. Besides, she could not know my real name unless Croft told her."

"What about me, then?"

"Your work here is finished, so you'll have to come with us." Kondo smiled. "I'm quite certain that Mr. Lee will give you everything that you deserve."

Sandy Patterson looked like she was on the verge of collapse. But it was obvious that she understood she had no other options.

"Naturally you'll have to stay here until we're finished, and then you'll be getting out of the country with us," Kondo said. "We'll talk later, after I finish the briefing, and figure out what role you can play for Mr. Lee."

Fort A.P. Hill, Virginia

Otto Rencke untied a bundle of file folders that he had secured with one of his shoelaces and spread the documents on the map table. After McGarvey left he had entered the photographs of the students at the

Berlin Wall into a computer recognition program that from time to time spit out a possible match.

Within the first ten minutes he'd come up with a name so surprising that it took even his breath away, and he'd returned for the Berlin station's annual summaries for 1978, '79 and '80, searching for further possible references to the incident Mac had been involved with, or with repercussions because of it. If Mac was right and the kids were graduate students and postdocs, their egos would have demanded that they do something in retaliation. Vietnam was the major issue, and the CIA was the enemy. But nothing of any consequence was showing up except for the one name.

The computer was giving a 58 percent probability that the photograph and name were a match and asked for more photographs or further data. But there was nothing else in the Berlin files. Apparently it had been an isolated incident.

Rencke stared at the photograph and the name for several minutes, his thoughts lost in a maze of floating, flowing, blending colors. Years ago he'd been trying to devise a series of tensor calculus transformations involving complex bubble memory systems. He'd hit on the question of how to explain color to a blind person. With mathematics, so sweetly elegant that even a person who could not even begin to understand the notion of color could "see." If it worked one way, he figured there was no reason it shouldn't work in the opposite direction. Since then, whenever he had to deal with something complex, he thought in colors. Lavender this time.

He slid over to his computer, brought up an outside line and within seconds was in the mainframe computer system for the United States Senate.

Seawolf

It was 0530 GMT and Captain Harding couldn't sleep. He was hunched over one of the plotting tables in the control room studying their track. They were five miles behind the Japanese submarine *Natsushio*, which was continuing southwest, its projected course taking it through the eastern channel of the Korean Strait south of Tsu Island. The last message they'd received from CINCPAC confirmed that the Chinese fleet of six surface ships and two submarines were headed into the Sea of Japan through the western channel. It didn't seem likely that the *Natsushio* was trying to make an end run on the fleet. It could not match their speed, so it would never be able to catch up. CINCPAC thought that it was possible the MSDF sub was heading to Tokyo, but that didn't make any sense to Harding either.

"You're supposed to be getting some sleep, Captain," Rod Paradise said at his shoulder.

Harding looked up. "I'm trying to figure out what this guy's up to. He kills a Chinese submarine, then bugs out like he's getting ready to attack the entire fleet. But he's not going to do that."

"You don't think he's going to Tokyo?"

Harding shook his head. "With the Seventh gone, Yokosuka is theirs. Nothing left in Tokyo Bay to challenge them, so why bring in another submarine when all the action is on this side?"

Paradise studied the chart. "Nothing else makes any sense." He looked up. "Of course he could be heading up the Korean coast. Maybe stand off Chungsan. Pyongyang is only thirty miles inland. If something did start up, they'd be in a good position to strike back."

"That's a cheery thought," Harding said. "But it'll be another twenty-four hours before he has to start his turn. North to Pyongyang or south toward who knows?" Harding picked up his coffee cup. "How's it looking behind us?"

"So far so good," Paradise said. "We've been stopping to clear our baffles every six hours."

"Make it every two hours, Rod," Harding said. "It'll slow us down, but we won't lose the *Natsushio*, and I want to make damned sure that no one is sneaking up on us."

Washington

Rudolph watched as the contents of the safe were laid out on a conference table. It was better than he expected. In addition to reams of documents, they'd found more than one hundred thousand dollars in small bills, in bundles of a thousand dollars each. Some of the bundles were actually marked with names, almost all of them U.S. senators and representatives, others marked simply The White House. Antus had become increasingly nervous, but the Far East Trade Association's attorney Calvin Wirtz maintained his composure. Rudolph figured he would have an answer for everything they were finding, but whether or not it would hold up in a court of law was another matter. From what they'd already seen—and this was just the preliminary search—he had a feeling that Sam Blair was going to be one happy camper. This would almost certainly end up another media field day when it came out, because already Dan Parks and his people were coming up with connections not only to Joseph Lee, but to Tony Croft as well. It was a bonanza.

Parks looked up from the counting and shot him a grin. It didn't do much for Antus, who looked as if he was ready to bolt at any moment. But Hailey stood next to him waiting for exactly such a move.

Rudolph's cell phone chirped, and he stepped out into the corridor to answer it. "Rudolph."

"Sir, this is George Keane, night duty officer. I'm holding an urgent call for you. It's a young woman who says she talked to you earlier about the Croft investigation."

"Do you have a trace on it?"

"She's calling from a pay phone in front of the convention center on H Street."

"All right, patch me over and then roll whoever's available. I want her picked up."

"Yes, sir."

The call was switched. "This is Fred Rudolph."

"I called you before," an obviously distraught woman said. "I'm ready to talk to you now. I need your help. I think."

Jack Hailey came out of the conference room, and Rudolph held up a hand for him to stay.

"We'd very much like to help you. Can you tell me your name?"

Rudolph could hear traffic noises from the other end. He put a hand over the pickup. "Handle the situation here, Jack. Something's come up. I've got to go."

"Not yet," the woman said. "They killed Tony Croft and I think maybe Sandy knows something about it."

That got Rudolph's attention. "Sandy who?" he asked, cautiously, as he sprinted down the corridor to the elevators. "Can you tell me at least that much?"

The woman hesitated. "Sandy Patterson. She was the one who got me together with Tony."

Rudolph could scarcely believe his luck, and he had to work hard to keep his voice calm. The elevator came and he took it.

"Have you talked to her tonight?"

"A little while ago. She told me to stay put and she'd come get me. But I don't know."

"Are you still there, where you called her from?"

"No. I'm across the street."

"Where was she when you called her?"

"I don't know. I used her cell phone number. She could be anywhere. Home, maybe. Or at work. I don't know."

"There isn't much I can do for you unless I know who you are? Can you tell me that?"

The woman hesitated again.

The elevator reached the ground floor and Rudolph raced across the lobby.

"My name is Judith Kline."

"Okay, Judith, if you're somewhere in the city I can reach you in a few minutes."

"I took pictures. I got one of the guy Tony met with. He was coming out of the hotel right after Tony died, and he was carrying something. Looked like a big manila envelope."

"Was it the Chinese gentleman you told me about?" Rudolph got his car started, shot out of the parking lot and headed down Massachusetts Avenue, traffic still heavy despite the fact it was after midnight.

"Yeah, same guy," Judith Kline said. "I don't want to turn out like everybody else in this town. I can't handle that."

"What do you mean?" Rudolph asked. He needed to keep her on the line and calm until his people got to her.

"Tony kept talking about the White House. But he was weird about it. Didn't make any sense."

"What didn't make any sense, Judith?" Rudolph asked. He could hear sirens in the distance, and for a moment he couldn't tell if he was hearing them through his open car window or over the phone. He decided he was hearing the sirens on the phone. "Did he talk about his job? About the President?"

Judith Kline heard the sirens too, and she was distracted. She said something that Rudolph couldn't quite make out.

"Judith?" Rudolph said.

"He kept saying it wasn't *that* White House."

"I don't understand." The sirens were a lot closer now, and Rudolph, who was only a few blocks from the convention center, was hearing them through his open window too. If there hadn't been any on-duty agents to send, Keane might have asked Metro police to pick her up.

"You traced my call!" she cried. "You sent the fucking cops."

"Judith!" Rudolph shouted. "Listen to me. I want to help you."

The sirens were much louder now, and the closer to the convention center he got, the heavier traffic became.

"Judith!" Rudolph shouted again, but she was gone.

They were going to lose her, and it was his fault because he had not explained the situation to Keane. Stupid.

He was about to toss his cell phone down when he heard a woman scream, the squeal of tires and a second later a horrific thump and the crash of breaking glass, then more sirens.

National Reconnaissance Office

Louise Horn was operating on cigarettes, coffee and adrenaline when Major Wight called her a few minutes after 2:30 A.M. He sounded excited.

"Anything new on *Natsushio?*"

"Nothing in the past four hours," she said.

"I have a new course line for you. That burst transmission from the sub has finally been decrypted and translated. Submarine Flotilla Headquarters Yokosuka has ordered her to make best possible speed for Tanegashima Island."

"The space center?" Louise asked, surprised.

"They have a launch coming up in a couple of days, and I'm told it's SOP to station a couple of MSDF ships just offshore for rescue operations."

"But a submarine?" Louise asked in wonder. *"That* submarine?"

"We're going to need confirmation ASAP, so I want as many people as you can spare on it. If the *Natsushio* shows up anywhere along that track it'll be to communicate with Yokosuka. I want to know about it."

"What's going on, Bert?"

"Wish the hell I knew. But it's starting to get interesting out there."

"That it is."

Langley, Virginia

McGarvey met Fred Rudolph at a roadside café just off the George Washington Parkway near CIA Headquarters at 7:30 A.M. When Rudolph called he'd been mysterious, except that the meeting couldn't wait and he preferred that it be held on neutral ground. The place was busy and therefore anonymous.

"This is getting completely out of hand, and I'm going to have to make some tough decisions today," Rudolph said. It was obvious he hadn't slept last night. His suit was rumpled, and his eyes were red. He looked done in.

"How'd the raid on Far East's offices go?" McGarvey asked. "Did you find something?"

Rudolph laughed, and glanced at the four men in the booth across from them. "Joseph Lee was funneling money not only to the White House, but to nine senators and twice that many representatives. We found cash, payment records and lobby points. We're still working on that, but on the surface it looks as if Lee was representing the Japanese. Specifically the Ministry for International Trade and Industry." MITI was as close to a Japanese central intelligence agency or intelligence clearing-house as any governmental bureau in Tokyo. Their stated goal was the domination by Japanese business, and therefore political interests, in the eastern hemisphere.

The fact wasn't surprising to McGarvey, only the extent of it. "Have you turned that over to Sam Blair yet?"

Rudolph shook his head. "That's one of the decisions I have to make. Because once I do, it'll leak to the media and all hell will break loose. After everything else that's happened, Congress will almost certainly start impeachment hearings." He rubbed his eyes. "Christ, what a mess."

"Did you pick up Sandy Patterson?"

"We have a warrant for her arrest, but she's disappeared, and that's not the half of it. Apparently she was the one who introduced Tony Croft to the call girl. Her name is—or was—Judith Kline. She's dead. Run over by a taxi in front of the convention center last night." Rudolph looked beseechingly at McGarvey. "I had her on the phone, and she panicked. An accident."

"She's the one who told you that Croft was murdered?"

Rudolph nodded. "The ME says he killed himself, no doubt about it. But the woman took some photographs of a man she saw meeting with Croft. Right after Tony killed himself, she said she saw this guy coming out of the Hay Adams in a big hurry, carrying what looked like a manila envelope. And it's a break, if you want to call it that. We got the film from her purse and developed it. He was registered at the Hay Adams under the name Thomas Wang. His real name is Bruce Kondo, and he works for Lee."

McGarvey sat back. All the pieces were starting to come together. Trouble was he had no idea what it all meant or where it was leading.

Rudolph read something of that from his face. "What the hell is going on?"

"Lee is buying influence for the Japanese, and Tony Croft was giving them information," McGarvey said. "That part's easy. Question is, why'd they come after me, and why'd Croft pick this time to kill himself? Did the woman say anything else?"

"Nothing that makes any sense, except that Tony Croft was worried enough about what he was doing that he kept mentioning to her something about the White House. But she said he told her that he wasn't talking about *that* White House, whatever the hell that means."

"The cabby who hit her comes up clean?"

"Yeah. It was an accident. She was there in front of him, and he couldn't do a thing about it."

"Anything else on the film?"

"Nothing that means anything, unless she was planning on blackmailing Croft."

"What about Far East's records?"

"We're just starting to sift through it all. Dan Parks and his people are still hauling stuff out of there. But it's going to take weeks before we're through it all. In the meantime what am I supposed to do?"

"Your job, Fred. You're a cop investigating a crime."

Rudolph nodded. "Dr. Pierone said the President wants to be kept informed."

"I'll bet he does," McGarvey said, but his mind was elsewhere, spinning out connections between what was happening here in Washington to what was going on in the Sea of Japan. Something, some link between the two, was tickling the edges of his consciousness. Anomalies. The one fact that didn't seem to belong. But he wasn't quite seeing it yet.

"How is your daughter doing?" Rudolph asked, breaking McGarvey out of his thoughts.

"She's on the mend, thanks," McGarvey said. "Have you found out who put the safe house on the Web?"

"That's like looking for a needle in a haystack. But Croft had a lot of friends in the Bureau, so if you want to carry a dark thought in that direction, it could be one of them. We're still checking."

McGarvey dropped back into his thoughts.

"Whatever it is, it's going to happen soon, isn't it," Rudolph said.

McGarvey looked up, another piece of the puzzle suddenly falling into place. "That's it."

"What is?"

"They have a time table," McGarvey said. "All we have to do is find it."

SIXTEEN

Morningside, Maryland

Kondo checked the plain gray government vans to make sure that nothing was missing. They'd brought them inside with Sandy Patterson's blue Toyota van and loaded them last night. Then everyone had spent the night resting. After this operation there would be others, of course, but nothing would ever have the same urgency and flavor as this, because Japan would no longer have to hang her head in shame for something that had happened more than a half-century ago. India with her large navy and nuclear arsenal, China with her vast population and even ridiculous North Korea with her nuclear weapons, the triggers of which were held by a rabid madman, would no longer threaten the home islands. Japan would, at long last, take her rightful place in the eastern hemisphere, and no power on earth could resist her. It was a heady feeling. Melodramatic, but it had symmetry. The U.S. would be the dominant superpower in the West, and Nippon the new superpower in the East. Nothing on earth could stop them now.

This morning the team was in a subdued mood as they checked and rechecked their weapons, night-vision oculars, radios and other equipment.

Kajiyama came back from the front of the warehouse. He was dressed, as the others were, in street clothes. They wouldn't change into their all-black uniforms until nightfall and time for deployment. "It's ten o'clock. Time to head out."

"Is everybody ready?"

"*Hai*," Kajiyama said. His mood was bright, full of nervous energy. He glanced up toward the offices on the second floor. "What about the woman?"

Kondo followed his gaze. "Has she made all the final arrangements?"

"So far as I know, she has."

"I'll check with her."

Kajiyama looked at him. "And then what, Kondo-san?"

"Get the men aboard the vans and pick up the boat at Riverview. We'll rendezvous up river at Barton at five."

"Is she coming with us, or with you?"

"Neither," Kondo said.

"Kill her now," Kajiyama said simply, and he went to gather the men as Kondo went upstairs.

Sandy Patterson was watching CNN on a small television in the manager's office, where she'd slept last night. She switched the set off and looked up guiltily.

"Was there anything about you or the Far East Trade Association?" Kondo asked.

"No," she said, shaking her head. She looked like she was on the verge of cracking up. There were splotches of color on her forehead and high cheeks, and her lower lip quivered.

"Did you call this morning to make certain the boat is ready for us?" he asked calmly, gentling her like a trainer might do with a skittish horse.

"Yes, you have the slip number."

"The helicopter pilot has his instructions?"

She nodded.

"The Bonanza pilot is ready for another sight-seeing tour?"

"He's waiting for you at Woodmore."

"Did you tell him that you would be coming along for the ride, the same as last time?"

Her eyes narrowed in surprise. "No. You told me that it'd be best if I stayed here until . . . afterward."

"Very good," Kondo said.

Cropley, Maryland

Rudolph's speculation that whatever was going to happen would happen soon bothered McGarvey. Back at his office he started work on the daily intelligence report that Murphy would use to brief the President later in the day, but he couldn't keep his mind on the paperwork. He told his secretary that he would be gone for a couple of hours and drove out to the safe house, calling ahead so that Isaacson's people would be expecting him.

Nothing had changed out here. The weather remained beautiful, and the house and grounds looked like a summer camp or health spa. Idyllic, calm, peaceful. But he couldn't shake the dark cloud that seemed to hang over him. It was a sixth sense of impending disaster that an Agency psychologist had once explained was nothing more than a highly developed and finely tuned subconscious awareness of everything and everybody around him.

He parked his Nissan Pathfinder in front, and like before an armed guard appeared from around the corner of the house.

"I won't be long, so don't bother putting it in the garage," McGarvey told him.

The guard waved, then said something into a lapel mike and went back around the corner.

Paul Isaacson and Todd Van Buren were in the dining room operations center having a cup of coffee when McGarvey came in.

"How's it going this morning?" he asked.

"Quiet," Isaacson said. "How about you? Anything new?"

McGarvey cocked his head to listen to the sounds of the house. Music was playing somewhere, and he thought he could hear someone talking in the kitchen. Normal sounds. Nothing out of the ordinary, but he was spooked. Someone was walking over his grave.

"Nothing that makes any sense," he said distantly.

"But you've got the feeling."

McGarvey laid a copy of the photograph Rudolph had given him on the table. "His name is Bruce Kondo, and he's here in Washington."

Isaacson studied the picture and handed it to Van Buren. "Do we have anything on him?"

"He works for Joseph Lee, we've got that much. And it looks like Lee is working for MITI. But if he's the same guy we have in our files, he was involved in the Yokosuka riots a couple of years ago, working for the same group that I came up against."

"It's a revenge thing?"

McGarvey shrugged. "Unknown. There were no photographs in our files, and the Bureau doesn't have much on him either."

"But they could have sent him after you," Isaacson pressed.

"It's possible," McGarvey conceded. "But if it's the same guy, he was involved in Tony Croft's death. So we're looking for some kind of connection."

"Is this guy any good?" Van Buren asked.

"Another unknown." McGarvey shook himself out of his funk "I just came out to see how Katy and Liz were doing, and to tell you to keep on your toes, because I think if something's going to happen, it'll go down pretty soon. Maybe in the next twenty-four to forty-eight hours."

Isaacson had been studying him. "You're worried."

They went back together long enough that McGarvey wasn't offended by the observation. "The Georgetown bomb was overkill. And if Kondo somehow drove Croft to suicide, he has finesse."

"Quite a combination."

"That it is," McGarvey said. "Are they upstairs?"

"Yes, sir," Van Buren said. "They went up to get ready for lunch. Will you be staying?"

"I have to get back," McGarvey said. "I'll see how they're doing then get out of your hair."

Isaacson got up and went out into the stairhall with him. "They're as safe here as they would be anywhere else."

It wasn't very comforting, but McGarvey nodded. "I know," he said. He went upstairs, knocked once and went in.

Kathleen, her hands on her hips, stood in the middle of the sitting room watching Elizabeth, who'd opened the window and was trying to pry open the latch that held the security shutter in place. The shutters on all the windows had been closed last night.

"Are you trying to escape?" McGarvey asked.

"They're treating us like prisoners," Elizabeth snapped crossly, a table knife on the latch. She grinned sheepishly. "Hi, Daddy." She put the knife down, came over and gave her father a hug.

"If Paul wants the place buttoned up, leave it be, will you?"

Elizabeth nodded.

McGarvey gave Kathleen a hug. Dressed in a cream-colored skirt, matching blouse and flats, she looked as if she'd stepped out of the pages of *Vogue*.

"You look tired," she said.

"I'm not an administrator, and if it wasn't for some good people out there I'd go crazy," McGarvey said, trying to keep it light, but it was obvious Katy saw through him.

She gave him a questioning look. "Are you okay?"

McGarvey hadn't been quite sure what he was going to say to them, but he decided that no matter how bad the truth was, it was better than a lie. He'd been telling them lies for too long a time.

"I don't think the situation will last much longer," he said to both of them. A look of concern crossed Kathleen's face, but Liz lit up.

"Good," she said viciously. "I want to get it over with."

"What is it, Kirk?" Katy asked.

"I don't know. Maybe nothing, but I've got a feeling that whatever they've planned is going to happen within the next day or two, so I want both of you to keep your heads down and listen to what Paul tells you." McGarvey motioned to the window. "That means no screwing around with the security measures."

Kathleen studied his face. "Are you going to be all right, Kirk?"

"If I don't have to worry about you two."

"I'll behave," Elizabeth promised.

On the way back to Langley, McGarvey's cell phone chirped. It was Rencke and he sounded completely strung out.

"Oh, boy, Mac, you gotta get down here right now!"

"Have you found something?"

"The whole enchilada. Or at least the first course, and it's a pisser!"

"I'm on my way."

"Mac?" Rencke said, his tone suddenly guarded.

"Yeah?"

"Watch yourself. Really watch yourself this time."

In the Air Above
Cropley, Maryland

On the second pass, McGarvey's gray Nissan SUV was gone, and at first Kondo thought that it had been put in the garage. But then he spotted it on the river road heading south toward Interstate 495.

"I've seen enough," he told the Capital City Aviation pilot. "We can head back to Woodmore now."

"Did you want to try the other side of the city, sir?"

"Next week," Kondo said pleasantly.

McGarvey had come out to check on his wife and daughter this morning, which might mean he would be back this evening. It would be perfect, because they could make a clean kill and get out of the country without having to do a kidnapping, which was always more risky than an assassination. But they were running out of time and options, and McGarvey had to be stopped. Once they had the women, they would lure McGarvey to an isolated spot and kill them all. Not elegant, but it would work.

Catching a last glimpse of the safe house as the pilot banked to the southeast, he was bothered that the security team down there had shuttered all the windows in the house. That fact, along with McGarvey's visit this morning, meant they were expecting trouble. Had there been a leak from Sandy Patterson's office, he wondered? If so, it was too late now to find out. And too late to change their plans.

The operation would happen tonight, and Kondo found that he was truly looking forward to the challenge. He'd read McGarvey's file and was struck by the obvious exaggerations in it. No man, he decided, could be that good.

Fort A.P. Hill, Virginia

Weekday traffic was a bitch on I-95, so it was after 2:00 P.M. by the time McGarvey reached the CIA's Central Archives on the military reservation. The small parking lot in front of the two-story concrete block administration building was full, and security procedures were tougher than they were at night. But he was the DDO and was admitted to the elevators without delay, reaching the main floor of the storage vault eight hundred feet underground a few minutes later.

Rencke was not waiting for him this time, so after he signed in, a nervous air force staff sergeant drove him back to the map room.

"Sir, my supervisor, Captain Parker, asked if you could have a word with Mr. Rencke."

"Has he made a mess of the files?"

"Yes, sir, but that's not the problem. He's pretty well locked down our mainframe. We have work to do here, but he's somehow restricted our access to the system."

"I'll talk to him," McGarvey promised. "But he's just about done with his project. And it's top priority right now."

"Yes, sir," the sergeant said.

Rencke, his sneakers off, lay flat on his back on top of the files, computer printouts and photographs strewn on the long map table. His arms were crossed on his chest, and his eyes were open, staring up at the fluorescent lights and acoustical tile ceiling. For a split second McGarvey thought he was dead, but then Rencke turned his head.

"Mac," he croaked, his voice harsh, as if he had a bad cold.

"Are you okay?"

Rencke shook his head. "No." He sat up, crossed his legs and ran his fingers through his totally out-of-control hair. He shook his head again. "And neither are you . . . going to be okay, you know. It's lavender. Oh, boy, really deep shit lavender, you know?"

McGarvey made his decision. "Come on, I'm getting you out of here. You look like shit, and you need a shower, something decent to eat and some sleep."

"Now that I've finally hit pay dirt you want to fire me?"

McGarvey took him by the arm and helped him down off the table. "You can tell me on the way back to my apartment. Now what the hell did you do with your shoes?"

"No, Mac, it's not done," Rencke cried desperately, clutching at McGarvey. "This is big shit, the biggest, you know. None of us is safe now. Pandora's box. Open it and all the shit is going to come out. Except hope. That's it, hope."

McGarvey had never seen him so agitated, so strung out, even frightened. "In English, Otto, I'm not following you."

"Well, follow this," he started viciously. "You're not going to be safe in your ivory tower at Langley, nor are Mrs. M. and Liz no matter where you stash them. I don't even think I could run and hide this time even if I wanted to."

"What are you talking about?"

Rencke pushed McGarvey aside and rummaged through the files on the table, coming up with a photograph of a young man, possibly in his midtwenties, wearing a tattered Oxford sweatshirt. His hair was down around his shoulders, and he wore a full beard.

"Recognize him?" Rencke asked.

The eyes were familiar, but McGarvey couldn't place him. He shook his head.

"He was the kid you pulled off the wall in Berlin. The one who was so pissed off."

"Who is he?"

"Wait," Rencke said. He found a thick bundle of files, brought them around to where McGarvey stood and slapped them down on the table. "Santiago, Chile. Remember that operation? All here in living black and white." His lips twisted into a snarl. "Correction, Kemosabe, *almost* all here."

McGarvey didn't have to look through the records. Santiago had been his last official assignment for the CIA. He'd been sent to the Chilean capital to assassinate a general who'd been responsible for the deaths of hundreds, if not thousands of people. It was the last of the Carter days in which the Agency had its guts torn out by an idealistic President who saw evil lurking everywhere.

The assassination had been called off. It wasn't in the national interests. But it had been too late to reach McGarvey because by then he'd already gone to ground in Santiago, and three days later he had taken the general out. When he returned home, the Agency fired him and Kathleen had kicked him out.

Bad times, he thought, reliving those years in his mind. He'd run to Switzerland, where he'd hidden until the Company came to him for the first of several freelance assignments, but by then he'd lost everything that was dear to him.

"You remember it?" Rencke pressed.

"Yes I do."

"The Senate Subcommittee on Central Intelligence had oversight duties in those days. The administration could fart in the wind all it wanted to, but the subcommittee held the real power. It was the committee who axed the hit, and it was the committee that—" Rencke picked up a document. "And I'm quoting now: 'It will be the committee's responsibility to advise the director of Central Intelligence on all matters before it.'" Rencke looked up. "'In a timely manner.'"

"I'd already gone deep by then."

"Wrong answer, recruit," Rencke said. "The decision to call you off was made two days before you made your final call to the Santiago COS." Rencke's eyes were bright. "Somebody dragged their feet until they knew for certain that you would be unreachable."

"Darby Yarnell," McGarvey said.

"He was one of the senators on the committee. The one you thought screwed you. But he wasn't given the assignment to notify Langley. It was someone else. A junior senator. And I'll give you three guesses who it was, but the first two don't count."

McGarvey glanced at the picture of the young man with the Oxford sweatshirt. "Him?"

"Bingo," Rencke hooted. "One and the same. Rhodes scholar in those days. Came home, went into politics in a big way. Oklahoma state representative, U.S. representative, then U.S. senator."

McGarvey supposed he'd somehow known in the back of his mind since after Georgetown. It was one of the reasons for his increasing unease. "You have to believe in something," his father had told him. "Or else you'll have nothing, you'll never get anywhere and you'll never be anything."

He shook his head. "No guessing, Otto."

Rencke pulled out another file folder, slapped it on top of the Santiago file and opened it to an eight-by-ten glossy photograph.

"Shit," McGarvey said softly, still wanting to deny what he finally knew the truth to be. "Revenge? All those years since Germany, and he went that far just to get back at me?"

"Okay, so maybe he was manipulated into it," Rencke said, though it was clear he didn't buy that theory. "But records wouldn't show anything like that. And most of the guys on the subcommittee are either dead or doddering old idiots somewhere." He glanced at the photograph. "Our guy was the junior member on the committee. One of the youngest senators ever to be elected."

"No."

"You'd better believe it, Mac, or else come up with another plausible explanation, because your life depends on what you do next. So do the lives of Mrs. M. and Liz."

"Is that why you've locked down the mainframe here?" McGarvey asked. "You didn't want anyone to know?"

Rencke nodded diffidently. "The President of the United States, James Lindsay, has sold us out to the Japanese—for political expediency to keep the peace out there, or for whatever reason—with help from Joseph Lee, who funneled money into the White House through the Far East Trade Association, and with the help of Tony Croft, his adviser on foreign affairs, who passed information back to Lee and therefore the Japanese. At the very least he's a traitor—"

"A fool," McGarvey broke in. "Not a traitor."

Rencke inclined his head. "A fool, then. And a murderer."

"The White House went along with my appointment," McGarvey said, trying to find fault with Rencke's insane conclusions.

"He was damned if he supported you and damned if he didn't," Rencke said. "Think it out, Mac. Murphy put you up for the job. If the White House hadn't gone along with it, questions would have been asked. And someone might have discovered what I did. But if he did get behind your nomination, he had to know that you might go looking." Rencke shrugged. "So they tried to kill you."

"Not Lindsay."

"Maybe not him. But Croft knew the score, and he passed the concern over to Joseph Lee. It was probably one of the reasons Croft killed himself. He knew that once this all came out he'd be the one left holding the bag. And I'm sure that Lee's people made that perfectly clear."

"Have you been in the FBI's system?"

"From the start, so I know all about Judith Kline and Bruce Kondo and Sandy Patterson. The only thing I haven't nailed down yet is who it is over there leaking shit onto their public access Website. But I've got the list narrowed down to a half-dozen guys, all of them Tony Croft's pals."

"Why?" McGarvey said.

"It has something to do with the Japanese, that's a pretty safe assumption," Rencke said. "And it takes no leap of faith to figure out the nuclear explosion at Kimch'aek means something. A lot of other people think so too, because Lindsay has sent the Seventh Fleet into the fray."

McGarvey looked at him with a mixture of pride and pity. Rencke was too smart for normal society. He saw things differently than everyone else. Left on his own he would eventually self-destruct, and that would be a terrible waste of a very good man.

"You don't do anything by halves," McGarvey said.

Rencke grinned. "I never thought you wanted me to."

"Let's find your shoes, then clean up this mess. You're coming back to Langley with me. For the time being you're going to bunk out there."

Rencke clutched McGarvey's sleeve. "Something else is going on, Mac. Something very big. Deeper than lavender." He shook his head. "I just can't see it yet." He was frustrated.

"We'll work it out together, my friend. You and me. One step at a time."

Otto's grin spread into a smile, and he hopped from one foot to the other. "Oh, boy."

Cropley, Maryland

"What the hell are you doing out here?" Todd Van Buren said.

Elizabeth, who had been going stir crazy, had slipped out to the front veranda to have a cigarette while no one was looking. She didn't bother turning. "Smoking, what does it look like?"

"Well, you're coming back inside."

"When I'm finished."

"Now," Van Buren insisted.

Elizabeth turned languidly to him, and took a deep drag on her cigarette. Her pistol was stuffed in the waistband of her jeans, and she felt in control except for the look of exasperation and worry on Van Buren's face. She realized all at once that he was frightened, and he was using anger to hide it. She softened.

"Sorry," she said. She tossed her cigarette away. "It's just that I'm going crazy being cooped up. It's not what I was trained for."

Van Buren softened too. "I know," he said. "It's getting to all of us. But you just got out of the hospital, and you've got to take it easy." He grinned. "Besides, I don't want to cross your dad."

She smiled back. "Not a good idea." He really did have a nice smile, she thought. And she loved his butt. She let her eyes take a last sweep of the lawn that led to the woods lining the driveway, then went back inside with him.

Barton, Maryland

The forty-five-foot Bertram fly-bridge trawler, *Just-N-Time*, with its large afterdeck, pulled up at the public dock at precisely 5:00 P.M. Kondo, who'd parked the government sedan out of the way behind the marina, stepped aboard and went below as the commando up on the bridge pulled away. Only two other men were on deck handling the lines, the others were out of sight in the crowded main cabin.

Kajiyama was seated at the table in the main saloon, a chart of the Potomac River spared out in front of him. "Any last-minute changes, Kondo-san?"

"McGarvey was out there, but he left," Kondo said.

"He might come back tonight."

"That's what I thought," Kondo said. Barton was only four miles downriver from Cropley. "Let's head upriver, to about White's Ferry, and then take our time coming back. We'll hit them sometime after ten."

"Did you see anything else interesting up there?" Kajiyama asked.

"They've secured the storm shutters on the windows."

"Then they're expecting trouble."

"So it would seem," Kondo said, and he searched Kajiyama's eyes for any sign of apprehension, but he found nothing other than anticipation. It was the same with all of them. Good men, he thought.

"Did you kill the woman?"

Kondo shook his head. "No. We might need her. We'll see."

CIA Headquarters

McGarvey walked into his office a few minutes before five-thirty. They'd left Rencke's car at Archives after retrieving his knapsack with a change of clothes and a few personal items. For the time being he would be staying here, where he could continue working and still remain out of harm's way.

Ms. Swanfeld looked up from a letter she was typing, then did a double take when she saw who McGarvey had brought with him.

"I'd like you to meet a friend of mine, Otto Rencke," McGarvey said. "Otto, this is my secretary, Ms. Swanfeld."

"Oh, boy," Rencke said wiping his hands on his trousers. "Pleased to meet you."

"Mr. Rencke," she said. "Your reputation has preceded you."

"Otto's going to be bunking here for the next couple of days. If you're up for some overtime, we need to get him cleaned up and fed, then set up with an office on this floor and a place to get some sleep."

"Very well," Ms. Swanfeld said. "In the meantime Mr. Murphy wanted to see you the moment you came back. But Mr. Adkins would like to have a word with you first."

"Okay, tell Dick to come right over. And as soon as you get Otto settled in, I have some work for you. Might be an all-nighter."

She smiled faintly. "If you're going back out, you'll be needing a shave and a fresh shirt," she said. "I've laid your things out for you." She phoned Adkins's office then got up and motioned for Rencke to come with her. "Actually I've been expecting you for some time now, Mr. Rencke," she said. "In fact I think we may even be able to find you some Twinkies in the executive dining room, though how anyone could subsist on such things is beyond me."

"Oh, boy," Otto said, grinning on the way out the door.

Cropley, Maryland

Elizabeth stood at the open window, the security shutters partially ajar, looking out toward the woods across the long lawn. She was jumpy, and she didn't know why. It was more than boredom or claustrophobia, but she was unreasonably bitchy and she knew it.

"Todd will go through the roof if he sees you like that," Kathleen said.

Liz held back a sharp retort. "I'll close it when it gets dark," she said instead. "Right now the fresh air feels good."

Kathleen came over and placed the back of her hand on her daughter's cheek. "You're a little warm. Do you feel sick?"

"I'm fine, Mother."

Kathleen looked critically at her. "No, you're not. I've seen that same expression on your father's face just before something was about to happen."

"I don't know what it is," Elizabeth said, glancing out the window.

"Your period?"

Elizabeth shook her head. "I'm so nervous I'm shaking."

"Maybe we should say something to Paul."

Again Elizabeth shook her head. She turned back to her mother. "What Daddy said this afternoon just got me thinking, that's all. It's my overactive imagination."

"Maybe," Kathleen said after a beat. "But I think we'll mention it to Paul at dinner tonight. After all, you *are* your father's daughter."

SEVENTEEN

CIA Headquarters

McGarvey had finished shaving and was putting on a fresh shirt in the bathroom when Dick Adkins walked into his office with a thick bundle of files and a sour expression on his square face.

"You missed the intelligence board meeting this afternoon and Murphy wanted to know where you were," Adkins said, laying the files on his desk.

McGarvey was sorry Adkins had to take the heat for him, but it couldn't have been helped. "What'd you tell him?" he asked, knotting his tie in front of the mirror. The worry lines around his eyes and mouth were pronounced, and he felt like shit mentally.

"I told him that you were running down a couple of leads and you sent me instead. Where were you?"

"Running down a couple of leads," McGarvey said, sitting at his desk.

The first two thick files contained the National Intelligence Estimate and Watch Report. Adkins had done the lion's share of the work, and he felt bad about treating the man this way.

"Look, you're the DDO, but if you want me to act as your chief of staff, you're going to have to let me know what the hell is going on."

McGarvey motioned for Adkins to have a seat. "You're right, Dick, and I'm sorry it has to be this way. But this time I'm going to have to keep you out of the loop."

Adkins started to object, but McGarvey held him off.

"I told you right from the start that there'd be no lies, no bullshit, no hiding anything between us, and I meant it. Neither of us can do our jobs very well any other way. I'm not running a Howard Ryan shop here. But this time you're better off not knowing, because the axe is going to come down on every exposed neck in the building."

"Okay," Adkins said. "You're up to speed here, and except for the routine crap, which anyone can handle for you, there's nothing more I can accomplish. You'll have my resignation on your desk within the hour."

"I won't accept it."

Adkins shook his head in irritation. "Not much you can do if I simply walk out the door."

McGarvey's private line rang. It was Murphy, and he sounded mad. "You're back."

"About twenty minutes ago," McGarvey said.

"Has Dick briefed you?"

"He's here now."

"I want to see you as soon as you're finished. The President has pushed back his briefing to nine-thirty tonight, and he's going to want some specific answers which I don't have, at least not beyond the NIE and Watch Report."

"I'll be right over," McGarvey said heavily. He was going to have to maneuver the DCI tonight, and in order to do that he was going to have to lie to his boss.

Adkins had risen to go, and when McGarvey hung up he motioned for the chief of staff to sit back down.

"I don't have all the answers, Dick."

"I'm not asking to be protected, Mac. Nobody here is. We've got jobs to do, and as you like to say, we can't do them by shitting the troops."

It was a fault he'd fought all of his life, McGarvey thought morosely. Not stepping up to his commitments under the guise of keeping his people out of harm's way. He despised that trait in other people, probably because he recognized the failing in himself. He wasn't a team player, he'd told himself. Which in itself was a load of crap. He'd never worked completely alone, despite what he kept telling himself. And he couldn't work alone now. The fact was he needed Adkins here running the DO, just as much as he needed Rencke's skills, and just as much as he needed his daughter's love and his ex-wife's respect and understanding.

"Otto's been digging through the files and he's come up with connections between the bombing in Georgetown, an outfit called the Far East Trade Association, Joseph Lee, the Japanese Ministry of International Trade and Industry, the *zaibatsu* that brought down all those airliners a couple of years ago and Tony Croft."

"The White House," Adkins said softly, as if he were afraid of being overheard.

McGarvey nodded, but kept his silence. He wanted to see if Adkins would head toward the same conclusions Otto had.

"None of this might have come to light if you hadn't taken the DDO."

"That's right."

"But there's more, isn't there," Adkins said. "Something to do with the incident in North Korea and the situation in the Sea of Japan."

"I think so."

Something else suddenly occurred to Adkins and his eyes widened slightly. "Tony Croft was feeding information to Lee." Now he looked frightened and angry. "What else, Mac? Are you saying it goes further?"

McGarvey took a moment to answer. Once this mountain was crossed there was no easy way back. "This office is clean and the tape recorder is off, so whatever is said here stays here until I tell you otherwise."

Adkins took his own time to reply, working out for himself the ramifications. "I won't lie."

"I'll never ask you to do that," McGarvey said. "But any report generated in the DO on this subject will not be released without my signature so long as I'm DDO."

Adkins thought that out, then nodded.

"Very well," McGarvey said, and he told Adkins what Rencke had discovered at Fort A.P. Hill.

Adkins was stunned. "Do you have any proof other than what Otto dug out?"

"No."

"But you're going to try to get it?"

"Tonight," McGarvey said. "But that's just half the problem, because I still don't know what the connection is between all this and the explosion at Kimch'aek and the standoff between the Japanese and Chinese."

"What's the point, Mac? If Lindsay's been bought and paid for by the Japanese—something I think is far-fetched—where's this going? Certainly not a war between Japan and North Korea, or China. That'd be suicide. And you can't honestly believe that the President is a traitor."

"No, I don't. At the worst I think he's been influenced into giving Japan more leeway than he should. Something a notch above most-favored trading status. Maybe to buy them some time."

"For what?"

McGarvey spread his hands. "I don't know," he said. "But I'm sure as hell going to try to find out, because I think whatever they've been waiting for is about to happen."

Tanegashima Space Center

Frank Ripley walked into the busy launch control center at 8:00 A.M. and felt the chill of angry indifference that had grown steadily over the past week. Nobody said hello or even looked at him as he went up to the console the Tiger team had been assigned for the launch. The shutters on the sloping glass wall facing the pad were open, sun streaming into the five-tiered room that was practically the twin of launch control at the Cape. In the distance the H2C rocket was sheathed in its prelaunch gantry, and even at three miles he could see a great deal of activity out there.

Before the mood had drastically changed he and the others had been besieged by the staff for words of wisdom and advice. Most of his team had been in space, and when they'd first got here they'd been treated like heroes. Ripley wasn't overly sensitive. He was an engineer used to dealing in hard facts. He could get lost in the technical problems of the moment. But he was a highly experienced astronaut whose knowledge could be useful to them if they wouldn't shut him out.

He sat down, powered up his console and put on his headset. The launch clock between the two main status boards was stopped at forty-eight hours. It was a critical point in the prelaunch sequence at which all systems were run through a second-to-final diagnostic test. Once they were assured that everything here in launch control, out on the rocket and at the six monitoring stations around the Earth was nominal, no glitches no problems with equipment, weather or personnel, the clock would start again.

From this moment on, Ripley was expected to monitor launch preparations but not offer any advice unless asked, or unless he spotted a possibly important anomaly. He had a job to do, despite the chilly mood, and he set about to do it.

CIA Headquarters

McGarvey had to remind himself why he was withholding vital information from the DCI. Sitting across the desk from Murphy, he was struck by the enormity of the situation he'd been pushed into. Wars had started with a lot less provocation than the Japanese had provided the North Koreans. At this point it came down to his ego, his understanding of an explosive situation that would almost certainly be at odds with Murphy's perceptions and his own willingness to do what he thought was the right thing.

Everything he knew led to the White House, he had to keep telling himself; Lee, Croft, the decision to send the Seventh Fleet into the Sea of Japan. And he was setting himself up to make an action that was nothing short of a challenge to the Constitution. The thought frightened him more than anything he'd ever faced in his life. He'd felt like this when he'd been led to believe that his parents had been spies for the Russians. But this was even worse.

"How are you doing, Mac?" Murphy asked, his face a mask. He was holding his anger in check.

"I may not be the man for this job, General. But as long as I have it I'll do my best."

"I've heard no complaints except from Archives."

"I pulled Otto out of there this afternoon. In fact he's going to stay here in the building until we're finished with his operation."

"Did he turn up anything?" Murphy asked patiently, as if he were trying to drag the answers from a reluctant student.

"He found out that Joseph Lee was pumping a lot of money into the President's election fund, along with the funds of a half-dozen senators and a bunch of congressmen. That's for starts. And he found out that Tony Croft was passing information back to Lee."

This part was news to Murphy, and his eyebrows rose. "What kind of information?"

McGarvey had to be careful now. "White House policy on the Japanese. Lee was probably working for or with MITI. But we're still looking into that part."

Murphy's jaw tightened. "Are you telling me that Lee was buying information? Croft was a spy for the Japanese government?"

McGarvey nodded. "It's probably why he committed suicide. He couldn't see a way out because of what's happening over there now. Sooner or later someone would have started to ask the wrong questions?"

"Like you," Murphy said.

"Yeah, like me."

"You were in Croft's way, so he had Lee arrange for your assassination, and they didn't care how many people they killed doing it."

"That's a possibility we can't ignore, General," McGarvey said. "And since I'm still in the middle of it, I'd like to come with you tonight."

Murphy took a moment to answer. "Croft is dead, so there's no reason now for them to come after you."

"Unless Lee is somehow involved in what's going on between Japan and North Korea. He might think that I'm coming after him. Which I am. I'd like to step the pressure up a notch."

"What are we getting from our Japanese networks?"

"Nothing. They're all closed down, either arrested or gone to ground, so we just don't have those answers yet. But the Japanese are making a concerted effort to keep a lid on what they're up to."

"War?" Murphy asked. "Are they actually going to try to invade North Korea?"

"They'd be justified," McGarvey said. "But I just don't know yet."

Murphy eyed him skeptically. "What's Otto working on now?"

"He's still trying to nail down a link between Lee and the Koreans."

"Why do you want to see the President tonight?" Murphy asked directly.

"Somebody has to tell him about Croft," McGarvey answered without flinching. Murphy wanted to ask the next question: Is Lindsay himself under suspicion? McGarvey could see it in his eyes. But he did not.

"The briefing has been pushed back again. This time to ten o'clock. It'll give you time for a final update to the NIE and Watch Report. There've been some new developments in the Sea of Japan that he has to deal with now because the Seventh Fleet is going to be in position soon, and nobody knows what's going to happen when they get there."

"I'll be ready by nine-thirty," McGarvey said

"I don't like surprises, Mac," Murphy said. "If you and Otto come up with something I want to know about it first."

"You're the boss."

Just-N-Time

It was still a full hour before nightfall as the Bertram trawler turned back downriver below White's Ferry. The lone man on deck was still in civilian clothes, and he kept up a running commentary on the intercom. River traffic was beginning to thin out. By nightfall there would be very few boats out and about. Even so they would have to be careful not to be observed when they launched.

Kondo and the others below had already changed into their black night-fighter jumpsuits, and he supervised the final preparations. Weapons, radios, night-vision oculars and black paraglider chutes. One man would remain aboard the trawler to drag them into the air on a long cable and then would ground the boat on the riverbank just below the safe house, where he would take up a defensive rear position near the driveway to warn if they had unexpected company. At the correct time he would meet up with them at the helicopter's landing zone.

Kondo looked out a window. The countryside was really quite pretty here, he thought.

Cropley, Maryland

When Elizabeth McGarvey came downstairs, her mother was in the corridor by the front door in deep discussion with Paul Isaacson and one of the outside guards, whose name she couldn't recall. She was famished, and now a little annoyed that she wasn't being included in whatever they were talking about.

"Am I interrupting anything?" she asked peevishly, reaching the bottom of the stairs. They looked up.

"I was just about to come get you for dinner," Kathleen said. "Are you feeling any better now?"

"I'm fine," she snapped. "What's going on?"

"Your mother says that you're getting jumpy," Isaacson said. "But there's no reason for it. You know the setup here; everything is covered. There's no way for anybody to get to you short of mounting an all-out invasion."

Liz glanced at the other man. His name was Stuart, she thought. He was an instructor at the Farm. "Maybe that's what they'll do."

"We're ready for them," Stuart said with a confidence she didn't share.

Todd Van Buren appeared at the kitchen door. "Soup's on," he announced.

"I had one of my people run the path, and we had him on the monitors before he got ten yards," Isaacson said. "If someone tries to get in we'll know about it. And if need be we'll call in reinforcements. The Maryland Highway Patrol knows what's going on out here, and they've agreed to come running if we need them."

"What about the river?" Liz asked.

"That's more than a mile away. Anyway, they'd still have to cross our perimeter motion detectors to get to the house. So no matter what, we'll find out they're coming long before they get within firing range."

Kathleen laid a hand on her daughter's arm. "You see, Elizabeth, we're safe here until your father straightens out this mess," she said. "How about something to eat? You must be starved."

Elizabeth looked at her watch. It was already 9:30 P.M. and dark outside. "Sure," she said, not really very hungry suddenly.

CIA Headquarters

"You didn't tell him," Dick Adkins accused.

"He wouldn't have let me get within a hundred yards of the White House if I had," McGarvey admitted. "But if Lindsay is involved in whatever the Japanese are up to, he'll have to think that I know something about it when I show up for the briefing." McGarvey pointed to the leather-bound folder. "I put in the stuff about the incidents in Germany and Santiago. If nothing else that'll send him a message he can't ignore."

Rencke had finally fallen asleep, practically on his feet, and they'd left him and come back to McGarvey's office where Ms. Swanfeld had put the finishing touches on the briefing.

"Murphy will cut you off at the knees when he finds out what you're trying to do," Adkins warned. "What if you lay this on Lindsay's lap and he doesn't flinch?"

"I don't think Lindsay's a traitor, nor do I think he ordered the Georgetown bombing. He probably doesn't even know what he's doing for Japan. He was manipulated from the start, just like a lot of presidents before him."

"If that's the case, ordering the Seventh Fleet into the fray has to be exactly what the Japanese want. But why?" Adkins shook his head. "North Korea probably asked the Chinese for help, so no surprise there. Nor was it very surprising that the Japanese knocked off one of their submarines.

They started the fight, so why back us into a corner where the only thing we can do is send our navy right back into the middle of it?"

"In the first place it's emptied Tokyo Bay. We don't have much of anything there now."

"That's a thought," Adkins said, a sour look on his face.

"And secondly it's got our attention squarely focused on the Sea of Japan." McGarvey shrugged. "Maybe that's where they want us looking so that they can pull off something else." The thought was there again niggling at the back of McGarvey's mind. Something he should know, some connection he should be making. One of those ideas that surprised you because of its simplicity. But he wasn't seeing it.

Just-N-Time

Kondo, Kajiyama and five commandos were in the water, strung out for 150 yards behind the Bertram. It was finally dark, but very few stars were visible because of the glow from Washington's lights. The commando on the fly bridge could not see the men because of their black outfits and blackened faces. But one by one they sent one click on their walkie-talkies, which meant they were lined up and properly connected to the tow cable. When he counted the seventh click, he scanned the river both ways to make sure there was no traffic, then shoved the throttle levers forward to their stops. At first the boat struggled against the dead weight in the water, but then as the seven men became airborne on their paraglider chutes, the Bertram surged ahead. Looking back he could make out only vague forms rising into the night sky. They could have been anything, perhaps a flock of birds, harmless.

George Washington Parkway

McGarvey rode with Murphy in the DCI's limousine, the bodyguard riding in front with the driver. Thursday night traffic was moderate, a lot lighter than it was during the day. A few clouds had come in, but there was almost no wind, and a thick haze of humidity had settled over the city.

"Was there anything new in the AMs from Tokyo station?" Murphy asked.

"No. The entire country has closed down. Nobody's talking," McGarvey replied.

Murphy tapped his briefcase in which he carried the briefing folder.

"I didn't get a chance to go through the new material. Anything I should know about?"

"It's mostly deep background. Tony Croft had apparently been seeing the call girl for about six months. Started about the same time Joseph Lee came to Sam Blair's attention. The poor bastard."

Murphy gave him a wry look. "Who's a poor bastard, Croft or Blair?"

McGarvey had to smile. "Both of them."

Murphy didn't pursue the thought, leaving McGarvey to his self-doubts and his increasingly uneasy feeling that something very bad was going to happen.

Cropley, Maryland

Elizabeth slipped down the back stairs and went outside to the rear patio. The pool lights were out, and with the windows shuttered and the lights in her room off, the grounds were pitch black.

The flare from her cigarette lighter destroyed her night vision for a minute or so, and until her eyes adjusted she instinctively stepped back under the roof overhang. It was like being temporarily blind, and she didn't like it.

She cupped her cigarette, conscious that out here in the darkness, she stood out like a beacon. She shivered. "Impatience is eventually going to get you in trouble." She could practically hear her father telling her something like that. But she simply couldn't stay inside doing nothing. At least out here she was another pair of eyes watching for an attack.

In the Air
Above the Safehouse

Kondo's night-vision oculars adjusted for the sudden light blossom at the rear of the house, but it had taken him by surprise, and he was momentarily disoriented. It took several precious seconds for him to straighten out his flight path and angle once again toward a small open landing area that would put ten meters of woods between him and the four guards he'd spotted on the way in.

They were at their most vulnerable now, coming in silently 150 feet above the woods behind the house. If one of the guards on the ground was equipped with night-vision equipment and happened to look up, the operation would be over before it began. But so far their luck seemed to be holding.

Just before he dropped below the tree line, he glanced back toward the pool area. A lone figure stood beneath the overhang, something glowing in its left hand. The figure raised a hand to its face, and the glow intensified in Kondo's oculars. The stupid fool was smoking a cigarette, Kondo realized in amazement, then he was down and gathering his chute as the two commandos with him touched down soundlessly.

Kondo directed them with hand signals. They moved swiftly to the edge of the woods, and immediately he spotted one guard leaning against a tree less than ten meters to his left. He clicked his comms unit once.

Within five seconds his two commandos, plus Kajiyama and his force of three men in the woods in front of the house, reported in with a total of another eleven clicks. In all they'd spotted twelve guards.

Now they would wait patiently until Kondo sent the tone signal which meant attack. But first he would allow time for the situation to stabilize in case they'd been spotted coming in. And he wanted to get a little closer to see who was smoking at the back door.

The White House

McGarvey entered the Oval Office with Murphy at precisely 10:00 P.M. The President and his national security adviser, Harold Secor, were seated across from each other in easy chairs, and McGarvey saw the brief look of irritation in Lindsay's eyes replaced almost instantly with the President's famous boyish grin. The President looked tired, McGarvey thought, as well he should considering everything that was happening.

"Good evening, Mr. President," Murphy said. "Mr. McGarvey will conduct the briefing tonight, because at the moment he has more of the answers than the rest of us."

"Very well," Lindsay said. "Let's get started."

Cropley, Maryland

Mindful that there were armed guards out ahead and on either side of him, Kondo crawled slowly beneath some scrub brush. His two men were waiting in the darkness behind him for the signal to attack, as were the others. They would wait, he knew, without moving until hell froze over if need be. Their training and discipline were nothing less than magnificent.

He moved his head slowly to the left in time to see his targeted man speak into a lapel mike. Seconds later the guard stepped around the tree and urinated.

Kondo waited until the guard was finished and had moved back into position before he turned his attention to the lone figure still standing at the back door.

He could tell that it was a woman from her slight figure, but he was completely surprised when she turned and looked in his general direction, giving him a full view of her face. She was Elizabeth McGarvey. The foolish woman had come outside. They knew something might happen, otherwise they wouldn't have taken the precautions they had: the guards, the shutters, the blackout. Yet they'd let McGarvey's daughter step outside and light a cigarette.

"Amazing," Kondo murmured.

The White House

McGarvey did not dwell on the military situation in the Sea of Japan or on the Japanese mainland, because the President was getting that information directly from his military advisers.

The leather-bound briefing folder was on the coffee table in front of Lindsay, but he hadn't opened it yet.

"I don't have very good news for you, Mr. President," McGarvey said.

"I wasn't expecting any," Lindsay shot back. "But I don't want to hear a lot of speculation. Won't do me any good. What I need are hard facts."

"Yes, sir," McGarvey replied. "Fact: Tony Croft committed suicide because he thought he had no other option. He was selling White House policy information to Joseph Lee for a considerable amount of cash that wound up in your campaign fund, and he knew that he was about to be found out."

The President went pale with anger, and Secor started to object, but he held his national security adviser off. "I've known and trusted both of those men for a long time. Tony was a close friend, and Joseph Lee still is. So you'd goddamned well better have some hard proof, Mr. McGarvey, or I'll personally rip your fucking heart out."

Secor and Murphy were both taken aback by the outburst, but McGarvey's eyes never left the President's.

"The money was funneled from Joseph Lee through the Far East Trade Association here in Washington. The FBI raided their offices last night and found money, documents and encrypted computer records showing payouts to your campaign manager though Croft, as well as to the campaign funds of a number of senators and congressmen."

Lindsay didn't blink, nor did he respond.

"In addition to the briefing Croft and his staff conducted for Lee here in the White House last week, the FBI also found documents and computer records in Far East's files with Tony Croft's name on them. We don't know exactly how he passed them the information, except that the call girl he'd been having an affair with for the past six months had been supplied to him by Far East's executive director, who the FBI have reason to believe once was Joseph Lee's mistress in Hong Kong."

"Is all of that included in the briefing?" Lindsay asked, glancing at the folder.

"Yes, sir." McGarvey nodded. "Fact: Joseph Lee, who went to some trouble to go into hiding in Tokyo, works with or for the Japanese Ministry for International Trade and Industry. Whatever information he got from Croft went directly to them. It means the Japanese government has known about your policy toward it and region for at least the past six months."

McGarvey could see connections and sudden understandings pop off behind Lindsay's eyes.

"Those are the facts, Mr. President. The speculation is that Croft didn't want me to become DDO because he thought, for some reason, that I would discover his nasty secret. So he asked Lee's people to have me assassinated."

"Pure fantasy," Secor exploded.

"Since the Japanese knew your policies, they knew that you would send the Seventh Fleet into the region. It's something they expected, and we have to assume it's something they wanted."

"Why?" the President demanded.

"That's one answer I don't even have a speculation for," McGarvey admitted.

Cropley, Maryland

Kondo checked the safety catch on his long-barreled suppressed .22mm semiautomatic assault pistol to make certain it was ready to fire. He took aim on the guard by the tree, then reached up to his lapel mike with his free hand, hesitated a moment and sent the tone signal to start the attack.

*   *   *

Elizabeth was about ready to go back inside when she spotted one of Isaacson's people beside a tree forty yards away. He was looking directly at her. She stepped out from beneath the overhang, waved and started around the pool. She wanted to have a few words with him, to see what he thought about all of this. She got ten feet when the guard seemed to take a couple of dance steps to the right and then crumpled to the ground.

For a split second she was confused, but suddenly she realized that he might have been shot. The attack they prepared for had just started.

"Ah, shit," she said.

She pulled out her gun, thumbed the safety catch off and keeping low, darted to the left.

DGSE officer Albert Level thought he heard a movement behind him in the woods near the driveway. He stepped out of the deeper shadows beneath a tree, all of his senses heightened.

The setup here was okay as far as it went. But he wished they'd been equipped with night-vision equipment. Without it they were at a definite disadvantage.

He picked out his partner, Louis Maurois, about thirty meters away. Suddenly Louis fell forward, and before Level could react something very hot stung his neck, causing him an instantaneous wave of dizziness and nausea.

"*Merde*," he swore falling back as a second bullet plowed into his shoulder.

He clawed for his M16 assault rifle slung over his shoulder as he dropped to the ground, arterial blood spurting from the neck wound. He keyed his lapel mike. "Control, we're under attack," he whispered urgently, remembering to speak in English. "Maurois is down, and I'm hit. We need help out here."

"I'm calling for it now," Isaacson came back immediately. "How many are there? And where the hell did they come from?"

"*Je ne sais pas*," Level responded. "I don't know."

A figure dressed all in black appeared on his left, and before Level could bring his gun around to bear, a thunderclap exploded inside his head.

*   *   *

An angry Todd Van Buren was on his way downstairs, looking for Elizabeth, when he heard the distinctive pops of several M16 rifles on full automatic outside. It was as if a quart of adrenaline were suddenly pumped into his bloodstream. He bolted, drawing his .10 mm Colt as he ran.

"Liz?" he shouted. He raced into the kitchen past a horrified Kathleen McGarvey, Pat Dyer right behind him.

"Todd, stay away from the door," Dyer shouted.

Van Buren ignored him. He tore open the kitchen door and barged outside.

Dyer switched off the kitchen lights behind him, and in the sudden darkness Van Buren couldn't see a thing.

A short burst from an M16 came from the woods in front of the house at the same moment Van Buren spotted Liz crouched low on the far side of the pool. He took two steps forward when he was hit in the chest, and suddenly he was lying on his side, the patio tile cool on his cheek.

Van Buren was down behind her, and Elizabeth reacted in fury, firing five shots in rapid succession into the woods, hoping that any CIA officers left were well concealed.

Someone grunted like a pig, and there was another flurry of M16 fire from the front.

She raced around the end of the pool, firing two more shots over her shoulder into the woods. Whoever was still standing back there wasn't returning her fire, but she refused to consider why, her concentration instead completely on Van Buren, who was struggling to sit up while firing into the woods.

There were twelve officers outside, and only Isaacson and Dyer inside now with Kathleen. Two others had gone back into town this evening because of personal problems, and Isaacson hadn't considered it necessary to call for their replacements. It might have been a big mistake, Elizabeth had the fleeting thought as she hauled Van Buren to his feet.

"We have to get inside! Now!"

"What the hell were you doing out here again?" he demanded. He was in a great deal of pain, and the entire front of his shirt was drenched with blood. Elizabeth was frightened for him. He needed help.

Reaching the overhang Elizabeth fired two more shots into the woods, and the Walther's ejector slide stopped in the open position. The gun was out of ammunition.

* * *

Jeff Stromquist didn't dare use his radio. He lay on the ground behind a
fallen tree about fifteen feet from where he'd been standing when the
attack began. Two ghostly black figures seemed to float through the woods
in front of him. They were looking for him, methodically searching the
area where he'd been standing.

The attack had taken less than twenty seconds, though to Stromquist
it seemed like it had lasted hours. He was almost out of ammunition
himself, and in the past several seconds he'd not heard any other shots.

He had no idea how they'd gotten inside the perimeter, or how many
of them there were. But they were here, and they were damned good. Too
good. But McGarvey had warned them.

The only option now was that the women were secure in the basement
vault until help came. With any luck he'd also be able to hold out.

He raised up a couple of inches so that he could get a better look
over the log, and he came face-to-face with one of the black-clad figures
towering over him less than five feet away. On instinct alone, Stromquist
raised his M16 and fired the last six rounds in his magazine, cutting the
terrorist down.

The second man came running.

"Fuck," Stromquist shouted. He leaped up and swung the assault rifle
like a club, three .22 caliber bullets plowing into his brain before he got
halfway through the swing.

Elizabeth reached the back door and kicked it open. Van Buren was helping as much as he could, but he was having trouble making his legs work,
and he was an impossible burden for her. She could feel the stitches in
the wound under her left arm pulling open and the sticky wetness of blood
running down her side.

Kathleen, her face white, her eyes wide, her mouth open, was suddenly
there, and she grabbed Van Buren by the lapels and hauled him inside
the kitchen with surprising strength.

Dyer shoved the three of them bodily aside and raised his pistol at
the same moment a small hole appeared in his forehead and he fell backward, his eyes registering complete surprise.

"Pat," Elizabeth shouted in desperation. She and Van Buren stumbled
over Dyer's body.

As they went down, Van Buren managed to pull free, swivel left and fire three shots outside before Kathleen finally slammed the door and rammed the deadbolt home.

Kajiyama and two of his commandos, one of them wounded but still able to fight, appeared out of the darkness in the woods opposite the rear of the house where Kondo and his remaining commando waited.

"We're clear in the front," Kajiyama said, out of breath. "But we have to abort the mission. I monitored two calls to the State Patrol. Help is on the way."

"Where is your other man?" Kondo demanded. It was suddenly difficult to keep on track. Lee did not reward failure, especially not something like this so soon after Georgetown.

"He's down, Kondo-san. We have to go."

Kondo keyed his mike. "Skybird, lead one. What is your best ETA to the primary pickup zone?"

"Five minutes," the pilot replied at once.

"Come now," Kondo said. They no longer had the element of surprise, but they still had five minutes to accomplish the mission. He cocked his head and listened for a moment. He could hear no sirens yet. They had time.

"Kondo-san?" Kajiyama prompted.

"You and your two men will take the front door while we take the back." He glanced at his watch. "Ninety seconds."

Kajiyama hesitated only a moment, then nodded. "*Hai*," he said.

"We've got incoming," Isaacson shouted desperately from the front hall.

Elizabeth scooped up Pat Dyer's pistol and with her mother's help managed to drag Van Buren out of the kitchen, away from the attacking forces at the rear of the house.

"Get back," Isaacson ordered them. "Go down to the vault. Help's on its way." The basement stairs were on the other side of the kitchen.

"They're coming that way too," Elizabeth replied, trying to keep her cool.

Isaacson took in their condition in a single glance, then nodded toward the stairs. "I'll hold them off as long as I can. But the State Patrol is on its way."

"We won't leave you—" Elizabeth tried to argue.

"For Christ's sake, Liz, follow an order for once in your life," Isaacson said almost gently. "You've got to get your mother and Todd upstairs while you still have a chance to save them." He snatched an M16 from where it was leaning against the wall and tossed it to her. It left him with only his pistol. "Go," he said. "Now."

Elizabeth was torn. For once she didn't know what her father would do.

"Paul's right," Van Buren said weakly.

"Goddammit," Elizabeth said. She took a last look at Isaacson, then she and her mother, Van Buren between them, started up the stairs.

Kondo saw the flash and heard the bang from the front of the house a moment before his grenade took out the kitchen door. He and his commando raced across the patio, keeping low. The problem was McGarvey's daughter. She'd not only fought back when the attack started, but she'd risked her life to save the downed guard who'd come for her. Taking her alive was going to be more difficult than he'd first suspected. Maybe impossible. But if they had to kill her and her mother, he thought, then so be it. They would take the bodies and use them to lure McGarvey.

He and his commando darted into the house, jumped over the body and swung their weapons left to right searching for targets. But nothing moved.

"Clear," he shouted to the front hall.

"Clear," Kajiyama answered.

Kondo reached the stairhall. He had just a split second to spot the downed American inside the shattered front door, Kajiyama and one of the commandos flanking the bottom of the stairs, when the second commando who'd started up was suddenly cut down by automatic weapons fire from the head of the stairs.

Van Buren lay on his side a few feet back from the head of the stairs as Elizabeth fell back after firing the short burst.

"One down," she whispered grimly.

"Give me the rifle," Van Buren said urgently. "I can hold them off from here while you and your mother get out the back way. You can jump from the balcony. If they're all inside now they might not spot you leaving. You can hide up in the woods."

"No way in hell, Todd," Elizabeth said.

Kathleen had darted down the hall to their sitting room. She returned with the spare magazine for Elizabeth's Walther PPK. "Nobody's leaving you," she told him firmly. She gave Elizabeth the magazine. "Give Todd the rifle, give me Dyer's gun and reload yours. Between the three of us we should be able to discourage them until the State Patrol decides to show up."

"You don't know how to shoot a gun."

Kathleen smiled grimly. "Never underestimate your mother, dear. Now, do as I say."

"If you surrender now, you do not have to die, Miss McGarvey," someone called from downstairs.

Elizabeth gave Van Buren the rifle and handed Dyer's pistol to her mother. "Go to hell," she shouted down in a steady voice, as she hastily reloaded her gun.

"All your people are dead and no one is coming to help you."

Elizabeth edged closer to the head of the stairs. "Why not come up here, and we'll discuss it, Mr. Kondo," she said.

Kondo could scarcely believe what he'd just heard. She knew his name. But that was impossible. A dozen thoughts raced through his head at the speed of light, building into a nearly uncontrollable rage. "Fucking Americans," he muttered tightly.

Kajiyama and the two commandos were looking at him. In the distance now they could hear the incoming helicopter, and over that they could hear sirens. A long ways off. But there were a lot of them. Too many.

"Kill them," Kondo ordered. "Now."

One of the commandos pulled out a coiled-wire grenade, yanked the pin and tossed it up the stairs.

Kondo saw the man's stupid mistake the instant the grenade left his hand. The fool had not waited long enough after pulling the pin.

He heard it thump on the carpeted hall upstairs, and a second later it clattered back down the stairs. Someone, the young woman who he thought was so brave, had the presence of mind to kick it back.

"Down," he shouted, and they all managed to fall back against the wall and bury their heads in their arms, as the grenade went off with a tremendous roar. Plaster and glass and splinters and chunks of flaming wood rained down all around them.

It seemed to take forever before Kondo could recover, and when he got up someone sprayed the stairwell with two controlled bursts from an M16.

They had failed again. The thought was so bitter that Kondo wanted to lash out in rage at anything or anybody.

Kajiyama and the one man had pulled back. The second commando was dead. At the doorway they hesitated, but Kondo waved them out, then raced after them, firing the last of his ammunition over his shoulder toward the head of the stairs.

The White House

McGarvey's cell phone chirped in his pocket. Lindsay shot him an angry look. It was the last straw.

"Sorry, Mr. President," he said. "It's my emergency number." McGarvey answered it on the second chirp. "Yes."

"Everybody's dead out here except for me, Elizabeth and Todd," Kathleen said in a rush, her voice cracking.

McGarvey's heart leapt into his throat. "Katy, are you all right?"

"We beat the bastards. They're going in a helicopter. And the State Patrol is finally here. But everyone else is dead."

"What about Paul?"

"He's dead! Can't you understand?" Kathleen shouted hysterically.

McGarvey was on his feet. He put a hand over the mouthpiece. "They attacked Cropley," he told Murphy. "I need a chopper down there now." He took his hand away. "Are you sure they're gone, Katy? Don't move unless you're absolutely sure."

"They're gone, Kirk," she shouted. "But it's not over. They got away. *Some* of them got away. But they'll come back. And keep coming!" She cried out in anguish, the sound of her voice cutting into McGarvey like a razor sharp knife. "Kirk, my God, I need you. Now! I need you!"

PART TWO

WHITE HOUSE

EIGHTEEN

En Route to Cropley, Maryland

Eight minutes after Murphy put in the call, McGarvey scrambled aboard a Bell Super Cobra Marine ground attack helicopter which touched down on the White House lawn. A half-dozen fully armed marines had come along in addition to the crew. Even as McGarvey buckled in and donned his helmet, the chopper lifted off and headed northwest, the tremendous acceleration of the twin Pratt & Whitney turboshaft engines shoving him against his restraining straps. The marines were all young and grim-faced. They didn't know exactly what they were heading for, except that there'd been a lot of casualties and there was no telling if any of the bad guys were still out there waiting for them to show up.

"Mr. McGarvey, this is Captain Don Casey," the pilot radioed back. "Our ETA to the target is seven minutes. Can you tell me what we're heading into, sir?"

"Probably just a mop-up operation along the perimeter." McGarvey spoke into his headset. "The Bureau and the state have people on the ground, but this is a determined group, so keep your eyes open."

"Yes, sir, we got that on the way over."

McGarvey was having trouble keeping on track. Starting with the attack in Georgetown, the situation had developed faster than he could keep up with. The bastards had a definite timetable, and there was no doubt that whoever was behind it was afraid that he'd screw them up. They wanted to get to him, to stop him from doing his job however they could. It didn't matter who got in their way or how many innocent people they had to kill. The worst part of it was that someone in Washington besides Tony Croft was feeding them information. It was as if half the city had been bought and paid for, though probably most of them had no idea what effect they were having, and that people were dying because of them.

"Captain, I need to make a couple of calls to the Agency. Can I do that from here?"

"Affirmative, sir."

McGarvey gave him the first number, and seconds later he was connected with Adkins in the DO's Operations Center.

"I'm on my way out to Cropley. Do we have people en route?"

"There are two teams just ahead of you," Adkins said. "I wanted them in motion before I talked to you. I figured they were more important. But the place has been secured, and your wife and daughter are okay."

"What the hell happened, Dick?"

"Looks like they came in from the air. Fred Rudolph is on the way out there too. His people on the ground found several parachutes or hang gliders. Probably dropped them from a plane somewhere upwind."

"Who's left on the ground?"

"Todd Van Buren, but he's already being medevaced to Bethesda. He was shot up pretty badly, Mac."

"Paul Isaacson?"

"Dead, along with all the others," Adkins said. "I'm still getting a lot of contradictory shit, but it looks like he fought a delaying action inside the house while Todd, along with your wife and daughter, held them off from the upstairs corridor until the cops showed up."

"What happened to the terrorists?"

"Four down, but a helicopter picked up the rest of them. We're looking for it now. It was a professional job, Mac. The bastards knew what they were doing."

"Can we keep a lid on this?"

"Not a chance in hell. The media is already screaming bloody murder for answers." Adkins hesitated a moment. "The good news is that no one is making the connection between this attack and the bombing in Georgetown or the incident on the Canal Bridge, but I don't know how long that's going to last."

McGarvey closed his eyes for a minute. The attack was meant for him, of course, which meant whoever was directing it was desperate. "I'll be on the ground in a few minutes. Keep me posted. In the meantime send someone out to Dulles. I want Joseph Lee's jet staked out. They might try to get out of the country that way."

"Will do."

McGarvey's second call was to Otto Rencke, and it went through as they crossed the Potomac just east of CIA headquarters.

"Oh, boy, Mac, I'm already on it," an excited Rencke blurted. "I'm in every Washington area LE system including the Bureau's."

"Have they found the helicopter?"

"Not yet, but it won't be long. There's not that many civilian choppers out there, and the Bureau has already accounted for more than half of them."

"It would have been chartered through Fast East or some dummy organization they set up."

"I'm on it," Rencke said. "Liz and Mrs. M. are okay."

"That's what I'm being told."

"We'll get the fuckers, Mac. I swear to God, we'll get them and hang them by their balls."

"You can count on it," McGarvey said tightly.

Walker Mill Regional Park

All hell was breaking loose, and Maryland Prince Georges County deputy sheriff Dale Zuber figured he wasn't going home anytime soon. Listening to the chatter on the radio in his police cruiser, it sounded as if every cop from Baltimore to D.C. had been called out. There'd been some sort of terrorist attack up in Montgomery County and the feds were hot to bag the bad guys. Every inch of the state was being searched with a fine-toothed comb, and he figured the cop who got lucky would get an extra stripe. It was a promotion he desperately needed because of the new house. The payments were killing him.

He'd been heading south on Ritchie Road parallel with I-95 toward Forestville, where he usually stopped for coffee around this time of night, when he decided to take a quick pass through the park. Sometimes on slow nights he made the panty run to roust out the kids parked up there, but as he came around a curve in the park road, his mouth dropped open and he pulled up short.

"Prince Georges, Zuber. I have a helicopter down in Walker Mill Park," he radioed. "Looks empty. Stand by."

"Roger," the dispatcher replied. "Approach with extreme caution. Backup units are en route."

Zuber got out of his car, put on his campaign hat and drew his service pistol and flashlight as he stepped off the road and headed across the grassy field. The chopper was parked about fifty yards away at the edge of a stand of trees. It was dark, but he could see that the side doors were open and no one seemed to be inside.

In the distance he could hear sirens, but other than that the night was very quiet.

He stopped twenty feet from the helicopter and shined his flashlight into the main compartment, then let the beam slide forward to the windshield as he slowly walked around to the front of the machine.

Something had splashed on the Plexiglas window. He spotted that at the same moment he saw a figure slumped forward in the pilot's seat. He shined the light on the figure and his stomach did a slow roll. The pilot, dressed in a light-colored shirt, was obviously dead. The entire side of his head and forehead were gone, nothing but a mass of blood. He'd probably been shot in the back of his head at point-blank range.

Zuber keyed his shoulder mike. "Prince Georges, Zuber, requesting a medical unit. The helicopter pilot appears to have been shot in the head."

He stepped around to the opposite side of the helicopter and shined his light in the main compartment again. It was empty, except for what appeared to be black uniforms or jumpsuits. "Jesus," he said out loud. The pilot had brought them here, they'd killed him for his efforts on their behalf, changed clothes and then took off.

Zuber shined his light on the ground around the helicopter, and immediately picked out several sets of footprints leading across the field toward the road.

This is going to be a long night, indeed, he told himself.

CIA Headquarters

Otto Rencke was in his element, finally doing something that had real meaning. But he was frightened, because for every answer he found, a dozen questions popped up, spreading outward faster than even he could keep up with.

The computers up here were even better than those down at Archives in Fort A.P. Hill, because he had designed much of the system. And yet there wasn't a decent computer that could do what even a stupid human was capable of doing, and that was think intuitively.

He sat back and idly stuffed a Twinkle in his mouth as his eyes roamed to each of the three screens and three printers that were pulling up information his specially designed search engine was looking for. Anomalies, McGarvey called them. The questions—answered or unanswered—that seemed to stick out. The ones that didn't seem to fit a pattern. Obvious questions, like where the thimble was hidden when it was in plain sight.

Three minutes ago he'd monitored the deputy sheriff's call about the downed helicopter and the dead pilot. He stared at one of the printers. Never mind how the terrorists got into the air to fly their paragliders to the safe house; he would find out about that later. They made their attack and got away aboard a helicopter which took them to a park southwest of Washington. But what happened next? Either someone was waiting with a getaway car, or they'd left an escape vehicle there. They killed the pilot and drove where? A hideout? In Rencke's mind he could see a car or van racing through the night, using back roads and deserted streets, finally pulling into a parking garage behind some abandoned factory somewhere.

He sat forward. The cars or vans they used and the hideout they escaped to, as well as the helicopter, had to have been arranged by Sandy Patterson and the Far East Trade Association.

He pulled up the file he'd been working with. Among the dummy groups Far East had set up were three on the Beltway: Digital Systems Engineering, the Quantum Research Group and Microchip Applications, Inc., all of them with lucrative government contracts.

He cleared the screen and began with Digital Systems. Two questions needed answering: Where did the escape vehicles come from, and where had the terrorists stored their equipment, planned the attack and bunked?

Cropley, Maryland

Since taking over the DO, McGarvey had gotten very little sleep and almost no rest. The position wasn't so much of a job as it was a way of life. No wonder so many Agency people had deep personal problems. The Company was a human meat grinder; steak in, hamburger out.

Coming in low from the southeast, he could see the flashing lights of a lot of vehicles on the highway and the driveway and bobbing lights crisscrossing the open fields and woods surrounding the house. It looked like a carnival, and from the air he couldn't see any outward signs that anything bad had happened. But it had. Paul Isaacson and a lot of good people had died down there. Giving their lives to protect his family, who'd been attacked simply because of what he was, because of what he did for a living. The same black rage he'd felt on the Canal Bridge after the Georgetown bombing threatened to block out his sanity, but he struggled to fight it. This time he was going to have to be much stronger. He needed to keep his head until he found the bastards and killed them. This time there would be no mistakes.

The marine helicopter touched down on the lawn in front of the house, completely surrounded by police cruisers, some unmarked government cars and a half-dozen ambulances. Bodies were being brought from the woods behind the house, and dozens of uniformed cops stood around with little or nothing to do.

McGarvey unbuckled and started to get out, but the six marines were faster. They jumped to the ground and formed a tight half circle in front of the door, their weapons at the ready.

"Clear," their sergeant said. He turned back. "Okay, Mr. McGarvey."

"What the hell?" McGarvey mumbled, but then he realized that Murphy would have ordered the marine guard for him in case there were any terrorists left behind in the woods who'd take the suicide shot in order to kill the DDO. It was a chilling thought, even for McGarvey.

Fred Rudolph came over from a knot of men who'd been having a conference in front of an evidence van. The marines kept a close watch on him.

He and McGarvey shook hands. "Nobody thought they'd come in from the air."

"Wouldn't have happened if this place wasn't on your Website," McGarvey said.

A pained look crossed Rudolph's face. He was under a lot of strain and it showed. "We have a place set up for them—"

McGarvey cut him off. "They're coming with me."

"Where are you taking them?"

McGarvey said nothing, and after a moment Rudolph nodded.

"Can't blame you, Mac. We screwed it up for your guys, but I'm not going to worry about that right now. First we have to catch the people who did this. Has the CIA come up with anything?"

"Not yet. But we're working on it. Have you found Sandy Patterson?"

Rudolph shook his head glumly. "She's disappeared without a trace. But we found the helicopter that pulled them out of here, which means they're still in the area." His jaw tightened. "We'll find them."

"Any IDs on the bodies they left behind?"

"Asians. Maybe Japanese, but hell, there's no way of knowing that for sure yet. They were well equipped. Night glasses, radios, silenced weapons. They knew the layout here, and they timed their attack to take out every outside guard at the same moment. Some of your guys just got lucky and shot back."

"Yeah," McGarvey said. "Real lucky. Now they're dead." He turned away from the FBI special investigator and walked across the lawn, his marine contingent surrounding him.

The house smelled like a gunpowder factory, and blood was splashed against the stairhall wall and the destroyed remnants of the front door. It was where Isaacson had died.

Kathleen and Elizabeth were seated at the dining room table in the makeshift operations center, drinking coffee. Several Company men were standing by with them. McGarvey motioned for them to get out and join his marine guard in the hall. Kathleen and Liz looked up, and they both managed to smile. Outwardly they looked no worse for the wear, but Kathleen had been crying and Liz looked shell-shocked.

"Hi, Daddy," she said in a small voice.

McGarvey kissed his daughter on the cheek, then sat down and took Kathleen's hand. "Are you okay?" he asked his wife.

She looked into his eyes, and he could feel her strength. She nodded almost imperceptibly. "We were lucky this time," she said simply. She studied his face as if she'd not seen it for a long time. "I don't think I'll ever feel safe again. But as long as I have you and our daughter, I'll be able to live with it."

"I'm sorry, Katy."

She squeezed his hand, a new intensity in her eyes. "It wasn't your fault."

"It's going to be okay now," McGarvey said. "They won't be coming after you again. We're very close to catching them."

"They were good, Daddy," Liz blurted. "Better than we expected. But if it wasn't for Paul we wouldn't have made it. And Todd—the medics say he'll be okay—God, he was fantastic. He saved our lives too."

Kathleen reached out and touched her daughter's cheek. "You were rather fantastic yourself."

Liz smiled, then started to cry, big tears that slid down her cheeks. Kathleen began to cry, and McGarvey's eyes filled as he held his family, the black rage inside him doing a slow fade to a temporary corner of his mind where he could pull it out when it was time to pay back the people who were responsible. And that would happen very very soon, he promised himself.

CIA Headquarters

Rencke was set up in a small office down the hall from the DDO's suite that was used by temporary research assistants the CIA brought in from time to time. He'd been going without sleep or anything decent to eat for a couple of days himself, but he was feeling no fatigue now.

"Bingo," he said, staring at one of the computer monitors that showed a stream of information scrolling up on a lavender background. Whoever had set up what amounted to a triple blind was very good, but not nearly good enough, Rencke told himself, grinning from ear to ear. "The magic," he whispered, excitedly tapping his feet like a kid getting a birthday present. "Oh, boy. I got the magic."

He activated a search program that would find and telephone McGarvey wherever he was. Five days ago Far East had given Digital Systems Engineering a contract to gather and collate information on the worldwide development of new satellite data transmission technologies. Digital Systems in turn subcontracted to Quantum Research the task of purchasing the latest equipment for study and evaluation. In turn Quantum subcontracted the job of transportation and storage of the equipment to Microchip Applications, which had done exactly that. At least for the record. The only flaw was that companies like Quantum and Microchip didn't do that kind of work, renting vans and arranging for warehouses.

The call went through to McGarvey. He was still at Cropley. "Can you talk?"

"Just a minute," McGarvey said. He said something indistinct in the background, and half a minute later he came back. "Okay, have you found something?"

"They're using two Dodge vans and a Ford Taurus. Government surplus. I came up with the license plate numbers, but what's better than that is where they're staying. It used to be a Kmart store in Morningside, Maryland."

"Did Far East set it up?"

"Last week, through a triple blind. But they used their own dummy organizations. Dumb, dumb, dumb."

McGarvey was silent for a moment. When he came back his voice was changed, lower, more precise. "I'm bringing Katy and Liz to my office for a couple of hours, maybe for the night. My secretary will take care of them until I get back."

"Do you want to talk to her?"

"No, I'll take care of it," McGarvey said. "In the meantime I want you to load everything you've come up with on a disk and give it to Liz. Everything, do you understand, Otto?"

"Gottcha," Rencke said. "Do you want me to tell the Bureau about Kmart?"

"No," McGarvey said flatly.

"Come on, Mac—"

"No, Otto. I'm going to take care of this myself."

"Oh, boy," Rencke whispered. "Oh, boy, Mac. Watch your ass. Big time, watch your ass."

"Now tell me exactly where this place is," McGarvey said.

Cropley, Maryland

"Okay, there's nobody aboard," the FBI special agent radioed.

"Maybe it broke loose from its dock and drifted downriver," Rudolph replied. He was outside at his car.

"No, sir. They definitely ran her up on the bank. Looks like our perps. Some civilian clothes below. They probably changed into their black gear down there. And there's some kind of a cable tow arrangement on the stern. Could have been used to lift them airborne on their hang gliders."

"Secure the site and don't touch anything. I'm sending the second evidence van down."

"Yes, sir."

Rudolph turned to look as McGarvey, surrounded by his contingent of marines, came out of the house with his wife and daughter and headed toward the helicopter. He tossed the microphone on the seat and walked over to them.

"Are you going into town?" he asked.

"We're heading to Langley," McGarvey said. "Won't be very comfortable, but it's safe."

Rudolph nodded. "We found a boat pulled ashore just across the highway. Looks like they might have come in that way and then got out by helicopter."

"Any idea where they got the helicopter?" McGarvey asked, and there was something in the way he asked the question that bothered Rudolph. He suspected that McGarvey knew something he wasn't telling. And Rudolph already knew the man well enough not to bother asking.

"We're checking on it."

McGarvey glanced toward the end of the driveway, which was lined with television vans, satellite dishes on their roofs. "Keep us out of it," he said.

Rudolph followed his gaze. "I'll do what I can."

McGarvey gave him a last look. "Keep me posted."

"You too," Rudolph said.

NINETEEN

Seawolf

I t was 0500 GMT, which made it two in the afternoon local. Harding was finally getting to sleep after tossing and turning in his bunk for three hours when his growler phone buzzed angrily.

He turned on the light and grabbed the phone. "This is the captain."

"Hate to bother you, but we've got a problem," Paradise reported.

Harding sat up. He felt like hell, and he wanted to bite off his XO's head. "What is it?"

"In the past two hours he's cleared his baffles three times. He just did it again, and he's slowed down. I think he knows we're back here."

"What's our range?"

"Five thousand yards."

"Okay, come to all stop and rig for silent running," Harding said. "I'm on my way." If the MSDF submarine they'd been following knew someone was behind them, rigging for silent running would either confuse the Japanese skipper or confirm that he was being followed by a submarine with hostile intent. Either way, the situation was one that Harding had wanted to avoid. But now that they were apparently in the middle of it, he wasn't going to back off.

Forcing himself to slow down, he splashed some cold water on his face, combed his hair, put on a fresh shirt and stopped by the officers' wardroom to get a cup of coffee before going forward to the control center. By the time he arrived he was his usual calm, collected self. It was good for the crew to see their captain unruffled.

Paradise was at the door to the sonar compartment. He came aft and joined Harding at one of the plotting tables. He looked worried and dragged out. None of the officers had been getting enough sleep since the *Natsushio* sank the Chinese submarine and *Seawolf* had been ordered to give chase.

"What's the situation?" Harding demanded.

"We're still clear aft, but something evidently spooked him into finding out if he had a tail." Paradise made a mark on the chart east of Goto Island at the entrance to the East China Sea. "He made his first turn to starboard here. We figured he was heading for the Korean coast after all. But when he shut down his diesels and I figured out what he was really doing, it was too late."

"He probably had us on the first pass," Harding said.

Paradise nodded glumly. "My fault—"

"Don't worry about it, Rod, I would have done the same thing," Harding said, although he wouldn't have. It was a major error that could mean the end of Paradise's career as a submarine officer.

Paradise nodded his thanks, though he would beat himself up over his mistake for a long time. "Since then he's made the same turn three more times."

"He's still holding the same course?"

"Definitely heading south. But each time he made his turn we managed to shut down ahead of him."

Harding studied the chart. If the *Natsushio* was heading for Tokyo Bay after all, it would take two days to get there, so they still had a little time to figure out what was happening. But it made no sense to him. Why pull a submarine from these waters, especially *that* boat?

"Should we call this home?" Paradise asked.

Harding looked up and shook his head. "Not yet. I want to see how far he's going to take this."

"He killed the Chinese submarine without warning."

"I know," Harding said. "Let's go to battle stations, torpedo. Load tubes one and two, but don't flood them just yet."

Natsushio

"*Kan-cho*, the submarine has disappeared," Seaman Mizutami reported from sonar.

"He's not disappeared. He knows we've detected him, and he's gone silent," Captain Tomita replied. "Were you quick enough to confirm his class?"

"No, sir. But what we do have indicates a strong possibility that he's a Seawolf."

Tomita glanced across the control room at his XO, Lieutenant Uesugi. "Keep a close watch now." He released the comms button.

"Does the American know where we're heading?" Uesugi asked.

"Not unless the Americans are intercepting and decrypting our communications," Tomita said. That was not likely, but certainly a possibility which he knew he had to consider. And it was more than possible that the American submarine had witnessed the attack on the Chinese submarine. Flotilla Headquarters had informed him that the Seventh Fleet had entered the Sea of Japan from the north, which was one of the reasons that the *Natsushio* was ordered out of the area. Not the only reason, however.

"Turn one hundred eighty degrees to port," he ordered. "We'll clear our baffles from a new direction this time."

Uesugi came over. "We are no match for them, *kan-cho*," he said, respectfully lowering his voice.

"That is correct," Tomita agreed. "Nevertheless I mean to deal with them here and now. Send up a slot buoy, and we'll call for help."

CVN 73 George Washington

Admiral James Hamilton hunched over a chart in the busy Combat Information Center one level below the bridge. "What's the situation, Dave?"

"Well, if Harding stayed on his projected track, it looks to me like they're trying to box him in." Captain Merkler spread several 50 × 50 cm satellite images on the plotting table. "They suddenly got real interested in a spot just west of Goto Island about an hour ago. The destroyer *Myoko* and frigates *Noshiro* and *Yubetsu* are already closing in, and a half-dozen other surface ships are within a couple of hours. Take that together with at least four Orion sub-hunters circling the same piece of ocean, and it looks to me like an all-out hunt for *Seawolf*."

"Seven hundred miles," Hamilton said. "It'd take us twenty-four hours to get down there. Way too long."

"We can send aircraft. At least it would counter the threat the Orions are posing. And if we tell our pilots to kick the pig we could be in the middle of it in under thirty minutes."

Hamilton looked at the chart and the photographs. "Okay, send a pair of Hornets. I want them down there as soon as possible, then I want them right down on the deck. Wave-top level."

"They won't be able to defend themselves effectively."

"That's the point, Dave." Hamilton's expression hardened. "God help the sonofabitch who takes advantage."

Merkler looked at the satellite images. "What the hell are they up to?"

"That's what we're here to find out. I want the entire fleet moved south at best possible speed. In the meantime I want an ELF message sent to Harding. He needs to be warned that he's heading into trouble."

"If he doesn't already know," Merkler said, and he turned to issue the orders, leaving Hamilton to wonder exactly what the Japanese were up to this time. They weren't simply defending against a possible nuclear threat from North Korea. Or were they?

Seawolf

"Sonar, conn. Have the bearings to the three surface targets changed?" Harding asked.

"Negative, skipper," Fischer reported excitedly. "They're all within twenty-five thousand yards and closing fast. Still spread out over a twenty-degree arc. They know we're here, or at least in the vicinity."

"How about the *Natsushio*?"

"He shut down after his last turn to port. He's out there, but I'm still getting nothing."

Harding released the phone button and studied the main tactical display on the overhead CRT next to the periscopes. Paradise was at the rail.

"Looks like he doesn't want us to follow him," Harding said.

"It's my fault he knows we're here—"

"Belay that," Harding said sharply. He knew what the Japanese sub driver was about to do and couldn't believe it. Right now he needed all the help he could get, because he didn't want to precipitate an all-out shooting war with the MSDF.

"He's not going to shoot at us," Paradise said.

Harding looked at his XO. "I think that's exactly what he means to do as soon as the help he called for arrives. And that's going to be soon."

"He's a diesel-electric boat."

"In his own waters, up against an allied warship. He's counting that we won't shoot."

"We won't," Paradise said.

"Not unless we're provoked," Harding replied calmly. "Let's start a TMA on his last known position, then send out a couple of noisemakers."

"That'll pinpoint our position."

"Exactly," Harding said carefully. He was losing his patience. "I want to see what he'll do about us."

Paradise lowered his voice. "Look, Skipper, as XO my job is to do more than follow orders. I'm supposed to give advice, which I can't give unless I know what you want to do."

"We followed him, he detected us and we both shut down. Then he called for help, which he knows we heard. Now, we can either bug out—which is what he wants us to do—or we can let him know that we're still here and we plan on sticking around. The next move will be his."

"If he shoots at us, he's got to know he'd be committing suicide."

"It'd sure tell us how serious they are," Harding said. He keyed the growler phone. "Sonar, this is the captain. If he floods his tubes I want to know about it pronto."

Natsushio

"Noisemakers in the water," Seaman Mizutami reported. "Relative bearing zero-eight-zero, range, four-thousand five-hundred meters."

"Stand by," Tomita ordered. He called ESMs. "This is the captain. Has there been any response from our surface ships?"

"*Iie, kan-cho.*" No, the electronic support measures officer replied.

"Sonar, conn. What is the range to our surface ships?"

"All of them are within the twenty-five-thousand-meter ring and closing fast."

"The American captain knows that our ships are closing in on his position," Uesugi said from his position in front of the BSY-1 consoles. "It's only a matter of time before they have him."

"So it would seem," Tomita said staring at the tactical display monitor.

"They mean to provoke us before we get help, knowing that we will not shoot."

"Sonar, conn. Is the *Seawolf*'s aspect changing?"

"No, sir," Mizutami said. "I was able to paint a partial picture because of the noisemaker bubbles. It looks as if he's beam on to us."

"Stand by," Tomita said. The American captain not only told them that he was there, but he'd moved his boat in such a position that its flank was presented to the *Natsushio*. He'd given them the perfect shot.

Uesugi was looking at him.

The American would not shoot. It was unthinkable. But even if he did, he would find himself in serious trouble from the surface ships that would find and kill him within a matter of minutes.

"Conn, sonar. Give me one ping for range and bearing."

Mizutami hesitated for a fraction of a second. "*Hai, kan-cho.*"

The sonar ping reverberated through the hull. Seconds later the return signal was entered into the BSY-1 computers.

"I have a shooting solution," Uesugi said, trying to keep his voice even.

"Flood tubes one and two."

Uesugi looked over at him.

"This is not a drill," Tomita warned. "Flood one and two."

"*Hai, kan-cho.*"

Seawolf

"Conn, sonar, he's flooding his tubes," Fischer called.

"Give me two pings for range, and a precise bearing to his propeller," Harding ordered.

"Aye, Skipper."

"Flood tubes one and two," Harding told his XO. "And prepare to get us out of here."

"Flooding tubes one and two."

"Prepare to fire only one," Harding said, fighting to remain totally calm, in control. "We're going to take out his prop before he gets off a shot."

Two active sonar pings reverberated throughout the ship. A second later the solution came up on the BSY-1 console.

"I have a firing solution," Harding said.

"Fire one," Harding ordered without hesitation.

The weapons control officer hit the button, and there was brief low-pitched vibration.

"Emergency crash dive, all ahead full, come right to course two-nine-zero." Harding reached up for a handhold on the overhead as his orders were relayed. With gathering speed the *Seawolf* heeled over hard to starboard, the bows canted sharply down and they accelerated. Now it was going to start getting real interesting, he told himself.

TWENTY

CIA Headquarters

McGarvey forced himself to go through the motions of getting his wife and daughter settled in with the help of his secretary, Ms. Swanfeld. They had brought along their things from the safe house, and while they were cleaning up, a couple of cots were brought from housekeeping and set up in the DO's conference room. It might not be comfortable, but it was safe.

The doctor came out to where McGarvey was waiting with his secretary.

"They're a little shook up. Other than that they're fine, which is amazing considering the injuries your daughter suffered in the bombing. She's a tough woman."

"That she is."

The doctor looked critically at him. "It looks as if you could use some rest yourself."

"I'm going to take a couple of days off."

"Make it soon," the doctor said, and he left.

A little smile curled the corner of Ms. Swanfeld's mouth. "For a Company doctor he certainly doesn't know what goes on around here."

McGarvey returned her smile despite the rage he was filled with. The heat had been turned up tonight and he was at the edge of boiling over. "Are you up to sticking around for another couple of hours? Just until they get settled in?"

"You couldn't pry me out of here, Mr. McGarvey." She glanced at the door. "Are you going to talk to Mr. Adkins before you go? He's in the Operations center."

"I'll see him when I get back."

Her left eyebrow rose. "Will Mr. Rencke know how to reach you—in an emergency?"

"Yes, he will," McGarvey said. He walked across the hall to the conference room, knocked once and went in. Kathleen and Elizabeth had finished dressing and Kathleen was making up their cots.

"Daddy," Elizabeth said brightly. She looked worn out.

"Hi, Liz," McGarvey gave her a peck on the cheek, then took his wife in his arms. "The doctor said you're both fine."

"Good thing he wasn't a psychologist," Kathleen said.

"You'll be okay here until morning. My secretary is going to stick around tonight, so if you need anything just ask her. She wants to help."

"Then what?"

"I have to leave for a couple of hours."

Elizabeth was watching them. "You found out where they went, didn't you? And you're going after them."

McGarvey nodded. He should have realized that Liz would figure it out. But he didn't have time to argue with them.

"I'm coming with you," Elizabeth said.

"You're staying here with your mother," McGarvey said firmly. "Otto is loading some information on a disk for you, and your job is to make sure nothing happens to it. No matter what."

Kathleen's nostrils flared in anger. "I suppose it would be futile of me to try and talk you out of whatever you're going to do this morning."

"They tried twice, Katy. And both times a lot of good people got hurt. It's not going to happen a third time."

Kathleen touched his weather-beaten cheek. "Now that you've started to come back into my life, I don't want to lose you."

"You won't," McGarvey said, and they embraced. Mixed with his rage was a sense of wonder that he had allowed all these years to pass without her. Empty, senseless years.

"Take care of yourself, my darling," Kathleen whispered in his ear.

He gave her an extra hug, kissed his daughter again, then walked down the hall to where Rencke was working on the computer.

"I'm going out to Morningside."

"They might not be there," Rencke said. He looked terrible, his eyes red and puffy.

"You're probably right," McGarvey said. He sincerely hoped that Rencke was wrong.

"I'm only giving you a couple hours, Mac. If I haven't heard anything by then I'm telling Fred Rudolph about Kmart. I don't care what you say."

McGarvey had to smile. "Fair enough. Did you load the disk?"

"Yeah. I'll bring it over to Liz as soon as I'm finished here. I set up a search program for Joseph Lee. Guys like him just don't disappear. Sooner or later he'll make contact with someone and I'll find out about it."

McGarvey nodded. "You know the score, Otto. Cover your tracks."

Rencke grinned like a kid at Christmas. "They won't even know I've been there." He got serious. "It's payback time, and I can't blame you. But watch your ass, will ya?"

"Count on it."

Private Aviation Terminal
Dulles International Airport

Kajiyama came back to the van in a big hurry and climbed in the front passenger seat. "Get us out of here," he told the commando behind the wheel.

"What's wrong?" Kondo demanded, though he'd half expected that something else would go wrong tonight. He sat in the back with the other commando, all that was left of his team.

"Somebody's watching the airplane, that's what." Kajiyama was practically jumping out of his skin.

The driver glanced in the rearview mirror. Kondo nodded for him to do as Kajiyama asked, and they headed out.

"Calm down. Who is watching the airplane?"

"I don't bloody well know," Kajiyama blurted. "They're parked on the apron just across from the Gulfstream. Government plates." Kajiyama turned and looked back. "The woman knew your name. No wonder they know about the plane. They have you connected with Mr. Lee, so now there's no way out for you. No way out for any of us, because of some stupid blunder you made. Someone probably saw you hanging around with Croft at the Hay Adams and made the ID."

"We weren't going to fly out until morning in any event." Kondo needed time to think out their next moves. "We'll go back to Morningside just as we planned—"

"You knew that something like this was going to happen," Kajiyama shouted. "It's why you wanted to come out here first, to see if they'd already made the connection."

"That's correct, Kajiyama-san," Kondo said patiently.

"That's also why I didn't kill Sandy Patterson when you wanted me to do it. The Gulfstream may no longer be an option for us. But she will provide us with another."

"How?"

"I don't know yet. But we'll work it out if you don't lose your head like a stupid *gai-jin*."

"It is you who are stupid. We failed, hasn't that sunk in? Or have you already worked out who you will blame when you talk to Joseph Lee? *If* you have the chance to talk to him."

Only a supreme effort of willpower and self-discipline stopped Kondo from pulling out his pistol and killing the man then and there. There was still an outside chance that they might get to the Gulfstream, and Kajiyama was their only remaining pilot. "We will work it out. And when we return home, both of us will make our reports to Mr. Lee. It is I who will take the blame, not you."

Cropley, Maryland

"What's your situation out there?" FBI Director Pierone demanded.

"The CIA got chewed up pretty badly this time," Rudolph replied. "But they've agreed to let us take over the investigation."

"Considering the circumstances, they don't have much of a choice."

"They're blaming us because of the Web site screwup. But they had some of their best people out here, and still they missed guarding against the one thing that would have saved them. Frankly I don't know if we would have done any better, but it's in our lap now. And there's a connection between this attack and the Georgetown bombing through the

Far East Trade Association. Looks like one of their people arranged for the helicopter the State boys found on the other side of the river. And I'm pretty sure that we'll come up with IDs on some of the terrorists tying them to Joseph Lee or one of his companies."

"What's the point, Fred?" Pierone asked. "Are you any closer to finding out why they want Kirk McGarvey dead? I've got to tell the President something. Presumably the CIA has kept him up to speed on its investigation. But I've got nothing to report. In the meantime the media is flooding our switchboard."

"I don't think McGarvey knows much more than we do," Rudolph said. "At least he's not saying anything to me, if he does. I guess the key is finding Joseph Lee and interviewing him. But as long as he remains in hiding in Japan there isn't much we can do except run down every lead we come across. We might get lucky and find the rest of the terrorists before they get out of the country."

"If they're Lee's people they might use his private jet."

"It's being watched," Rudolph said.

"Okay. I want to see you in my office at nine o'clock, along with Jack Hailey and Tom Moulton. Maybe we can start making some sense of this." Hailey was SAC for the District of Columbia, and Moulton was chief of the Bureau's Anti-Terrorism Unit. Both good men.

"See you then, Mr. Director," Rudolph said, and he broke the connection. Almost immediately he got another call, this one from Otto Rencke at CIA headquarters.

"Do you have a pencil and paper?"

"Just a minute." Rudolph cradled the cell phone and took out a notebook and pen. "Go ahead."

"Have you traced the helicopter yet?"

"The helicopter was leased by someone at Far East Trade, but we're still working on the boat. Did McGarvey ask you to call me?"

"Do you know about the car and two vans they're using?"

"No."

Rencke rattled off the makes and models of the car and vans, and the three license numbers. "Get that over to the Maryland Highway Patrol, maybe they'll get lucky."

"Where are they going? They must have a base of operations somewhere close. Do you know where it is?"

"Do you still have your pencil out?" Rencke asked.

"Yes, go ahead."

Rencke gave him three names, one of whom Rudolph recognized as a Bureau computer programmer. "They're all pals of Sandy Patterson's. They all knew about the Cropley safe house. And they all had access to the Bureau's Web site."

"How the hell did you find that, Rencke?"

"There'll be a few other names of Bureau people who fed information to Tony Croft. When this is over you should probably think about cleaning house."

"I want to talk to McGarvey—" Rudolph said, but he was talking to no one. Rencke had broken the connection.

For a moment he stood there vexed, but then he tore off the slip with the three license numbers, walked over to one of the Maryland Highway Patrol officers and gave it to him.

"We think the terrorists may be using these vehicles to get around," he told the officer. "Tell your people to take it easy. You saw what they did here."

Morningside, Maryland

Five minutes later the van carrying Kondo, Kajiyama and the two commandos took the Andrews Main Gate exit off I-95 and headed north to the old Kmart. On the way over from Dulles, Kondo had counted six highway patrol cruisers, the last just ahead of them as they turned off. The FBI and CIA knew about Joseph Lee's airplane, but they didn't know about the vans, which meant they didn't know about the warehouse yet. But they'd obviously pulled out all the stops.

It had been nothing but blind dumb luck that the whore had seen him at the Hay Adams with Tony Croft. It didn't explain how the authorities knew his name, but it was possible they got it from some intelligence file even he didn't know about. But, and this was the thought that caused him the most anger, it was more likely that the Bureau got his name in the raid on Sandy Patterson's office. The codes and blinds she thought were foolproof might not have been. She had screwed up in Georgetown, and now it looked as if she'd screwed up again. If the Bureau hadn't come up with something from the raid on her office, then the security agents out at the Cropley safe house would not have been alerted and the mission would have happened as planned.

Women in general were stupid. But *gai-jin* women were the worst because they didn't know their place.

The commando drove to the rear of the Kmart and stopped in front of one of the loading bays. Kajiyama jumped out, opened the overhead door, waited for the van to pull inside, then closed and locked it.

Sandy Patterson was waiting by the stairs when Kondo came from the rear of the store. She was wide-eyed and breathless.

"How did it go?" she asked.

Kondo forced a cold smile. "Just fine." He took her arm and they headed upstairs. "I'll tell you all about it, and then we'll make our plans for getting back to Japan."

"I thought we were taking Mr. Lee's jet—"

"Unfortunately the authorities are guarding it," Kondo said reasonably. "Which means we must find another way. But we have plenty of time. Not to worry."

McGarvey watched from his car across the street as the van pulled up and entered the old Kmart. The man in the front passenger seat had opened the service door, which probably meant that no one was inside. But there was no way of knowing how many other men in addition to the driver were in the vehicle. Possibly as many as a dozen, though he doubted it. They'd found seven paragliders and four bodies. Which meant that there were three terrorists unaccounted for, and possibly a fourth who had run the boat ashore. They could have left other men with the helicopter and the van, but he didn't think they would have split their force. There was no reason for it.

He was guessing four men, all heavily armed. But he'd faced worse odds than that before. He checked the load in his Walther PPK, transferred the two spare magazines into his trouser pocket and pulled off his light-colored jacket. His trousers were dark, as was his short-sleeved Izod. He glanced at his reflection in the rearview mirror. They had killed Jacqueline and two dozen others. They had seriously hurt his only child. And they had tried to kill his wife. There was no time now for anger, he had to remind himself. This was a tactical situation, nothing more, and he would rely on his training and experience.

He grinned viciously. "Bullshit," he murmured. He slipped out of the car and headed across the street to the east side of the Kmart.

Kajiyama was in what had been Kmart's cafeteria, which they'd used for a command center. He happened to look over at the bank of six closed-circuit television monitors in time to see a dark figure darting around the corner on the east side of the building. The other monitors showed nobody else. He put down the bottle of Evian he'd been drinking, switched off the lights and raced out into the main part of the store.

"There is someone out there," he called to the two commandos who were over by their cots preparing to get some sleep. "One man. In front, on the east side," he said gesturing toward the painted-over glass front doors.

The commandos reacted instantly, drawing their weapons and donning their night-vision oculars as they raced toward the front of the store.

Kajiyama grabbed a pair of Uzis and took the stairs up to the offices two at a time.

Sandy Patterson, her clothing in disarray, a trickle of blood at the corner of her mouth, was backed up against the wall, Kondo, his hand raised, advancing toward her.

"Take your revenge later; someone is outside," Kajiyama warned.

Kondo turned around in surprise. "Is it the police?"

"No. It looks like there is only one man." Kajiyama tossed him one of the Uzis. "He came around the front from the east side."

Kondo smiled. "It's McGarvey," he said triumphantly. He glanced at the woman. "Apparently you screwed up even this simple assignment, otherwise he would never have found us." He turned back. "Just as well that the arrogant bastard is here. Our mission will be a success after all."

"He's not dead yet."

"Even if he is twice as good as his file suggests, he cannot defeat four-to-one odds."

McGarvey ducked under the last of the closed-circuit television cameras along the east side of the building and raced around to the loading docks in the rear. He'd spotted the cameras almost immediately and figured that if someone inside was watching, he would make them believe that he was coming in from the front. With only four people they would be hard pressed to watch every approach. The building was simply too big.

There were two cameras covering the back of the store, one at each corner. He studied the layout, then screwed the silencer on his pistol. The cameras only covered the loading docks and not the second-story windows. He ducked beneath the nearest camera, then reached up and fired one shot, taking out the lens. Even if someone had been staring at the monitor, they would have seen only an indistinct blur, and then nothing.

Stuffing the gun in his belt, McGarvey shoved a Dumpster a few feet up against the building beneath a canopy over one of the service entrances. Directly above was a window. He scrambled up the Dumpster, then up on the flimsy fiberglass awning that crackled and nearly buckled under his weight. He paused a moment to make sure it wouldn't collapse, then looked in the window. Venetian blinds obscured his view, but he could see enough to determine that he was looking into an empty office. The door, to what appeared to be a corridor, was open. The only illumination seemed to come from outside the office, probably a security light at the stairs.

If they were on the ball it wouldn't take them long to figure out that trouble was coming at them from the rear of the building, not the front. They would be coming to investigate.

A woman appeared in the doorway, and McGarvey ducked down as she looked over her shoulder. She wouldn't be able to see outside, because of the light in the corridor, but she came across the room directly to the window. As McGarvey slid to the right, she undid the latch, slid the window aside, raised the venetian blinds and looked outside directly into the muzzle of McGarvey's gun.

"I hope to God that you're Kirk McGarvey," she whispered urgently. She showed him her hands. "I'm not armed."

McGarvey lowered his gun. "Sandy Patterson?"

She nodded. "That's right. They're waiting for you downstairs. They think that you're coming in from the front." She held the venetian blinds aside as McGarvey climbed through the window.

"I thought you were with them," he said, hurrying silently to the door. Nothing moved in the corridor, and he could hear no sounds in the building. He turned back and looked at the woman. A bruise was forming on her right cheek, and she looked like she was on the verge of collapse.

"I *was* with them," she whispered. "But after Georgetown . . ." She searched his face for understanding. "I didn't know it'd be like that."

"A lot of good people were hurt," McGarvey said, amazed with himself that he hadn't already put a bullet in her brain. She was at least indirectly responsible for the Georgetown bombing and the attack at the safe house. For what, he wondered?

"I know," she said lowering her head. "But it's gone too far." She looked up. "He's crazy. They all are."

"Okay, take it easy, Sandy," McGarvey said. He would have to make his judgments and decisions later. Right now he needed her help. "How many are there?"

"Kondo and Kajiyama, and I think only two of the commandos came back."

"Weapons?"

"Sniper pistols, Uzis, grenades. And they're all wearing night-vision equipment."

"How'd you know I was at the window?"

"I was upstairs and heard something on the loading dock. When I looked out my window I spotted you climbing up."

"They're going to figure out real soon that I'm not out front. So you better find someplace to hide, and keep your head down until it's over."

"You'll never make it that way." Sandy shook her head. "They're too good and too heavily armed."

"You got any suggestions?"

"If I can get Kondo up here, you can take him. I don't think the others will have a lot of enthusiasm once he's down. They'll probably run to save their own skins."

"If he thinks it's a trick he'll kill you."

Sandy looked into his eyes, and after a moment she shrugged. "You were thinking about it yourself when you came through the window."

McGarvey looked out into the still empty corridor. "Okay, see if you can get him up here."

"Don't miss," Sandy said. She brushed past him and went to the open office door across from the stairs. She glanced back at McGarvey, then stepped to the head of the stairs. "Kondo-san," she called out.

McGarvey studied her. She held herself as if she were in a lot of mental anguish. She had made one too many mistakes, for whatever reason, and she was trying desperately now to make it up with one daring act.

"Kondo-san," she called louder. "You must come up here now."

"What is it?" someone called from the foot of the stairs.

"It's Mr. Lee, on the telephone for Kondo-san."

Someone came up the stairs, and Sandy stepped backwards into the office. McGarvey ducked back just as a figure dressed all in black, night-vision oculars pushed up on his forehead, appeared at the head of the stairs and crossed the corridor into the office where Sandy had disappeared.

McGarvey waited just a second before he slipped into the corridor and silently raced the twenty feet to the open office door.

"The call is for Kondo-san, and nobody else," Sandy said.

McGarvey stepped around the corner into the office and laid the muzzle of the Walther's silencer against the base of the man's skull.

"This is Seijewa, one of their commandos," Sandy said.

"Take his gun and goggles," McGarvey told her. He shoved his pistol harder into the base of the terrorist's skull. "How many more men down-stairs?"

Siejewa said nothing, but his muscles bunched up as Sandy took his weapon and night-vision oculars.

"Was he involved in Georgetown?" McGarvey asked.

"No. But he was at Cropley. They were going to kidnap your wife and daughter and use them to get to you."

"Some friends of mine died there," McGarvey said. "So you either cooperate with me now, or I'll kill you."

"Americans don't have the courage—" Seijewa said contemptuously. He started to turn, when McGarvey fired one shot directly into the base of his skull. He started forward, then crumpled like an empty sack.

Sandy let out a squeak and stepped back, nearly tripping over her own feet, her eyes and mouth open wide. "My God—"

"Seeing it first hand isn't very pretty, is it," McGarvey said harshly. "Where are the switches for the main floor lights?"

She couldn't drag her eyes from the body. A puddle of blood was already pooling up beside the head.

"The light switches," McGarvey demanded.

She looked up, trying to gather herself. "Downstairs. Around the corner. A door to the utility panel."

"Is it locked?"

"No."

"Okay, we're going downstairs. As soon as I'm in position, you're going to switch on every light in the building." He glanced at the sniper pistol in her hand. "Unless you plan on shooting me in the back."

She shook her head. "I'd have to go back to Japan with them. I want to stay here. Even if it means jail."

McGarvey donned the dead terrorist's night-vision oculars and went down the dark stairs. Everything in front of him was bathed in an un-earthly green glow. He held up at the bottom to make sure no one was waiting for them in the corridor, then signaled for Sandy Patterson to go to the utility panel. He went left past some restrooms and then ducked down as the corridor opened onto what had been the main sales floor. It was littered with uneven stacks of desks, chairs, file cabinets, bookcases, lamps and other office equipment.

He scanned left to right, concentrating his attention toward the front of the store. But the building was huge. The only way he was going to find the remaining three terrorists was to make them come to him.

He glanced back at Sandy down the corridor. She had the utility panel door open and was looking directly toward him, but in his darkness he didn't think she could see him. Kondo's people had shut down all the security and fire exit lights, and now Sandy was waiting for some kind of a signal.

A pile of a dozen gray steel government-issue desks was stacked, some of them three high, just across from the corridor. Keeping low, McGarvey crept across to them, stuffed his pistol in his belt, climbed up on one of the desks and then putting his back to the effort, toppled one of the desks stacked on another, sending it crashing into a jumble of file cabinets with a tremendous crash.

He yanked off his night-vision oculars and pulled out his pistol, thumbing the safety off. "Now!" he shouted.

The lights came on, one long string after another, in quick succession. For a second or so the sudden light would completely destroy the vision of anyone caught wearing night-ocular equipment. All of the remaining three terrorists, McGarvey hoped.

Straight down the aisle a dark clad figure that had been crouched behind a pile of steel cabinets turned around as he yanked off his night-vision oculars. Compensating for the degradation in accuracy because of the silencer, McGarvey fired three shots left, on target and right, the third shot catching the figure in the chest and driving him backward into the cabinets.

Someone to his immediate left fired a long burst from an Uzi in his general direction, evidently still half blinded from the sudden light. McGarvey ducked right as a figure dressed in black appeared in the aisle. The terrorist started to swing his Uzi around when McGarvey fired two shots, both of them catching the man in the face and knocking him off his feet.

All the overhead lights went out, plunging the store into almost total darkness.

McGarvey stepped to the right and jumped down from the desk. Almost instantly the desks and cabinets piled above him were raked with automatic weapons fire. The weapon evidently was equipped with a flash suppressor, because McGarvey hadn't been able to pick out the shooter's position.

He pulled on his night-vision oculars in time to catch a movement at the end of the corridor as the last of the terrorists came out on the main floor. He fired a couple of shots, the rolled left. Sandy Patterson lay face down on the floor in front of the open utility panel door, her hands covering her head.

McGarvey held his breath and cocked his head to listen as he ejected his spent magazine and reloaded. There was no sound. Not even traffic noises from the highway a hundred yards away. The night was perfectly still.

"We can stay here all night until the FBI shows up." McGarvey called out. He scrambled around the corner on all fours. Someone moved to his right, then stopped.

"I don't think help is coming, Mr. McGarvey. I think that you are here this morning for revenge."

McGarvey rose up above the level of the desktop and looked in that direction. He could see desks and chairs, but no movement. He ducked back down. "I'm not interested in revenge unless you're Bruce Kondo."

"Yes? Why this man specifically?"

"Because he's not a *Bu-shi*. He's a coward."

The terrorist laughed, the sound coming from farther around the pile of desks McGarvey was crouched behind. "I'm Bruce Kondo, but I'm neither *Bu-shi*, as you call it, nor a coward."

"What then?" McGarvey edged closer.

"Why, an intelligence officer, just like you."

"Working for whom?" McGarvey switched directions and headed around the pile of desks from the back.

"Mr. Lee, of course."

"MITI?"

"There are certain powers in the Japanese government that are involved."

"With what?"

"You will not live long enough to learn about the plan, but the world will know all about it in a couple of days."

"Is it going to be another Pearl Harbor?" McGarvey asked. "Is that what you crazy bastards are going to try?" Is it Morning Sun again? The old men in the *zaibatsu*, looking for their moment of glory before they die?"

Kondo coughed, then laughed again. "Another Pearl Harbor will not be necessary—"

McGarvey had edged his way around the jumbled pile of desks and file cabinets to where Kondo was sitting on the floor, his back against one of the cabinets. McGarvey pointed his pistol at the man's head, less than two feet from his right temple.

Kondo turned and faced the Walther's muzzle. He smiled and slowly raised his left hand. He held a fragmentation grenade, the lever still attached but the safety pin gone. Blood seeped from a wound in his back. "Shall we get it over with now, or would you like to chat a bit longer?"

McGarvey stared at the man for several long seconds. In his mind's eye he was seeing Jacqueline as she was leaving the sidewalk cafe, the oncoming Mercedes, the bomb, the tremendous explosion. And he was seeing the look of pain and helpless defiance on his daughter's face as she lay in the hospital bed after the attack. And the look in his wife's eyes after the Cropley attack.

He lowered his gun, eased the hammer down, flipped the safety catch back and stuffed the gun in his belt at the small of his back.

"You're right. I came here for revenge." McGarvey shook his head disparagingly. "But you're not worth it." He started to get to his feet.

"I'll do it," Kondo shouted wildly, and he thrust his grenade hand out.

It was exactly what McGarvey wanted to happen. He grabbed Kondo's hand with his right, his powerful fingers curling about the man's fist and the grenade.

"*Iie*," Kondo screamed like a wild man. He pulled a stiletto out of a sheath strapped to his chest and stabbed at McGarvey's heart.

McGarvey deflected the thrust, then grabbed Kondo's wrist and bent the man's arm and knife hand back toward his own throat.

The lights came on again, momentarily blinding McGarvey until his night-vision oculars slowly began to compensate for the overload. Kondo was very strong, and it took every ounce of McGarvey's strength to force the point of the stiletto to the terrorist's neck just below his chin.

"Kill him," Kondo shouted. "Kill him!"

McGarvey looked over his shoulder. Sandy Patterson, a sniper pistol in her hand, stood five feet away, a determined look on her face.

"Kill him—" Kondo screamed hysterically.

Sandy didn't move, and McGarvey turned back to the terrorist. Without a word, without emotion, drained now of his feelings of hate and rage and even contempt, McGarvey slowly forced the blade of the nine-inch stiletto into Kondo's throat. The razor-sharp steel easily cut through the tissue and cartilage, the terrorist's body convulsing, blood gushing over McGarvey's hand and wrist. Then Kondo became still, his muscles slack.

McGarvey released his grip on the knife, then carefully pried Kondo's dead fingers from the grenade.

"Get down," he ordered Sandy. He tossed the grenade toward the front of the stairs then fell back behind the pile of furniture. A second later a tremendous explosion rocked the store, blowing the glass out of the front windows and sending it spraying across the empty parking lot.

TWENTY-ONE

Tanegashima Space Center

The gantry elevator bumped to a sudden stop ten feet below the open payload doors. Ripley pressed the button, but nothing happened; the power was evidently off.

"Hello," he called up to the technicians.

One of them came to the rail and looked down at him. *"Hai."*

"The power is off. I want to come up."

The technician said something over his shoulder, and Hiroshi Kimura appeared at the rail. Like everyone else he wore spotlessly clean white coveralls, booties and a paper head cover with the NSDA logo. He looked surprised and irritated. If anything, he and all the Japanese at the center had gotten even cooler toward the Americans in the past twenty-four hours. Something was going on, all the more disturbing to Ripley because it was so close to launch.

"What are you doing here? You belong back at launch control."

"I'm taking a last look before everything is buttoned up," Ripley said. "Is there anything wrong with that?"

"Evidently you haven't properly gone through sterile procedures. That is why the elevator stopped. It's programmed to do that so we can avoid contamination." Kimura said something to the technician, who disappeared from view. From his position Ripley could see the edge of the open payload hatch in the rocket's nose and the open door to the clean room where the satellite had been prepped prior to loading.

"I'll do the procedure again," Ripley said.

"There is no need for that, Major. We are nearly finished here. As soon as we secure the hatch, this level will be cleared."

Ripley shaded his eyes against the glare of the gantry lights. Something wasn't right about the satellite nestled in its compartment just beneath the nose cone. He stepped to the left to get a better look. The hatch swung shut, but not before he caught a momentary glimpse of a bit of the satellite's outer covering, and his eyes narrowed.

"I'll restore the power. But you must return to the pad."

The elevator lurched. "Wait a minute," Ripley said. "It's part of my job to see that everything is being done according to specs."

"The launch clock is about to start. Would you delay it?"

"If need be I'll not sign off my final compliance inspection form," Ripley said. He was confused, and he was trying to sound normal. Kimura was looking at him with a strange expression. Unusual for a Japanese.

"Very well, Major. If you insist."

The elevator went up the last ten feet, and Ripley stepped onto the steel mesh catwalk. The door to the empty clean room was open, but the rocket's payload hatch was closed, and two technicians were finishing with the last flush fasteners.

"I want to see inside."

"If you insist," Kimura said. The technicians looked over their shoulders. "But since you are not clean, we will have to return the satellite to the payload building where it will be disassembled and sterilized. Since that procedure will take at least thirty days, you and your team will be returned home. A new team would be requested in that case. One that would work with us, not against us."

Ripley weighed his options. He wasn't quite so sure of what he'd seen after all. And their final inspection of the satellite in the clean room had turned up no anomalies. There was nothing to be worried about. Yet he could not shake the feeling of the unease.

"Major?" Kimura prompted.

"You have a point. I'll meet you at launch control." Ripley stepped back aboard the elevator.

"Very well."

The rocket was being cleared, stage by stage, from the top down for launch. Once the final preparations were completed and each system signed for, the countdown clock would start at T-minus forty-eight hours. From this point he and his Tiger team would actually have very little to do. They would remain as observers. Theoretically they would answer questions if some critical problem were to arise for which the Japanese had little or no experience. It was unlikely, but possible.

At the bottom, he walked across the launch platform toward the ramp to ground level where a dozen vehicles were parked. At one point he stopped and looked back up the wall of the rocket rising above him. He wasn't sure what he had seen in the payload compartment, but he was certain of one thing at least. What he did catch a glimpse of was definitely not gold foil. The outer skin of the satellite they had checked in the clean room was gold. The one in the rocket was black. He took off his paper head cover and went to his car.

Morningside, Maryland

McGarvey hadn't known what he was going to accomplish by coming out here this morning. But looking back across the parking lot at the shattered front of the old Kmart store as the first of the tagged and bagged bodies were being wheeled out, he figured his mission had been a total failure. He'd wanted to strike back at the monsters who had tried to hurt his family and who had killed his friends, but he'd needed information more than revenge. As it stood now, he had neither.

Fred Rudolph broke away from a group of reporters and television people he'd been talking to and came over to where McGarvey leaned against a Maryland Highway Patrol cruiser smoking a cigaretee.

"Here we are again," he said sharply, obviously having trouble keeping his anger and disgust in check. "Four more bodies, no answers." He glanced toward the ambulances. "You knew they were here and you ordered your people to keep their mouths shut. Cute."

"I thought I could take at least one of them alive," McGarvey said. It was a lie, but it was better for Rudolph just now than the truth.

"What the hell am I supposed to do with a statement like that? From a high-ranking officer of the Central Intelligence Agency? Is that how our government is supposed to conduct business? I thought that's what we hated about the Nazis and the Soviets."

"I didn't have much of a choice, Fred."

"Yes, you did," Rudolph shouted. "You find out about a crime, you call the cops. That's how it works."

"Tell that to the families in Georgetown, and to the families of my people at Cropley," McGarvey shot back. He was tired and fed up with himself. It was hard to keep on track. A part of him wanted to run now, find a safe hole in which to crawl and pull the dirt over his head. You're just like a dog, Katy had once told him. When you get hurt you don't want anyone tending to your wounds. You just want to crawl under a porch somewhere and be left alone. But it wasn't over yet. The hard parts were yet to come. He was beginning to seriously doubt if he was up to the challenge. Run, something inside his head nagged. Run. Run.

Rudolph looked over to one of the Maryland Highway Patrol cruisers where Sandy Patterson was sitting in the back. "What about her?"

"She wants a lawyer, but she says she'll cooperate," McGarvey said. He told Rudolph what she had done this evening.

"The odds were against her, so she switched sides when she figured it would do her the most good." Rudolph shrugged.

"There were a couple of times when she could have had me. They would have gotten away clean by the time Otto blew the whistle. She realized that she was in way over her head, and she wanted out."

"You have to admire her sense of timing."

"I think it's more complicated than that," McGarvey said. "Billion-aires have a way of hypnotizing people. And Lee had her, just like he has half of Washington."

"Did she make the connection?"

"She doesn't know the specifics. Just that Lee has been working on some project for at least five years, which includes campaign funding for the White House and a bunch of congressmen. But whatever he's up to is supposed to happen very soon."

"Is that why they came after you?"

"She didn't know. Except that Tony Croft and I were their priority targets."

"Croft, because he knew too much, and you, because you were in a position to learn too much," Rudolph said. "But what? And what now?"

"I'm going to continue doing what they wanted to stop me from doing."

"Which is what, exactly?"

"I don't have anything concrete to tell you—"

"Bullshit," Rudolph exploded. A couple of cops nearby looked over. Rudolph lowered his voice. "You know exactly what's going on, goddammit." He was pissed off. "I'm in this investigation right up to my neck, and so far everything leads back to the White House. Am I wrong?"

"I don't know."

"Don't give me that, McGarvey. I've stuck my neck way out on this one, and I'll be damned if I'm going to end up a scapegoat." McGarvey didn't look away. "Give me something. Anything."

"It goes to the President."

"Are you telling me that the President of the United States is a traitor? That he's sold us out to Jospeh Lee and the Japanese for money, or for whatever reason? Because if that's what you really think is going on and you can prove that Lindsay was behind the Georgetown bombing and the attack on you and your family, then I quit. I'll just get out of the Bureau and say the hell with everything." Rudolph's lips compressed as if he wanted to stop himself from going on. But he couldn't help himself. "We've had some crooks occupying the Oval Office. But no one ever believed that they loved themselves more than they loved the country. Egotists, cocksmen, liars, bastards, but not traitors." He shook his head and gave McGarvey a bleak look. "I refuse to believe it."

Tanegashima Space Center

"They're just about finished buttoning up," Ripley said in the gallery above launch control. The center was busy and would remain that way until launch.

"Did you see Kimura?" Maggie asked. They were keeping their voices conversational so they would not attract undue attention.

"Yeah, he was there. He all but kicked me out."

"Why?"

"The elevator locked out just below the clean room. Kimura claimed it was because I hadn't gone through sterile procedures. But that was a crock of shit. He could see I had done it."

They glanced at the status boards. The clock, stopped at 48:00:00, would begin to count down as soon as Kimura acknowledged that the satellite was secured in the rocket.

"He's risking the launch window and he knows it," Maggie said. "So what the hell is he up to?"

"They're hiding something," Ripley said looking around to make sure they weren't being overheard.

"No kidding—"

"I mean something big, Maggie. It's not the H2C, it has something to do with the satellite. And they're nervous as hell that we're going to find out what's going on. At first I thought it was nothing more than extrastringent security, but these guys are really uptight. Kimura wouldn't let me up to the payload level until *after* the hatch was shut."

"If he really thought you hadn't gone through sterile procedures he was within his rights."

"He knew damn well that I was clean. But I got a glimpse of the satellite before they closed the hatch. It wasn't the same bird that we've been working on."

Maggie's eyes narrowed and she gave him a look of skepticism. "What do you mean?"

"Unless they painted the gold foil black for some reason, the satellite in the payload bay wasn't Hagoromo II."

"What about the lighting up there, Frank? Shadows?"

"Gold foil reflects everything. I would have seen it if it was there."

The activity on the floor of the launch center was beginning to pick up. More than half the consoles were lit up and operational now, including the positions for the Tiger team.

"Okay, so what are we going to do about it?" she asked. "Do you want to call Hartley and blow the whistle? I'll back you up. So will the others, you know that."

Ripley had thought about that option. "I wouldn't know what to tell him. But if we did stop the launch, providing the Japanese went along with us, and the satellite turned out to be legitimate, and it was just some shadow I saw up there, we'd be in some serious shit."

Maggie had to smile. "What do you want to do?"

"We have forty-eight hours plus before launch," Ripley said. "I'm going to spend the time doing a little research, and you and the others, my dear, are going to cover for me. I have a ton of paperwork to catch up with. A deluge."

Maggie joined Hammarstedt and the others at the Tiger team's consoles on the upper tier in launch control. They would stay at their positions until the forty-eight-hour countdown clock started. Afterward they would alternate shifts depending on what procedures and tests were scheduled.

The whole team would be on duty once again for the last few hours before launch.

"Oh, hi, Maggie," Hammerstedt said, looking up. "Where's Frank?"

"He had to go back to the office. Paperwork."

Hammerstedt smiled. "Better him than me."

The guards were no longer posted around payload building one, and the facility was deserted now that the satellite had been taken away. Ripley paused a moment in the middle of the main assembly bay and listened for a sound, any sound. But the place was as silent as a mausoleum. The lights were on, but turned low in the offices upstairs, and unless Kimura suspected something, he would still be out on the launch pad.

Ripley crossed the floor of the bay and took the stairs up two at a time. He would not be missed at launch control for at least another hour. After that he would either have to get back or be at his office, because questions would be asked.

He didn't really know what he was looking for. Evidence that the Japanese had switched satellites, perhaps. Or, at the very least, that they had removed or covered the gold foil on Hagoromo II. But for the life of him he couldn't figure out why they would do the latter.

Kimura's office was unlocked. Ripley let himself in and powered up the satellite engineer's computer, pulling up the launch menu. He entered the Tiger team's password, then brought up the database for the satellite. The language was Japanese, but the mathematics and engineering details were all in English, since the Japanese had no technical terms. Starting with the main frame on which the satellite's component subassemblies were attached, he began looking for inconsistencies. Something that might at least give him a hint what the Japanese were really up to. But, not knowing what he was looking for, and searching a database that was partially in a foreign language, Ripley didn't think he had much chance for success. But he had to try.

Joseph Lee was walking alone on the beach five miles from the launchpad when a Toyota Land Cruiser with NSDA markings pulled off the road and came toward him. He had come out to clear his mind of discordant thoughts. If Miriam were here she would have cut through his present difficulties with a word or two of advice. He missed her dearly.

Shinichi Hirota, Tanegashima's chief of security, got out of the Toyota and came over. He was dressed, as usual, in a military-style uniform without insignia. He saluted.

"Is it about Ripley?" Lee asked.

"Just as you expected, he broke into Kimura's office and is at this moment searching through the computer files. He may have seen something before the payload doors were closed, as Kimura suspected."

"He will find nothing in the computer."

"No, sir," Hirota said, somewhat impatiently. He had come with more important news. "The other matter you asked me to check."

Lee's mouth tightened. "Yes?"

"Our Washington embassy has received no direct news. But there have been unconfirmed reports about an incident or incidents in Morningside and Cropley, Maryland. An explosion, gunfire and police, plus the Federal Bureau of Investigation." Hirota shrugged. "It may be nothing."

Lee knew better, but he nodded and kept his true feelings of disappointment and rage from his face. Kondo should have called hours ago to report that the mission was a success. Once again his trusted aide had failed. The question uppermost in Lee's mind was the extent of the failure. The countdown clock was about to begin. They needed forty-eight hours. Two days, no more. Time enough, he wondered. If Kondo's mission had not been a complete failure he may have bought them enough time. However, the reverse could easily be true.

He glanced down the beach toward the launchpad lit blood red in the setting sun. "There is another problem that you may have to deal with," he said.

"Here?"

"Yes, here," Lee said. "His name is Kirk McGarvey, and there is an outside chance that he will be coming to us in time for the launch. You must be ready for him, because he is very deadly, and there is so much at stake here. Do you understand, Hirota?"

The security chief grinned. "*Hai*, Lee-san," he replied.

TWENTY-TWO

CIA Headquarters

The morning shift was just beginning to arrive when McGarvey finally got back and took the private elevator up to the seventh floor. Whatever was about to happen was going to break very soon, and he had at least one major hurdle to overcome before they were out of the woods.

Dick Adkins came out of an office as McGarvey emerged from the elevator. "Where were you? I've been trying to reach you all morning. Looks as if the Bureau might have got lucky down in Morningside."

"I was there," McGarvey said. He headed down the corridor to his office. His chief of staff fell in beside him, a look of exasperation on his face.

"Are you going to tell me about it? Or is it something else that you're going to keep to yourself for my protection?"

"I'm sorry, Dick, but it was my show," McGarvey explained. He felt bad that he was cutting Adkins out of the loop, but there had been no time to include him. Nor was there much time now.

"What the hell are you talking about?" Adkins responded angrily. "You're the deputy director of Operations, for Christ's sake. You're not supposed to move out of this building without a bodyguard. Murphy's having a fit every hour on the hour. He expects me to keep track of you."

"Otto found out where the guys who hit Cropley probably went. Wasn't much time to tell you about it. As it was I got there about the same time they did."

"Shit," Adkins said. "What happened?"

"They're dead."

Adkins gave him a hard glance. "Why didn't I think of that," he said, resigned. He studied McGarvey. "You were right about one thing. You sure the hell aren't an administrator." He shrugged. "I don't know what I'm supposed to do. What do you want me to tell Murphy?"

"The truth," McGarvey said, tiredly.

"He'll fire you," Adkins warned.

McGarvey stopped. "It was personal, Dick. They came after my wife and daughter. Twice. I wanted to make sure there wouldn't be a third time."

Adkins backed down. "Okay, Mac. I guess I can understand what you did. Doesn't take much of a leap. But what's next? If all the bad guys are dead, who do we go after now? Or are you going to hold that from me too?"

"What about Joseph Lee? Anything from our networks?"

"He hasn't returned to his house in Taiwan, and he hasn't come back here. But we're still beating the bushes."

"Is his wife still here?"

"So far as I know, she is," Adkins said. "The Bureau is watching her."

"I want to know the moment she leaves," McGarvey instructed. "She'll be taking the Gulfstream back to Taiwan. Probably in the next day or two."

Adkins stared at him for a few moments. "I thought it would be different, somehow, with you as DO."

McGarvey smiled. "I can't change now."

Adkins shook his head. "No, I don't expect you can. The Company is going to have to change, and I don't know if that's a good thing."

"Lean on our Taiwanese and Japanese networks. I'd like to know where Lee has gotten himself to."

"I'll double our assets out there. Beyond that there isn't much we can do."

"I appreciate that," McGarvey said. "But we'll have some kind of an answer one way or the other in the next couple of days."

"Are you going to be here for the rest of the morning?"

"Probably not."

Adkins smiled. "Keep me posted, Mac. Can you do that much? It'd make my job a hell of a lot easier."

"Sure," McGarvey said, but the answer convinced neither of them.

Ms. Swanfeld looked up from her computer when McGarvey walked in. He'd been on the job for nearly a week, yet he hadn't spent more than a few hours behind his desk. The day-to-day operations of the DO were overseen by Adkins and Ms. Swanfeld, and the strain was showing on her face. He had warned them. Nevertheless he felt badly for her.

"Boy, am I glad to see you." She gathered a stack of files and memos and got up. "Your phone's been ringing off the hook, Mr. Murphy wants to see you immediately and you've got one problem you're going to have to deal with first thing."

McGarvey held her off. "Have you been here all night?"

She looked at him as if he'd just asked a stupid question. "Naturally. I had work to do."

"Go home."

"Not a chance, boss. We're still swamped here." She smiled. "Besides, I still don't feel half as bad as you look."

"I could fire you."

"That you could."

McGarvey shook his head. "Okay, but when we get past this, you're taking a vacation, and that's an order."

"Right," she said. "First off—"

"First off I want you to get the President's appointments secretary Dale Nance on the phone. Then I want to see Otto."

"He asked me to let him know the moment you arrived."

McGarvey went to his office. "Oh, and see if you can rustle me up some breakfast. I'm starved. Lots of coffee."

Ms. Swanfeld was already dialing the White House. "You're going to want to see Mrs. McGarvey as soon as you can."

"After I talk to Nance and Otto." McGarvey took off his jacket, tossed it over a chair and went into the bathroom where he splashed some cold water on his face. He was haggard, but he'd looked and felt a lot worse. Killing the terrorists had done nothing for him. It was as if it had never happened. They'd made some stupid mistakes, and he'd taken advantage of them. Routine. Nothing out of the ordinary.

He studied his face and he tried to order his thoughts. Killing those four men was no more important to him than stepping on four bugs. And that frightened him to the bottom of his soul. He had seen the same lack of emotion in the eyes of one or two shooters he'd killed. *Mokrie dela.* Wet work, in the old KGB parlance. Department Viktor had attracted men, and some women, who were completely devoid of emotion when it came to taking human lives.

Not a night went by, however, when McGarvey did not see the last look of surprise on the faces of every person he'd assassinated. The number wasn't huge, but each night they came to him in his sleep, haunting his dreams, so that each morning when he awoke it was as if he was returning from a graveyard.

But he didn't feel that way about the men he'd killed on the bridge, or the four tonight. And he studied his eyes to make sure that he wasn't seeing the same utter lack of emotion he'd seen in the eyes of at least two of the shooters he'd killed. Bad men. Sociopaths. Emotionless killing machines.

Staring back at him in the mirror was the reflection of a man who'd done so much that he was hurting and frightened. Somehow, just now, those emotions were comforting.

He went to his desk and lit a cigarette as his telephone rang.

"It's Mr. Nance," his secretary called from the outer office.

McGarvey picked up his phone. "Mr. Nance, this is Kirk McGarvey. I'd like to have a couple of minutes with the President this morning to finish last night's briefing."

"Good morning, Mr. McGarvey. That won't be necessary. The general will be briefing the President this afternoon at two."

"I have some new information—"

"I'm sorry about the attack on your family; it was an outrageous act. The President asked me to pass along his concern as well. Everything is being done to find the people responsible."

"He'll either see me this morning, or I'll go to Sam Blair."

"That's your prerogative," Nance said coolly. "Although it would probably mean your position."

"Tell the President that I have some new information."

"We're busy over here just now."

"Do it," McGarvey said. "He'll want to know about this right now. I'll hold."

"Send it over."

"I don't think so. And neither would you. Now tell him, goddammit. I'll hold."

"Very well," Nance said after a moment. He was gone for about a minute and when he came back he sounded angry. "Ten o'clock."

"Thank you," McGarvey said.

"Don't be late."

McGarvey hung up and went to the door. Otto was just coming in. He looked like he'd been put through the wringer, his out-of-control red hair practically standing on end. But he had a gleeful look in his eyes.

"Oh, boy, you did it again," he said, his boyish voice hoarse.

"Have you eaten anything this morning?" McGarvey asked. "Other than Twinkies?"

Rencke shrugged indifferently, as if the thought of food was the farthest thing from his mind.

"There's enough breakfast coming for both of you," Ms. Swanfeld said. "But Mr. Murphy called again, and you have to speak with Mrs. McGarvey."

"Is she awake already?"

"She didn't get much sleep last night," Ms. Swanfeld explained. "But she insisted on speaking to you the moment you arrived."

"Okay. Stall the general for as long as you can, and tell my wife I'll be right there."

"What about Mr. Adkins?"

"I've already seen him," McGarvey told her. "And if anyone else calls, I'm out."

Ms. Swanfield gave her boss a faintly amused look. "Yes, sir."

McGarvey took Rencke back into his office and closed the door. Standing next to the computer expert was like being near high voltage lines. A low-pitched hum of energy seemed to radiate from him.

"Maryland H. P. put on the wire that they had gunfire, an explosion and four unidentified males down at Morningside," Rencke said. "Since your name wasn't mentioned, I figured you'd done okay."

"Sandy Patterson was out there with them. But she decided to switch sides."

"Good thinking," Rencke said. "Did you get anything useful from her?"

"This is all some Joseph Lee plot that's been in the works for a couple of years," McGarvey explained. "After Croft killed himself I was their number-one target. She was sure about that part."

"Lee thought you could hurt him somehow," Rencke said dreamily. "Something out of your past."

"Lindsay is the only connection I can see," McGarvey said. "But I still don't know how deeply he's involved with Lee, or what they're up to."

Rencke blinked. "Tanegashima," he said. "Joseph Lee is at the Japanese space launch center."

"How do you know that?"

"NSA recorded a portion of a phone message before the encryption device was activated. The call originated at the space center and was directed to MITI headquarters in Tokyo. The computer said there was a ninety-six percent probability of a match between the voice calling from Tanegashima and a file recording of Lee."

McGarvey turned that over in his mind. Lee was at Tanegashima for the upcoming launch of the space station module. So what? Security at the center was very tight, so he could simply have gone there to lay low. But that didn't seem right. "There's still no tie between Joseph Lee and myself."

"Not directly. But there is a connection between you and President Lindsay, who has, in turn a strong connection with Lee."

"And the space shot?" McGarvey wondered out loud.

"Could be Lindsay arranged a transfer of technology to the Japanese in exchange for campaign funds. Lee could have been the intermediary. It's happened before."

McGarvey shook his head. "It has to be something more than that. I don't think they'd try to kill me merely because of some engineering advice or NASA trade secrets."

"It's got something to do with the launch," Rencke said. "Lee's being there isn't a simple coincidence."

"That only gives us a couple of days to figure it out."

"Yeah," Rencke said, resting his weight on one foot. He did that whenever he was deeply in thought. "We better not forget North Korea's nukes," he said softly. "That's how all this started, you know." Rencke blinked again. "The connection is there, Mac. I just don't have it yet."

"I'm going to see someone this morning who might have the answers. Or at least some of them. But you're going to have to stick around to backstop me. In the meantime tell Adkins where Lee is hiding out."

Rencke's eyes focused on McGarvey. "David is going after Goliath? Storming the White House?"

"Something like that."

"Nothing's going to be the same."

"It never is," McGarvey said.

As a breakfast cart was being wheeled in from the executive dining room, McGarvey walked next door to the conference room where his wife and daughter had set up housekeeping last night. Kathleen, still dressed in the same clothing she'd been wearing at the safe house, her hair a mess, her makeup smudged, was pacing. She looked up in relief.

"I tried to stop her, Kirk. But she wouldn't listen to me."

McGarvey went around the long table to her, the same vise clamped around his heart. "What are you talking about?"

"It's Elizabeth. She went over to Bethesda Hospital about an hour ago, and there wasn't a thing I could say to talk her out of it." Kathleen's lower lip quivered but she was refusing to give in to her fear or her tiredness. "At least Dick Yemm is with her."

"Is she hurt? Sick?"

"No. That's where they took Todd Van Buren, and she wanted to be with him," Kathleen said. "She figured that since you were going after the terrorists she didn't have to stay here any longer. She was sure that you would take care of them, so she didn't have to worry."

McGarvey forced himself to calm down. In this instance his daughter was probably right. Lee had failed twice, his people here were all dead, Sandy Patterson, his stateside manager, had defected and he had hidden himself at Tanegashima. He wasn't going to try again.

"You don't need to stay here any longer, Katy," he told her.

She looked at him, the expression on her face a mixture of relief and uncertainty. "You caught them?"

"Yeah." McGarvey thought of everything his family had gone through because of him. It was over for them, and he was grateful for at least that much.

"There's no possibility they'll escape?"

McGarvey shook his head. "They're dead."

Kathleen shivered, as if a cold draft had come from somewhere.

"Get your things and I'll drive you home."

"Will you be able to stay—"

"My part's not over with yet, Katy," McGarvey said. "Could be a couple more days."

"In that case you'd better take me over to Bethedsa. I want to be with our daughter."

"I'll have our people keep an eye on both of you. Just in case."

"Good idea, Kirk."

The White House

McGarvey arrived at the White House from Bethesda a couple of minutes before ten, assured that Dick Yemm would keep a close eye on his wife and daughter for as long as it took to straighten this out. But he had no idea how long that might take, because what he was about to do this morning was nothing short of challenging the Constitution. He was about to go farther out on a limb than he'd ever been before, and he was still clutching at straws, because he didn't know the entire story. He couldn't even guess at some of it yet, yet he was going up against the President of the United States.

Dale Nance came from his office, a look of contempt on his face. "Is this really necessary, McGarvey?"

"Yeah."

"Stay here. I'll see if he's ready for you." Nance went into the Oval Office, and came out a half minute later. "I hope you know what you're doing," he said. "Go on in."

President Lindsay was seated at his desk, while Harold Secor poured a cup of coffee at the sideboard. One of four television screens in a bank of monitors was on and turned to CNN, but the sound was low. Two co-anchors were talking about something, their voices just audible.

"We were happy to hear that your family came out of the attack unharmed," Secor said, bringing his coffee and sitting down across from the President. "Dr. Pierone has been instructed to pursue the investigation with the utmost vigor."

"It won't be necessary," McGarvey told them. "We found the rest of them."

"They're in custody?" Secor asked his face lighting up.

"They're dead. But we arrested Sandy Patterson, who worked for Joseph Lee. She's agreed to tell us everything." McGarvey looked directly at the President. "She and I had quite a talk this morning. About Tony Croft and me, and about Joseph Lee and his connection with the Japanese space program. We found him. He's at their space center now."

"You know this for a fact?" the President asked.

McGarvey nodded. "Yes, sir. NSA monitored some of his telephone conversations with MITI in Tokyo."

"CNN is doing a piece on the launch right now," Secor said indicating the television. An aerial view of the space launch facility could have been taken from above Kennedy Space Center. Tanegashima was a miniature version of the Cape.

"Our satellite pictures are better," McGarvey said.

"I'm sure they are," the President said. "But I wasn't aware that we were monitoring them so closely."

"You need hard intelligence, Mr. President. Not guesswork. Especially with what's going on over there right now."

"Harold, could you leave us alone for a few minutes? There's something I'd like to say to Mr. McGarvey in private."

Secor gave the President a look of surprise, but then left the room, closing the door softly.

The President touched a button on his telephone console, then looked at McGarvey standing in front of his desk like a principal might look at a student in trouble.

"Okay, mister. We're alone, and I've switched off the digital recorder. Obviously you have something to say to me. Well, now's your chance." The President sat back in his leather chair.

"I don't have everything yet, but I do have enough to know that at the very least you are a liar and a fool. At worst you're a traitor." McGarvey had psyched himself up for this moment, but now he wasn't so sure he was doing the right thing. But Lindsay reacted about the way McGarvey thought he would.

"You can't talk to me that way, McGarvey. Not even in private."

"I sincerely wish I didn't have to, sir. But a lot of very good people are dead either because of you directly, or because you allowed your staff to do it for you. And the hell of it is, when the heat was turned up, you let your friends like Tony Croft take the fall for you."

"You don't know what you're talking about," the President said angrily. His face was red.

"Croft was in direct contact with Joseph Lee not only to accept payments to your campaign fund, but to pass along information which made its way to the Japanese government."

"No secrets were passed."

"That's up to a congressional review committee to decide, Mr. President. And there *will* be an investigation when I turn over what I know. But beside trading information for cash, and allowing Croft to kill himself for your sake, why come after me and my family?"

"I had nothing to do with any of that," Lindsay said shaking his head. Most of his anger had dissipated. He seemed numb. "I swear to you."

"Are you still holding a grudge against me after all these years?"

A puzzled look came over the President. "What are you talking about?"

"Santiago," McGarvey said. "You were on the Senate watchdog committee that withdrew authorization for my assignment to kill General Paolo. Do you remember that?"

"I remember serving on the Senate Subcommittee on Central Intelligence. But no specific incident."

"I have the file, Mr. President. You were the senator who was supposed to inform the Agency about the decision to pull me out. But you waited until you knew it was too late for me. Why?"

The President shook his head again. "I don't know what you're talking about."

"How about New Year's Day, nineteen seventy? Berlin. Checkpoint Charlie."

The President's jaw tightened.

"I probably saved your life, Mr. President, but I embarrassed you in front of your friends. Made you look like a fool."

"What's your point?"

Out of the corner of his eye McGarvey noticed that CNN was displaying a cutaway model of a launchpad gantry at Tanegashima.

"The Japanese have no love for me, but Lee had no reason to order my assassination simply because I had been appointed to head the Directorate of Operations."

"Do you honestly think that I ordered your death because of some incident that supposedly happened thirty years ago?"

"I think that in discussions with your staff about Joseph Lee and what you and he were doing for each other, the fact that he was connected with the Japanese government, and not Taiwan, came up. As did anything that could possibly hurt your arrangement, such as my appointment."

"That doesn't make any sense."

"Not on the surface. But you knew from past experience all about me, and Lee was told. Your people may even have told him about Berlin and Santiago, and he made the decision on his own to have me killed. Maybe he was concerned that if I started snooping around as DDO, I might uncover your real connection with him. And his actual agenda."

McGarvey glanced again at the television screen. The various parts of the launch gantry were being labeled and their functions explained. He could just make out the newsman's words.

"What do you think that agenda is?"

A large, enclosed elevator ran up the outside of the gantry to a sealed chamber at the top, opposite the rocket's payload section. As the announcer continued to talk a label appeared beside the chamber: The White House.

The bottom dropped out from beneath McGarvey. He turned back to the President and looked at the man in amazement. Lindsay was not a traitor, McGarvey had been wrong about that part. But the President had been manipulated, as had the twenty or thirty senators and congressmen who Joseph Lee had bought. They had given him exactly what he had wanted to buy when he came to Washington. The incredible part of the entire affair was that it was completely out in the open. It had been from the start.

McGarvey looked at the TV screen again. Japan had been awarded a bigger slice of the international space station than it had been previously awarded at the behest of Lindsay and a group of senators and congressmen paid for by Lee. This, despite the fact Japan's economy was nearly in shambles and building and launching the bigger module was straining their financial abilities to the breaking point.

Was it simply for a space station module? McGarvey didn't think so. Whatever the Japanese were about to put into orbit would have nothing to do with *Freedom*, and Tony Croft knew or guessed something about it. According to the call girl he'd been sleeping with, his biggest worry was the white house. But not the White House at 1600 Pennsylvania Avenue. He was worried about the one at Tanegashima. And whatever the Japanese were going to launch also had something to do with North Korea's nuclear capability and the explosion at Kimch'aek. He could think of a number of possibilities, none of them very comforting because Lee was willing not only to suborn a U.S. President, he was willing to assassinate a deputy director of CIA Operations, no matter what the cost or political fallout might be.

"I asked what you think that agenda is," the President said.

"Mr. President, I owe you an apology, sir," McGarvey said.

Lindsay gave him a wry smile. "Yes?"

"You're not a traitor, sir, but your people are guilty of murder, or at least complicity to murder. A stink goes all the way back to Taiwan, Hong Kong, Korea and Japan. Your foreign policy is a joke. And you've unwittingly made a lot of questionable deals because of it." McGarvey shook his head. "But no, Mr. President, you're no traitor. You're a fool."

"You're fired," the President shouted, enraged. "You're finished. If I can arrange it, and I think I can, you're going to jail for a very long time."

McGarvey turned and walked out of the Oval Office.

"You sonofabitch," Lindsay shouted after him. "You sonofabitch!"

TWENTY-THREE

Seawolf

Conn, sonar. Sierra seventeen is turning inboard to port," Seaman Fischer reported excitedly.

"Does he have positive contact on us yet?" Harding demanded.

"I don't think so, Skipper. The current is probably messing up his sonar, but he suspects something. And if he keeps it up he's going to find us."

The problem was they lay on the bottom in three hundred feet of water at the southwestern extremity of the Eastern Channel below Tsushima Island. They weren't deep enough to enjoy the protection of a thermocline, and they didn't have much maneuvering room. The only things going for them were the fierce current in the channel, ten foot seas on the surface and the fact that when *Seawolf* was rigged for ultrasilent operations she was extremely quiet. In addition, it was thirty minutes past midnight. Despite radar and collision avoidance systems, operations like this in which so many ships were in close proximity to each other—sonar had identified eleven surface targets—the darkness of night made everything all the more dangerous. Accidents could and often did happen.

On the surface their most immediate threat was from the MSDF destroyer *Myoko*, which had been running a grid pattern search for the past two hours, the legs of which kept getting smaller and smaller. *Seawolf* was being effectively boxed in. And when *Myoko* found them it would be an uneven fight that *Seawolf* couldn't possibly win. Despite her awesome nuclear capability, she simply could not prevail against eleven-to-one odds, not counting the threat from however many ASW Orion aircraft that were circling overhead and however many MSDF submarines that were lurking about.

Paradise handed the captain a cup of coffee. "We need another ten hours and the *George Washington* will be here."

"We're probably not going to get that much time." The ELF message they had received ten hours ago was sketchy. But Admiral Hamilton had warned them about the trouble they were heading into and promised a pair of Hornets on scene within thirty minutes and the entire fleet in twenty hours.

"Then the jets are going to have to hold them off." Paradise gave Harding a worried look. "We're not going to fire again, are we?"

Harding shook his head. "The moment we did, they would come after us with everything."

Paradise looked relieved. "We can make a case for shooting at *Natsushio*. All we did was disable her. She's up there on the surface now, her skipper mad as hell. But I think he had every intention of shooting first. And not merely to cripple us."

"I agree," Harding said. "But the *Myoko* won't have to start it. Once they find us, they'll send one of their choppers out to wherever their submarines are hiding, drop a dipping buoy and give them our position. If we're fired on and we either move or retaliate, then the surface ships can make a case for declaring us hostile, possibly a Chinese submarine, and they'll come after us and win."

"I see," Paradise said after a moment. "But we're not just going to wait here until it happens."

"We might have to, Rod. But we're not beat yet." Harding picked up the growler phone and called sonar.

"Sonar, aye."

"Mel, I want you to feed us the position of every surface ship within fifty thousand yards. I'll need constant updates as fast as you can get to me."

"Ah, yes, sir," Fischer said. "Skipper, it might help if I knew what you wanted. Help me come up with the right numbers, in the right sequence."

"We're going to start a TMA on every ship up there. I want continuous shooting solutions on each of them. Simultaneously." Harding let that sink in. "Can you handle that?"

"Yes, sir. But it's going to get a little busy back here. How long do you want to keep it up?"

"Maybe as long as ten hours. But probably a lot less than that."

Fischer hesitated only a moment. "You've got it. Skipper," he said.

Natsushio

There were lights all around him. Captain Tomita, standing on the bridge, studied the lights of the ocean-going tug connected to his boat by a three-hundred-meter steel tether. His orders were to return to Maizuru at all possible speed for repairs, but for the first time in his naval career Tomita was not obeying a direct order. He wanted to stay here to witness the destruction of the American submarine that had bested him. He'd ordered the tug to maintain steerage way in the three-meter seas, nothing more.

Thinking about the incident that had sent his boat limping to the surface made him tighten his grip on the binoculars so hard that the knuckles on his fingers turned white.

"Bridge, communications."

Tomita lowered his binoculars and answered the growler phone. "This is the captain."

"*Kan-cho*, I have the captain of the *Myoko* for you."

"Very well." Tomita raised his binoculars with one hand and searched for and found the 2+2 Kongo class destroyer about two miles off his starboard bow. "Kurosawa-san, how is the search going? Have you found him yet?"

Shintaro Kurosawa, captain of the *Myoko*, sounded rushed. "We may have picked up something with the sidescan sonar on our last pass. We're doubling back now for another set of sweeps."

"He's there, listening to us."

"How can you be certain?"

"I know this captain," Tomita said. "He's a cowboy, waiting for the fleet to arrive."

At that moment one of the two F/A-18 Hornet fighter/interceptors screamed low overhead from the north, the tremendous roar drowning out all sound. Tomita lowered his binoculars and raised a fist to the sky in a perfectly futile gesture.

". . . shoot them out of the sky," Kurosawa was saying.

"It would be a mistake to destroy them."

"That's what I said. But we have other resources. If we find him, Tomita-san. If he's down there."

"He's there. I'd stake my life on it."

"You should start for base."

"Not yet."

"I understand," Kurosawa said. "But now let me get back to my work. If we can pinpoint his exact position perhaps we can flush him out of hiding."

"Better to kill him without warning, lest he fire on us again. The fact is, he's probably a Chinese submarine. Perhaps even North Korean. We don't know for sure who he is, simply that he fired on my boat."

"We'll take care of it," Kurosawa said.

"Good hunting," Tomita replied.

Orion 3311

Flying an operation so low and slow in restricted visibility, the ASW aircraft's two radar operators were the most important crew members aboard. The pilot, Lieutenant Hitoshi Kuroda, a slight line of sweat on his narrow upper lip, was flying by the numbers. He had to trust his radar people because the slightest mistake could send them crashing into one of the other two Orions out here on patrol or the two American jet fighters. In fact, he was surprised that an accident hadn't already happened with so many ships and aircraft so concentrated in so small an area.

"Captain, ELINT. Ready to deploy on your mark."

"Stand by," the pilot said.

Their search pattern was being coordinated by the Combat Information Center aboard the *Myoko*.

"Home plate, this is aircraft eleven. We're ready to make our turn now and deploy on your mark."

"Turn left to new heading one-eight-zero . . . now."

Kuroda hauled the big four-engine turboprop ASW aircraft in a tight turn to the left. When he was on his new heading, the *Myoko*'s CIC operations officer was back. "Deploy on my mark . . . now."

"ELINT, deploy now," the pilot relayed the order.

"Deploying now, *hai*."

"Radar, this is the captain, how are we looking?"

"Clear on this heading, *kan-cho*," the chief radar operator reported.

"Sensor is wet," the ELINT operator Kuminori Godai advised.

They were flying at five hundred feet, trailing a one-meter-long fin-shaped sensor connected to the aircraft's sensitive computer system by a titanium/ceramic composite cable. Since the American submarine was not moving, presumably sitting quietly on the bottom, their magnetic anomaly detector would not work to pick it up. However, a new laser-detection device had been developed in the past year that solved such a problem. Sea water was all but opaque past two hundred feet, except in the blue/green spectrum. The sensor, trailing five meters beneath the surface, sent out a beam of blue-green laser light, and sensor-head detectors watched for a reflection of the light off a metallic object.

Almost immediately an excited Godai came back. "Positive laser contact. Definitely a submarine, identified as probably American Seawolf class. Bearing one-nine-nine. Position has been transmitted."

Myoko

"Bridge, CIC, we have a confirmed target," *Myoko*'s executive officer Lieutenant Commander Tono Ogawa reported. "Range five thousand meters relative, bearing zero-seven-zero."

Captain Kurosawa snatched the growler phone. "This is the captain. Do we have an independent confirmation from our own sonar?"

"*Iie, kan-cho*. Aircraft eleven and seventeen have both reported positive B/G L-1 contacts. It's a Seawolf."

"We're not sure of the type," Kurosawa said. "Conditions are too difficult. It could be another Chinese submarine."

"*Hai, kan-cho*," Ogawa responded.

Kurosawa turned to his first officer on the bridge. "Sound battle stations, submarine. This is not a drill."

"*Hai, kan-cho*. Sound battle stations, submarine."

"Turn to course zero-seven-zero, make your speed twenty-five knots."

"Turn to course zero-seven-zero, make my speed twenty-five knots, *hai, kan-cho*."

Kurosawa turned back to the growler phone and his XO in the CIC as the nine-thousand-four-hundred-ton destroyer heeled sharply to starboard and the battle stations klaxon sounded throughout the ship.

"Get this off to the *Noshiro*, but hold your active sonar search until we're within one thousand meters of their reported position. I don't want to alert them."

"*Hai, kan-cho*," Ogawa said. "But, *kan-cho*, this is an American submarine."

"You are mistaken, Ogawa-san. But I will not hold that against you. Now carry on."

"*Hai, kan-cho!*"

Seawolf

The continually changing positions of every surface target in their vicinity was being worked out in the computers. Nevertheless, Harding made a paper plot at the starboard chart table. It helped him visualize what he was going to try to do if all his other options ran out.

"Conn, sonar, I think they're on to us," Fischer called the control room.

Harding pulled a phone from the overhead. "This is the captain, what have you got, Mel?"

"We had that unidentified dipping buoy about three minutes ago, and now all of a sudden the *Myoko* and the *Noshiro* are heading right for us and beatin' feet."

"We heard nothing from the buoy?"

"Negative, Skipper. But it found us. Maybe they worked out that blue-green laser detector we were briefed on back at Pearl."

"Give me ranges and bearings."

"Sierra seventeen, range four thousand eight hundred meters, bearing two-five-zero, making turns for twenty-one knots and accelerating. Sierra twenty-five, seven thousand three hundred meters, bearing one-five-zero, making turns for eighteen knots and definitely accelerating."

"Stand by," Harding said. He quickly plotted the new positions, courses and speeds, projecting their tracks, which intersected directly over the *Seawolf*. "Okay, good job, Mel. Keep a sharp watch now. We're almost there."

Harding wrote out a brief message to CINCPAC in Pearl outlining their present situation, the possibility that the MSDF had developed the blue-green laser system after all and what he was doing.

He motioned Paradise over and handed him the message. When his XO finished reading it he looked up in appreciation. "I would never have thought of it."

"Get that back to comms and tell them to send it in the clear as soon as the antenna breaks the surface."

For a moment Paradise wanted to discuss the order, but suddenly it dawned on him what the captain was trying to do. *Everything* the captain was trying to do, and he grinned. "Yes, sir," he said, and he headed forward.

Myoko

The XO, Tono Ogawa, rushed up from the Combat Information Center, a confused, urgent expression on his round face. "*Kan-cho*, we have a definite sonar contact."

Kurosawa gave him an amused look. "Is the ship's communications system inoperative?"

"No, sir. May I speak to you frankly, and in confidence?"

Kurosawa pursed his lips, but nodded. They stepped onto the port wing deck. "We're in the middle of a hunt, Ogawa-san. We have found our prey, and we are about to engage it. What troubles you?"

"That is an American submarine. If we attempt to destroy it, there's no telling what the American captain will do in retaliation. I urge caution, *kan-cho*, until we can sort out the reason that the American fired on Captain Tomita."

"In the first place, you are mistaken about the nationality of that warship sitting on the bottom beneath us. It is definitely a Chinese nuclear submarine. An improved Han class, as a matter of fact. It violated our waters despite repeated urgent warnings to the contrary." His eyes narrowed. "Now we shall kill it. But if we fail, then our comrades will take up the fight until it is finished." He nodded. "Is this clear to you?"

"It is the reason the American jet fighters are here, *kan-cho*. If we fire our weapons they will fire on us—"

Kurosawa silenced him with a gesture. "One further word and I shall place you under arrest pending a court-martial."

Ogawa was clearly struggling with what he knew to be the truth versus his sworn duty to uphold the orders of his commanding officer.

"Let us finish this operation, and then we'll talk. There are certain aspects that you are not aware of." Kurosawa gave him a friendly smile. "Can we do this together? Do I have your support?"

Ogawa bowed. "*Hai, kan-cho.*"

"Very well. Return to your duties."

"*Hai.*"

312 D A V I D   H A G B E R G

Seawolf

The sound of the sonar pulse hammering the hull was unmistakable to everyone aboard. Nonetheless Fischer called the control room.

"Conn, sonar, they have us."

"We heard it, Mel," Harding said dryly. He switched to the ship's intercom. "This is the captain, stand by for an emergency blow."

A horn sounded through the boat.

Harding glanced at the chart. He had one opening in the pack of ships above. "Come right to three-four-zero degrees, make your speed five knots."

"Come right three-four-zero, make my speed five knots, aye, Skipper," the diving officer responded.

Paradise was positioned at the ballast control station, his hands hovering above a pair of small handles at the top of the panel. They controlled the manual emergency blow valves which, when opened, would send high-pressure air into the ballast tanks all at once. The boat would head to the surface like a rocket.

"Blow all tanks," Harding said gently. "Emergency blow all tanks."

Paradise turned the levers with both hands, and the *Seawolf* came off the bottom, started to accelerate, then suddenly came alive.

Myoko

"Bridge, CIC," Ogawa's excited voice reported. "The target is on the way up. Very fast."

This wasn't what Captain Kurosawa expected. "What is his depth?"

"He's already passing fifty meters and accelerating. Bearing still zero-seven-zero, but his range is opening, six thousand meters now."

"He's making an emergency blow," Kurosawa said. "Go to battle stations, surface." He stepped over to the radar screen and pulled a phone from the overhead as battle stations, surface, was announced throughout the ship. The moment the American submarine broke the surface he would give the order to destroy it.

Natsushio

The *Seawolf* broke the surface two hundred meters off *Natsushio*'s port bow, two-thirds of its hull shooting out of the water like a breaching whale. For a second Captain Tomita stood watching as a huge phosphorescent wave spread outward from the submarine. "Fantastic," he said softly.

"Bridge, ESMs."

Tomita snatched the phone. "This is the captain."

"That submarine just sent a burst transmission. But it's going to take at least a half hour to decode it, if at all."

"Never mind that," Tomita shouted. "Uesugi, this is the captain. Open torpedo doors one and two and target that submarine. I want two snap shots as soon as possible."

"*Hai, kan-cho,*" Lieutenant Uesugi replied instantly.

Myoko

With the submarine on the surface and illuminated by many radars, there was no doubt that it was an American Seawolf.

"Bridge, CIC. We have a confirmation of submarine type—"

Captain Kurosawa angrily overrode him. "I want a positive lock on that target now," he shouted.

"*Kan-cho,* that is no longer advisable," Lieutenant Commander Ogawa came back.

"Prepare to open fire—"

"*Kan-cho,* we have an incoming air-launched missile now," Ogawa shouted.

Before Kurosawa could react, a tremendous flash seemed to rise up from the sea fifty meters dead ahead. An instant later the sharp bang of the explosion hammered the bridge windows, and a second after that the American jet fighter/interceptor that had fired the shot roared overhead from the starboard.

Natsushio

Captain Tomita was about to give the fire one, fire two order, when a similar flash/bang erupted off his bow between him and the *Seawolf.* Two seconds later the second F/A-18 Hornet screamed overhead less than a hundred meters above the *Natsushio*'s sail, and Tomita ducked down beneath the steel coaming, his insides seething like a boiling cauldron.

TWENTY-FOUR

Tanegashima Space Center

The countdown clock had been restarted a few hours ago, around 9:00 P.M. Ripley looked up from his console as the numbers changed to T-minus 40:00:00, then 39:59:59. After searching Kimura's computer and finding nothing, he'd come back to his console at launch control. If nothing else at least he'd be with his own team, although Johnson and Wirth had gone back to the guest quarters for a bite to eat and a few hours' sleep around midnight and Maggie and Hilman were busy at their consoles. Ripley flipped a switch to show him a view of the launchpad. There was still a lot of activity out there and would be until a few minutes before launch.

Maggie slid over beside him and looked over his shoulder at the monitor. "I'm about finished with my stage. Do you want to leave Hilman here? We could get something to eat and go over to my room."

Ripley looked up at her and smiled tiredly, but shook his head. "Nothing I'd like better."

"Well, you didn't get anything from Kimura's system, so what's next?"

"Unless my eyes were playing tricks on me last night, the answers are out there on the pad."

"Short of shutting down the clock and unbuttoning the payload hatch, there's not much you can do about it, Frank."

Ripley glanced back at the monitor, his brows knitting in sudden concentration. "We don't need to do that, at least not yet. But you just gave me an idea. If I was right, and what I saw in the payload section *wasn't* the satellite we worked on, where is it?"

"Do you think they switched satellites?"

"It's possible."

"Why?"

Ripley tore his eyes away from the screen. "That's the million-dollar question. But if I can find the bird that we worked on, it'll prove that what's loaded aboard the H2C isn't what we signed for." A look of triumph crossed his face. "In that case you better believe I'll blow the whistle."

"Where are you going to start?"

"We saw the original satellite being moved to the launchpad and taken up to the white house on the elevator. At least one of us has been on duty out there or here at the monitors at all times since then. The only place the original satellite could be is somewhere near the launchpad."

"So what, Frank? They're not going to let you wander around out there."

"Why not?" Ripley asked. "I still have my pass. I'd simply be doing my job."

Maggie leaned a little closer and lowered her voice. "Think about it. If they are hiding something and they think that you're on to them, they'll stop you."

Ripley smiled again. "That'd be just about as good as finding the old satellite, because if they did it I'd shut down this launch in a New York minute."

"He's making the connection," Hirota said.

"As we expected he might," Joseph Lee said. They were in the Tanegashima security chief's office listing to Ripley's conversation with Margaret Attwood. Despite the late hour, Lee was keyed up because of the events in Washington and the possibility that McGarvey might be putting it together too. Nothing his remaining Washington contacts were telling him warned that McGarvey was on the way, but he had gut feelings about these matters. As he did with the chief astronaut on the American Tiger team. "But he hasn't actually found anything yet."

"If he does, he could delay the launch, Lee-san," Hirota said respectfully. He looked like a compact, hard-muscled Buddha, except his eyes were cruel and calculating. Lee had more respect for him than he had for Kondo.

"If we interfere with his movements he could also cause trouble," Lee suggested, wanting to hear Hirota's answer.

The security chief nodded sagely. "There are ways around that."

"At all costs the launch must not be delayed, except for technical reasons. It must not fail."

"If I am given a free hand in this, the launch will go off on schedule and Major Ripley will cause no further trouble."

They were the answers that Lee wanted to hear. He smiled inwardly. "With a delicate touch, Hirota-san. There are four others on the Tiger team, among them his lover, Captain Attwood."

Hirota flushed slightly with pleasure at Lee's use of the polite form of address. He nodded again. "With delicacy, Lee-san, I assure you. But accidents do happen."

The launchpad was a beehive of activity. Technicians were going over every square centimeter of the rocket and its launch gantry. The guard at the last checkpoint stepped out of his box and held up a hand for Ripley to stop. He came around to the driver's side of the Toyota, a fake smile on his round face.

"Good evening, Major Ripley."

"I need to take a look at something." Ripley handed out his pass. He had the uneasy feeling that the guard had expected him.

The man took a perfunctory look at the pass, then handed it back. "Yes, of course. Let Mr. Kato know that you are on site, please." Akio Kato was the launchpad director. He smiled again, stepped back and raised the barrier.

For a second Ripley was nonplussed. The guard should have checked with the launchpad director first. Ripley's name wasn't on the prelaunch directory. Technically he wasn't supposed to be out here at this stage of the countdown except by permission. He'd been expecting to do some quick talking to get himself admitted.

He flashed the guard a smile, waved and then drove the last couple of hundred yards to the pad, where he parked on the west side of the loading ramp. The H2C rocket, bathed in hundreds of lights, towered 230 feet into the night sky, taller now in its final configuration than even the huge vehicle assembly building. The lower service towers and umbilical cord gantries were still in position, but the payload service tower had been swung on its central core out of the way to the right. Its primary purpose was to secure the payload to the upper stage of the rocket. Since that task was completed there was no further use for the tower, most of which was now in shadow.

Something was definitely wrong. This launch was very important to the Japanese—more so for some reason than Ripley could not figure out yet—so they were being superfastidious with their inspection routines and their security. Nothing was going to get past them. Nothing. And yet the guard had not raised so much as an eyebrow when he'd shown up at the gate.

Ripley was an engineer. Every effect had a cause, every action a re-action. He did not believe in spiritualism, touchy-feely group encounters, going with the flow and all that karma bullshit that some of his old college friends, now working in California, were into these days. Everything for him had a clear-cut reason, and therefore a clear-cut, understandable cause.

For some reason the Japanese no longer wanted Americans involved with this shot. During the last week they had made the Tiger team's job almost impossible. The reason had to be a very good one, because the freeze-out was universal. Nobody was talking to them. Nobody.

He'd come to understand if not the actual reason, at least the effect, and so much as possible he and the others had managed to work around it. They had a job to do here, and they were doing it.

This morning, however, was completely out of character. If the Japanese were true to their recent form he would not have gotten past the first checkpoint, let alone this far. Even last week, before the dramatic shift in attitude, he would not have been allowed out here without a lot of questions being raised.

So what the hell was going on, he asked himself. If their console had been bugged and his conversation with Maggie recorded, they wouldn't have let him out of the building. At least he didn't think they would, because there'd be no reason for it. If they were hiding something out here, they'd want to keep it from him. If they *weren't* hiding something, they'd still keep him away from the launchpad because he had no reason to be out here now. It bothered his sense of orderliness. He didn't like unexplained mysteries, and this one was starting to piss him off.

He put on his hard hat and headed over to the payload gantry. A dozen other vehicles were parked around the pad, and twenty or thirty technicians were busy at work. At this stage of the countdown they were concentrating on mechanical glitches: loose screws or fasteners, missing access plates, disconnected launch cables or hoses, rust, metal fatigue— any of hundreds of little problems that could have a serious effect on the mission. The inspections would not end until the rocket lifted off the pad. It was the same at the Cape.

No one paid any attention to him. He was expecting someone to come after him, or at least shout for him to stop or ask him what the hell he was doing here. Kato ran a tight crew, nothing escaped his attention. But nobody did.

At the base of the tower, Ripley glanced over his shoulder; still nobody was coming after him. It was incredible. He ducked inside the big service elevator, half expecting to see that the power was down and he would have to climb the stairs to the white house. But the buttons were lit. For just a moment he had the feeling that he was being set up, being led by the nose exactly where they wanted him to go. But that made no sense either.

He closed the gate and pressed the button for the top level. On the way up he looked across at the activity on the other tower and umbilical gantry. He could see the technicians because they were bathed in light, but they could not see him because the payload tower was in darkness. Which was another bothersome thing. The power was on, but there were no lights other than the red warning lights on top.

He tried to work out all the possibilities in his mind, to find an innocent, logical explanation. But no matter how he looked at the information he had available, he came back to the satellite in the rocket. Whatever he'd seen wasn't covered with gold foil. He knew that much. So why hadn't he brought it up with Kimura, he asked himself. Kimura would have told him something, and he could have made his decision then and there on the spot. He had held back, he decided, because of everything else that had happened in the past seven days. Something wasn't right. He didn't know what it was, but he damned well was going to find out tonight, or he'd stop the launch clock, and the hell with the consequences if he was wrong.

At the top, the tower swayed a little in the light sea breeze. The red warning lights above in the scaffolding flashed pink against the stark white walls of the empty clean room, the tall door to which was clipped in the open position.

He stepped off the elevator and stood a few moments in the flashing red lights, still debating with himself. He was on a wide catwalk across from the clean room which capped the tower's enclosed central core. The room was empty, except for test equipment mounted on the walls, and the low-slung titanium dolly on which the satellite had been moved. No one was up here with him, and yet he had the feeling that he wasn't alone.

Four closed-circuit television cameras were mounted overhead on the scaffolding, but the lights were off indicating that the circuits were not in use. The nearest technicians were seventy-five or eighty feet away on the service tower. He looked over the rail, but no one had come to check out his car or to find out why the elevator wasn't at the ground level. Kato would notice sooner or later, so he didn't have a lot of time to screw around. Still, he couldn't shake the feeling that someone was watching him.

"Nerves," he muttered, hesitating a moment longer, then he stepped across the catwalk and went into the white house.

The flashing red lights acted like strobes; they were disconcerting. Ripley went back out, unclipped the dust-proof door and pulled it closed. Lights came on automatically, and the test equipment powered up.

He stood, head cocked, listening for any sounds, for an intruder alarm to pop off or for someone to call on the phone to demand what the hell he was doing up here.

He stepped over the dolly and moved cautiously to the center of the circular room. White plastic padding covered the walls, and the floor was covered with spotless white tiles.

He let his eyes move from one piece of test equipment and power point to the other. But there was nothing wrong here. Nothing.

The floor lurched slightly. For a second Ripley thought a sudden gust of wind had rocked the tower or that something had hit them, but he suddenly realized that the floor was sinking.

The room, or at least the floor, was an elevator. For some reason his coming inside the white house and closing the door had activated it, and he was heading down, slowly and silently.

"The bastards," he said, suddenly understanding what was going on. The original satellite had been brought up to the white house, and after his Tiger team had completed their final checks, it had been moved below the tower, where it had been switched for the satellite he'd spotted in the rocket's payload. It had been done in secret through the enclosed central core. It was something the Japanese had planned for when the tower had been designed. This wasn't some last minute add-on.

The question in his mind was, why? The NSDA was publicly getting set to launch a module up to the *Freedom* space station. That's what they wanted the world to believe. Instead, they had switched the satellite for something else. Something as massive as a Greyhound bus, ten metric tons, sheathed not in gold foil, but in some black material.

There were no longer any innocent explanations, as far as Ripley was concerned. For the first time since coming to Tanegashima he was worried about his safety and the safety of his team. Whatever the Japanese were doing here was not meant for outsiders to see.

Five minutes after the floor of the white house started down, the smooth walls of the shaft suddenly opened on a large, white-tiled room that was almost the twin of the clean room at the top of the tower. Sitting on a dolly in the middle of the room was the original satellite, its gold foil gleaming in the dim lights.

The room was empty, except for the satellite. A huge door, the twin of the one above, was closed, and test equipment like above lined the walls.

Ripley tried to take it all in, to made some sense of it. Whatever was going on here had to be stopped. There would have to be explanations, full disclosure, before whatever was strapped aboard the rocket was lifted up to the space station.

He stepped off the elevator and started toward the satellite when the floor silently began to rise again. He caught the movement out of the corner of his eye, and without thinking, jumped back on before it got out of reach. He did not want to be stuck down here. He had to get topside and use his satellite phone to call Houston. It was coming up on eleven in the morning over there, and Hartley would be in his office. There was no other option, Ripley decided, because the plain fact was that he and his Tiger team were strangers in a strange land, outnumbered and out-gunned. They were astronauts, not spies.

CIA Headquarters

McGarvey walked into his office a couple of minutes after twelve. He'd stopped first at Bethesda Hospital to make sure that Kathleen and Liz were doing okay, then had gone back to his apartment where he packed an overnight bag with a few items of dark clothing and a pair of soft boots. He tossed in his passport and cash, along with a Belgian passport, credit cards and IDs under the work name Pierre Allain.

Ms. Swanfeld's mouth dropped open. "Heavens. You're the last person I expected to see again today."

"Grab your notebook. I want you to sit in on a meeting," McGarvey told her. He glanced in his office. His desk was piled with files and memos, and the light on his voice-mail was blinking furiously. "When we're finished, you haven't seen me since this morning."

Ms. Swanfeld looked dubious. "Mr. Murphy is screaming for your hide—"

"I need your help, Dahlia, more than I've ever needed anybody's help," McGarvey said urgently. "I'm doing nothing wrong. In fact I may be the only person in Washington who's doing anything right. But I need you to trust me a little longer."

"And cover for you?"

He smiled wryly, and nodded. "You should have gone home when you had the chance."

"No way, boss," she said, grinning. She grabbed a steno pad and pencils.

McGarvey checked the busy corridor to make sure that Murphy wasn't charging his way, then led his secretary down to Rencke's cubicle. The room was a mess, papers strewn everywhere, two wastepaper baskets overflowing with computer printouts, milk cartons and empty Twinkies packages littering the floor. Otto, his fingers flying over a keyboard, streams of numbers flashing across a lavender-hued monitor, didn't bother looking up.

"Just a second," he said excitedly. "Just a second." He stopped typing, and the data stream on the monitor began to speed up, so fast that the numbers became an indistinct blur. He hesitated a moment, then pointed a finger at the screen. "Bang," he cried in triumph. The numbers flashing across the screen stopped, leaving only one. "There," he said.

"What is it?" McGarvey asked.

Otto looked up, an odd, frightened expression on his face. "I know what you're thinking, Mac, and it won't work. This time you gotta listen to me. No shit, you're going to get your ass shot off this time."

"We're running out of options. The White House isn't going to do a thing to stop it, and convincing someone down in Houston without proof isn't going to get us anywhere."

"That's right. But NASA's got five people out there to help with the launch. Technical support, you know. That kind of shit. The head guy is Frank Ripley and I came up with his satellite cell phone number."

"He's probably just as much in the dark as everyone else," McGarvey said. "They sure as hell aren't in on it."

"Call him and ask."

"Excuse me," Ms. Swanfeld broke in. "Would you two mind telling me what's going on?"

"Mac wants to stop the Japanese from launching their satellite, and he thinks the only way to do that is to go over there and do it himself. But if you can convince Ripley that something's rotten in Jap-land, maybe he can come up with the proof—something we can take to Houston. There's only thirty-nine hours left, but maybe Ripley could buy us some time."

"I don't understand."

"Whatever the Japanese are going to launch has nothing to do with the space station. I don't know what it is, but it has something to do with the nuclear explosion in North Korea. Maybe an orbiting laser weapon or something to knock out a missle attack. You know, Star Wars?"

"Mr. Murphy can take this to the President—" Ms Swanfeld said. Then she got a funny look on her face. "Mr. Nance . . . oh. You already told him." Her eyes widened as she took the thought to the next step. "They didn't believe you, and the President fired you. That's why Mr. Murphy is screaming bloody murder."

"Exactamundo," Otto said. "What your boss wants to do is fly over there, sneak onto the base past all their security—and by now you gotta figure they know he's going to try something like that—find Papa-san Lee and twist his arm."

"That's crazy," Ms. Swanfeld said, then her face dropped. "I'm sorry, Mr. McGarvey, but Mr. Rencke's right, you'd never get away with it. You'll get yourself killed."

McGarvey couldn't face them. He looked at the number on the computer monitor. A CIA psychologist had once told him that he was a man with unrealistic expectations, not only for himself, but for everyone around him. He judged the world through his own viewpoint, which was distorted by the things he had done in his life. Soldiers returning from a war took years to come back to normal, to see the world around them in noncombat terms so that they wouldn't wake up in the middle of the night in a cold sweat and blind panic thinking the noise they heard wasn't an enemy soldier sneaking up on their position. It was called battle fatigue. The psychologist had kindly suggested that McGarvey quit the Company before his battle fatigue killed him. What the psychologist didn't understand was that McGarvey could not change. It was who he was, right to the core. In old-fashioned terms, he was simply a man who when faced with a job to do, got on with it in whatever way he could. Nothing could dissuade him. His problem was that the jobs he picked always seemed to be the impossible ones.

"Call him," he told Otto.

"All right," Rencke said, relieved, and he turned back to his keyboard.

McGarvey turned to his secretary. "I'm still going to need you to cover for me here."

A look of genuine anguish crossed her face. She shook her head, but then girding herself, finally nodded. "I can stall Murphy at least long enough for you to get out of here, but I'm going to have to tell Mr. Adkins something."

"Use your own judgment."

She nodded again. "We have a lot of military traffic heading east just now. Some of it out of Andrews. I know that because my nephew is a squadron commander over there." Her lips compressed. "I can get you a ride at lest to Okinawa without having to go through channels. And as DDO you carry a lot of weight."

McGarvey smiled. "Will he keep quiet about it?"

"He will if I tell him to," Ms. Swanfeld said. "Do you want Tokyo station alerted?"

"No," McGarvey said.

She shook her head. "I think you're being a foolish, reckless man," she blurted.

"Aren't we all?"

Otto looked up. "The call is going through."

Tanegashima Space Center

As soon as he got back up top Ripley knew that he was in trouble. The clean room's lights were off and the door was open.

He jumped up onto the platform and flattened himself against the padded wall, feeling silly even as he did it. But his heart was beginning to pound, and he had the strong feeling again that he wasn't alone up here. The only illumination came from the flashing red tower lights, which left most of the loading bay platform in shadow.

He took a quick peek around the corner. The elevator was gone. In the ten minutes he'd taken to ride down to the old satellite and return someone had been up here and then left again. That's why the payload lift had been recalled to the clean room. They knew his car, and now they knew that he'd seen the old satellite.

But what's the worst that could happen, he asked himself. Kimura would be pissed off, but he wouldn't be surprised. He once told them that nothing about Americans surprised him now that he was working with a Tiger team. At the time Ripley and the others had been amused, but now he wasn't so sure exactly what the payload manager had meant by the remark. Like the shadows up here, everything was beginning to seem ominous to him.

The fact that he was on his own and no one, not even Maggie, knew exactly where he was or what he'd just seen was getting to him. He took his satellite phone out of his pocket, extended the antenna and was about to enter Hartley's number, when the display lit up and the phone chirped. No telephone number came up on the screen.

Ripley pushed the Talk button. "Hello?"

"Is this Major Frank Ripley?"

"Yes, it is. Who the hell are you, and how did you get this number?"

"Are you someplace right now where you can talk freely?"

"Who is this?"

"Listen to me, Frank, you could be in some danger. Can you talk?"

Ripley looked out again at the empty payload platform, trying to keep calm. "I can talk."

"My name is Kirk McGarvey. I'm the deputy director of Operations for the CIA. I don't know how I can prove that to you right now. But we think that something is going on over there that the Japanese government is trying to keep secret from us. And probably from you. It has something to do with the satellite they're getting ready to launch."

Ripley felt as if he'd been punched in the stomach. This could be a Japanese trick, of course. He had to make sure. He forced himself to calm down, to concentrate. He sure as hell wasn't going to tell what he knew to someone on the phone who identified himself as CIA.

"Okay, hold on," Ripley said, getting his mental bearings. "Are you at the CIA now?"

"Yes, I am."

"Hang up. I'll call the switchboard, and ask for you—"

"Tell them you want Yellow Light," McGarvey said, and the connection was broken.

For a moment Ripley stood there, his heart racing. Goddammit, he was an astronaut, not a spy. He entered the international numbers for the U.S., then the area code for Washington, D.C., and the number for information.

"What city, please," an operator answered.

"I'm trying to call the Central Intelligence Agency. I don't know if that's a Washington listing."

"No, sir, that's Virginia. I have an 800 number for you." The operator was replaced by a mechanical voice which gave the CIA's 800 number.

Ripley broke the connection and dialed the number. It was answered on the first ring by a recorded woman's voice. "You have reached the Central Intelligence Agency. If you want employment information please call—" She gave another 800 number. "If you have information of an intelligence value, please give your name and number."

"Wait," Ripley said. "I want Yellow Light. Yellow Light."

Three seconds later McGarvey was on the phone. "Okay, Frank, at least you know that I work in the building. And since you called back, something's going on over there that has you bothered."

"You can say that again," Ripley said, relieved that he was finally talking to someone from his own government. "What do you mean, I could be in some danger?"

"Where are you right now?"

"On top of the payload gantry, across from the rocket. But they know that I'm up here, so I've got to get back right now."

"Go someplace where there are a lot of people, we'll talk on the way," McGarvey said.

Ripley stepped out of the clean room and pressed the elevator's call button. "They switched satellites," he said.

"How do you know that?"

"I saw the one we worked on. It's hidden in a room beneath the payload tower. The one they loaded in the rocket was a different color." The elevator started up. He could hear it. His eyes happened to light on the railing where two of the bolts holding it in place were missing. His heart went bump and he stepped back.

"What do you mean, a different color?"

"The one we worked on is gold, the one I saw in the rocket was dark. Black maybe." Ripley looked around. Someone was up here with him. He could almost feel the other presence.

"Anechoic tiles," McGarvey said, and that caught Ripley's attention.

"It would make the satellite invisible to radar."

"That's right. Whatever they're going to launch tomorrow won't rendezvous with *Freedom*—"

A dark figure shot from the deeper shadows at the back of the catwalk. Ripley reared back and raised his left hand to ward off a blow. "No," he cried.

"Frank?" McGarvey shouted.

The man, dressed all in black, his face covered by a balaclava, batted the phone from Ripley's hand, sending it flying out over the rail. Before Ripley could defend himself, the man shoved him backward, his hip catching the disconnected railing, which gave way with a metallic bang. Suddenly Ripley was falling backward off the catwalk in utter disbelief. It couldn't be happening! He was an astronaut, goddammit, not a spy.

TWENTY-FIVE

Seawolf

We have a firing solution now on four targets, but there're just too many of them," Paradise said. There was a lot of tension in the control room.

"Nobody's going to shoot at us," Harding told him calmly. He was swinging the search periscope in a complete 360-degree circle. There were slowly moving navigation lights in every direction, but at the moment none of the ships was heading toward him. He picked out the stacked lights of an ocean-going tug, and moving the periscope left he found the *Natsushio* wallowing in the three-meter seas. He could imagine the captain on the bridge, fuming that he had lost this time.

He stepped back and called the comms shack. "This is the captain. Did you get the message off?"

"Aye, Skipper. We have confirmation, but there's been no reply so far."

Paradise gave him a questioning look from across the control room where he hovered over the BSY-1 computer displays. Harding shook his head.

He'd taken a big chance, surfacing like that, not only risking crashing into a ship but having some excited, trigger-happy weapons officer fire off a snap shot in the heat of the moment. After the first couple of minutes, however, the situation had settled down. Sonar was painting a picture of eleven surface ships, plus the damaged *Natsushio*, slowly circling, while electronically illuminating the *Seawolf* with everything they had. It was exactly what Harding had hoped for. Now there could be no doubt in anyone's mind what type of submarine the *Seawolf* was and what country she belonged to. The Japanese could no longer maintain a pretense that they thought the *Seawolf* was a Chinese submarine.

"Conn, ESMs."

"This is the captain."

"Skipper, I'm receiving four airborne radar units. Two of them are Japanese Orions, but the other two are ours. Hornets."

"What are they doing, Ballinger?"

"Sir, it looks like our guys are just flying back and forth right over us. They're putting themselves between us and the Japanese navy."

"Very well," Harding said. They were maintaining steerage way, but nothing else. The entire flotilla with the *Seawolf* in the middle was slowly moving south.

He switched back to the communications shack. "This is the captain. See if you can raise the *George Washington*. I want to talk to Admiral Hamilton. *In the clear.*"

"Aye, Skipper. We're picking up some of their signals now."

"Have any of the Japanese ships tried to communicate with us?"

"Negative, Captain."

"Okay, get me the admiral."

"Stand by, sir."

Harding gave Paradise a faint smile. The hard part had been getting his boat and crew out of immediate harm's way. But the next step wasn't going to be very easy either. He was just glad that poker hadn't caught on with the Japanese as big as American baseball had. It was going to put the MSDF at a definite disadvantage. But he needed every edge he could get just now.

"Skipper, the admiral is on the *open* channel for you."

Harding switched phones. "Admiral, thanks for the help. The timing couldn't have been better."

"Glad to do it, Tom," Hamilton said. "I'm told that you made quite a big splash. What's your situation now?"

"Did you get my flash traffic?"

"Just in time to give you a little assist."

"We're right in the middle of it here," Harding said, letting a note of desperation creep into his voice. The admiral knew him well enough to understand why he'd called on a nonencrypted circuit and pick up the completely out-of-character tone of voice.

"Okay, take it easy. We're less than six hours out. Can you hang on that long?"

"I'm not sure, Admiral. I have half the Japanese fleet staring down my throat and the Chinese flotilla not too far away either." He gave a big grin for the benefit of his control room crew. "But I'll tell you one thing, I've got every one of them targeted, and all my tubes loaded. If one of those ships so much as farts, I'm going to fire everything I have. I won't get them all, but I sure as hell will make a serious dent in their fleet."

"Take it easy, Tom," Hamilton said. "There's going to be no further gun play down there."

"If I'm threatened, I'll shoot."

"Not unless someone fires first."

"I hear you, Admiral. But, goddammit, the Japanese are supposed to be our allies."

"They are, and we're working on getting this straightened out, you have my word on it. In the meantime I'm sending you some more air assets."

"Very well."

"Tom, can you hold out just a little longer?" Hamilton asked. "I want you to be part of the solution, not the problem."

"Yes, sir. I'll do what I can for as long as I can."

"I know you will. And we're with you."

Natsushio

Captain Tomita, his rage nearly uncontrollable, played the powerful beam of the spotlight along the length of the American submarine less than two hundred meters away.

His fleet was arrayed all around him, but they were impotent to do a thing against the bastard. These were Japanese waters, and he'd been sent to defend them against any and all intruders—that included Americans. Now he was being ordered again, in most emphatic terms, to stand down, and the shame was nearly unbearable. He was glad that his young son was not here to see it.

Two figures appeared on the bridge of the *Seawolf*. Tomita locked the spotlight on them, then raised his binoculars. The shorter one on the left was Capt. Thomas Harding. Tomita could not make out the man's facial features from this distance, but he'd studied his entry in the Foreign Warship Personnel Profiles on the computer below, and he was certain now that the men he was looking at were Harding and his executive officer Rod Paradise.

He gripped the binoculars so tightly that his knuckles turned white.

"*Kan-cho*," his third officer prompted respectfully at his elbow. "Tug three-one-two advises they are ready to get underway."

Tomita continued studying Harding and Paradise.

"*Kan-cho*—"

Tomita's jaw tightened, and he gripped the binoculars even harder. He counted slowly to five, then nodded. "Proceed," he said.

"*Hai, kan-cho*," the relieved officer replied.

Seawolf

When the *Natsushio*'s spotlight was extinguished, Harding studied the bulk of the MSDF submarine through his light-intensifying binoculars. He could make out two ghostly green figures on the bridge as the warship's bows turned slowly to port.

Paradise was doing the same thing. "Looks like he's heading out."

Harding shifted to the ocean-going tug well out ahead of the submarine. The sea at her square stern boiled with phosphorescence as her massive propellers dug in against the strain of getting underway with a two-thousand-ton tow.

"He wanted to stay and fight," Paradise said. "His two forward tubes were loaded and flooded." He lowered his binoculars. "He would have lost."

"We all would have lost," Harding replied tiredly, relieved that the tough part was over with. No one was going to open fire now.

The ship's com buzzed, and Harding answered it. "This is the captain."

"Skipper, this is the radio shack. We just received a for-your-eyes-only encrypted message for you."

"From who?"

"The Joint Chiefs, Captain. An Admiral O. Rencke."

"On my way," Harding said, and put the phone back. "Ever heard of Admiral Rencke, Joint Chiefs?"

Paradise shook his head. "Doesn't ring a bell."

"Well, he just sent me an eyes-only. God knows what they've cooked up now." Harding glanced again toward the departing Japanese submarine. "Stay here, I'll go see what he wants."

George Washington

"Say that again?" Captain Merkler shouted into the phone. He nodded again and turned to Admiral Hamilton. "Harding bugged out."

They were on the bridge, and Hamilton gave the captain a hard stare: "Bugged out where?"

"One of our Hornet drivers said the *Seawolf* submerged."

"Did we try to make contact?"

"There was no time."

"What the hell is going on down there now?" Hamilton said, an angry set to his features. He did not like surprises.

"I don't know, but I sure as hell think we ought to find out."

Seawolf

"Sonar, conn, are they still looking for us?" Harding asked.

"Aye, Skipper. They're all over the place up there. I'm counting at least nine active sonars. They're stepping all over each other."

Harding glanced over at Paradise, who gave him an uncertain grin. Their latest orders from Admiral Rencke were crazy, considering what was going on out here, but not quite as crazy as the sonofabitch they were ordered to pick up. It seemed to Harding the the entire world had gone nuts, and he didn't think it was going to change for the better anytime soon.

"Sooner or later they're going to figure out what we've done," Paradise said. They could hear the rhythmic swish of the tug boat above them. They had sugmerged in the confusion and had tucked in under the *Nat-*

sushio under tow. Hopefully by the time the MSDF ships searching for them figured out what had happened, they would be in the clear and be able to submerge deeper and slip away.

Harding looked again at the message flimsy. He had no idea who Admiral O. Rencke was, but in a way he was grateful to the man, because he much preferred rescue missions to peacetime battles.

TWENTY-SIX

En Route to Japan

McGarvey was trying to get some sleep. His seat was reclined in the nearly empty cabin of the air force VIP Gulfstream V jet, the steady hum of the engines fading to a dull rush, like water running in a small river. His head was turned toward the window, the early afternoon western sun blasting on the thick cloud cover below.

Getting out of CIA headquarters with everything he needed had been relatively simple. The only people who knew he was back weren't talking to Murphy, and it had taken his staff less than an hour to work up his legend and the necessary paperwork to match his Pierre Allain Belgian passport.

He was a journalist with the Associated Press, currently on assignment as a travel writer in Japan. Using a news service as a CIA cover was sharply frowned upon by the media, and was rarely done. But if some curious

Japanese official called either AP Tokyo, or AP's world headquarters in New York, his background would hold up. There was, for the record, a Belgian journalist by the name of Allain currently on assignment in Japan. Rencke had inserted his personnel file in the AP's computer system without their knowing about it. When the assignment was over, Rencke would quietly extract the file. As long as there was no trouble, no one would be the wiser.

His secretary's nephew, Captain Elias Swanfeld, had been happy to help out. Traffic going west was heavy, and in fact the Gulfstream was heading to Japan via Elmendorf Air Force Base in Alaska with a full bird colonel and two majors. The officers had been briefed not to ask Mc-Garvey any questions. The only problem was that the Gulfstream was going to Misawa Air Force Base on the far northern coast of Honshu, three hundred fifty miles from Tokyo and a farther seven hundred miles to the south coast of the Japanese island of Kyushu. McGarvey had checked the flight ops schedule to see if anything was going over in the next few hours that would put him closer to Tanegashima, which was fifty miles off the coast of Kyushu, but there was nothing.

"We can get you there, sir, but after that you're on your own," Captain Swanfeld said. McGarvey could see the family resemblance with his secretary.

"Sounds like a B movie, but I was never on this flight," McGarvey told him.

The captain grinned just like his spinster aunt. "You got it."

His staff had briefed him on Japan's transportation and communications systems and had supplied him with the guides, maps and phrase books that a journalist might carry. But the difficult part was going to be the Japanese officals he came in contact with. At the moment anti-American sentiment was running high. The rumor had swept across Japan that somehow the U.S. had been involved in the Korean underground nuclear explosion. It was the same rumor that had gone around when India exploded its nuclear weapons: The United States had supposedly encouraged India to go ahead to counter the threat that China's alliance with Pakistan was causing instability in the region. It was nonsense of course, but McGarvey could only hope that the sentiment did not include all westerners, especially Belgians.

The other difficult bit was the timing. The launch window opened in a little more than thirty-six hours. It would take at least twelve hours to get to Misawa, leaving him only a day and a night to make it nearly the entire length of the two main islands, somehow get across the fifty miles of sea to Tanegashima, penetrate the heavily guarded space center and somehow stop the launch.

On top of that they were expecting him. Any doubts he'd had on that score had been dashed when his call to Frank Ripley had been abruptly cut off. Otto had tried to get through again, but Ripley's phone was out of service.

The smart thing would have been to convince Murphy of what he suspected and put pressure on NASA to somehow stop, or at least delay, the launch until an investigation could be mounted.

McGarvey's lips compressed. He'd blown that option by confronting the President. He'd been charged up. Twice he'd nearly lost his life and his family put in harm's way, so he'd not been thinking straight. Stupid. The President had undoubtedly called Murphy and demanded Mc-Garvey's removal as DDO. He might even have ordered McGarvey's arrest. So this was his last shot at figuring out what was going on and stopping it. If he failed this time his effectiveness would be zero.

The steward, Sergeant Wilkes, touched him on the shoulder, and he looked up.

"Sir, we're at cruising altitude now. The captain says it's okay for you to use your phone. Or, if you want, you can use our comms equipment."

"Mine's encrypted," McGarvey said.

"Yes, sir."

"Can I get something to eat? Maybe breakfast?"

Sergeant Wilkes smiled. "It'll take ten minutes. In the meantime how about a cup of coffee?"

"Sounds good."

The lieutenant colonel glanced back at McGarvey, but then turned away.

McGarvey straightened his chair and then phoned Rencke, who picked up on the first ring. A moment later the encryption circuits cut in, and reception cleared.

"Still no word from Ripley," Rencke said.

"Have you talked to anyone in Houston?" McGarvey asked.

"A guy by the name of Hartley. He's in charge of the Tiger team, and he admitted that he hasn't been able to get through to his people over the last few hours either."

"What are the Japanese telling him?"

"Nothing that makes any sense," Rencke said. "I didn't tell him what Ripley told us, because I didn't think it would make any difference down there. They're all hung up on their own bureauacracy. And we're talking about beaucoup bucks here."

"Okay, what about Murphy?"

Rencke chuckled. "He knows I'm lying through my teeth. I told him that I didn't know where you were—which strictly speaking *was* the truth right then. But he just gave me a smile, and said to tell you to watch your ass, because the big dogs were gunning for you."

McGarvey was surprised by the DCI's apparently soft attitude. But then he'd been floored when Murphy first offered him the job as DDO and accepted Rencke back into the fold. "Keep an eye on my wife and Liz, would you?"

"Will do, Mac," Rencke said with conviction. "Just take care of yourself and get back home. There're a lot of people depending on you."

"Count on it," McGarvey said, and he broke the connection.

Sergeant Wilkes came back with the coffee and set it on the pulldown table. "Not exactly regulation, but I think this'll hold you until breakfast, sir."

McGarvey took a sip of the coffee and smiled. It was laced with brandy. "This'll do just fine."

"I think you should try to get some sleep. It's a long slog to Misawa." Sergeant Wilkes looked out the window. "At least it's not bumpy." He went forward to the tiny galley.

McGarvey was too fired up to sleep, thinking about Ripley. He did his homework, studying the Japanese guides and maps his missions and programs people had supplied him with. Sometime after two in the morning local, they touched down at Elmendorf Air Force Base outside Anchorage for refueling, the apron harshly lit by violet lights. He went into the base terminal cafeteria where he ate another breakfast, the only meal they were serving at that time of night, and an hour later he was back aboard the Gulfstream. This time the aircraft was nearly full with seventeen of the twenty seats occupied by air force officers, none of them below the rank of major. They'd been briefed too, and left McGarvey to himself at the rear of the plane. A half hour out he finally managed to drop off, his mind back in Katy's Chevy Chase house the night they made love for the first time in years. He wanted to get back from this operation more than he'd ever wanted anything in his life. There was so much he wanted to tell her, so much lost, uselessly wasted time to catch up on.

Misawa, Japan

McGarvey woke up, a gummy taste in his mouth, his muscles cramped, and he looked out the window. The sun was low on the hazy horizon,

which meant it was late afternoon already. For a second he was confused
about the time, until he realized he was seeing land ahead of them, which
meant they were approaching the coast of Japan. Flying time combined
with their westerly direction meant, in effect, he'd lost a day, although
his body clock was still on U.S. Eastern time, five in the morning.

Sergeant Wilkes came back with another cup of brandy-laced coffee.
"The time change screws everybody up," he said with a chuckle.

McGarvey took the coffee. "When do we land?" Now that he was
coming awake he felt rested.

"About twenty minutes. You okay, sir? Because I talked to Captain
Palmer. He says we can put you up at the BOQ for a day and a wakeup."

McGarvey quickly did the arithmetic in his head. When he'd left CIA
headquarters the launch clock was around thirty-six hours. Now it stood
at twenty-one. He shook his head. "I'd like to take a shower somewhere
and then catch a ride into town, if that's possible."

"No problem, sir. I'll take you over to the crew ready room, and when
you're ready I'll run you out to the main gate. There's a cab stand there."

"Do the locals treat you guys okay?"

Sergeant Wilkes gave him an odd look, but he shrugged. "We pump
a lot of money into the economy. Business is business."

McGarvey nodded. That's what was so weird about what had been
going on between Japan and the U.S. over the past few years. They were
major trading partners. Their economies were so closely linked that when
the Dow Jones twitched, the Nikkei average did a nose dive. And when
the value of the yen took off, the American economy felt the effects
almost instantly. Of course the situation had been nearly the same in the
twenties and thirties. It wasn't a very comforting thought.

The Gulfstream touched down at Misawa Air Force Base at 8:00 P.M.
local, and coming in McGarvey had a chance to study the layout of the
coastal city of 100,000 people. The chief industry was fishing, of course;
sardines, if he remembered his briefing book correctly, although there were
a few very small copper mines to the south.

He waited until everybody else was off the aircraft before he rode with
Sergeant Wilkes over to flight operations housed in a low, concrete block
building. He had the shower room to himself, and when he had finished
and gotten dressed, Wilkes was waiting in the day room with a couple of
hamburgers, french fries and a can of Budweiser.

"I don't know how long you're going to be in-country, but I figured
you might like a home-cooked meal while it was available."

McGarvey dug in as Wilkes watched him, an expectant look on his
face.

"I know I'm not supposed to say anything, but you're a spy, aren't you?"

McGarvey took a drink of beer, and grinned. "Let me guess, you're a James Bond fan."

"Le Carré, Clancy, Cussler, Flannery, all of them."

McGarvey shook his head. "Sorry to disappoint you, Wilkes. What I'm doing here is secret, but I'm not James Bond."

Wilkes shrugged good-naturedly. "Oh well. Even if you were you wouldn't be able to tell me."

After the meal, Wilkes drove McGarvey across the bustling base to the main gate. The guards were dressed in combat fatigues and wore sidearms in addition to the M16 riffles they carried. But there didn't seem to be much tension. In fact as they approached the gate, a half-dozen airmen walked around the barriers and climbed into two cabs waiting on the narrow road. It was a Saturday night, and, as Wilkes explained, they were heading into town just like GIs did wherever they were stationed.

"When do you go back?" McGarvey asked.

"In the morning," Wilkes said. They shook hands. "Have a good trip."

"You too, Sergeant. Thanks for the burgers."

Tanegashima Space Center

Shinichi Hirota pulled up in front of the living quarters of the space center director, hurried up the walk and went inside. Lee and Tomichi Kunimatsu were having dinner together with several pretty young women. It took Hirota several minutes to get the attention of one of the girls, who came out to the front hall to him. It would not have done for him to barge in and thus interrupt their peace.

The girl bowed respectfully.

"Tell Mr. Lee that I am here."

She hesitated, her eyes lowered.

"It is most urgent."

"*Hai*, Hirota-san," she said demurely, and she turned and shuffled back inside.

Hirota stepped back out of sight. His daughter, in school in Tokyo, was about the same age as the young women with Lee and Kunimatsu. He felt an instant of shame thinking what it would be like if she were doing this instead of studying chemistry, but then his heart hardened. Nippon was under attack. Difficult and problematic steps were necessary, sometimes even for the most innocent.

Lee, wearing a hand-embroidered silk kimono, came out a minute later, a neutral expression of his face. "What is it?"

"It's him. Kirk McGarvey. He is here in Japan."

Lee's expression did not change. "Where?"

"Misawa. It is a small fishing city in Aomori Prefecture on Honshu's far northern coast."

"I know where it is," Lee said, showing the first sign of impatience. "What is he doing there?"

"I alerted all the prefecture police captains to watch for him. He was spotted less than an hour ago leaving the American air force base."

"In uniform?" Lee asked incredulously.

"No, Lee-san, the man is dressed in civilian clothes," Hirota replied. "He took a taxi to the train station, where he purchased tickets on a local *futsu* train to Hachinobe, from there to Morioka on a limited express *tokkyu* and then the *shinkansen* bullet train to Tokyo."

Lee considered this information for a moment. "Was he seen actually boarding the train?"

"*Hai*. I can have two men meet it at Morioka where they can intercept him before he gets the *shinkansen*."

"Why did you come to me with this?"

"I must know if the man is to be arrested."

A faint smile curled the corners of Lee's narrow mouth. "Two men, you say?"

"*Hai*," Hirota replied respectfully.

"Very bad odds."

"I wanted to make sure there were no mistakes—"

"I meant for your men," Lee said. He thought again. "Does the Hachinobe train make any stop before Morioka?"

Hirota consulted his notebook. "At Ichinobe. About halfway."

"Have your men intercept Mr. McGarvey there. It is a smaller city, with fewer people and less opportunity for him to make an escape."

"*Hai*."

"Get him away from the train and then kill him no matter what it takes. That must be your *only* priority."

Hirota bowed. "He will not reach Morioka alive."

En Route to Morioka

The *futsu* train was old and small, but spotlessly clean. There was only one class of seats, most of them occupied by families. Everyone was quiet and very polite, and although McGarvey was the only westerner aboard his car, no one so much as stole a glance his way, although his presence was unusual.

The local followed the coastline south fifteen miles to the slightly larger city of Hachinobe, stopping at every tiny hamlet, finally pulling in the small railroad station at 10:45 P.M., where almost everybody transferred to the larger, newer, faster *tokkyu* train which had just pulled in on an adjoining track.

This time McGarvey sat in a rear seat near the connecting door to another second-class car. The one forward was a green car, for first-class passengers. Although westerners might be expected to travel first class, McGarvey had decided against it for exactly that reason. If the authorities were looking for him, they might start there. It would give him a slight leeway.

As the train pulled smoothly out of the station precisely on time, McGarvey sat back. Lee's people might suspect that he was coming, but they couldn't know about his Allain identity, nor was it likely they knew he would be entering Japan at one of the air force bases. Most likely they were watching Tokyo's Narita Airport with his name, passport number and photograph. Of course, if they were watching Dulles too, they might not even know that he'd already left the States. It wasn't much to count on, but it was something.

The night was pitch black, but the lights in the car were turned low so that McGarvey could see the lights of distant farms and villages. Morioka, the capital of Iwate Prefecture, was surrounded by mountains, and he could feel that they were steadily climbing away from the coastal plain, sometimes slowing down for the steeper grades.

Just like aboard the train from Misawa, the passengers on this train were very polite, mostly families, many of them with small children who slept in their parents' laps. A few people were eating snacks, and across the aisle from McGarvey two old men played a game with colored tiles, the board set up between them on their knees. Although they made their moves with lightning speed, they made no noise. Everyone looked happy.

The train pulled into the station at Ichinobe at 11:15 P.M. McGarvey looked out the window. A few passengers were waiting on the platform to board, but there seemed to be some sort of a delay. A minute later the lights in the car came on. A uniformed conductor wearing white gloves came to the door and made an announcement in Japanese and then in English that there was trouble with the engine and that everybody would have to leave the train until it was repaired.

It struck McGarvey all at once that although the Japanese were very efficient they would not make such an announcement in English for the sake of only one passenger. They could not possibly know that the foreigner spoke English. In fact at Misawa he'd used a French-Japanese phrase book to make himself understood with the ticket clerk.

The passengers got up, good-naturedly, and shuffled to the front of the car. McGarvey glanced over his shoulder. A conductor stood blocking the rear door. He considered taking out the man, who looked old and not very fit, and jumping off the wrong side. But there would be an immediate manhunt for him. And it was just possible that there really was trouble with the engine and his imagination was getting away from him.

But he had to figure on the worst-case scenario, that they were somehow on to him, and figure out how to deal with it.

He followed the passengers off the train and looked around. There were several dozen people on the platform, most of them milling around in confusion. He started toward the exit gate when two men in suits and ties who'd been speaking with a uniformed police officer broke away and came over to him. They looked like cops; their eyes missed nothing, and one of them held back a couple of paces, his hand in his jacket pocket.

There was no place to go now. Whatever happened in the next few minutes, McGarvey decided, would depend on how well he kept his composure and what their orders were.

The one cop bowed warily. "Mr. McGarvey, if you would please come with us, there is a gentlemen waiting to speak to you."

"What are you talking about?" McGarvey said, feigning fear to cover his surprise. They knew his name!

A second uniformed police officer joined the other at the ticket barrier and they were looking this way.

The plainclothes cop took McGarvey's arm at the elbow, his grip strong enough to cause pain. "Sir, there is no trouble here, I assure you. In fact you will be able to get the next train, and you will be in Tokyo only a half-hour later than your schedule."

There it was, their first error. It was unlikely that Lee had come up from Tanegashima to talk to him. These two had been sent to make sure that he never got near the space center. Their orders were to kill him, but someplace private.

McGarvey willed himself to relax, a look of resignation on his face, a defeated note in his voice. "May I see some identification?"

"Yes, sir. If you will just come with us, we will identify ourselves. There should be no trouble here, among innocent people."

The other cop took McGarvey's bag, and he let himself be led away from the platform and into the nearly empty arrivals hall where they headed directly for the front doors.

Somehow they'd found out that he was on that train. The only explanation was that Lee had sent word to every possible entry point into Japan to be on the lookout for him. But they still didn't know about his Pierre Allain identity, which gave him an opening, no matter how slight.

His second break came when they emerged from the station. A black Toyota Land Cruiser was parked at the curb, but there were only a few taxis, a city bus and a few passengers: no other policemen. Lee had sent his own people to take care of McGarvey. It was a mistake.

They crossed to the car.

"Hands on roof, feet spread," the cop said. The other cop stood at a respectful distance, his right hand still in his coat pocket.

McGarvey did as he was told. The cop efficiently frisked him, coming up with his Walther and one spare magazine of ammunition, but leaving his wallet and passport. The silencer and a second spare magazine were packed in his leather overnight bag.

They put him alone in the backseat of the Toyota, which was isolated from the front by a heavy steel mesh. There were no inside door handles.

The city was very quiet and dark, all the shops and offices closed for the night. There was very little traffic, and as they headed away from the station, the cop riding shotgun looked back at McGarvey with a neutral expression on his face.

"Where are you taking me?" McGarvey asked politely.

The cop said something to the driver, who laughed, then he turned back. "You should not have come here."

"My government ordered me to Japan. And I think that you should tell that to Mr. Lee. We know all about the launch."

The cop said nothing.

McGarvey looked out the window. Ichinobe was not a large city, and within minutes they were away from the downtown section and into what looked like an industrial area of warehouses and buildings that could have been small factories. These gave way quickly to open countryside of farm fields dotted with stands of trees silhouetted in the night. In the distance McGarvey spotted moving lights along what was probably a major highway.

At any moment they would pull over to the side of the road and simply fire through the steel mesh, and there wasn't a thing he could do about it. He was a rat caught in a cage waiting to be executed.

If he waited, which is exactly what they were counting on.

The cop looked away momentarily. McGarvey let out a cry, clutched his chest and threw himself on the floor behind the driver. He curled up in a fetal position, his feet against the driveshift hump, his legs cocked like springs. They could not shoot him from that angle.

The cop shouted something, and the Toyota immediately slowed down and pulled to a stop off the road. "Get up! Get up!" the cop screamed through the mesh.

McGarvey groaned and pretended to try to rise, but then he slumped back. "Help me," he cried weakly.

He heard both front doors open, and then the rear door on his side was pulled open and hands were grabbing him. It was all he needed, but he knew that he would only get this one chance.

He suddenly uncoiled, driving upward and forward with every ounce of his strength. His head and right shoulder connected with the driver's midsection, bowling the much slighter man backward onto the macadam. McGarvey landed on top of him and yanked the pistol out of his hand.

The second cop came around the front of the car, his pistol drawn. He stepped left and dropped into a crouch as he brought his gun hand up.

McGarvey rolled the momentarily stunned driver over on top of him and fired three shots, the first missing the cop, but the next two hitting the man in the right thigh and his chest, flinging him backward.

The driver smashed a karate blow into the side of McGarvey's neck and shoved him aside.

The blow knocked McGarvey on his back, and he dropped the gun. The driver scrambled for his pistol. McGarvey recovered, rolled up on his left hip and swung a roundhouse right cross that connected with the driver's chin, breaking it. The man wasn't expecting the blow, and his head snapped to the side as if he had been hit by a pile driver. He fell on his back, his head bouncing limply on the roadway.

McGarvey grabbed the pistol and covered the driver. But the man lay absolutely still, his head lolling at an impossible angle. His neck was broken.

The second cop lay on his side in front of the car, his eyes open and already glazed. His jacket was open, and there was a thin splotch of blood over his heart. He too was dead.

They had picked him up not to place him under arrest, but to kill him and dump his body somewhere out here in the countryside. So killing them had been a matter of self-defense. But it didn't make it any easier for him, and bile rose up at the back of his throat. He looked at his hands in the darkness, certain he could see blood dripping from them. A river of blood. Wherever he went, whatever he started out to do, seemed always to end in bloodshed.

He didn't want this. He knew it was inevitable, but he didn't want it.

He glanced both ways up the road. No traffic was coming. In that, at least, his luck was holding. He dragged the bodies back to the car and stuffed them on the floor in the back, covering them as best he could with their jackets. Someone casually looking through the window tonight might not be able to make out what was lying there. At least not with a cursory glance.

He recovered his own gun and spare magazine, then got behind the wheel and checked his watch. It was nearly midnight. If the countdown had not been delayed, the launch would take place in a little over sixteen hours.

He considered his options. They knew that he'd entered Japan at Misawa, and they were already coming after him. But they might not expect these two to call in for a while longer yet, which gave him a little time.

He unfolded a highway map and figured out where he was. The road to his right was one of the main north-south toll roads. Although it would be the fastest way to travel, the toll roads were highly regulated. It wouldn't take long for this car to be spotted once the alert was raised.

His only real chance, he figured, was making it to Tokyo, or some other large city, where he could ditch this car and find another means of transportation to Kyushu's south coast. But the south island was one thousand miles away. He was a foreigner in a stolen car with the bodies of two men he had killed, the authorities were looking for him and he was running out of time.

He pulled out and headed south. Driving on the left felt odd, but that was the least of his troubles. The fact of the matter was, he had no other choice and he no longer gave a damn. The blood lust was rising in him. They had hurt his family and it was payback time. He was going to have to find an airfield or a *shinkansen* station and start taking chances he didn't want to take.

Tanegashima Space Center

By four in the morning, Hirota knew that he had lost control of the operation to neutralize McGarvey. He had waited with mounting anxiety for his people in Ichinobe to telephone. They were to have met the train shortly after eleven last night, arrest McGarvey, drive him out into the countryside, kill him and then dispose of his body. But something had gone wrong, and he wasn't ready to tell Joseph Lee that he had failed. Not until he was sure of his facts, though in his heart of hearts he knew that he was in trouble.

He got up from behind his desk in his office and went to a sideboard, where he poured another cup of tea. He turned back and looked at the photograph of his wife and daughter. His father had been too young to fight in the war, but his grandfather had been killed on Okinawa in some of the bloodiest fighting against the Americans. He wondered if his grandfather had taken out a photograph of his wife and son, who were back home in Kobe, before that final battle to reassure himself, as Hirota was doing now, that he was following the correct path, that what he was doing was not only for the emperor and Nippon, but for his family.

He glanced at the clock for the third time in the past ten minutes as the telephone rang. He rushed to his desk and picked it up. The caller was his contact on the Aomori Prefecture Police.

"Have they called yet?"

Hirota's grip tightened on the phone. "No. Have you heard anything?"

"Nothing," the police lieutenant said. "Something must have gone wrong."

Hirota bit off a sharp reply. "Begin a search within thirty kilometers of Ichinobe."

"There should be no problem finding the car—"

"You're not looking for the car," Hirota said, cutting him short. "You're looking for two bodies."

"*Hai.*"

Hirota calmed down. "You're looking for the car as well, of course. I want you to look everywhere, including the train station in case our man doubled back and took the next train."

"Yes, sir."

Hirota broke the connection and dialed another number. This one rang seven times before it was answered by Shiego Shimoyama, chief of Tokyo Police, at his home.

"This must be bad news," Shimoyama said.

"Our people at Ichinobe haven't reported in."

"Have you instituted a search of the immediate area?"

"*Hai.*"

"Very well then, we must assume the worst, that's he is on the loose and heading south."

"Yes, but time is on our side now. There are less than twelve hours to launch, which means he will have to take a *shinkansen* or an airplane. He can't get here in time otherwise."

"That's helpful. It means his choices are limited, and we can concentrate our search efforts."

"He must be found, Shimoyama-san. At all costs."

"Yes," the police chief replied dryly. "It is in the national interest."

"Nothing has been so important since Pearl Harbor."

Shimoyama laughed. "With different results this time, one would hope."

Nagano

McGarvey entered the Buddhist pilgrimage city of Nagano shortly before seven in the morning. It was a weekend and traffic was reasonably light. At first he didn't know where he was because the few road signs that existed were difficult to understand, and often contradictory. He knew that he was south and west of the Tokyo megalopolis, and that he was in the mountains. But it wasn't until he actually entered the city that he knew precisely where he was, and that he would never make it in time to stop the launch unless he could find an airplane and pilot to take him there.

The H2C was scheduled to lift off in a little more than nine hours, but the space center was seven hundred miles farther to the south. At least eighteen hours by car just to Kyushu's south coast, plus however much longer it would take to cross the fifty miles or so of open water to the island.

He stopped at a roadside rest area that contained a Shinto shrine and studied his maps. The nearest airport was fifty miles south at Matsumoto where he was reasonably certain that he could find a plane and pilot. He had enough money to pay for the trip, but he would have to invent a plausible story that the air service would buy. That was providing private aviation hadn't been grounded because of the military alert.

In addition, the two cops who'd come to kill him in Ichinobe would be missed by now, and the authorities would be searching for this car in ever widening circles. Sooner or later he would be caught in their net unless he got rid of the car very soon.

He decided that would have to be his first priority. He studied the Nagano city map, then drove into the city, careful to watch the speed limit and traffic that came from his right. It would be terrible to get a traffic ticket or get involved in a fender bender now, because once the civilian police had him he could not fight back. They were innocents in this.

He stopped for a red light a half block from the ornate railroad station at the end of a broad cul de sac. A bus had just pulled around the traffic circle and stopped in front of the station, ahead of a taxi rank with three cabs. As McGarvey waited for the light to change, a police car, its blue lights flashing, came through the intersection from the right, sped around the circle and pulled in behind the bus. Two cops jumped out of the car and rushed inside the station.

It was no coincidence. But even if it was, McGarvey felt that he would have to operate on the assumption that the authorities were guarding every train station between Ichinobe and the south island until after the launch. They would be looking for a tall, well-built westerner. They would stop all westerners, because there were so few of them traveling around Japan at any time, and especially now.

The light changed. McGarvey turned right and headed away from the station. If they were watching all the train stations, they were probably watching all the airports between Ichinobe and the south island, including Matsumoto. Lee's people would have figured that McGarvey's only way to Tanegashima in time for the launch was either a *shinkansen* or an airplane. Any other means of transportation would be too slow.

Of course he did have the option of doing something totally unexpected. He could turn around and drive back up to the air force base at Misawa, where he would be safe. But he would have failed in his mission. It was a bitter thought, but one that he knew he was going to have to consider very soon.

The solutions to both of his immediate problems—time and transportation—came ten minutes away from the railroad station near a magnificent Buddhist temple at the foot of which was a very old traditional *ryokan*, the Hotel Fujiya, when his satellite cell phone chirped. He answered the phone as he cruised slowly past the long pedestrian entrance to the temple. It was Rencke.

"Oh, boy, I can't get a fix on you, Mac. Where are you?"

"Nagano. But I don't think I'm going to make it in time."

"Are you okay, Mac?"

"For the time being," McGarvey said. He quickly ran through everything that had happened since he'd landed at Misawa. "I'm going to have to get rid of the car and try to make it back to the base."

"You've got an extra thirty-one hours, if that'll help," Otto gushed. "They're having trouble with one of the onboard guidance computers, so

the launch has been pushed back until tomorrow night. The new window
is from 11:02 to 11:24."

McGarvey was passing the hotel entrance, and it suddenly occurred
to him how he was going to make it at least to Kyushu in time for the
delayed launch.

He headed back into the city.

"Okay, I've still got a shot at this," he told Otto. "Has NASA made
contact with their people yet?"

"No. Hartley wants to go over, but the Japs are dragging their feet.
Nobody seems to know or care what the hell is going on."

"Keep pushing on them," McGarvey instructed. "I can use every extra
hour you can give me."

"Gotcha—"

"But you can't call me again. This time we were lucky, I was alone.
But if I'm in a tight spot and this phone pops off I could be in trouble."

Otto didn't like it. "I see your point. But keep in contact, willya?"

"Will do," McGarvey said, paying attention to traffic, which was picking up. "Gotta go."

"Hang in there, Mac. We need you."

McGarvey broke the connection and tossed the phone in his bag on
the passenger seat. He circled around the downtown area, approaching to
within a couple of blocks of the railroad station from a different direction
than before. Parking on a weekday would have been difficult, but Mc-
Garvey found a spot in the parking lot of a small shopping district two
blocks away. He circled until there was no activity in the lot, then pulled
in, grabbed his bag, locked the car doors and walked away without looking
back and with the air of a man with all the time in the world.

There was some pedestrian traffic, but no one paid him any particular
attention. A block from the parking lot he stopped to look at the cameras
in a shop window and to check behind him. No one was tailing him. At
this point they would be concentrating on the train station.

He walked another couple of blocks toward the railroad station, finally
finding a taxi waiting in front of a department store, its vacant light on.

McGarvey got in, and the driver turned and smiled.

"L'hôtel Fujiya, s'il vous plait," McGarvey said.

"Fujiya?" the driver said, his smile widening.

"Hai."

Tanegashima Space Center

Joseph Lee was having trouble maintaining his composure in the wake of the launch delay and his security chief's inability to find and deal with McGarvey. He sat in front of a low table, his back erect, an austere expression on his narrow features, as two girls served him his lunch.

Kunimatsu was busy at launch control and with the international news media at the media center five thousand meters from the pad, so he wasn't available to explain the trouble with the rocket's computer system. Nor was Miriam here to lend him her good counsel. He didn't dare telephone her at their Washington home, because he knew the lines were bugged. He was alone with his thoughts, a rare occurrence that he did not enjoy.

Time was against them now. The extra thirty hours gave McGarvey a chance to somehow make it here, and the time gave the media that much more of an opportunity to find out about the death of Major Ripley, even though the rest of the American Tiger team had been isolated from the news people and were being denied access to outside telephone lines or cell phones.

Hirota telephoned from Nagano, and Lee dismissed the two young women.

"It was my people in the car," the security chief said. "He shot one of them to death and somehow broke the other's jaw and neck."

Lee held himself in check. "Were there no witnesses?"

"Not after they arrested him at the train station in Ichinobe," Hirota said. "Every *shinkansen* station and every airport in Japan is being watched, but so far he hasn't shown up."

"You should have sent more men. You underestimated him."

"There was a need to keep this contained," Hirota said, respectfully. "But flying across the Pacific and driving all night, he has to be tired. And without transportation he must be hiding somewhere here in Nagano."

"No," Lee said emphatically. "I disagree."

"*Hai,*" Hirota replied immediately. Lee appreciated the security chief's instant compliance; it was so much unlike Kondo.

"He is long gone from Nagano, and well on his way here by now. Come back and we will plan for his arrival."

"But how will he get to the island?"

"He's going to steal a boat," Lee said. He looked out the window that faced the launchpad, the rocket standing tall in the azure sky, and he felt powerful, all-seeing, as if he could foretell the future. "You must admire this man, Hirota-san," he said dreamily. "Before he dies I wish to talk with him. You will see to that."

"*Hai,*" Hirota said, but this time his answer wasn't so quick in coming.

Kyushu

It was dark by the time the congested four-lane highway crossed the narrow strait from Shimonoseki and McGarvey arrived on the south island of Kyushu. This was Japan's most ancient region, and the feeling of the lush but volcanic countryside changed immediately from the hustle-bustle frenetic pace of the north, to the more rural, relaxed atmosphere of the south.

Traffic thinned out, and a light, gentle rain began to fall, with a mysterious mist rising from the Inland Sea. The main highway bypassed the coastal town of Kokura, splitting southeast toward Beppu and southwest to Kyusho's largest city, Fukuoka. He headed southwest.

He had checked into the Fujiya Hotel in Nagano. The desk clerk at the three-hundred-year-old *ryokan* had been very helpful renting him the royal suite for three days at ¥30,000 per day and arranging for a rental car for the entire period. McGarvey had taken a long, leisurely bath, changed clothes and was on the road by 9:00 A.M.

The Lexus ES400 was supremely comfortable and very fast. Since he was driving a car with the proper paperwork, he got on the main north-south toll road and made excellent time, stopping only for something to eat when he refueled the car.

By noon, when he was well away from Nagano, he telephoned Rencke with his new plans.

"They'll never expect that," Rencke said. "It'll take me about twenty minutes. Can I call you back?"

"Yes."

Traffic had been very heavy on the toll road, but it moved fast, though not as fast as the interstates in the U.S.

Rencke was back a half hour later. "Okay, you want to go to Fukuoka. I've booked you a room at the Hotel New Otani Hakata under your Allain work name. Everything else should be set within the next couple of hours, and I'll fax the package to you at the hotel."

"You might take some heat for this, so cover yourself."

"Don't worry about me, just watch yourself," Rencke warned. "It's you with your ass hanging out in the wind, and when Lee looks up and sees you standing there, he's going to be one unhappy camper."

McGarvey had to laugh. "I hope so."

TWENTY-SEVEN

Tanegashima Space Center

When Maggie finished packing, it was coming up on 8:00 P.M. She looked out the window where two guards were waiting with the van that was to take them to the airstrip. The countdown clock was at T-minus three hours, and activity at the launchpad and in launch control was heating up. But she and the rest of the Tiger team would miss it.

She went back to the bed where she zippered up her B4 bag and folded it. She could not get the vision of Frank's broken, bloodied body out of her mind. She'd lived with it for nearly forty-eight hours, going over and over the part where she'd bent down to touch his cheek, but then recoiled. She was frightened that she didn't have better self-control. She was an engineer, a pilot, an astronaut, and yet she'd been afraid to touch the body of the man she'd loved.

She went into the tiny bathroom, where she splashed some cold water on her face, brushed her hair and then studied her haggard reflection in the mirror. They had murdered Frank for what he had seen, or thought he had seen, and for once in her life she didn't know what to do. The enormity of it was staggering. And the past two days of house arrest had been surreal; her isolation made all the more complete because the one man she could have talked to about what was happening was dead.

Frank had made an unauthorized trip to the top of the payload service tower, where he apparently lost his balance and fallen over two hundred feet to his death. There were no witnesses. Kimura and another man who'd been identified as chief of security for the center were sympathetic but skeptical when Maggie and the others swore they didn't know why Frank had gone out there.

Afterwards, when she had tried to telephone Hartley, her call had been blocked, and she and the others had been taken to their quarters where they were placed under house arrest. They had served her meals in her room, refusing to answer any of her questions about what was going on, why they were treating her like this and what was happening to Hilman and others. Her laptop had been taken away, the phone and television were dead and she had nearly lost her mind with fear, anger, boredom and guilt about Frank.

A half hour ago, one of the security people in white coveralls with the NSDA logo on the breast had come up and informed her that she must pack; she and the others would be leaving the space center sometime before the launch.

"Once we get back everything will come out, you bastard," she blurted.

The security officer looked at her without blinking, then turned and left.

She sat down on the bed now, her hands clasped between her knees, and tears of rage and frustration slipped down her cheeks. She was being foolish; she knew that, but she didn't think that she would ever trust a Japanese again. They had murdered Frank, and they were arrogant enough to send the rest of the team home without so much as a word of explanation.

"Bastards," she said softly. "Bastards."

Joseph Lee, dressed in a dark blue business suit, rode in the backseat of a Mercedes limousine from his quarters to launch control. In the distance, the giant H2C rocket was brightly lit on the pad, and the entire base was alive with last-minute activity. He looked out a window at a ten-passenger van which came from a connecting road and headed directly for the media center and viewing grandstands across a field from the vehicle assembly building. The decision to allow the international media to witness the launch had been made in Tokyo, overriding his strong suggestion that the center be placed strictly off-limits to the outside world. His driver pulled into the launch control building parking lot and went directly to the back entrance.

Miriam was on her way over finally. Once she was airborne she'd called to tell him that she'd been followed to Dulles but that no one had interfered with her movements. For at least that much he was relieved. He thought it might have been a mistake leaving her there. He'd considered the possibility that McGarvey might have gone after her in retaliation. But now that she was safely away he no longer had to worry about her. He could concentrate his complete attention on McGarvey, who had dropped out of sight as if he had never existed.

He'd seen a partial transcript of the man's dossier, but until now he had dismissed most of the fantastic report as the probable figment of someone's imagination. But after everything that had happened, he was no longer sure about his assessment. By all accounts McGarvey was an extraordinary man. He was in Japan at this very moment, of that there was no doubt. And on the drive over, Lee had trouble keeping his own imagination in check, wondering if the man had somehow gotten here to the space center and was lurking in the shadows or crawling up the beach like some nocturnal sea monster.

The countdown clock on the side of launch control switched to T-minus 1:28:00 as Lee got out of the limo and went inside. The armed guards knew him by sight. Hirota was upstairs in the security operations center. Three walls of the long narrow room were filled with television monitors that were connected to hundreds of lo-lux closed-circuit cameras around the space center. Every centimeter of the perimeter, and especially the approaches from the beaches, was covered, as was nearly every square meter of the entire sprawling base. Embedded in the security pass that everyone wore were computer chips that contained the personal data of the bearer, his or her specific job, as well as a transponder that radiated a locator signal. Anyone unauthorized anywhere on base would be detected immediately and the appropriate closed-circuit television camera would home in on them.

"Any sign of him yet?" Lee asked.

"He's not here," Hirota said, looking up from a bank of monitors he was standing in front of. "Everyone is accounted for, unless he somehow managed to steal a valid pass. But he would have had to get on base first. And that's impossible."

The center's fourth wall was made of one-way glass that looked down on the launch control center, extremely busy now that the clock had reached and passed the T-minus-ninety-minute mark. Lee looked down at the launch director's console, where Kunimatsu was holding a conference with a half-dozen people.

Hirota came over. "Even if he got as far as Kyushu, he's simply run out of time."

Lee looked at his security chief. He wanted to argue, but he couldn't. The base was tight. And even if McGarvey was here, there was nothing he could do now to stop the launch short of blowing up the rocket or the launch control center, both of which were under heavy guard. For that he would need a substantial quantity of explosives. But something Hirota said suddenly struck him.

"What do you mean, 'Even if he got as far as Kyushu'?"

Hirota's lips compressed. "A man who roughly matches McGarvey's description might have checked into a hotel in Nagano about the same time we found the missing men from Ichinobe."

"Why wasn't he arrested?" Lee demanded sharply.

"We didn't find out about it until a couple of hours ago. He rented a car yesterday, and he never came back. But it wasn't until this afternoon when the hotel reported it."

"It's him."

"Possibly, Lee-san. But even if he made it to Kyushu, and we're checking every hotel and parking lot on the island, he still had to face the problem of crossing eighty kilometers of open sea. No boats have been reported missing in the past forty-eight hours."

"What about a light airplane?"

"None have been reported missing." Hirota said. "In any event we would have picked him up on radar. And there aren't that many places on the island where he could have landed. But even if he somehow *had* got that far, someone would have spotted the airplane." Hirota shook his head. "McGarvey is not here, and the launch will go on as scheduled."

Lee looked down at the tiers of consoles. Kunimatsu had finished his conference and had returned to his own desk on the upper level. Lee's eyes strayed to the consoles reserved for the American Tiger team. The monitors were lit up, but no one was seated there.

"When does the American team leave?" he asked.

"They're giving us some trouble, as we expected they would. But my people are with them, and they'll be leaving at any minute." Hirota looked more sure of himself than he sounded. "The problem will come afterward," he went on. "They'll demand an investigation."

Lee managed a slight cruel smile. "By then it won't matter."

McGarvey climbed out of the airport van and hurried into the media service center with the half-dozen other last-minute reporters he'd joined in Fukuoka. His credentials were checked for the fourth time, and just inside the door he was issued a base pass, which hung around his neck. He went with the others to the briefing room where they were given media packets, watched a five-minute tape on the mission and were quickly advised on the use of the facility's communications center.

On the short drive from the airstrip, he had pretended to be asleep in the backseat while through half-lidded eyes he watched out the window for an opening, anything that would help him. Tanegashima was very much like Kennedy an hour or so before a launch; there seemed to be traffic and activity everywhere, and they had to pass six security checkpoints in as many miles. Now that he was here, he needed to figure out how to stop the launch, and for that he needed more information.

The press credentials and launch invitation package that Otto had worked up and faxed to the hotel were perfect. The Japanese media officers and security people didn't raise an eyebrow when he presented himself for this morning at the Tanegashima offices in the Fukuoka Prefecture Police Department. His name and description had to be posted in every police department in Japan, but they were looking for Kirk McGarvey, an American spy trying to steal a boat, not Pierre Allain, a Belgian journalist here to cover the launch.

He had missed the morning plane to Tanegashima, but he'd been told that a few reporters were coming down from Tokyo at the last minute and would be meeting at the Hotel New Otani. A final flight was being arranged to get them out to the space center in plenty of time for the launch.

Back at the hotel, McGarvey kept out of sight for most of the day, checking from time to time with the front desk for the latest information on the last flight to Tanegashima. He was committed to this course of action, and there was very little he could do except wait. It would have been practically impossible to steal a boat in the daylight hours and make it to the island without being spotted. And by the time it got dark it would be far too late for him to try, unless there was another delay in the launch, something he could not count on. Nevertheless, it had been a long, difficult afternoon for him with nothing to do but keep out of sight.

"You have a little less than twenty minutes to prepare your initial dispatches for filing," Tsuginoni Moriyama, the media rep, was telling them. His English was impeccable, and he constantly smiled. "We would like you to move to the viewing stands no later than T-minus sixty minutes. Or, if you wish, you may elect to remain here and watch the launch on the television monitors. Tapes will be provided for you after the launch. But I must caution you that we have only a limited number of telephones and digital feeds off the island. Because of other sensitive equipment here, you may not use cellular or satellite equipment from now until T-plus thirty minutes."

There were a number of groans, and several heads shot up.

The press officer looked around the room. He was still smiling. "If there are no questions, *other* than the use of cellular or satellite equipment, this will be your last briefing until after the launch when we will meet here at T-plus thirty minutes."

An attractive, middle-aged woman raised her hand. "Judith Rawlins, *New York Times.* I would like to interview the American Tiger team before the launch."

"I'm sorry, that is not possible," the press officer said. "At this moment, as you might guess, they are extremely busy at the launch control center."

McGarvey, who was sitting a few feet away from the *New York Times* reporter, heard her say, "Bullshit."

"No more questions?" The press officer looked around the room, then nodded. "Well then, wish us luck, and we'll see you back here once we're in orbit." He stepped away from the podium and disappeared through a door in the back.

The *New York Times* reporter remained seated and took some notes while the others headed down the corridor to the media communications center. A table was set with a coffee and tea service. McGarvey poured two cups of coffee and came back to where the reporter was seated. He held a cup out to her.

"I didn't know if you used cream or sugar," he said.

She looked up, smiled pleasantly, and took the coffee. "Black will do fine," she said. "Thanks. Do I know you?"

"Pierre Allain, AP Brussels."

"Judith Rawlins, *New York Times.*" They shook hands, and McGarvey sat down beside her.

"I had an ulterior motive bringing you coffee," he said.

She laughed warily. "Most men do. What's *your* story?"

"I'd like to get an interview with Frank Ripley too, or at least with one of his team members, before the launch. But if they're in launch control I'm afraid I'm out of luck. But you didn't seem to think the press officer was telling the truth."

"They're not there. They've been taken off the mission."

"How do you know that?"

She eyed him speculatively, then shrugged. "I have a friend in Houston. What's your interest in Ripley?"

"I have a friend in Houston too."

"What'd he tell you?"

"He's lost contact with his people and he's worried. What did you get from your source?"

Her attitude suddenly got chilly when she realized that he knew nothing more than she did. "I'm really sorry, but I can't share that with you," she said. "You know how it is." She got to her feet. "But it doesn't matter if we're stuck here until the launch."

"If they're not at launch control, where would they be?" McGarvey persisted, looking up at her.

"In their quarters, I imagine."

"Where's that?"

The woman was done with the conversation, but she put down her notes, took the briefing package from McGarvey and pulled out a map of the space center. She circled one of the buildings and handed it back. "Good luck." She smirked, then left the briefing room and headed down the corridor to the communications center.

McGarvey studied the map until she was out of sight. He was going to need some information, and the only people here who would be willing to help him were the Americans on the Tiger team. It was worrisome that he would have to place them in danger, but he could see no other way around the problem. And he was going to have to get to them very quickly, because he was running out of time. It meant he was going to have to start taking some even bigger chances.

He put his coffee aside and stood up. Media reps, or information specialists as they were called at Kennedy, had the free run of the facility as part of their jobs. He hoped it was the same here.

He crossed the room and went through the door that the media rep had used. A short corridor led straight back to an exit door. Two empty offices were on the right, and two offices, both occupied, were on the left. He found Moriyama in the last office, talking to someone on the phone. The press officer held his hand over the mouthpiece. "Go back to the communications center, you do not belong here."

"Ms. Rawlins had a problem. You must have seen her pass this way."

Moriyama said something into the phone, then hung up and came over to McGarvey. He wasn't smiling. "What are you talking about?"

"I thought she came to see you, but she must have gone outside."

Moriyama sprinted down the corridor and out the exit door. McGarvey came right behind him. When they were outside in the parking lot, he pulled out his gun.

"I won't kill you, if you do exactly as I say," McGarvey told him.

Moriyama could hardly believe what was happening. He stepped back a pace. "What do you want?"

"I have to talk to someone on the Tiger team, and you're going to drive me to their barracks."

"Impossible—"

McGarvey raised his pistol directly at the man's head. "I'll shoot you right now if I must."

Moriyama glanced at one of the Toyotas. "I don't know what you think you're going to accomplish."

McGarvey cocked the Walther's hammer.

Moriyama stepped back, his hands out. "Okay, okay, I'll take you there," he said. He got in the car and McGarvey hurried around to the passenger side and climbed in beside him.

The media rep started the car, pulled out of the parking lot and headed the few blocks over to the visitors' housing building. "They're being guarded. You'll never get inside."

"You're going to get me in," McGarvey said. "I'll have my gun in my pocket, and if there's any trouble you're the first one I'll shoot."

"You're crazy."

"Yes, I am."

They drove the rest of the way over in silence. A van was parked in front of the building. Moriyama pulled in beside it, and he and McGarvey got out of the car and went up to the two guards. Moriyama flashed his pass, and the guards waved them on without a word.

Inside, they found themselves in an empty dayroom. A corridor led to the back of the building, and there were stairs to the left.

"Okay, we're here, now what?" Moriyama asked.

"I want to see Frank Ripley."

Mariyama blanched. "You can't," he stammered. "He's not here."

McGarvey pulled out his gun. "Where is he?"

"I don't know. He's gone. He flew out this morning. Maybe he's up in Sasebo."

"What about the rest of the Tiger team?"

Moriyama hesitated just a second, and McGarvey raised his pistol, pointing it directly at the man's face. Moriyama turned and took the stairs up to the second floor and down the corridor to the last room on the left.

"Who's room is this?"

"Captain Attwood. She's in charge now that . . . Major Ripley is gone."

McGarvey screwed the silencer on the end of the Walther's barrel, and keeping his eyes on the media rep, knocked on the door. "Captain Attwood?" he called softly. He tried the doorknob, but it was locked.

"Who is it?" a woman called.

"A friend. Do you have the door locked from the inside?"

"No, they locked me in."

"Do you have the key?" he asked Moriyama, who shook his head. "Stand back, Captain, I'm going to shoot the lock off."

"Okay," she called hesitantly.

McGarvey fired one shot into the locking mechanism, the silenced shot nothing more than a dull pop. He pushed the door open, and waiting just a moment to make sure that no one was coming to investigate, he shoved Moriyama inside, went in himself and closed the door.

Maggie stood next to the bed, her suitcase packed and ready to go, a frightened, but determined expression on her narrow, pretty face. "Who the hell are you?" she demanded.

"I talked to Frank Ripley the day before yesterday. He was on top of one of the launch gantries. He told me they'd switched satellites."

Maggie's hand went to her mouth. "My God."

"I'm here to stop the launch. Where's Ripley?"

"He's dead," Maggie said. "They pushed him off the top of the launch gantry. Doesn't anybody in Houston know about it?"

"No," McGarvey said. "When did it happen?" He looked at Moriyama, who flinched.

"It must have been when you were talking to him. Who are you? What are you doing here?"

"I'm here to stop the launch. How do I do it?"

"You don't," Moriyama blurted.

"Captain Attwood?" McGarvey prompted.

Maggie glanced at Moriyama. "The launch can be delayed if there's a glitch somewhere in the system. Evidently they ran across something yesterday because it was pushed back until tonight."

"Who makes that decision?"

"The launch director on advice from his systems controllers."

"Can anyone else stop the launch?"

Maggie thought about it for a moment. "Someone in Tokyo, I suppose. The head of NSDA."

"How about here at the center?"

"Other than Mr. Kunimatsu, I wouldn't know."

"There is no one else," Moriyama said smugly. He was regaining some of his composure. "And unless you mean to take launch control center by storm, you can't get to him."

"How about Joseph Lee?" McGarvey asked. He watched Moriyama's eyes very closely.

The media rep blinked, and fumbled. "Who?" He was lying.

McGarvey turned to Maggie. "Do you know how to reach the launch director by telephone?"

She nodded.

He took out his satellite phone and handed it to her. "I want you to call over there and demand to speak to Joseph Lee."

"You can't do this," Moriyama objected.

McGarvey silenced him with a look. "When he comes on the line tell him that Kirk McGarvey called you from Fukuoka. Tell him that you know about Kimch'aek, and that I want to cut a deal, otherwise the launch will be stopped."

Moriyama lunged for the door. McGarvey reached him before he could get out into the corridor and hauled him back. He lightly tapped the much slighter man on the temple with the butt of his pistol, and Moriyama went down like a felled ox.

"Call him now, Captain, we're running out of time," McGarvey said. She got on the phone as he shoved the suitcase off the bed, pulled the covers back and pulled off the top sheet, from which he tore several long strips.

He was just finishing tying and gagging the media rep, who was starting to come around, when Maggie motioned that she had Lee on the phone.

"Mr. Lee, this is Captain Attwood, and I think you and I have a serious problem. You'd better come over here right now so we can talk about it."

McGarvey rolled Moriyama over on his side so he wouldn't choke to death.

"Don't hang up, Mr. Lee. I just spoke with Kirk McGarvey. I think you know that name." Maggie's face lit up and she flashed McGarvey a big smile. "No, sir. He called me from someplace in Fukuoka with a message for you."

She nodded.

"Your security people missed this phone. The point is that we know what really happened at Kimch'aek, and Mr. McGarvey would like to cut a deal with you, through me."

She laughed bitterly.

"You'll have to come here alone to find that out, because I want my safety and that of my crew assured."

She looked at McGarvey and shrugged then turned sharply back to the phone.

"No, sir. The launch *will* be stopped. And I can assure you that Mr. McGarvey has the means to do it unless you cooperate with us." She smiled again, and broke the connection. "He'll be here in five minutes."

"How did he sound?"

"Shook up," Maggie said. "Now, would you mind telling me who the hell you are, who Joseph Lee is and who or what the hell is Kimch'aek?"

"It's a long story, Captain, and we don't have the time." He gave her a smile. "Besides you don't want to know."

He took the phone from her and pocketed it, then went to the window. The two guards were still by the van. One of them was speaking into a lapel mike.

"What about the others on my team?" Maggie asked after a couple of minutes.

"They'll be better off staying out of this for now. When Lee shows up we're going to go downstairs, get in his car and he's going to take you over to the media grandstands. I want you to find a woman by the name of Judith Rawlins. She's a reporter for the *New York Times*. Tell her that you believe that your life and the lives of your team are in danger. She'll help you."

"Just like that?"

McGarvey nodded. "Just like that."

"What do I tell her about you?" She glanced at Moriyama on the floor. "About all this?"

"Nothing, she'll work it out on her own."

"How the hell am I supposed to do that?" she blurted. "What about Frank?"

McGarvey looked her in the eye. "Listen to me, Captain. There's going to be a lot of confusion around here, and your life might depend on you keeping your cool. Do you understand?"

She nodded tentatively.

"You're going to have to trust me, even though that sounds stupid."

"If I don't?"

McGarvey looked out the window again. A limousine was passing under a streetlamp at the entry to the parking lot. "He's here."

"You didn't answer my question."

McGarvey turned to her. "Call me at the CIA."

His reply took her breath away, and she was visibly staggered. "I think you're right," she said in a small voice. "I don't think I want to know what happened here."

"Are you ready?" McGarvey asked her. The limo was pulling into the driveway.

"Yes."

"No matter what happens, don't say anything to anybody, don't answer any questions and keep moving until you reach the *New York Times* reporter."

The corridor was clear, and by the time they got downstairs to the dayroom the limousine was parked next to the van. McGarvey took Maggie's right elbow, and keeping his pistol out of sight behind his right leg, went outside and headed directly for the limo's rear door which was starting to come open.

The two guards by the van, their attention distracted by the limousine, turned around. One of them started to raise his hand. The limo's door was all the way open. McGarvey shoved Maggie into the arms of a startled Joseph Lee and then climbed in behind her, pulling the door shut behind him.

He jammed the muzzle of his silencer into the base of the chauffeur's skull. "Drive right now, or I'll put a bullet in your brain."

The driver hesitated for a fraction of a second, and McGarvey pressed the gun harder into the man's head. "*Ima,*" now.

The guards were dragging out their pistols when the chauffeur finally stomped on the gas and the limo shot across the parking lot.

McGarvey switched aim to Lee, who was just beginning to realize what was happening. "We're dropping Captain Attwood at the media grandstands, and afterward we're going to have a little chat."

"You're insane—"

"Tell your driver now, or I'll kill you and worry about how to escape later."

Lee was weighing his options. McGarvey could see it in his eyes. He glanced disdainfully at Maggie, then said something to the driver in Japanese.

"*Hai,*" the chauffeur responded, and he drove left out of the parking lot in the direction of the media center.

Lee had calmed down and it seemed that he had come to some decision. "What are you planning on doing?" he asked conversationally. "It was really quite clever of you to get this far, but you're running out of time, you know." He smiled pleasantly. "You can't stop a rocket with a handgun, and I'm certainly not going to order such a thing, no matter what silly threats you make against me."

McGarvey let his face sag a little. "If my government wanted to stop the launch they would have done it politically. I was sent to get information."

"To spy on us," Lee retorted sharply.

"We're helping with your North Korean problem. But nobody in Washington knows what the hell is going on. Do you honestly want war?"

"Actually we want to prevent a war."

"By sabotaging Kimch'aek?"

Lee laughed. "I understand that you have become an unpopular fellow in the White House. You don't even have a job, so you're here without your government's sanction."

"But it's me with the gun pointed at you."

Lee shrugged.

They had come to the media center, and the driver asked Lee something in Japanese.

Lee again seemed to weigh his options as he stared at McGarvey. But then he nodded. *"Hai."*

The chauffeur drove around back and across to the media grandstands, which were filled to capacity. He pulled up at the gate where a guard turned and looked at them.

McGarvey gave Maggie his media pass and opened the door. "Lose yourself in the crowd and don't let them get you alone until after the launch."

Maggie gave him a significant look, then scrambled past him and got out of the limo. She flashed her pass at the gate guard, who waved her through, and she was gone.

The countdown clock in front of the grandstands read T-minus 00:28:00.

"Where do we go now?" Lee asked, indifferently.

"The launch control center."

Hirota picked up the call from the guard at the visitors' housing building.

"It was Captain Attwood and a man. They got into Mr. Lee's car and drove off," the guard said.

"Was it one of the other Americans?" Hirota demanded.

"I don't know, sir. But he had a gun."

Hirota crashed down the phone. At one of the consoles he brought up the video of the visitors' building parking lot. The limousine was gone.

"Mr. Lee is on his way back here," one of the security technicians said. "But his driver has keyed the emergency beacon."

It was McGarvey. Somehow Hirota knew there was no other explanation, and he could see everything he had worked for, his entire career, this launch, all of it going up in smoke.

He telephoned his OIC of security downstairs. "McGarvey is on his way here in Mr. Lee's car. I want you to stop him."

"Is Mr. Lee with him?" the man asked uncertainly.

"That is not a consideration," Hirota screamed. "McGarvey must not get within one hundred meters of this building, no matter what it takes! Do I make myself clear, Major!"

"*Hai.*"

"By now the guards at the visitors' barracks will have notified security that I'm in trouble," Lee said. "I should think that we'll be picking up an escort at any minute."

McGarvey had run through a short list of possible scenarios in his head: Somehow sabotaging the space center's power plant, storming the launchpad and parking the car beneath the rocket or forcing his way into the launch center, with Lee at gunpoint, demanding that the launch be postponed, then holing up with Lee while he telephoned Murphy so that pressure could be brought to bear from Washington. But none of those plans were very satisfactory, and they depended upon how important Lee was to the launch. They also depended upon some kind of proof of what the Japanese were up to. Murphy would not move without it.

"They won't do anything to this car, of course, but they won't let us get near the launch control center," Lee continued. "They'll force us to stop, or to drive around in circles until the launch is over, and then it won't really matter what you do. In fact, if you don't shoot me, you'll probably be allowed to return home."

"You switched satellites," McGarvey said. "The one that you're launching is covered with anechoic tile. We know at least that much. Why?"

"You're hardly in a position to demand anything from me," Lee said. "You're a very long way from home."

"I came here to get some information. Either I get it from you or I'll be forced to shoot you and get it from someone else. I think you know that I have the motivation."

Lee shrugged. "What will you do with this information?"

"Send it back to the CIA, who will in turn inform the White House. It's the way our system works."

"All that will take time."

McGarvey sat with his back against the door, his legs crossed and his gun pointed in Lee's general direction. He took a moment to light a cigarette, even though time was what he didn't have. But he had to be certain of what he suspected, and Lee had to believe that he cared more about information than about the launch. "Your satellite will not rendezvous with *Freedom*. I think I have that much figured out. Either that or it will approach *Freedom*, but since it's covered in radar-absorbing tiles, they won't see it coming. In fact it'll be undetectable from our ground stations." McGarvey smiled disparagingly. "Is that it? Are you going to attack the space station?"

"You're correct about the satellite's radar invisibility. But it won't come anywhere near *Freedom*. Eight minutes after launch, the satellite will develop a problem and it will be destroyed."

"But it'll still be up there, in low Earth orbit."

"Five hundred kilometers."

"Okay, so you spent what, six years bribing some U.S. senators and congressmen, not to mention the President, into allowing Japan to put up a satellite in such a way that no one would ever question what you were doing. That was a pretty expensive operation, not to mention the actual cost of building a real *Freedom* module, plus the satellite you guys are putting into orbit tonight. Where's the profit?"

"The survival of Japan."

"The North Koreans have nuclear weapons and the Taepo Dong missiles to deliver them to the Japanese mainland. You've convinced the world, so now let us deal with it."

"Like you dealt with India and Pakistan?" Lee shot back. He shook his head. "We can't depend on the U.S. to defend us any longer. It's up to us now if we're going to continue to exist."

"Is it a laser weapon? Something to shoot down incoming missiles?"

They came around the corner, and the chauffeur suddenly braked. One block away the launch control center building was ringed with the flashing blue lights of a lot of vehicles. The driver said something to Lee.

"Tell him to turn around right now," McGarvey said. The launch clock on the side of the building read: T-minus 00:17:00.

Lee hesitated a moment but then gave the order, and the driver made a U-turn and headed back the way they had come.

"Is it a laser weapon?" McGarvey asked again.

"We considered that option," Lee answered. "But you weren't having much success with your Star Wars program, and we didn't think it would work for us either." Everything about Lee's attitude, posture and bearing just then was supremely confident. "What we needed was a real deterrent. Not only against North Korea, but against India and Pakistan and China, all of them nuclear powers. We're surrounded."

"You're putting nuclear weapons into orbit?" McGarvey asked, incredulously.

"We thought about ground-launched missiles, or perhaps air- or sea-launched rockets, but all those bases and ships and aircraft are subject to attack. A radar-invisible satellite is, for all practical purposes, invulnerable."

"Once you fire your nuclear weapon on Pyongyang, you'll be back to square one."

"Four MIRVed missiles, each with three independently targetable warheads, moving at nearly thirty thousand kilometers per hour. Our enemies will have no defense against us. We'll be truly safe for the first time in our history."

"But the satellite won't be in a geosynchronous orbit. It'll take ninety minutes to make a complete orbit. Which means at any given moment, targets in North Korea could be an hour or more away."

Lee nodded sagely. "Thirty-one minutes, actually, when the speed of the missiles' rockets are taken into account. This is merely the first launch."

McGarvey glanced out the window. They were on the main road that led from the launch control center to the launchpad. The H2C rocket, liquid oxygen fumes venting from its flanks, stood bathed in lights, poised to fire.

"At any given moment, your missiles would be thirty-one minutes from targets in the United States as well."

Lee shrugged indifferently. "The U.S. is not our enemy."

"Yet," McGarvey said. "Why did you try to eliminate me?"

"Because you are a dangerous man. Everyone knows it."

"Even the President?"

"He's not in on this, if that's what you're getting at."

"Then why did you come after my family?"

Lee's lips curled at the edges. "It was a mistake," he said, arrogantly, obviously lying.

"Yes, it was," McGarvey said. He raised his pistol a fraction of an inch and fired. The bullet caught Lee in the middle of his forehead. "A very big mistake."

Hirota was watching the retreating limo on one of the monitors when the OIC called from downstairs.

"He turned around. Do you want us to go after him?"

"Send two units," Hirota ordered. "Everyone else stays put. Nobody gets close to this building. Nobody."

"*Hai.*"

Still watching the monitor, Hirota called down to Kunimatsu. "He might be heading to the launchpad."

"He won't get anywhere near it if you keep your security people there until the last minute," the launch director replied. He sounded harried, but in control.

"I can't hold my people past T-minus three minutes."

"It won't matter after that. He won't be able to do anything to the rocket. And if he's close when it lights off he'll be incinerated."

"So will Mr. Lee, you fool," Hirota shouted.

Kunimatsu took a moment to reply. When he did his voice was hard. "The launch cannot be delayed. Our next window won't be until tomorrow night. Mr. Lee's life is not a consideration," Kunimatsu said. "Have I made myself clear?"

Hirota stood up and glanced down at Kunimatsu's position on the top tier. The launch director turned around and looked up. Their eyes met.

"*Hai,*" Hirota said.

McGarvey held the barrel of his pistol against the back of the chauffeur's skull. "If you don't speak English, we're both going to be in a lot of trouble."

They had slowed to a crawl, still two miles from the launchpad. The driver, his face a mask of rage, stared at McGarvey's reflection in the rearview mirror. He nodded slightly.

"I have no reason to kill you, if you cooperate with me. Do you understand?"

Again the driver nodded.

"Drive to the launchpad."

"The guards won't let us pass. And the crash barriers will be down."

"This is a heavy car, we'll see what it'll do."

"It will get us killed," the driver said tightly. He'd gotten his rage in check.

McGarvey stole a quick glance out of the rear window. Two vehicles with flashing blue lights had pulled away from the launch control building and were coming their way.

"You'd better speed up now, or I'll pull the trigger."

The chauffeur had seen the approaching cars, and he'd been stalling for time. He stepped on the gas and they accelerated.

"How many guards are out there?" McGarvey demanded.

"A squad. Thirteen or fourteen men, plus a sergeant and an officer."

McGarvey didn't like the odds. They'd be spread out around the perimeter, especially on the main approach road, but there were too many of them. "How soon before the launch do they pull out?"

"I don't know."

McGarvey jabbed him with the pistol.

"They lock the gates at the ten-minute warning and drive back to the security post."

Ten minutes. It was coming up on that time. The rocket was fully fueled and ready to go right now. It was like a time bomb sitting on the pad. Even if the launch went without an accident, the heat radius would stretch a couple hundred yards; anything within that distance when the main engines lit off would be cooked or suffocated in the intense heat. If something went wrong, if the rocket exploded, the radius could extend a mile or more. The base of a launchpad was a very dangerous place to be.

A green sky rocket rose into the night from near the launchpad.

"What was that?" McGarvey asked.

"The ten-minute warning." The driver glanced again in the rearview mirror. "You're too late."

Ahead there were several vehicles at the launchpad's main gate. Their blue lights were flashing, and McGarvey could pick out several men standing in the middle of the road.

He looked over his shoulder. The blue lights from the launch control center had gotten much closer. They were boxing him in.

"You can't stop a rocket with a pistol," the driver said. He'd slowed down again.

McGarvey sat stock still. Ahead on the right was a low poured concrete building, a gravel parking lot in front. Behind it was a thick jungle of sea oats and tall grasses that led down to the beach. He had run out of options, but Japan, or any nation for that matter, in control of nuclear weapons in space was simply unacceptable, no matter what the personal costs were.

"Stop here and roll down your window," he said.

The chauffeur did as he was told. As soon as the limo came to a halt, McGarvey opened the rear door and jumped out. The driver looked at him.

McGarvey pointed his gun at the man's face. "Get out of here," he ordered. "If you come after me I'll kill you."

The driver nodded.

McGarvey waited until the limo made a U-turn and headed back the way it had come, then sprinted across the road. He crossed the gravel parking lot in a dead run, raced around to the back of the building and plunged into the dense grass jungle.

Shinichi Hirota stared in disbelief at the monitor as a dark figure disappeared into the tall grass behind the maintenance vehicle storage building. It was McGarvey.

His excited OIC called from downstairs. "He shot Mr. Lee and he's on the loose."

"I have him on the monitor," Hirota replied, trying to keep some semblance of calmness in his voice. But this was falling apart in front of his eyes.

"The ten-minute warning has passed. What do you want us to do?"

"Escort Mr. Lee's driver back here and hold your position," Hirota ordered. He called the squad leader at the pad. "He's coming your way."

"We saw him. What do you want us to do?"

Hirota glanced at the launch clock. It was passing T-minus nine minutes. "You have six minutes to find him before you have to pull out of there."

"*Hai.*"

The launchpad guards weren't doing what Lee's driver said they should. McGarvey watched from the shadows behind a pair of unmarked steel storage tanks seventy-five yards from the base of the rocket. By now they should have locked the gates and headed away from the pad. But they had left their two trucks on the road and had spread out along a line that directly cut him off, their M16 rifles at the ready. If he moved out of the shadows they would spot him.

They knew that he was back here somewhere. They could not stay this close to the rocket until the launch. At some point they would have to pull out. But all they had to do was keep him at bay until it was too late for him to do any harm, or to get out of there himself.

Keeping the steel tanks between himself and the patrol, McGarvey ran back into the tall grasses. Crouching low, he worked his way another fifty yards around the far side of the launch gantry. He could see the top of the rocket from his vantage point, but not its base or any of the installations around it. He couldn't see the patrol but neither could they see him.

A white sky rocket rose into the night to the west of the gantry. McGarvey checked his watch. It was five minutes before launch.

A sense of desperation welled up inside him. He was a David with a 9-millimeter pistol going up against a Goliath rocket that developed a million pounds of thrust from a main engine and two solid fuel boosters. A peashooter against a bazooka. Impossible. Yet he couldn't allow himself to think about backing off now. Even if the odds were a million to one against doing any harm to the rocket engines or the satellite, he had to take that chance. There was no other way for him.

He popped up for an instant, then dropped back down. The launchpad was empty, the guards were gone. He got an impression of a low, bunkerlike structure, its steel door open, to the right, just off the pad. But there'd been no movement.

He checked the action on his pistol and made sure he still had the spare magazine of ammunition, then unscrewed the silencer and put it in his pocket. Switching the safety off, he ran in a low crouch directly toward the rocket, stopping every few yards to look up and check for the guards. But they were nowhere in sight.

The grass abruptly ended twenty yards from the bunker, and McGarvey held up just within its protection. The launchpad was empty. By leaning forward he could see the main gate. The two trucks were gone, and the steel barrier was down, blocking the access road.

A red sky rocket whistled into the sky, followed immediately by a klaxon. T-minus ninety seconds.

"There he is," a technician at one of the monitors shouted.

Hirota spun around in time to see a man racing directly for the base of the rocket, his right hand up. He had a gun and he was shooting at the rocket. Hirota couldn't believe it. He snatched the telephone and got the launch director's direct line.

"He's on the pad! He's firing at the rocket!"

The countdown clock was approaching sixty seconds.

"Stand by," Kunimatsu's maddeningly calm voice came back.

"Don't you understand, you idiot? Stop the launch!"

"We're showing only a slight fluctuation in lox pressure in number two tank," Kunimatsu shouted Hirota down. "The launch goes as scheduled."

"No!"

The line went dead.

McGarvey ejected his spent magazine and rammed the spare one in the grip as he continued running directly toward the base of the launch gantry. But it wasn't doing any good. He wasn't doing any real damage to the giant rocket.

He fired three more shots, when something very hard slammed into his left shoulder, spinning him around and knocking him to his knees.

One of the guards had been left behind. He stood at the corner of the bunker, firing his M16 rifle, but he was taking too much time with each shot, trying to hit McGarvey and not the rocket. It was a mistake.

McGarvey fired two shots from a kneeling position. The first one missed, but the second took the guard in the chest, knocking him backward off his feet.

McGarvey jumped up, waves of dizziness and nausea coursing through his body. He stumbled back to the downed guard who was already starting to recover. The man was wearing a bullet-proof vest and had merely been stunned.

McGarvey pocketed his pistol and snatched the rifle out of the guard's hands. Using it like a club he tapped the butt into the guard's forehead, and the man fell back, unconscious.

His left arm nearly useless, McGarvey turned, raised the weapon awkwardly, and began firing at the rocket. His shots stiched up from the base toward the nose cone, having the same lack of effect his pistol had.

He stopped a moment, something coming to the back of his head. *Challenger.* The shuttle had been brought down because a simple seal in one of the solid fuel boosters had leaked.

A rush of water suddenly entered the trough beneath the pad. The rocket motors lit off at the same moment McGarvey fired the last of the M16's rounds into one of the solid fuel booster rockets. All of a sudden a spurt of flame shot from the side of the booster, growing almost instantaneously into a huge bloom of exploding gasses.

McGarvey grabbed the downed guard by the collar and dragged him around the corner of the bunker and through the open steel door, while all around him the night came alive with flames, the heat rising so fast it sucked the oxygen out of the air, making all rational thought impossible.

Hirota picked up the phone again and was about to call the launch director with a last-minute plea to stop the launch, when his mouth dropped open. The entire base of the rocket was suddenly engulfed in flame, blotting out everything on the pad, including Kirk McGarvey and the downed guard. They had lost.

He carefully replaced the phone on its hook, turned and without a backward glance left the security operations center, his future up in flames, as pandemonium broke out all around him.

Margaret Attwood had been in the middle of explaining her plight to Judith Rawlins when the rocket exploded on the pad. Both women turned toward the glowing ball of flames.

Fifteen seconds later the deep-throated boom of a very large explosion reached them, and Maggie's first thought was for Kirk McGarvey, who was out there, and she shook her head in wonder.

The lights were on in the emergency bunker. The guard, huddled in a corner, watched as McGarvey hurriedly pulled on a silver fire-retardant suit. He was having a great deal of difficulty with the task because of his shoulder wound and the burns on his back where his jacket was scorched. But it would only be a matter of minutes before the first squads reached the pad.

"Do you understand English?" McGarvey asked.

The guard nodded hesitantly. "*Hai.*"

"If you come after me, I'll kill you. Do you understand?"

"*Hai.*" The guard's entire body was trembling. Not only had he failed in his assignment, but the man he'd been left behind to kill had saved his life.

McGarvey pulled on the gloves, picked up the M16 and donned the helmet. The air inside the suit would have to last until he got clear, because he was in no condition to carry the extra weight of the bulky oxygen bottle.

He went to the door, took off one of his gloves and touched the steel.

It was too hot to touch, but there was no other way out. Putting the glove back on, he drew back the latches, girded himself, then yanked open the door and stepped outside into an inferno, slamming the door behind him.

The launchpad was on fire. Puddles of fuel and flaming wreckage lay everywhere. Visibility was near zero.

McGarvey took a couple of steps away from the bunker, then stumbled and fell to one knee, dropping the rifle. The heat inside his suit was already almost impossible to bear. It was hard to think, to make himself get back up on his feet and move.

He had come this far, goddammit. He wasn't going to stay here and die in the fire or return to the bunker where the Japanese authorities would take him.

He struck out blindly away from the core of the fire, not sure if he was heading in the right direction away from the flames, or what he was going to do if he made it to the beach.

Minutes or hours later, he stumbled and fell again, but this time he found himself in a wide patch of already burned grass. He looked over his shoulder. All the flames were behind him now. They shot up into the night sky, the core as bright as a welding torch, making his eyes water.

He got up again, and as he ran away, he pulled off his helmet and tossed it aside, drinking in the relatively cool air. He pulled off his gloves, dropping them by the wayside, and finally at the edge of the grass, just above the beach, he struggled out of the still smoldering fire suit, the outside of which was so hot it was impossible to touch.

He could hear a lot of sirens that sounded like air raid warnings wailing over the noise of the solid fuel in the boosters still cooking off.

Somewhere along the beach he would have to find a boat; it was the only way off the island for him. The manhunt would start the instant they found out he had not been killed in the explosion. He had the sinking sensation that he had forgotten something vital. Then he had it. There would have been a phone in the emergency bunker. He should have taken the time to destroy it, because by now the guard would have told his superiors what had happened.

He stumbled down to the beach, and headed to the right—the south, he thought—when several dark figures rose up from the ocean, pulling something behind them.

McGarvey stopped, his heart sinking. He fumbled for his pistol, but it was hard for him to make his burned hands work, or to remember if he had used all of his ammunition.

Two of the dark-clad figures rushed up the beach to him, and he raised his wounded left arm to ward off the blow. A wave of intense bitterness passed through him. He had come this far. All he wanted was one final piece of luck.

One of the figures pulled off a diving mask. "Mr. McGarvey?" he shouted. In English.

"What?" McGarvey tried to back away.

"Are you Kirk McGarvey?" the man insisted. The others had taken up what appeared to be a defensive position.

McGarvey managed to nod. "I'm McGarvey."

"Thank God we found you, sir. I'm Ensign Demaris, sir. Navy SEALS, aboard the *Seawolf*. Admiral Rencke asked us to stop by and give you a lift."

McGarvey looked at him. "Rencke?"

"Yes, sir."

McGarvey could only smile, as they hustled him down the beach to the waiting rubber raft. "Rencke," he said again. "Good man."

EPILOGUE

Ladies and gentlemen, the President of the United States."

President Lindsay, looking gaunt, shuffled to the podium in the White House map room, fiddled with his notes for a moment, then gazed into the television cameras. It was ten in the morning, two weeks after the Tanegashima explosion and standoff in the Sea of Japan.

"Last night, with the advice of my national security team, I ordered our armed forces to strike at four separate military targets outside the city of Pukch'ong, North Korea.

"Over the past weeks, after the underground nuclear explosion at Kimch'aek, U.S. and South Korean intelligence services confirmed the existence of a well-advanced nuclear weapons program there.

"Satellite photographs pinpointed the installation of four nuclear weapons, attached to long-range Taepo Dong missiles. The missiles were on their launchers, and we believe that technicians at each of the sites were preparing to launch attacks on the city of Seoul, in South Korea, and three targets in Japan, including the city of Tokyo.

"Had we done nothing, and the attacks had taken place, we believe that the loss of life would have been staggering."

The President paused and glanced up from his notes. His complexion was pale, and a slight tic had developed below his left eye. It seemed as if he had aged twenty years in the past few weeks since his last news conference.

"I am happy to report that the mission was a complete success. All four of the missile installations were destroyed, and there was no loss of American lives.

"One of our primary fears was that by attempting to destroy armed nuclear weapons, our strikes would themselves cause the weapons to explode, enveloping much of North Korea's east coast in a nuclear fireball. My technical advisers assured me that this could not happen, and in fact did not happen."

The President's resolve seemed to harden. "Let me make one thing perfectly clear. While we understand and respect the right of any sovereign nation to defend itself, the United States will no longer sit idly by while irresponsible governments attempt to build and deploy any weapons of mass destruction. In this, we are firmly resolved."

When Louise Horn emerged from the photo interpretation center she was surprised that it was a bright, sunny morning. She stopped under the overhang to take a deep breath of fresh air, and she coughed. "Goddammed cigarettes," she muttered under her breath.

"It's a bad sign when you start talking to yourself, Louise."

She turned and smiled as Major Wight walked over to her. "The air smells funny, Bert. Why do you suppose that is?"

"You're just not used to it," Wight said. He looked at his watch. "How about a late breakfast? I'm buying. Unless you have something better to do, like sleeping."

"Sure," Louise said. They started to the parking lot. "That was something last night. What do you suppose is going to happen now?"

"I don't think Kim Jong-Il is going to make any noise about losing his entire nuclear weapons stockpile and four of his missile batteries, if that's what you mean." He grinned. "Seventh creamed them."

"He was stupid not to have spread them out after Kimch'aek."

"He didn't have the time."

"Do you suppose he would have actually launched an attack?" she asked.

Wight shrugged. "We'll probably never know. But you saw the pictures. Four bombs, four modified missiles on their launchers. Their threat radars were up and active, and they got off three SAMs. They were serious."

The morning shift was straggling in. Louise waved at a few people she knew and wondered what sort of crises they would be looking at in the next eight hours.

She smiled wistfully and glanced back at the sprawling center. The job was like a drug, she decided. Worse than cigarettes, worse than pot, because once you got started you couldn't quit until you became a basket case and they carried you out.

"You did a hell of a job, Louise," he told her. They reached his car, three slots away from Louise's. "IHOP okay?"

"Sounds good. I'll follow you," she said. "The thing I don't get is the Tanegashima explosion. What happened out there?"

"One of the solid fuel boosters blew. Just like *Challenger*. It's part of the risks of the business."

"Thank God nobody but Frank Ripley was hurt."

"Amen," Wight said. "They'll rebuild. *Challenger* didn't finish us, and the Tanegashima explosion won't stop the Japanese. They're tough. If they want something badly enough they'll keep trying until they get it."

"Do you think so?"

"Count on it."

It was McGarvey's birthday, a fact he had completely forgotten until he was discharged from Bethesda Naval Hospital and the nurse wheeling him down the corridor mentioned it.

He was feeling pretty good. The gunshot wound in his shoulder was healing nicely, and he had cut out the pain medications for the second-degree burns on his back, neck and arms. He wasn't going to need skin grafts, although the doctors said that had he been exposed to such extreme heat for another few seconds he would have probably been in and out of hospitals for the next year. He was a lucky man.

Kathleen and Liz had stayed by his side around the clock, except during his extensive debriefings, first by his own people, and then under CIA supervision by the FBI's Fred Rudolph.

Not once during that time did anyone make the suggestion that what he'd done was not only foolish in the extreme, but criminal, though he saw it in their eyes and heard it in the tone of their questions.

He had sent Katy home last night, over her weak objections, and this morning Liz had to go down to the outpatient clinic to have some stiches removed. Afterwards she was going out to Chevy Chase to pick up her mother. They would be coming back to the hospital later in the afternoon.

In the meantime, McGarvey convinced his doctor to release him this morning, two full days earlier than planned. Instead of the big argument he'd expected, McGarvey had been pleasantly surprised when the doctor had simply shrugged and let him go.

Dick Yemm was waiting for him downstairs in the busy lobby, and he took over from the nurse who would not allow McGarvey to get out of the wheelchair until he was actually outside the building.

"You look a hell of a lot better this morning than when the navy brought you in," Yemm said.

McGarvey laughed. "I wouldn't recommend this place as a vacation destination."

"Next time duck, boss."

"I'll keep that in mind," McGarvey said. It really was good to be getting out.

"Did you catch the President's announcement this morning?"

"Yeah," McGarvey said, his stomach tightening again. Lindsay had announced to a stunned nation that he was resigning, only the second president in history to do so. He'd had a minor heart attack two nights ago, and to continue in the job would almost certainly mean his death. Vice President Lawrence Haynes would be sworn in at ceremonies in the Rose Garden tomorrow afternoon.

It was over, Lindsay's part finished. For all his mistakes and wrongdoings he would completely escape any sort of punishment or censure, but McGarvey supposed it was for the best. There was no reason to drag the country through any more turmoil. The North Korean nuclear program had been wiped out, and Japan's plans for nuclear domination were just as effectively stopped. From this point on the U.S. would be closely monitoring their nuclear program as well as their space launch capabilities.

"Did somebody bring my car over?" he asked.

"Your secretary told me that I'd be driving from now on, and I wasn't about to argue with her."

A Lincoln limousine with government plates was waiting in the driveway, and he was happy to see that Murphy hadn't come out for a final word. He was going to be pressured into getting ready for his Senate confirmation hearing in a few weeks, and once again he wasn't sure that he wanted the job.

There were a few people around, and Yemm pulled up short as a dark Chrysler minivan came up the driveway and stopped behind the limo.

The driver got out, took some flowers from the back and went inside the hospital, nodding pleasantly as he passed. McGarvey noticed that Yemm's eyes never left the man, and he had an inkling how Murphy felt everytime he went somewhere with a bodyguard at his side. It gave him pause. It was another aspect of the job he didn't know if he could handle. He was used to taking care of himself. Besides, McGarvey thought, people around him tended to get in the line of fire. It seemed sometimes like he was a magnet for every sonofabitch out there with a grudge against Americans. He smiled bitterly. In spite of all the anti-American sentiment worldwide, nobody was beating a path to immigrate to Iraq or Libya or Afghanistan. Everyone wanted to come here, the crazies included.

Yemm insisted that McGarvey ride in the backseat. And that was an odd feeling too. He felt like a pretentious jerk. Another Howard Ryan.

When they pulled out, Yemm glanced in the rearview mirror. "Do you want to go over to your apartment first?"

"First before what?"

Yemm got a funny look on his face. He shook his head. "I just thought maybe you needed to get something."

"What's going on, Dick?"

"What do you mean?"

"If you're going to work for me, I don't want any bullshit," McGarvey said.

Yemm looked at him again in the rearview mirror. "I'm in trouble," he said. "Mrs. McGarvey doesn't want you out there until noon. Gives us an hour."

"What's happening at noon?"

"Mr. McGarvey, you're going to have to cover for me," Yemm said. "They've got a surprise birthday party laid on for you. If Mrs. McGarvey finds out I blew it, my ass is grass."

McGarvey couldn't help but laugh. "On second thought we do have to get back to my apartment. I need some cigarettes, and I could use a stiff brandy."

"Yes, sir." Yemm was watching him. "She's invited half of Washington, boss. So maybe you should think about changing clothes too."

Again McGarvey couldn't help but laugh. "Is this the way it's going to be from now on?"

"Yes, sir. So you might as well sit back and enjoy it, because between Mrs. M. and your secretary I don't think you've got much of a chance."

McGarvey sat back, and this time his smile was private. It did feel good to be home. He just had to wonder how long it would last this time.